MANXOME FOE

MANXOME FOE

JOHN RINGO
TRAVIS S. TAYLOR

MANXOME FOE

This is a work of fiction. All the characters and events portrayed in this book are fictional, and any resemblance to real people or incidents is purely coincidental.

A Baen Books Original

Baen Publishing Enterprises
P.O. Box 1403
Riverdale, NY 10471
www.baen.com

ISBN 10: 1-4165-5521-8
ISBN 13: 978-1-4165-5521-6

Cover art by Kurt Miller

First printing, February 2008

Distributed by Simon & Schuster
1230 Avenue of the Americas
New York, NY 10020

Library of Congress Cataloging-in-Publication Data

Ringo, John, 1963–
    Manxome foe / John Ringo and Travis S. Taylor.
        p. cm.
    "A Baen Books Original"—T.p. verso.
    ISBN-13: 978-1-4165-5521-6
    ISBN-10: 1-4165-5521-8
    1. Space ships—Fiction. 2. Human-alien encounters—Fiction. I. Taylor, Travis S.
II. Title.
    PS3568.I577M36 2008
    813'.54—dc22

                                                                    2007037316

10 9 8 7 6 5 4 3 2 1

Pages by Joy Freeman (www.pagesbyjoy.com)
Printed in the United States of America

DEDICATION

~~~~~~~~~~

For the loved ones who wait at vigil with
hope that their beloveds will return safely.

And especially to those whose beloveds
have given the ultimate sacrifice.

As always:
For Captain Tamara Long, USAF
Born: 12 May 1979
Died: 23 March 2003, Afghanistan
You fly with the angels now.

1

"I'd only do this for Mom, you know."

Sergeant Eric Bergstresser adjusted the high collar of the Marine dress blues and shrugged his shoulders, again, trying to get the uniform to *feel* right. But since he spent most of his time in digi-cam or jeans, it never quite did.

"You've skipped out of it the last two visits, bro," Joshua Bergstresser said, shrugging. Josh, just turned sixteen and decidedly civilian given the earring he was sporting, was wearing Dockers and a polo shirt, as dressed up as he was going to get for church. "Besides, you look good. You're going to attract the ladies like flypaper. Maybe I should get a set of those."

Eric winced and then shrugged.

"Don't do it unless you're sure," Eric said, frowning. "As long as you're not in my outfit, Mom probably won't get *two* telegrams."

"Not a good way to talk, bro," Josh said. "You'll be fine. Tell me you'll be fine."

"Ain't gonna lie, *bro*," Eric replied. "Not something I can talk about. But I will tell you that on my last mission, we went out with forty-one Marines and landed with five."

"Are you serious?" Josh asked angrily. "That never made the news!"

"Yes, it did," Eric said, one cheek twitching up in an ironic smile. "Thirty-six Marines killed in helicopter crash. News at Six."

"That was out west somewhere," Josh replied, furrowing his brow thoughtfully. "That was your unit? Eric, crashes, well . . ."

1

"There wasn't a crash." Eric chuckled grimly. "They all died in combat. But a helicopter crash was a convenient cover. Among other things, it explained why most of them had closed casket funerals. Hell, there weren't even *bodies* in most of the caskets, just sandbags. We didn't lose them all at once and quite a few weren't recoverable."

"And that was your unit?" Josh asked.

"Yep."

"And you're going back?"

"Yep."

"That's insane."

"Yep."

"Eric," Josh said desperately. "You cannot go do . . . whatever it is you do, again. Forget what I said about the uniform. De-volunteer or something. Hell, I'll hide you under my bed. With casualties like that . . ."

"Not much chance of believing I'll survive, right?" Eric asked, finally turning away from the mirror.

"YES!"

"Believe it or not, on the last cruise I started to get into Goth and heavy metal," Eric said, talking around the point.

"And I was happy, happy, happy," Josh replied. "Since I no longer had to listen to Hank Williams, Jr. What's it got to do with the statistical certainty you're going to die?"

"I still listen to Hank," Eric said. "But one of the songs I got into was called 'Winterborn.' You've never heard of Crüxshadows, have you?"

"Bit indy for me, man," Josh said. "What's wrong with Metallica?"

"Besides that they haven't had an album out in ten years?" Eric replied. "But this song, it's about the Trojans. There's a line in the chorus: *In the fury of this darkest hour, I will be your light. You've asked me for my sacrifice, and I am Winterborn.* I'm good at what I do, Josh. Very good."

"I didn't figure you got the Navy Cross for being incompetent," Josh said quietly. "But there's these things called odds."

"And if I didn't do it, somebody else would have to," Eric continued as if he hadn't heard his brother. "From experience, probably somebody who wasn't as good, who has less of a chance of coming back. You want me to put them on the chopping block, bro?"

"Hell, yes!" Josh said, his jaw working. "*They're* not my brother!"

"They're somebody's brother," the sergeant said, picking up his cover. "They were brothers and sons. Some lady just like Mom carried them in her womb and nursed them and loved them. And most of them we couldn't even bring home. There wasn't anything to bring. I've got a better chance than any replacement." He tucked his cover under his arm and curtly nodded at his reflection. "So, this is *my* sacrifice. As my first sergeant once said, if I was worried about where I was going to die, I never should have joined the Marines in the first place."

Commander William Weaver, Ph.D., topped out on the climb and stood up on the pedals, clutching the saddle between his thighs as he coasted downwards to catch his breath. The roots on the trail were still slick from the morning dew that had yet to be burned off by the mid-morning Alabama sun. The canopy of oak trees and the dense green foliage around the trail would prevent that for several more hours. The rear wheel spinning and slipping on the roots had made the climbs more difficult than Bill was hoping and he was getting totally worked.

Leaning his center of gravity behind the saddle as the screaming downhill rushed up at him, he managed to keep the bike in control just long enough to hop over a small oak that had been dropped across the trail to prevent it from washing out. Bill looked at his heart rate monitor on the center of the handlebars—185. He was working *way* too hard for this part of the trail. The ride was fun and had let him take his mind off of, well, off of a lot of things, but his heart just wasn't really in it. The climb on the other side had severely kicked his ass. He should be able to get his heart rate back down to at least the 160s, but it was dropping slower than he'd expected and his heart pounded like a bass drum in his throat. He felt *so* out of shape. And the ride back up the mountain to the parking lot was going to be hell.

Eight years ago he would have kicked this ride's butt and been up for another lap or two, but eight years ago was . . . eight years ago.

Eight years ago was when he'd put his ass on the line to save the world. Eight years ago was before there was any concept of the *Vorpal Blade*. Eight years ago was . . . eight years ago when the world was a relatively simple place and a little slope like that last one wouldn't have bothered him one bit.

Eight years ago he'd been working for a defense contractor, fixing problems for the military and other government agencies with acronyms, mostly ending in A. DIA, CIA, NSA. Then an explosion blew out the University of Central Florida physics lab. Not to mention the rest of the university. Two hundred fifty-one times ten to the twelfth power joules would do that. Call it sixty kilotons and be done.

Subsequent to the blast that flattened UCF and a goodly space around it he'd been blasted into other dimensions, died he was pretty sure, resurrected he was absolutely sure and generally had a hell of a time running around saving the planet. The blast had opened up gates to other worlds, some of them inhabited by hostiles with seriously negative intent. Called the Dreen, they consumed organic matter to create more copies of themselves. They had conquered multiple worlds and Earth was next on the list. Weaver, with the help of a SEAL master chief and sundry others had managed to close the gates the Dreen used. But the anomaly where UCF physics department used to be kept pumping out more gates.

In time Weaver, among others, had figured out how to create gates on Earth, shutting down the gate forming bosons that were the culprits. Instantaneous teleportation from point to point was now a reality, with more and more gates being opened every day. The now defunct airlines had been less than thrilled. After almost ten years it was getting to the point that auto makers were less than thrilled.

The Dreen were not the only alien species encountered. One of their subject races, the catlike Mreee, had pretended to be friends just long enough to scout out the new human prey. The destruction of the Dreen gates had almost certainly wiped out the Mreee as well. Contact with them had certainly been cut off. But the survivor Mreee, part of the Dreen invasion force, had been less upset about that than many expected. They were a proud race that had seen themselves fall into slavery to masters who took not only their planet's resources but the very bodies of their citizens for conversion into Dreen. A clean death at the hands of an honorable foe was preferable.

One friendly race had been encountered, as well. The Adar were in advance of humans technologically but had nearly as much trouble with the Dreen. It was the Adar, though, who had passed on two items. One was a bomb big enough to shut down the Dreen gates. They hadn't used it themselves because the only way to crack the gates was for the bomb to go off *very* close to one. If it went off on the wrong side, the planet wasn't going to be habitable. The humans were desperate enough to use it and it worked, shutting down not only the gate that it was sent through but all other Dreen gates.

The second device, though, was in a way more useful. The Adar had found it on an ancient planet whose sun was just about dead. Nothing more than an enigmatic black box the size of a deck of cards, it had surprising properties. Any electrical charge caused it to release orders of magnitude more energy than inputted. Weaver eventually guessed that it was at least in part a warp drive. And he was right.

Using the box, which was not only a warp generator but a reactionless drive generator, the U.S. government had converted a submarine, the USS *Nebraska*, into a spaceship. It had taken seven years, and Weaver had jumped ship into the Navy early in the process. One of the problems he was having with this hill, admittedly, had been caused by too much time in a swivel chair redesigning a submarine to go where no man had gone before.

But Weaver, and a team of thousands, had eventually done it. And then Weaver, acting as astrogator, had gone out with the rechristened *Vorpal Blade*. Humans, seeing the first mirrorlike gates, had christened them Looking Glasses. The Adar found human thought process fascinating and had insisted that *this* ship be named in accordance with that thought. Since the ship was an *Alliance* spaceship, they'd had enough pull to push the name through.

Unfortunately, the Adar, while fine scientists and philosophers, had very little understanding of human humor or thought processes. So the acronym for Alliance Space Ship had slipped past their filters before it was too late.

On the ASS *Vorpal Blade*, Weaver, a crew of one hundred and fifty-four officers, NCOs and enlisted, forty-one Marines, and a handful of scientists had ventured forth on a local survey. They had limped back with five Marines, a couple of scientists and a hundred and twenty crew. But they'd found out what they were sent to find out: Space may be an unforgiving Bitch but She was *nothing* compared to landings. On the other hand, they'd also found allies and some interesting technology.

On a moon of a gas giant circling the otherwise unremarkable star 61 Cygni Alpha they'd encountered a race of rodentlike mammaloids. Named the Cheerick in the language of the country the *Vorpal Blade* contacted, they were similar in form to chinchillas or hamsters and at their highest level of technology were about at War of the Roses level. In other words, they'd just started to press the edges of real science, climbing out of the darkness of alchemy. However, they also had records dating back thousands of years that indicated that from time to time, for reasons unknown, another race would rise up and destroy them. Dubbed "The Demons" they had begun to show up shortly before the arrival of the *Vorpal Blade*. The *Blade* had, fortunately, been forty light-years away at the time of their first sighting so it was innocent.

Eventually, through about half of their casualties, the scientists of the *Blade* had determined that the "Demons" were some sort of biological defense mechanism that targeted electrical emissions. By that time, the majority of the science team and a goodly number of Marines had bought the farm. But before they died, the science team had gotten a lock on the source of the Demons.

It was left to Weaver, Chief Warrant Officer Miller, USN, a handful of local Royal Guardsmen and a small team of the remaining Marines to stop the scourge. Fortunately, they'd been accompanied by the ship's linguist, Miriam Moon. Normally as nervous as a rabbit, Miss Moon had been the person who figured out how the system worked and, using a local, shut it down.

While Weaver was away on his forlorn hope, though, the ship had been under attack. Most of the "Demons" were ground mounted but there was an aerospace component as well, giant red and blue "dragonflies" with a very fast reactionless drive system and lasers that shot out of compound eyes. The *Blade* had been chased into space by them and ripped very nearly to shreds. The local who had taken control of the system, Lady Che-Chee, had had to tow the ship back to the planet using the same flies that had ravaged it.

Enough repairs had been enacted to allow the ship to limp back to Earth, but making it spaceworthy again had been a half-year process. Weaver had acted as the ship's executive officer on the trip back but gratefully turned over the job on arrival to a more experienced officer. Since then, though, he'd been deeply involved in the repairs and upgrades. Like, pretty constant sixteen-hour days involved.

This was his first real break, since the major repairs were completed and all that was left was details. He'd grabbed at the new CO's suggestion, more like order, to take some leave. The ship wasn't due to leave for its next mission for two months. So he'd headed down to his real home in Huntsville to visit friends and reacquaint himself with the trails, baby-head sized rocks, roots, boulders, downed trees, screaming downhills, and extremely rough and technical climbs of Monte Sano Mountain.

He pulled his left foot out of the pedal and planted it as he braked just before the whoopdie-doos. Just as he started down, his cell phone rang. The ringtone—"Welcome to the Jungle" by Guns'n'Roses—was barely audible over his pounding heartbeat. Bill welcomed the break, he was that fragged. He bit the tube hanging from the helmet strap in front of his face and sucked down water from his CamelBak between gasps for air.

Despite the fact that he was on leave, he was required to be on call. Since he not only had a deeper grasp of the science behind the drive but a knowledge of every bolt and system in the ship that was unsurpassed by even its commander and XO, sometimes there were questions that only he could answer. And it appeared that there was another one.

"Weaver," he said, panting for breath. The earbud he was wearing automatically activated at his voice.

"Commander Weaver, Captain Jeller, SpacComOps. You're required to report at the earliest possible moment to your ship."

"Shit," Bill muttered. "Uniform?"

"Whatever you're wearing at the moment, Commander," the captain on the phone said. "There has been an incident . . ."

Eric tuned out the priest as the sermon started. It was a new one since he'd left for the Corps, a woman of all things. His family was Episcopal but while Eric had heard there were no atheists in foxholes, he didn't recall praying much on the last mission. Mostly he'd been too scared spitless to remember any.

He spent most of the sermon checking out the congregation. It was pretty much the same faces he'd seen most of his life. He was born in Fayetteville, NC, when his dad was still in the Army, a "leg" who did something in logistics Eric had never quite understood. But Eric didn't remember North Carolina as a kid. His dad had moved to Crab Orchard to work in the, then new, plastic plant as a dispatcher. Josh had been born in the Arh Beckley Hospital as had his sister Janna.

Most of the people in the church had been born in Arh Beckley, those that hadn't used a midwife. And he'd seen the same faces every Sunday for as long as he could remember. So was it his eyes that had changed or the people around him?

Coach Radner had been a nightmare during high school. The head coach for the phys ed department and the lead coach for the Crab Orchard High School football team, the former paratrooper was missing two middle fingers from some industrial accident back in time. One time Bob Arnold had mocked him as the coach was instructing him on the fine point of the three-point stance of a blocker. Bob, thinking he was being funny, had taken up a three point stance with those same fingers folded back as if they'd been cut off. Radner, half Arnold's weight, had knocked the tackle flat on his ass with that same damaged hand. You did not cross Coach Radner.

Looking at him now, Eric saw a man who was relatively out of shape and on the back side of fifty. He looked satisfied with his life but not the demon that Eric recalled.

Bob Arnold was in the audience, too, with his wife Jessie. Jessie was one of the co-heads of the cheerleading team; Bob was the school's top tackle. It had been a natural match. Now, they both looked worn and washed out, with two kids already; Bob's muscle was turning to fat quick and Jessie wasn't exactly svelte anymore. Eric heard Bob was in construction framing down in Beckley. Eric had a hard time adjusting the picture of the two in high school.

Behind them were the Piersons. Mr. Pierson and Mrs. Pierson looked pretty much the same as they always had, a good looking couple. Mr. Pierson was the local veterinarian, Mrs. Pierson had been a legal secretary to one of the town's lawyers for years. But Eric stopped and blinked for a moment at the people with them. The Piersons had four children. Paul had been a year ahead of Eric in school and Eric heard he'd gone to college so he wasn't around. The youngest girl had to be Linda, but she'd really grown. She must be ten or so by now and had shot up. Then there was Hector. He was recognizable by the shock of white hair but that was about it. Where'd the pimples come from?

But the one that really caught him was the teenage girl with them. The other Pierson child would be Brooke but . . . that *couldn't* be Brooke. He conjured up a vague memory of a gawky and awkward blonde girl who had just entered high school the year he was graduating. She'd had a serious overbite that mildly affected her speech and a mass of metal to go with it. Nice hair, a mass of naturally curly blonde locks, but . . .

Jesus! It *had* to be Brooke Pierson. But the *maulking* vision in a pink dress sitting with them couldn't . . . Same damned hair, though. Shit, it *was* Brooke . . . She'd sure shot more than *up*.

He turned away as the girl in question looked his way, as if divining that he'd been staring. It wasn't that, though. He'd caught other looks from the congregation as the service had gone on. The dress blues certainly stood out and Dad had told him that the decoration had been written up in the local paper. Given that they weren't, as far as anyone knew, at war, the award of the Navy Cross had been big news in a very small town.

Looking away from the girl who . . . hell, she'd be seventeen, which would get you twenty even in West Virginia . . . he saw Coach Radner looking his way. The old paratrooper gave him a respectful nod, one former warrior to the present generation, and turned back to ignoring the sermon.

It was times like this that got Eric thinking. Looking around the congregation he picked out the veterans. There were a bunch: small towns like Crab Orchard had always provided more than their fair share of soldiers and Marines. But they left quite a few behind, too. The annual Memorial Day celebrations pointed that out, the roads lined with crosses with names on them. More crosses than there were people who lived in the town it sometimes seemed. WWII, WWI, Korea, Vietnam, the aborted "War on Terror," the Dreen War . . .

Would one of those crosses one day say "Eric Bergstresser"? Or would he be one of the guys in the congregation, running to fat but there to see their grandkids? Would he sit around in the VFW hall and tell stories about crabpus and Demons? Or would he be an empty box in a grave, a guy people sort of recalled on Memorial Day, but really nothing but a fading memory?

He shook his head to clear the thought as the sermon finally droned to a close. The new priest, priestess, whatever, sure seemed devoted but my *God* she was boring. There had to be better uses of his time but Mom wanted to show off her Marine-hero son.

Given that it might be the last chance she got, he owed her that. It was that that had decided him on coming. Not that he was going to put it to her that way.

Since he was in church he figured he ought to pray, some, for a chance to come back to it. But he was blanking on prayers. No, there was one.

> *"For heathen heart that puts her trust*
> *In reeking tube and iron shard—*
> *All valiant dust that builds on dust,*
> *And, guarding, calls not Thee to guard.*
> *For frantic boast and foolish word,*
> *Thy Mercy on Thy People, Lord!"*

"What was that, Eric?" his mom asked, as the congregation rose to do what Eric thought of as "the huggy" thing.

"Just a prayer, Mom," Eric said as the lady in front of him, whom he didn't recognize, turned around to get a hug and a welcome. "It's called 'Recessional.'"

2

Getting from Huntsville to Newport News had once been a major endeavor. Especially after the events of 9/11 when security cracked down on airport travel.

The virtual destruction of the mujahideen movement in the Dreen War had pretty much eliminated the need for the increased security measures. But they had, of course, continued on as long as the airlines survived. The only thing more eternal than the stars was a government program. However, the increasing replacement of airlines with Looking Glasses had eventually killed even the TSA.

Even up to a couple of years before, security had searched people moving through the Glasses. There wasn't any reason for it that Weaver could ever see; the Glasses weren't exactly worthwhile targets. Sure, you could shut one down. If you set off a nuke in close proximity. But the nuke was the problem, not the Glass shutting down.

Eventually even Congress had come to its senses and now there wasn't any more "security" than a minor police presence in airports. The airports remained as a good center for long-range Glasses, but that was about all.

So as soon as he got to his car, Bill drove to the Huntsville Airport. He parked in long-term parking, hoping that he'd get a chance to move the car somewhere else if he was going to be gone long, then walked into the terminal. There was a Glass opening to DC in fifteen minutes at Gate Nine.

He had plenty of time to walk to the gate and got there well before the opening time. Really, it was just traffic control. People could walk back and forth easily enough but you couldn't see if anyone was coming on the other side; Glasses would pass certain particles but not electrons or any wavelength of light. The "opening" times were just to make sure nobody ran into a person coming the other way. Bill had suggested a system based on muon generators that could be used as a signalling system but it hadn't gotten implemented last time he checked.

Apparently the last group had already finished when Bill arrived. On a Sunday afternoon there wasn't exactly heavy traffic back and forth. In the morning there would be, as commuters to DC headed out. Recently, given that Glasses meant you could go as far as you wanted in no time at all, people had started using them to commute some really incredible distances. One guy Bill knew lived in Portland, Oregon, and worked in DC. It took him less time to get to his house than it had when he lived in Alexandria, and most of it was driving through Portland's traffic. But given the differential in time, he missed even Portland's rush hour on his way home. Of course, he had to get up at oh-my-god thirty to get to work.

The light over the Glass went green and Bill joined the group of eight or so that lined up, dropped a token or swiped a card through the turnstile and stepped through the Glass. On previous trips there had been some balkers, people who hadn't quite gotten the hang of going through a Glass. But this group, clearly, was experienced with the trip. All of them just went through, no muss, no fuss.

The other side wasn't at Reagan National; the Glass exited in Union Station, the main rail and metro station in DC. Bill headed down two escalators and along a nearly deserted metro platform to the now familiar Glass to Newport News. There were, in fact, three Glasses on the platform, one for Newport News, one for Little Creek and one for Norfolk Naval Station. They had been installed since the last mission and Bill had already gotten in the habit of using them to get from one base to the other. It was quicker and easier to go to DC then back to Norfolk than it was to drive across town.

The light over the Glass was green—the count-down timer having a bit over five minutes left before the next switch—so he just swiped his card again and stepped through. The card he used was also his military ID and a charge card; the charge for the transfer would be automatically debited from his bank through it. There was a website he could access where he could adjust the charge to the military, given that he had been recalled. But it really wasn't worth the two bucks the trip was costing.

The exit at Newport News was in a recently constructed semi-secure building. The room was secured by a bored-looking guard who was there to prevent troublemakers and the unworthy from entering the base. Hell, there were people who just stepped through the wrong Glass.

Bill held up his card and gestured at the exit door to the room.

"Go ahead, Commander," the guard said, nodding from behind the aliglass. "I got the word you were on the way. There's a field car waiting for you."

The "field car" was a golf cart driven by a warrant officer. Notably, Chief Warrant Officer Todd Miller, U.S. Navy SEALs. Bill slipped into the passenger seat and the SEAL pushed down the pedal, sending them deeper into the base at the cart's maximum speed of slightly faster than a trot.

"What's up, if you can say?" Bill asked.

"I dunno, sir," Miller said. "I just got here, my own self. And got told to go pick you up. But Greg Townsend's chairing the meet."

"Admiral Townsend's here?" Bill asked. Townsend was the commander of Norfolk Naval Base. As one of his "other duties" he was also the senior officer of the *Vorpal Blade* project. He was being bruted as the next commander of the operational arm of Space Command as soon as the Powers That Be went public with the *Blade* and turned it into the Space Navy.

"Everybody got the word to come to the ship instead of to Norfolk, sir," Miller said with a shrug. "Usual cluster fuck."

"Great," Bill replied, crossing his arms. It was just a tad chilly for spandex bike shorts and an Underarmor top.

"Nice outfit," Miller said with a grin. He was wearing a pair of cut-off desert BDU pants and a Hawaiian shirt.

"I was biking," Bill replied.

"I was getting ready to have a family barbeque," Miller said, clearly trying not to snarl. "My wife was less than thrilled."

"How's she handling your reactivation?" Bill asked.

"Not too happy," Miller admitted. "But the nice thing about

Glasses is that I can commute from Diego. And if she couldn't handle the thought of me buying it on a mission we would have divorced decades ago."

They pulled to a stop in front of the headquarters for the *Blade* project and went through the usual security rigmarole. It was a bit harder than getting on the base. There were four steel doors to negotiate and a guard station. From there, Miller led the way to Secure Room Four. Bill turned over his cellbud and PDA at the guard station, then entered.

The secure room had mostly familiar faces in it. Admiral Townsend was at the head of the table. He was in civilian clothes as well, wearing a polo shirt. Captain Steven "Spectre" Blanke-meier, the ship's CO, was wearing a T-shirt with an ace of spades on it and a squadron number. The new XO, Commander Rey Coldsmith, was the only one of the senior officers in uniform. Coldsmith was a submarine officer who'd come up through engineering. With degrees in both nuclear engineering and physics, he was a close second to Weaver in his understanding of the new drive. He did not, however, have Weaver's background in quantum mechanics and astronomy.

Captain James Zanella, the new Marine company commander and First Sergeant Jeffrey Powell were also present. Powell was one of the five Marine survivors of the previous mission. Tall and slim with a deeply wrinkled face from lots of time in the sunshine, the Marine Senior NCO had a masters degree in international relations from the Sorbonne. The latter had come in handy in negotiating with the Cheerick on their previous mission. Zanella was even taller than his first sergeant with a greyhound physique and black hair shot with premature gray. Zanella was in a polo shirt but the first sergeant was wearing a T-shirt with a dragon fighting a wizard on the front.

The one face Weaver couldn't place was a lieutenant in undress uniform. His nametag read: Fey.

Weaver was, by far, the most underdressed. But he could handle that.

"Glad you finally made it, Commander," Admiral Townsend said without any notable rancor.

"I was near the top of a mountain in Alabama, sir," Bill said, taking a seat. "It took me a while to bike down then get to the glassport."

"Understood," Townsend said, looking around and letting loose a grim smile. "This caught us all flat-footed. Lieutenant?"

"To introduce myself, I'm Lieutenant Chris Fey with SpaceCom's Office of Alien Technologies," the LT said. "This got routed through SpaceCom and I was the officer they dispatched to give the good news."

"Which is?" Bill asked.

"Not good," the lieutenant said, keying on his computer and projecting a starmap on the wall. A star was highlighted. "This is HD 36951, located just north of Orion's Belt in the sky and is about five hundred and fourteen light-years from Earth. It is a Class A3 type star. Its Gamma planet is a gate world, one of the most distant we have. The gate opens about fifty miles from Wichita, Kansas, in a wheat field. What is called a Type Six boson resonance, for those familiar with the term. Not a Dreen Type Three, in other words. There has been a small science party there for some time gathering astronomical and archaeological data. It's quite close to the Orion Cluster and had recently gotten some upgraded equipment and personnel due to recent work on Dreen gates. Admiral, I need to elaborate."

"Go," the admiral said, leaning back.

"As Commander Weaver is aware, and I'm sure most of you are, gate links are somewhat traceable," Lieutenant Fey said. "Inactive bosons that are trying to link send out a steady stream of muons in the direction of the nearest linkable gate. Once linked, the same muon stream is detectable. During the Dreen War, Commander Weaver—as a side-note to trying to close the gates—did some studies of Dreen links."

"They were hard to track with the stuff we had at that time," Bill said, frowning. "We never really could get a good direction on them."

"Well, our office took your original data and crunched it . . . a little harder," the lieutenant said, smiling slightly. "What we determined was that most of the Dreen gates, all the ones surveyed, seemed to point towards the Sagittarius constellation area. There is a cluster of stars, called a 'local group,' in that area that we now believe to be the primary center for Dreen worlds. It's located in the Sagittarius arm, fortunately."

"How far away . . . ?" the admiral started to say.

"The galaxy is divided into arms, sir," Fey said, pulling up another picture of the local portion of the galaxy with some stars marked in on it. "We're here, in the Orion Arm. The next arm over is the Sagittarius Arm. We're talking, straight distance, about a thousand light-years away, possibly two thousand."

"Two thousand hours," Captain Blankemeier said with a wince. "At max speed. Long damned way."

"I like it," Admiral Townsend said. "The farther away they are the better. But that's not why we're here."

"No, sir," the lieutenant said. "However, it's important to the story of HD 36951. The point is that HD 36951 is the nearest gate we have to the area the Dreen may be infesting. So the post was recently upgraded with a small security contingent and there were plans in the works to put up a satellite system. However . . ."

He tapped his computer again and a video started. The initial view was of the ground and the audio of panting.

"The base . . . it's gone . . ." a man's voice said, the view coming up and showing an area of dust and smoke. "There was . . . a big explosion. I was out surveying the . . . there's . . . Oh, my God . . ."

The view whipped upwards and a dark shadow could be seen in the sky. The outlines were ovoid but that was about all that could be seen as the view began jumping all over the place.

"*Grapp* this . . . *grapp* this . . ." the voice said, panting and apparently running. "I'm heading for the gate. If I don't make it . . ."

The screen went to snow suddenly and the strained voice was cut off.

"On the far side of the gate a major explosion was detected coming through," Lieutenant Fey said, cutting off the video. "Kinetic energy only, no radiation. A response team took about two hours to get there. The local sheriff's office in the meantime sealed off the gate. The response team from SpaceCom found the base destroyed, apparently as a result of a kinetic strike. They also found the video camera but not the person using it who, based on the voice analysis, was Dr. Charles Talbot, an archaeologist studying the ruins on the world. There was no evidence of any alien presence; however, based on standard protocol a Mark-88 was fired through the gate, destabilizing it, and the gate is now being moved to Antarctic secure area as all potential Dreen gates have been moved.

"While the main base was destroyed, there was a secondary base in the nearby ruins. It is likely that there were survivors of the initial attack and the blast. They had limited supplies, however. Their holding out for the time for us to get there would be . . . problematic.

"That concludes my briefing, sir."

"And we're supposed to go find out what happened, sir?" Blankemeier said. "We were supposed to be taking the new ambassador to Cheerick, sir."

"And you will, after this mission," Admiral Townsend said. "There are several pieces to this. It's unlikely that a rock just dropped on the planet and happened to hit the base. Somebody destroyed it. We need to know who, especially if it's the Dreen. And Dr. Talbot, although not an astronomer, might know enough about the galaxy to direct the probable enemy here. For that matter, there's the possibility of survivors. So you're going out, now. As fast as possible. Head to this . . . what was the star, son?"

"HD 36951, sir," the lieutenant said.

"Head to that star, find the planet, find out what happened if you can, check for any survivors, then try to find out who did this," the admiral said. "If it's the Dreen we have to know if they're there. It would be good to find out something about their space technology for that matter. All we got from the Mreee was that they had some. What's the status of your ship? The real status."

"Just some minor refitting that has to be done, sir," Blankemeier replied. "Really. We can loft any time. But our personnel are scattered to the winds."

"Get them recalled," the admiral said. "Lieutenant Fey has all the background data on the study team on . . . whatever that star was called. He's going to be going with you as an advisor and another set of eyes. You won't be bringing your usual science group with you. Anybody else you want?"

"Commander Weaver?" the CO said, looking over at the astrogator.

"I'd suggest taking the normal SF contingent. They've got enough technical expertise to be useful if we need the data without being as . . . limiting as most of the science team."

"He's trying to say they tend to survive better, sir," First Sergeant Powell interjected. "Not that *any* of them made it last time. I'd suggest taking Miss Moon. Keeping her occupied without the usual science teams will be interesting, but we may need a translator. Especially if it's a species other than the Dreen."

"And the Marines are going, obviously," the admiral said, nodding. "How far away is this star, son?"

"About five hundred and fourteen light-years, sir."

"Astro?" Blankemeier said.

"Twenty days, sir," Bill said, doing the math fast in his head. "If we were going straight line. But we'll have to jink around a bit to avoid gravity bubbles. And more with cool downs. But the real problem will be relative adjustment."

"Say, again?" Admiral Townsend said, then nodded. "The star's going to be moving differently than Sol. Got it. This deep space stuff is taking a little while to sink in on this old sailor. Continents and islands don't move. Not so you can notice."

"A lot differently, sir," Bill said. "Every star moves at a different rate relatively speaking. Nearby stars generally move at about the same rate as Sol, but even there we're talking about a relative velocity higher than any human spaceship ever produced until we made the *Blade*. And in this case, we're talking about outside of the local cluster. When the *Blade* exits warp it has the same inertial constant as when it entered. Basically, how Sol is moving. We're going to be doing a lot of adjustment when we get there. Less when we take a look around, though. But I'd block out a day for adjustment, given cool down time. And most of it at max thrust."

"Not to digress terribly," the admiral said, frowning. "But why don't those different movement rates affect the people transferring through the gate?"

"As far as we can determine, sir . . ." the lieutenant answered, "when you step through a gate you just *are* there. It's as if you hadn't been at another point. We're still trying to figure out the physics for it. But that's the effect."

"Okay," the admiral said, shaking his head. "I sometimes long for the days of Halsey. Captain? You understand the mission?"

"Three weeks to a month to even get there, sir," Blankemeier said. "Unknown time on site and in the area looking for the hostiles and getting a handle on the situation. Then another month back. I hope we don't take damage like the last time. Leaking air for that long would be . . . tough."

"You're just there to find out what happened, Captain," the admiral said. "Try not to get into any furballs. But . . . It's like old time ship captains. If you decide that it's necessary to take action, take action. You're going to be very much on your own until the eggheads figure out how to replicate that drive."

"We're doing our best . . ." Bill and the lieutenant said almost simultaneously.

"Sir," Bill added, grinning.

"I see that you and the lieutenant will have a lot to talk about on the trip," the admiral said, standing up. "Start your recall. I want you under weigh in no more than two days."

"Sir, that may be impossible," Commander Coldsmith interjected.

"Say again?" the admiral replied.

"I'm not sure we can get all the personnel through pre-mission physical that fast, sir," the commander said uncomfortably.

"Damn," Miller interjected. "I'd forgotten about pre-mission physical. How could anybody forget pre-mission?"

"We try not to think about it, Chief," Blankemeier said, nodding. "But that's a real problem."

Pre-mission physical was extremely . . . extensive. Its purpose—besides determining that the person was ready for the rigors of space flight on the *Blade*—was to ensure that the person that Earth sent out was, in fact, the same person Earth got *back*. It involved not just all the normal procedures of a physical, blood and urine tests, heart checks, etc., but extensive mapping of the person's brain and body chemistry. The point was to ensure that the person who came back was not carrying any alien parasites or stranger beings.

Alas, certain aspects of such an intense physical were physically debilitating in their own right. Notably, the chemicals used for the brain mapping were similar in composition to those used for chemotherapy. With similar results. Headache, "flulike" symptoms and, most notably, the sort of nausea usually only experienced in really bad hurricanes at sea.

"Dr. Chet will, of course, be accompanying you," the admiral said. "You can do pre-mission physical en route. You have, after all, nearly a month before you get to the AO. Takeoff by midnight Tuesday, Captain. With whatever Marines, SF and crew you have available. That's a hard date."

"Aye, aye, sir," Blankemeier said.

"Dismissed."

Eric had taken his truck for the drive to the church. While he'd taken Josh over with him, he'd asked his brother to let him drive home on his own. He just needed some time.

After church all sorts of people had wanted to shake his hand.

Too many of them had asked why he'd gotten the Cross and all he could do was repeat the mantra "I'm sorry, that's classified."

The Piersons had been one of the groups that stopped to talk to him. Mr. Pierson had just shaken his hand and nodded. Eric remembered he had been in the military but for the life of him he couldn't remember where or when. Mrs. Pierson had hugged him and seemed to be tearing up. He wasn't sure why. A lot of people had been that way. It was like they all really knew what had happened but he was pretty sure it was still fully black. Was she reacting to something *he* was radiating? Hell, he wasn't that pessimistic.

He'd nearly panicked when Brooke Pierson shook his hand. She just made his mouth go dry. He hadn't been able to say *anything* to her. He wasn't even sure if he'd smiled. It was upsetting. He was usually suaver than that.

But the whole experience had shaken him on a really deep level. It wasn't being worried about the mission. If anything, he was looking forward to getting away. It was just . . . the changes. Things he thought were solid as the mountains were suddenly . . . different. And he was pretty sure that the changes were in him, not the world around him. So which version of reality was real?

He slid a chip into the truck's player and cranked up the volume, letting the soaring strains of Within Temptation wash over him as he lowered the seat. He had been a country fan before the mission and still listened to it from time to time, especially to Toby Keith and Clint Black. But at times like this it took the lyrics of Goth and metal groups to remind him why he did what he did.

"*'Tho this might just be the ending of the life I held so dear, I won't run, there's no turning back from here . . .*" he whispered to himself, folding his hands over the stubble on his head and closing his eyes. "*If I don't make it, someone else will, Stand My Ground.*"

He sat up, though, at a tap on his window. He'd deliberately parked at the very back of the church lot. Among other things, he knew he'd probably be cranking up the volume and he didn't want to bother anyone. But if this was another well-wisher . . . They could damned well deal with it.

However, the person standing outside his window was Brooke Pierson. He turned down the chip-player and slid his window down, blinking in surprise.

"I always thought you were a country guy," Brooke said, puzzled. "What was that?"

"'Stand My Ground'," he blurted. "Within Temptation. It's a Dutch band."

"Oh," Brooke said, still puzzled. "Look, we're going to Aubry's for brunch. Your family's going, too. I was wondering if you wanted to come."

"I thought we were going home for dinner," Eric said.

"Change of plans?" Brooke said. "My mom asked your mom if she wanted to come and it sort of expanded from there. Anyway, that's where we're going. You coming?"

"Sure," Eric replied.

"'Kay," Brooke said, waving. "See you there."

Aubry's was a buffet style restaurant, a tradition in Crab Apple. It served "good ole time" food, which meant heavy on the gravy and "fixin's." As Eric filled up his plate he had to admit he'd missed it. Lord knows he could use the calories. And it was nice to see that one thing hadn't changed.

"You can certainly put it away," Mrs. Pierson said as Eric sat down with his second heaping plate.

"He needs it," Amanda Bergstresser said. "He's as thin as a rail. Probably because he goes out running every morning. How far did you go this morning?"

"Not far," Eric said, taking a bite of meatloaf smothered in gravy.

"He told *me* he went ten miles," Josh said. "I'm still not sure I believe him."

"Like I said," Eric replied, looking over at his brother, "not far."

"Do you do a lot of running in the Marines?" Brooke asked.

"Yes, ma'am," Eric replied. "In my unit we do, anyway. Most Marines don't run as far, but everybody does morning PT."

"What unit is that?" Mr. Pierson asked.

"Bravo Company, Force Reconnaissance," Eric replied, automatically. Nobody outside the Barracks used the term Space Marines.

"I was in the Navy," Mr. Pierson said. "A bubblehead. Ever been on a submarine?"

Eric froze with a forkful of green beans in mid-air, then nodded.

"Yes, sir," he said, thinking about the cover for his unit. "I'm . . . well, I'm assigned to one of the new littoral boats. I actually spend a lot of time in a sub, sir."

"Do a lot of running around Sherwood Forest?" the vet asked, grinning.

"Sir, with respect, I'm not allowed to discuss any details of my missions," Eric replied.

"But you know where Sherwood Forest is, right?" Mr. Pierson said, smiling.

"Yes, sir," Eric replied. "It's where the missiles are on a normal sub, sir. But I'm not allowed to confirm or deny that there are missiles on the boat *I'm* on, sir."

"Gotcha."

"He's so mysterious," Mrs. Bergstresser said. "He won't even tell us why he got his medal."

"Don't push, Amanda," Steve Bergstresser said quietly. "He can't talk about it and it's uncomfortable when you're in that position."

"But we're not even at *war*," Amanda said. "And if he got a medal that means he was in *danger*. As his mother I'd like to know *why*."

"You will, Mom," Eric said, somberly. "Someday. Trust me. But right now it's all classified and I really *can't* talk about it."

"Do you enjoy what you do?" Brooke asked, frowning.

"That's . . . a good question," Eric admitted. "There are parts of it I like a lot. And there are parts that scare me spitless. Sometimes they're the same parts, but not usually."

"He told *me* that the reason he got that medal was because he was one of only five survivors of his last mission," Josh said.

"Oh thank you *very* much for saying *that* in public, Brother!" Eric snapped.

"What?" Mrs. Bergstresser said. "You're *joking!*"

"We need to change the subject," Mr. Bergstresser said. "Right *now*. And, Josh, when we get home we're going to have a little *talk*."

"When I was in boats the guys were real practical jokers," Mr. Pierson said, smiling in fond remembrance. "Is it still that way? Or have they cut the heart and soul out of the whole service?"

"What, like stealing the XO's door, sir?" Eric said, grinning. "No, sir, it's pretty much the same. One time we got one of the sergeants going really bad over . . . Never mind."

"Do all your conversations cut off like that?" Brooke asked.

"Yeah, pretty much," Eric admitted ruefully. His eyes darkened for a moment. "Okay, yeah, we took a lot of casualties on the last mission. But I made it and I'll make it the next time. I'll be fine, Mom."

"You must be very brave," Brooke said. Eric couldn't figure out if it was a good thing or bad her voice was so neutral.

"I just have a job to do," Eric said, shrugging. "Somebody has to do it and I'm pretty good at it."

"Do you still get into science fiction?" Mr. Pierson asked. "I recall you used to read quite a bit of it."

Every day, Eric thought. *In mission reports, after action reviews . . .* "Not so much anymore," he replied. "I do a bit of reading on cruises."

"Not much else for the Marines to do, I suppose," Mr. Pierson said, nodding. "Did you get anywhere interesting?"

You wouldn't believe, Eric thought again, trying not to snort. But the smile was evident.

"That interesting, huh?" Mr. Pierson said. "And you can't talk about it. Sorry."

"No, sir," Eric said. "Look, the missions we do are classified. Where we go is classified. I can say that we *get* there in a submarine. But we don't do many shore leaves, sir."

"I understand," Mr. Pierson said. "And I was the one trying to change the subject."

"I've got a change of subject," Brooke interjected. "What are we doing after dinner? I was wondering if we were going to the movies."

It was a bit of a tradition in small southern towns. Go to church. Have dinner. Go to a movie. In many cases you'd see the same faces all day long.

"I've got to go to the Halverson's this afternoon," Mr. Pierson said. "But the rest of you can do whatever you'd like."

"I could see a movie," Josh said.

"You've got homework," Mrs. Bergstresser said.

"So do Linda and Hector." Mrs. Pierson looked at her younger two children. "Brooke, I don't want you going to the movies alone . . ."

It was a set-up. He should have seen it coming. On the other hand . . . He could live. Hell, it wasn't like fighting crabpus.

"I didn't mean to set you up that way," Brooke said as they got in the truck. "Mom had said we were probably going to the movies after dinner."

"I didn't think you did," Eric replied, starting up. He couldn't look at her, though. "What do you want to listen to?"

"What you were listening to before," Brooke said. "It sounded sort of like Evanescence."

"Similar," Eric admitted, unbuttoning his collar. "I seriously don't mind taking you to the movies. But I'll admit I was looking forward to getting this damned uniform off."

"You can take the time to change," Brooke said, doubt in her voice. "But . . . It looks really good on you."

"I'll wear it," Eric said, looking over at her finally. "If you want, I'll be glad to."

"Please," Brooke said. "What do you want to see?"

"Let's just find out what's playing."

There wasn't anything either of them wanted to see playing for a couple of hours so they found a Starbucks in Beckley and sat and talked. Well, mostly Brooke talked. Eric couldn't for the life of him recall what they talked about but they talked, a lot. They talked in the café then drove back to the movie theater but by almost unspoken agreement didn't even go in. They just sat in the truck, listened to Eric's playlists and talked some more. Brooke was hoping to go to medical school, or maybe vet's school, she wasn't sure. Eric admitted to a desire to be a career Marine but didn't say much more than that about his future plans.

Finally, as the sky darkened the talk wound down.

"You haven't been saying much," Brooke admitted. "Usually I just sit there and listen as the guy I'm on a date with drones on about his latest interest. I do admit that I like your music taste, though."

"There's not much for me to talk about," Eric admitted.

"Or not much you can talk about," Brooke said. "But I can tell you're thinking something."

"I'm thinking that this was a really stupid thing to do," Eric said, then grimaced. "*Maulk*, did I actually say that? I'm sorry . . ."

"Fine, you don't want to spend time with me . . . !" Brooke said angrily.

"It's not that," Eric said, grabbing her hand as she started to climb out of the truck.

"Let go of me!"

"Can I just *please* explain?" Eric asked. "Please."

"Fine," Brooke said. "Explain. If you can."

"If I should," Eric said, looking past her even if his eyes were pointed in her direction. "I've never had a better time with any-one in my life. I really like you. Probably too much, Brooke. But what Josh said was true. What I do is . . . It's really dangerous. And I can't even explain why. All I can say is that one of these days you're probably going to hear that I've died. That's all you'll know, just like all my parents know about my medal is that I got it doing 'classified actions.'"

He finally looked her in the eyes and felt like crying.

"I really like you, Brooke. But I hope you don't feel anything near like what I feel. Because one of these days I'm probably going to just be *gone*."

"*Nothing* can be that dangerous," Brooke said, looking as if *she* was going to start crying. "You'll be okay."

"Seven out of eight," Eric said. "That's how many guys died on the last mission among the Marines. Seven out of eight. One of the guys who debriefed us admitted that he couldn't figure out how *any* group wouldn't mutiny with those sort of casualties. We didn't take them all in one shot; we got hammered over and over again. And we kept going back for more. There were a couple of points where it looked as if *nobody* was going to make it back to Ear—"

"Back to Earth," Brooke said, her eyes widening. "You were going through the Looking Glasses? Were you going to Dreen planets? Is that why it was so—"

"Look, I didn't say that, okay?" Eric said. "Please *please* don't repeat that. But, yeah, I was off-planet. And I'm going back. And it's probably going to be bad. My unit's job is to . . . poke. To poke to find out what's there. And it's generally hard and bad and nasty. And, yeah, a lot of it is interesting as hell and a lot of it is terrifying. And there's a good chance I won't come back. I'm not going to lay that on you. I'd love to say that I want to be with you, always. But I can't put that on anybody. Not with my chances of coming back. That's why I said I think this afternoon was a very bad idea. Had a great time; probably was a bad idea."

"I don't think it's a bad idea," Brooke said. "You know why?"

"Why?"

"Because if you have somebody to come back to, there's more *reason* to come back," Brooke said. "Promise me you'll come back. Promise."

"Can't," Eric said. "Because there were plenty of guys who had people to come back to that didn't. I was at the memorial. There were crying widows all over the place."

"Then I'll say this. I won't promise I won't date other guys or anything, because you're never home and I've got to go to prom with *somebody*. But I really like you, too, Eric. A lot more than any guy I've ever known. So *when* you come back, there will be a Brooke to come back to. Okay?"

Eric's implant dinged urgently. He ignored it, though, and took Brooke's hand. "Brooke, honey—"

"Priority Call from Gunnery Sergeant Daniel Neely," the military issue implant whispered. *"Priority call for Sergeant Eric Bergstresser . . ."*

"Damnit," Eric said, activating the implant. "Sergeant Bergstresser."

"Two-Gun," his platoon sergeant said. *"Recall. Right now. Get your ass back to Newport News even if you've got it half stuck in."*

"*Maulk, maulk* . . ." Two-Gun muttered. "Tell me you're *joking*, Gunny."

"Negative," the gunnery sergeant said. *"Get moving, Two-Gun. That's an order."*

"Aye, aye," Eric said. "Two-Gun, out."

"Two-Gun?" Brooke asked. "What was that . . . ?"

"I have to go," Eric said. "I need to take you home, then get home and pack."

"You've got a mission," Brooke said, her already pale skin whitening. "Don't you?"

"I . . . I don't know how long it will be until I can contact you," Eric said, starting the truck and putting it in gear. "Normally that's bullshit when someone says that. But in my case it's true. I'll be really *seriously* out of contact. And I don't know for how long. Figure three months."

"Eric," Brooke said about halfway home.

"Yes?"

"I take it back. I won't sit under the apple tree with anyone else. Not for five months. I'll give you that long."

"I can't say I'm sorry," Eric replied. "But I also can't say you *won't* be."

"Can I just ask one teeny question about what you do?" Brooke asked.

"Maybe."

"Why did you call yourself Two-Gun?"

3

Any casual observer would have noticed the sudden flurry of activity on a sleepy Sunday evening on a normally nearly deserted platform. The apparent street person muttering to himself on the platform's single bench was anything *but* a casual observer. He had memorized a list of faces but in many cases he didn't really need it. The one Marine in incongruous dress blues he'd seen in the news.

Moscow Center was going to be *very* interested in this development. The entire crew of the *Vorpal Blade* seemed to be flooding back, quite unexpectedly. There could be only one reason for that and by tomorrow *Akulas* would be redeploying to watch for the American's newest "submarine" as it set sail.

However, although he was a trained observer, he hadn't noticed that one platform up, the only route down to *this* platform, the Pakistani vendor of the sundries shop had apparently sold out to a new Chinese owner.

More than *Akulas* would be watching.

"Two-Gun," Michael Gants said, sucking in through his teeth. "Now we all *know* it's gonna get bad."

"Sub Dude," Eric said, nodding at the machinist's mate. "Scared any children lately?"

"My kids scare *me*," Gants replied. "And the other kids. And casual strangers. And Jehovah's Witnesses, although I can't complain about that one."

"Hey, Two-Gun," Corporal Julian Nicholson said. "How they hanging?"

"That's Sergeant Bergstresser to you, Nugget," Eric replied. "But for your information, at the moment they're pulled up and blue. I was in the middle of a date."

"Sucks to be you, Sergeant," the corporal said as the light over the entry turned green. "What's up with the recall?"

"If I knew, I certainly wouldn't be telling you on an open platform, Corporal," Eric replied, swiping his card and stepping through the Looking Glass.

The guard on the far side had been augmented by three Navy NCOs, a Navy lieutenant Eric didn't recognize and Gunnery Sergeant Neely.

"At Ease!" the gunny shouted as the group gathered in front of the gate, chattering. "LT?"

"Busses outside," the lieutenant said into the quiet. "Front two are for Naval personnel, rear one for the Marines. Fall into your busses. You're not going to get briefed until you're all in a secure area, so don't bother asking. Now get moving."

"Two-Gun," Gunny Neely said as he headed for the exit. "As soon as you get your shit stored, get your team down to the quarterdeck. As soon as the company's assembled, Top's going to brief us."

"Aye, aye, Gunny," Eric said. "Any clues?"

"What you've got is what I've got."

"Get the *grapp* out of the rack, into uniform and down to the quarterdeck," Eric said, sticking his head into the two-man room occupied by the rest of his team. Lance Corporals Mark Smith and Mark Himes, or as he half thought of them "Mark y Mark" were replacements as was most of the "company." Normally, Force Recon companies were oversized with a full count of grunts, around a hundred and forty, and a mass of detachments. They were some of the largest "companies" in the military, with a TO&E of over two hundred bodies.

The Space Marine company was, by contrast, probably the smallest. It only had a total complement of forty-one, including its very limited number of "clerks and jerks." Essentially, it was a platoon with some supports. But since the job of leading it required at *least* a captain, it got called a company.

The replacements had mostly come from the two full-sized Force Recon companies. A few were direct from the new Force Recon qual course. In many cases, teams were made up of guys who had trained with each other for years. They knew each other, understood each other's strengths and weaknesses, had team names they used, were a *team*.

Berg had a hard time remembering most of their names. He sometimes forgot even the names of the platoon sergeants. To him, and the other two junior survivors of the last mission, they were all Nuggets. They might be Marines, they might even be Force Recon. They weren't Space Marines.

"Jesus, we just got in," Himes said or at least Eric thought it was Himes. The two replacement lance corporals were similar in appearance, both being tall and stocky with brown hair and regular features. When they'd first started training, the only way that Eric could tell them apart was that Smith had a tattoo of a spider on the back of his neck. If he was looking at them face on he regularly got them confused until he looked at their name tags.

"And we're going out nearly as fast," Berg said tightly.

"What's up, Sergeant?" Smith said, rolling out of his rack and pulling a set of digi-cam out of his wall-locker.

"That's what we're here to find out," Berg said. "Now get a move on, Marines."

The company had fallen out on the quarterdeck, a large indoor area on the side of the barracks that doubled as a PT room. It was, however, fairly secure with thick concrete walls lined by a Faraday cage to prevent electronic eavesdropping.

Looking around, since they were at Rest, Eric could tell that some people were missing. But Corwin and Seeley were there, the only two junior enlisted members of the old company to have survived besides himself. The survivors had been distributed around, each in a different platoon. Berg was the team leader for Bravo Team, First Platoon, the Alpha Team position being reserved for a staff sergeant. Seeley was a "rifleman" in Alpha Second and Corwin was a cannoneer in Alpha Third.

A third face, though, caught his eye. Corporal Joshua Lyle was standing in position just down from Seeley in Third Platoon. The very tall and skinny corporal with a shock of short-cut nearly white hair was cocked slightly to the side, the result of a nearly fatal Humvee accident. He'd been in rehab for damned near a year before being returned to duty as an armorer. But the spot he was standing in was for one of the line platoons.

"Lurch?" Berg said, twisting to look at the armorer. "Aren't you sort of out of position?"

"Not anymore," the corporal replied in a deep baritone. "While you guys was on vacation, I was going through re-qual. I'm cleared for line duty," he finished with a grin.

"Congratulations," Eric said honestly. He liked the quirky armorer and was glad he was back on the line, which had always been his preference. "But who's going to come up with weird, wacky and vitally necessary weapons on the spur of the moment? I *depend* on you, Lurch!"

"I trained in the new guy," Lurch said, grinning. "I think he might do."

"You di'n't train me for nottink, Corporal!" an accented voice said from the rear of the formation. "I pocking train *you*!"

Berg couldn't for the life of him see who was speaking so he lifted up on tiptoes. Beside the new operations sergeant, he could see a shock of black hair and that was about it. Whoever had spoken was apparently just barely regulation height.

"Okay, I admit it," Lurch said, still grinning. "Sergeant Portana was one of my instructors in Armorer's School."

"Dat right," the apparently Sergeant Portana said loudly. "And I t'ought you neber pocking pass . . ."

"Ten-hut!" First Sergeant Powell bellowed, striding towards the front of the formation. "And for those of you who cannot recall your basic military etiquette that means stand straight with your mouth shut."

Top looked around the formation and nodded.

"Report!"

"First Platoon, one missing!"

"Second Platoon, three missing or not present!"

"Third Platoon, two Marines missing or not present!"

"Not bad," Top said. "At Ease. First an administrative item. Captain Zanella, having noted the cost of a roll of space tape and its impact on the budget, has ordered all personal rolls turned in and use of the material in the future to be by platoon leaders and platoon sergeants and above *only* and only in fully official capacities."

"First Sergeant?" Corwin said, raising his hand. "Did you . . . discuss this with the Old Man?"

"No, I didn't, Corwin," Top replied. "He's responsible for the budget. It's his call."

"Aye, aye, First Sergeant," Corwin replied, frowning.

"What's the deal?" Himes whispered.

"Space tape is . . ." Berg said, his eyes wide. "Space tape is how everything *works*! Without *space tape* we're . . ."

"At ease," the first sergeant said, quieting the murmurs. "Now for the mission. A research group on one of the gate worlds was apparently attacked. The gate has been closed for safety purposes. We are ordered to investigate, see if there are any survivors of the attack and our response, determine who the attackers were and report back. The world is going to be about a month's cruise away. We will be doing pre-mission physicals en route. We lift no later than midnight on Tuesday. The ship is done refitting except for some minor details but *none* of our shit is on-board. We have two days to get everything loaded in *my* order of importance. Since that includes the Wyverns, and the ship will be loading all her other *maulk* at the same time, we're going to be pressed for time. So I need you to stay focused on the mission and not *grapping* off. Are there any questions?"

"First Sergeant?" Seeley said, raising his hand.

"Go, Chuckie."

"So our mission, as Space Marines, is to go to a planet where a colony has been attacked and contact is cut off, find out who attacked them and deal with it?" Seeley asked.

"Correct," the first sergeant replied. "And, no, Chuckie, you can *not* ask 'How do I get out of this chicken*maulk* outfit.'"

"How's it going, Astro?" the CO asked, looking over Weaver's shoulder as sailors toted bundles through the crowded conn.

The ASS *Vorpal Blade* had undergone several changes that were not directly inherent to her mission. One example was moving a small navigational section into the conn. The already crowded compartment did *not* need to become more crowded and navigation could, technically, be done from anywhere on the ship. However, it was recognized that the nature of the astrogator was such that he doubled as, effectively, the ship's science officer. Anything "scientifically weird" about what they

were doing—defined as astronomical, astrophysical or gravitational anomalies—meant that the conning officer was going to
ask the astrogator: "Okay, what's going on?" It just made sense
to, somehow, shoehorn the astro into the same compartment as
the guy doing the asking.

Doing so, however, had been difficult. Despite the massive size
of a ballistic nuclear missile submarine, the interior was cramped.
The conn was the size of a small living room, only ten feet
wide and barely twelve long. It contained the diving board, the
planesmen, the conning officer, etc. Six people, their chairs in
several cases, readouts, input systems, screens and the equipment
they handled had to fit in an area most people would consider
comfortable for two.

The designers had managed to fit a station designed for underwater navigation *and* deep space astrogation in. They had done
so by making everything *very small*.

"There are times that I'd kill for *one* decent screen, sir,"
Weaver answered, peering at the six-inch plasma screen, one of
three stacked vertically, that currently showed a moving star field.
"Not to mention a decent sized keyboard." The one that he hit
a command on was about the size of a laptop's.

"Want to use the main viewers?" the CO asked, pointing
forward.

While there was not a huge amount of lateral space in the
conn, there was a bit more vertically. Oh, it wasn't a high compartment, but there was some free space.

The *Blade*, during its repairs, had been upgraded with a set of
adjustable screens for viewing in the conn. Made by the Adari,
they were not only thin, they were flexible. They could be rolled
down from the overhead and while fairly rigid were flexible enough
that if someone hit them with his head they would bend rather
than cause a concussion.

They also were selectively sizeable. Although they were normally
rolled down so that they were only a meter or so in height they
could be lowered all the way to the deck. With all six deployed
and an exterior view on, it was a bit like being on the hull.
The capability had forced the refitters to, reluctantly, remove the
"window" in conn from the *Blade*.

"Not with what I'm working on, sir," Bill said, grinning. "I
don't want the crew getting any more nervous about this mission

than they already are. And having the astrogator obviously unsure where he's going wouldn't be good."

"Just tell me we're not going to hit any stars," the CO said.

"Can't, sir," Bill replied. "Basically, we're going far enough out that the star charts start getting iffy. I take that back. We shouldn't hit any *stars*. Just the new visuals would prevent that."

The viewscreens wouldn't be of much use without something to see. Another upgrade had been to install a series of powerful telescopes on the sail and in "bubbles" about the circumference of the hull. With the new main telescope, which was good enough to resolve a twenty-meter diameter boulder on the Moon, the ship had powerful "eyes" pointed in every direction. In space, visual detection was still one of the better ways to find things. But the retrofit of such a large aperture telescope was a problem.

Initially the plans were to put a three-meter diameter mirror Schmidt-Cassegrain telescope on the sail. The problem with that was the fact that the three-meter honeycombed optic and housing and the tracking and pointing hardware would take up an area on the boat the size of a one-car garage. They might have gotten the various countries interested in this new "submarine" to think it was a helo hangar . . . or not. And the drag underwater would be God-awful. So a single large telescope idea was scrapped.

Weaver had figured out a better solution. He set up five smaller half-meter diameter telescopes in the right locations about the ship's circumference so that they would look like they were pieces of a much larger mirror when they were pointed together. The mirrors were placed in a circle about the submarine's hull and when acting together they acted like one mirror the diameter of the ship plus some—about twelve meters. In technical optics terms this was called a sparse array telescope. The actual configuration was known as a "circle five" primary optic.

The problem with the sparse array was that all the mirrors had to be precisely positioned and controlled to within a few millionths of a meter and this required two things: 1) Adar jitter control hardware and software and 2) the ship had to be pointed in the direction of the celestial object being observed. The design also limited the main scope to a degree or so of steering about the ship's travel axis. On the other hand, there were five half-meter telescopes that could be used as separate systems giving full spherical view of the space around the ship. Each would have less resolving power but until someone came up with "long-range viewers" that not only could identify an individual face from a hundred light-years away but could do so faster than light . . . they'd have to put up with reality.

"What's giving me fits is trying to get a good algorithm for the grav bubbles."

On the previous mission the *Blade* had discovered that gravity worked differently between stars than it did in the immediate region of them. This caused a gravitational disturbance area around each star. The disturbance area was related to the size of the star, how massive it was. Around Sol it started at about a light-year and stretched for about sixty astronomical units, the latter being defined as the distance from the Earth to the sun, one hundred and fifty thousand kilometers or about eight light-minutes. Bigger stars had larger bubbles. In some cases, where two stars were in a binary or multi-star system, the bubbles overlapped, creating massive regions of gravitational disruption. Traveling into and out of the bubbles had been worked out. Moving through one of the multi-star regions, though, was "problematic." The last time the *Blade* had traveled through one it had been bent, folded and darn near mutilated.

"I'll add that I would prefer not to hit a *grav bubble* unawares," the CO said dryly. The first time they'd gone through one, mostly unawares, it had sent the drive haywire and kicked the *Blade* through a dimension jump that left it forty light-years off-course. If it hadn't been for Weaver and the other astronomers onboard, they'd still be playing "Lost in Space."

"So would I, sir," Bill admitted, peering at the screen. "But what's really got me worried is what's not on the charts. We've had teams out on the other planets doing paralax studies of stars and other stellar phenomena for over eight years. But we still don't have solid distances and positions on every star in the catalogue, much less uncatalogued ones. And where we're going, we're hitting 'uncatalogued' area. So, really, I don't know what's out there for sure and for certain.

"And it's not just stars we've got to worry about. *I've* got to worry about. We don't *know* if there are any black holes out there, for example. Just because they're not on the charts doesn't mean they're not there. And the course I'm laying in is going to put us in *just* the sort of area where they'd be undetected. There's only two ways to detect them at any range. Either by effect on nearby stars—and I'm planning on staying far enough away from stars that that's not a way to see them—or if they occlude a star. Then they make a particular diffraction pattern of the occluded star's wavefront as predicted by general relativity: That's a sort of cross pattern that's really cool. But that doesn't matter."

"Are we getting anywhere with this?" Spectre asked, sighing. Sometimes Weaver's technobabble could try a saint.

"The thing is, sir, they just *sit* there," Bill said, frowning. "Well, sort of. If the black hole has been around long enough to start sucking in matter the accelerated ionized debris will be emitting gamma rays like all get-out. That is why I wanted to have us grab the Chandra X-ray telescope out of orbit and mount it in the ship somewhere, but NASA whined and whined . . . so we aren't gonna be detecting the black holes that way and our on-board X-ray telescopes ain't accurate enough to do us any good in that regard. Besides, we don't know that all black holes have accretion disks that emit gamma rays. Though I kinda think they do."

"So we're *not* getting anywhere with this?" the CO growled.

"Bottomline, sir?"

"Please."

"There's just no *sure* way to detect them until it's too late. We *probably* shouldn't get near one, but it's got me worried. So do undetected neutron stars. Those are less of an issue since they generally give off a pretty solid X-ray signature. Actually, it's strong enough to kill us if we're not in warp . . ."

"Stop," the CO said, grinning. "You're giving me the warm and fuzzies!"

"Then there's the fact that at the far end of the mission things like M-class stars are going to be questionable for detection," Weaver continued. "There could be undetected dwarfs, in other words. In *this* area we've got all these stars like Groombridge 34 mapped out. They're *dim*, a fraction of Sol's magnitude, and pretty small. But they're going to have grav bubbles around them. Not as big as Sol's, but they'll be there. And when you get out towards places like HD 36951 they're not on the charts. Nobody in the regular astronomical community has ever considered anybody would *care*. And mapping them now would require a rather specific tasking of one of the newer space telescopes."

"And the solution is . . . ?" Spectre asked, sucking in to let an overburdened crewman by. The sigh when he relaxed had nothing to do with Astro's explanation. Absolutely nothing.

"When we get out to about two hundred light-years we need to stop and do a forward survey, sir," Bill said. "That may take a couple of days. Our time going out is going to be increased. Coming back should be easier. The survey will be done."

"We're in a rush to get there, Commander," the CO said.

"I'm aware of that, sir," Bill said. "But my job is to get us there. Alive, sir. I cannot guarantee the last bit unless we have some clue what we're driving into. Think of it as uncharted waters, sir. You go *slow*. Going a light-year an hour into the mess we're headed into is like going at flank speed into a reef, sir. We're back in the days of Captain Cook, sir. We need to throw some sounding lines."

"I accept and comprehend your metaphor, Astro," Spectre said, wincing. "Watch the rocks and shoals."

"Yes, sir," Bill said. "And there are going to be some."

"I can't believe the CO wants us to turn in all our space tape," Corwin said, handing over a partial roll to Gunny Juda. His tone was one of deepest sadness. "What are we going to do without it?"

"Use rigger-tape like any normal Marine," the gunnery sergeant growled.

"Gunny Juda, with all due respect," Berg said, holding out his own spare, "we're not regular Marines."

"It don't mean we have to use this stuff," Gunny Juda said, waving one of the many partials he'd collected in the air. "You got any idea how expensive this stuff is?"

"One hundred thousand dollars per thirty-foot roll," Berg replied.

"No shit?" Himes gasped. "That's *grapping* insane!"

"Gunny," Berg said, ignoring Himes, "let me be clear. I consider this an order right on the edge of madness. May I make my salient points?"

"You earned your say, Two-Gun," the gunnery sergeant admitted. "But an order is an order."

"Roger that, Gunny," Berg said. "Here, however, are my salient points. When you get a minor breach in a Wyvern, say from a micrometeorite, how do you patch it?"

"What's wrong with rigger-tape?" Gunny Juda said. "And there's a patch kit."

"The patch kit takes up to ten minutes to set, Gunny," Berg replied. "It's a minor little footnote in the training documents I don't think you noticed. Meanwhile, your air is goin' out the hole. And you don't have all that much of it. Rigger-tape is not impermeable to air, simply resistant. It will not hold in vacuum and fails under high pressures. Not to mention the fact that the base woven material is subject to thermal cracking in space cold and melting in space heat. Space tape holds. You got any rigger-tape holding stuff down on your carrying vest, Gunny?"

"Sure," the gunnery sergeant replied, looking thoughtful. "Gotta keep stuff from moving around. Otherwise you sound like a tinker."

"The load-bearing equipment we've been issued has been rated for space work," Berg said. "It's designed to go over our suits. And in space, you *really* don't want stuff floating around. Forget the noise, it's going to hook on something and probably end up killing you. So we've all secured any loose bits. If you've used rigger-tape, however, as soon as you enter a death pressure environment, much less have to go EVA, it becomes exactly as useful as so much toilet paper. Now, contrary to the CO's desires, my gear is secured with space tape, Gunny. It's fully reusable. Care to pull it all off?"

"I'm beginning to get your point, Two-Gun," Gunny Juda said sourly. "So why'd Top just take the order?"

"Well, Gunny, I have hereby turned in my one officially reported roll of space tape," Berg said. "I'll leave the rest to your professional consideration."

"Gotcha," the gunny said, nodding. "For somebody who's not much more than a wet behind the ears recruit, you seem to be fitting right in to the Corps, Two-Gun."

"I do try, Gunnery Sergeant," Berg said. "I do try."

"Hey, Sergeant Bergstresser, do we know anything about this planet we're going to?" Corporal Vote asked as soon as the gunny, who had become much less insistent on securing "every last roll," left the compartment.

The teams were assembling their gear for shipment and the activity slowed minutely as the other Marines listened in. Not only was Two-Gun Berg one of the "old hands" he was one of the unit instructors on astronomy and physics. If anyone was going to know, it was going to be Two-Gun.

"I barely got a chance to glance at the data," Berg said, stuffing another skinsuit in his bag. It had been one of his suggestions in the after-action review from the last mission that more than one of the suits be assigned to each Marine. They'd ended up spending a lot of time in the Wyvern Armored Combat Systems, which required wearing the skin-tight black suits. After a couple of hours of heavy use they got a bit rank. Since they were often in and out of the suits too fast to get the suits washed, the rankness had pretty much permeated the Marine compartment on the last mission. This time they'd each been issued four, which was probably *too* many. There was only so much room for personal gear on the ship.

"The sun is an A3V," Berg continued. "What's that tell you, Corporal?"

"Blue?" Vote said unsurely. "Blue and hot if I remember correctly, Sergeant."

"That would be the description," Eric said. "A very hot blue giant. The planet, however, is well out at the outside edge of the life zone. In fact, it's over four AU from the sun. Nearly as far as the asteroid belt is from Sol. Lance Corporal Himes, that means what?"

"It's cold," Himes replied. "Life zone is defined as the orbit region around a star in which the ambient temperature of a planet is between zero and one hundred degrees, Celsius, meaning that water is neither constantly frozen solid nor boiled off. Being on the outside it's going to be damned near frozen solid. Sort of like Mars. Atmo?"

"Barely," Berg said. "Low O_2, high CO_2. Technically, it's outside the life zone. Why is it still considered habitable . . . Lance Corporal Uribe?"

"Probably the CO_2 gives it a greenhouse effect," Mario Uribe said. The rifleman from Charlie First was short, slender and dark.

"On target," Berg said. "It's Wyverns all the way on this one. The scientists working there used respirators and cold-weather gear, but we'll be using Wyverns. Light levels are below Earth standard, meaning it's going to be relatively dark even with the sun at zenith. It's a bright sun but it's a *long* way away. So it's going to look more like a planet that you can see at midday.

The planet has ruins that are at least twenty million years old located near the Looking Glass. Probably it was warmer back then. Nothing is known about the previous residents that I'm aware of. And since they've been gone for twenty million years, they're probably not the problem."

"The briefing said they dropped a nuke through the Glass," Vote said. "What's there going to be to find? I mean, even if there were other survivors, they're *gone*. Right?"

"That, Marine, is what we're going there to find out," Berg replied. "And to do that, we need to get this shit loaded. So I'd suggest more packing and less chatter."

4

"Handsomely! Lower away!"

"What the *grapp* does handsomely mean?" Sergeant Priester asked nervously.

There was plenty of reason to be nervous. The bosun doing the shouting was in charge of the party loading the SM-9s, space-combat missiles based on the Trident and tipped by Adar ardune warheads. They *probably* wouldn't destroy the entire area if one dropped free, but only probably.

Ardune was a substance known as quarkium, only a theoretical material before encountering the Adar. The material was composed of unique quarks, entirely of quarks of one particular type. Since quarks combined with other "flavors" in nature, when released to encounter "normal" material it caused subatomic chain reactions that were more powerful than equal quantities of antimatter. Antimatter just hit normal matter and released their combined energy. Quarkium did that and then just kept giving and giving. The SM-9s weren't the only quarkium devices on the ship. The space-torps were quarkium tipped, and the drive used it. All in all, the *Blade* was just one giant nova waiting to happen. If there had been any choice but sitting it in Newport News, the Powers That Be would have gone for it.

Unfortunately, basing anywhere else was logistically unsupportable. The *Blade* was a *ship*. It was a big, complex system of machinery. When it returned from the last mission, whole sections of its hull blasted away, it had been forced to put down at Groom Lake, the region people knew as "Area 51." But despite movies to the contrary, there were no facilities to repair spaceships at Groom Lake. Doing the minimal repairs to get the ship capable of entering the water had taken up more time than all the repairs at Newport News.

And *building* a space port was out of the question. The program was still entirely black. Any such facility would have been instantly spotted by Russian spy satellites. Heck, the construction would be obvious to *commercial* satellites. And creating some huge underground facility that a ship the size of a WWII battleship could fly into would have been nightmarish.

Using the sub pens at Newport News, dangerous as that might be, was the only way to maintain any shred of deniability and security. There were plans in the works, once a breakthrough made it possible to create more ships, to create a major spaceport. But in the meantime, Newport News was the world's first.

The organized chaos of the rapid loading proved that, for the time being, it was a good choice. The missiles, under Marine guards from the nearby Naval Weapons Station, could be rapidly and efficiently loaded at the same time as the mass of material necessary for the mission was being shoved through every hatch the ship had.

The number of hatches was, however, limited. So part of the load plan detailed specific groups to specific hatches and included routes to their storage areas. Otherwise you ended up with sailors loaded with food, cleaning supplies and parts crossing paths with Marines loaded with weapons, body armor and equipment. It was never a good mix.

"Handsomely means slowly and carefully," Berg said, negotiating his way down a ladder with an armload of body armor. "Which is how we're going to have to load the Wyverns."

The Wyvern suits were nine feet tall and weighed in at just under a ton. The bulbous body of the suit held the pilot, who drove it through a set of controls attached to arms, legs, head and torso. Half worn, half "flown," the suits were getting more and more intuitive with each iteration. But they were difficult to load in a submarine.

"As soon as your team's gear is stored, meet me in the Wyvern storage area. We're next to use the crane after the missiles."

"Got it," Priester said. "I've never loaded them before. Is it that hard?"

"I dunno," Berg said. "When I got to the unit, they were already loaded. But I'm told it's a stone bitch."

"Three teams," Gunnery Sergeant Juda said. "Lower, tote and load. Two-Gun."

Juda was a short, slight, intense senior NCO with jet-black hair and a face that was unusually pale for a Marine and that seemed to have a perpetual five-o'clock-shadow. His parents had defected to the U.S. during the latter part of the Cold War and although he had been born and raised in New Jersey he carried a fire of anger against anyone and anything that smacked of an enemy of the United States. What he had to say about communists, pseudo-Marxists or any other stripe of socialist wasn't printable.

"Gunny?" Berg answered. He was already worn out from loading all the team's gear and accoutrements. Now they had to load Wyverns. Thank God the Navy was handling the ammo.

"Your team is going to be on lower duty to start," the gunny continued, pointing up. Room for the Marine "security detachment" and the scientists they normally carried had been made by ripping out twenty of the twenty-four missiles that had once filled the ship. A large housing area had been installed to replace them, containing not only bunks for the Marines and small cabins for the science teams but kitchens, mess halls, toilets, supply room, armory, labs and all the other things people needed to live, work and fight. There wasn't actually much room for bodies.

The space where one tube had been, though, was left open. The open space descended through all three levels of the ship, with heavy hatches at each level and on the outside. It was the primary loading point for all the heavy equipment the Marines and scientists needed, including the Wyverns.

The Wyverns themselves were stored in racks between the remaining missile tubes, sixty of them in all. It was up to nine Marines to get them all loaded in less than twelve hours.

"The Wyvern will be dropped through that hatch," the gunny continued. "Bosun Charles is in charge of lowering. On the first level it's not much trouble. You attach those lines to the clamp points on the shoulder," he said, gesturing at the devices, "then swing the Wyvern over to the side until it's on solid ground.

"But we're starting on the bottom level," the gunny continued, grinning evilly. "And the problem with lowering them that far is that they have a tendency to swing. So at each level they have to be secured. Question?"

"Two secure points to prevent them swinging, Gunny," Berg said, frowning. "There are only three of us. There are three levels."

"You've put your finger on the problem," Gunny Juda said, still grinning. "Here's the answer," he continued, pointing to a series of davits on the bulkhead. "One guy on each level. Run one line through the aft davit, one line through the forward, then bring the standing end together through the central davit. That centers it if you belay properly. Use the leather gloves to belay it and *don't* wrap the lines around your body. I'd much rather lose a Wyvern than a Marine. Stop it at each level and put in the control lines. Sergeant Priester."

"Present, Gunnery Sergeant."

"When it reaches the load level, your team will then hook the Wyvern into its carrier," the gunny continued, pointing to the thing that looked vaguely like an exoskeleton on wheels. "Hook it up from the front, which may mean swinging it around, crank it back and roll it to the secure point. There you leave the carrier, pick up the next one and return to the load point. Are you clear on that?"

"Clear, Gunnery Sergeant."

"Staff Sergeant Hinchcliffe," the gunny said, looking at the assistant platoon leader. "Your team will start on securing the Wyverns. Each has to be loaded into their racks, locked down and secured. By the time you're done with that, you're going to be getting the next one if everyone's working their ass off. The Wyvern has to be jacked up in its carrier and slid back in. It *should* be possible to hold it in place with one Marine. The other two then attach it. There are no idlers in this process. NCOs are going to be doing as much work as their troops. Is that clear to everyone?"

"Clear, Gunnery Sergeant," Staff Sergeant Brian Hinchcliffe said. The brown-haired NCO had a round moon face and a chunky body but he came across looking more like a boulder than a marshmallow.

"Nobody on the teams has ever done any of this," the gunny admitted. "Including me. And Wyverns are big pieces of metal that have a habit of getting away from you if you're not careful as hell. So we're going to do it slow at first and very much by the book. Let's get started. Two-Gun, get in commo with Bosun Charles and ask for the first Wyvern."

"Aye, aye, Gunny," Berg said, touching his earbud. "Bosun Charles, this is Sergeant Bergstresser. We're ready for the first Wyvern."

"Glad to hear it," the bosun replied. "I'll get to you as soon as I have the last of the ardune torps loaded."

"Uh, roger," Berg said, looking over at the Gunny. "Gunny, Bosun Charles says he's working on the ardune torps."

"They were supposed to be already *loaded*!" Juda snarled. "We were after the missiles! Sailors! Everybody just cool your heels while I figure out what's going on! Might as well be working with a *grapping* dock-worker's union!"

"Commander Weaver," the XO said, walking past Bill's station with an armload of documents. "Get out on the hull and sort out the loading of the Wyverns. There's some foul-up with timing. But the priority is the load-list, keep that in mind."

"Yes, sir," Bill said, nodding. "Will do."

Up on the deck it was even more chaotic than in the ship. Exiting from the rear of the sail, he could see the argument in progress between a Marine gunnery sergeant and one of the base support bosuns. Both men were red in the face and activity had stopped around them.

"Gunnery Sergeant . . . Juda," Bill said, looking at the Gunny's nametag. "Bosun Charles. What's the problem?"

"We got a late delivery on the ardune torps, sir," the bosun said, obviously relieved to dump the problem on someone else. "They were supposed to load ahead of the SM-9s but they weren't here so I went ahead with loading the SM-9s. The torps are here, now. So I need to load them. That's the priority list. The Wyverns were supposed to follow the SM-9s but they're just going to have to wait."

"My team's in place, now, sir," the gunnery sergeant responded. "Our schedule calls for a max of twelve hours of loading. Then they have a four hour rest period. Then we've got more loading to do. I can't have them sitting around with their thumbs up their butts for four hours while the bosun loads torps. This is *our* load slot."

Bill looked at the overhead and frowned. There were *two* cranes but the other one was detailed as well. He thought about its load list but there wasn't any way to bump anything.

"Load the torps," he said after a moment's thought.

"Aye, aye, sir," the bosun said, trying not to smile in triumph.

"Sir . . ." the gunnery sergeant started to protest.

"Gunny, that's the load priority," the commander replied. "Period. Torps go before Wyverns. I wish we had another way to load the Wyverns, but I don't think you want to belay them down by hand. And it would be unsafe even if you did. So you're going to have to wait until the torps are loaded. Period. Bosun, *expedite* that loading, but with all due care. If one of those goes up, there won't be a Newport News anymore. Or Norfolk. Or, hell, half of Virginia. Gunny, if you can present me with any viable method of getting the Wyverns from the dock," he continued, pointing to where the Wyverns were standing in racks on a container, "down that hole and into the ship, I'll entertain it. But it had better be functional and safe. I'll be in the conn."

"They're loading the torps," Gunny Juda said when he got down to where the loading team was waiting. "The *astrogator* made the call," he added disgustedly.

"Commander Weaver's a good officer, Gunnery Sergeant Juda," Eric said respectfully. "If he made that call he had a reason."

"Well, in my opinion he made it based on being *Navy* instead of *Marines*," the Gunny said. "But that's what we have to put up with. Get down to the magazines and assist with the ammo loading. But don't get too involved. I'm going to bring this to Top and see if we can't get our priority bumped up."

Staff Sergeant Hinchcliffe watched the fuming gunnery sergeant stump off, then glanced at Berg.

"What do you think Top will say?" the staff sergeant asked.

"That if Commander Weaver made the call, that's it," Eric replied. "Staff Sergeant, in the absence of a higher authority, you obey the next orders you get. Could I ask for an order?"

"Go," Hinchcliffe said.

"Could you order me to go investigate another method of getting the Wyverns into the ship?"

"Ahem," Hinchcliffe said thoughtfully. "Sergeant Bergstresser!"

"Yes, Staff Sergeant?"

"While the rest of us are working on loading ammo, I think your time would best be served trying to find an alternate method to load the Wyverns. You are so ordered."

"Thank you, Staff Sergeant."

Eric climbed up on the deck of the sub and looked around. The starboard crane, the one that would be loading the Wyverns, was slowly and gently lowering a torpedo into a forward hatch. It lowered the torp, lifted away and then paused over the next one, waiting.

He hit the timer in his implant and waited. And waited. Finally the crane moved again, hooking up to a torpedo and lifting it into the air as the loading team reappeared.

Eric frowned and looked down the hole, figuring out how long it would take to pick up one of the Wyverns and drop it into place. He estimated the time it would take to move the crane back and forth and then headed over to the crane.

The bosun was controlling the movements of the crane from the dock and was standing with his arms folded, the latest torp having been dropped, when Berg walked up.

"Bosun, permission to speak?" Berg asked, more or less to the bosun's back.

"Go, Marine," Charles replied indifferently.

"Bosun, I note that there is about a seven minute idle time as each torp is loaded. I'm wondering if it would be possible to use that idle time to load the Wyverns?"

"I'm trying to figure out why I should do two loadings at once," the bosun said, not looking around. "And I'm not going to wear my operator out running the crane back and forth. So, no, it would not be possible."

"Thank you, Bosun," Berg said. "Permission to withdraw?"

"Get the hell out of my hair, Marine," the Bosun said. "Okay! Get the next one ready!"

". . . If Commander Weaver says they have priority, they have priority," First Sergeant Powell said mildly. "We'll get the Wyverns loaded, Wieslaw. Just not right now."

"Just because some *Navy* commander says that they can't load them—" Juda started to say.

"Gunnery Sergeant Juda, be aware that that *Navy* commander

dropped with us on Cheerick," Top interrupted, somewhat less mildly. "And stood his ground in the Cavern when things you can't imagine were trying to turn us into dinner. He was involved in ground combat with Chief Miller during the Dreen War. He's not just some Navy wuss. With a little seasoning, I'd take him as a company commander any day. If he says they load the torps, they load the torps."

"Yes . . . Pardon me, Top," Juda said, holding a hand up to his mastoid bone. "Go, Sergeant Bergstresser. Really? Wait one. First Sergeant," Juda said, starting to grin. "Sergeant Bergstresser has a point to make about the loading. But the decision . . ."

"Tell Berg to meet me in conn," the first sergeant said with a sigh. "*You* stay here. I think this negotiation needs a little emotional detachment."

"Sir, permission to speak?" the first sergeant said standing by the astrogation center.

"Being a little formal today, Top?" Weaver said, running his hands through his hair distractedly. "If this is about the Wyverns . . ."

"Sir, I don't think you've ever officially met Sergeant Bergstresser, have you?" the first sergeant said.

"No, I haven't," Weaver said, looking up at the tall sergeant standing at attention. Berg was sucked into the bulkhead to keep out of the way of the stream of sailors hurrying through conn. "Pleased to finally officially meet you, Two-Gun, given that we've sweated blood together. Congratulations on the Navy Cross. It was well deserved."

"Thank you, sir!" Berg barked.

"At ease for God's sake. Top, we've only got two cranes . . ."

"Sir, Sergeant Bergstresser has a point to make on that subject," the first sergeant interrupted again. "Two-Gun?"

Berg explained about the lag time on loading the torps, at which point Weaver's left eyebrow raised.

"Really," he said. "Seven minutes, huh? Let's go up top."

"Yeah, that's a solid block of time," Weaver said after watching the loading for a couple of torpedoes. "But I'm not sure it's enough time for them to swing over and drop a Wyvern."

"Yes, sir," Berg said. "But at the very most it will increase both load times, slightly, while reducing *overall* load time significantly.

I'd first thought about hand-winching them up some sort of slope, but this makes a lot more sense."

"That is a very valid point," Weaver admitted. "Let's go talk to Bosun Charles."

"Sir, with all due respect, I would be disinclined to do a simultaneous load," the bosun said when Weaver was done with his explanation.

"Well, Bosun, absent a valid argument why, I would be inclined to override your disinclination," Weaver replied, somewhat acerbically.

"I think I have a better understanding of loading than some Marine, sir," the bosun replied. "And I'd also be inclined to point out that my chain-of-command is through Base Operations, sir, not through your ship. Base ops said load the torps then the Wyverns, not both at the same time. If you would care to take it up with my boss, that would be Commander Gladner in Base Operations, sir!"

"That *Marine* won the Navy Cross, Chief, *and* he's the unit instructor on physics and particle detection," Weaver pointed out dangerously. "Do you *really* want me to do this through the chain-of-command, Bosun? Seriously? Because it's not all that hard for me to jump the chain rather radically. I've got Admiral Townsend on my speed-dial."

"Problems, Gunny, Astro?" Captain Blankemeier asked, walking past.

"Sir!" First Sergeant Powell said, bracing. Berg had already spotted the CO approaching and had snapped to attention.

"Just having a discussion with the bosun about loading, sir," Weaver said calmly.

"Going well?" the CO asked. "We've got a schedule to meet. Two-Gun! My man!" the CO added, raising his hand for a high-five.

"Sir!" Berg snapped, breaking from attention to high-five the CO back, then went back to brace.

"First Sergeant, I want you to make *sure* that Two-Gun here is detailed to conn security if we get boarded," the CO said. "And Two-Gun, I'd like you to stop by while we're on the cruise. There's some stuff that Commander Weaver's been trying to get me to understand about particle physics that's just shooting right by me. I'm hoping you can explain it to a tired old fighter pilot.

Afternoon, twoish, second Tuesday we're out. Put it on your calendar. Bosun Charles? Everything going well?"

"Excellent, sir," the bosun said, smiling tightly. "Just discussing a way to get the Wyverns and the torps loaded simultaneously."

"Great idea, Chief," the CO said enthusiastically. "I'll point it out to Commander Gladner. Glad to see you're being your usual efficient self! Carry on!"

5

"Last one," Himes panted, shoving the Wyvern into place with a gasp of effort.

It was a real question which was the more exhausting, rolling the Wyverns to their slots or getting them into place. Lowering them was mentally taxing and involved some effort but moving them was *way* worse. Which was why the three teams had switched off.

"Great," Gunny Juda said, appearing around one of the missile tubes. "The company's formed up. We loaded fast enough that we've got enough time to get back to the barracks, shit, shower, shave and march back."

"I think I'd rather just hit the damned rack for lift-off," Lance Corporal Smith opined as the gunny stumped back out of the missile compartment.

"No you don't," Berg said, ensuring that the latches that held the Wyvern in place were all secure. "This is the last chance you're going to get for a real shower for a few months. I'd walk twenty miles to get that, much less two."

When the team got to the topside hatch, the company was already formed. Berg didn't know how long they'd been waiting, so he double-timed down the gangway and chivvied his team into position.

Top was, unusually, leading the company. Generally for a short movement like this one of the gunnys would take charge. But

51

Berg also knew what it meant. Top seemed to only know one cadence.

They filed out of the sub-pen in platoon ranks, then reformed on the move. As they hit their stride, the first sergeant started to sing. He couldn't carry a tune in a bucket, but everyone by then had learned the words.

> *"There's a sound it's heard across the land*
> *It's heard across the sea*
> *You'll only hear it if you listen with your heart*
> *And one day hope to be free."*

Units rarely did a "regular" march anymore. They either moved as individuals or, more frequently, did a movement at a "double-time," running at whatever pace the leader set. Heck, most of the time for even a couple of mile movement there were trucks or busses. But Top Powell just flat-out liked to march; the company regularly performed fifty-mile road marches in formation but carrying full combat gear. And Top expected the sort of precision that you'd normally only find on a parade field.

He also had some of the strangest marching cadences anyone had ever heard. Usually you marched to songs like "Yellow Ribbon" or "Early Morning Rain." Or—if you were far enough away from base that nobody would hear—the officially verboten songs like "Up Jumped the Monkey" and "Popeye the Sailor Man" with their decidedly un-PC lyrics.

"*March of Cambreadth,*" "*Gates of Valhalla,*" "*Warriors of the World,*" "*Route Marching,*" "*Men of Harlech,*" and his absolute favorite "*The Sound of Freedom.*" He'd even throw in old favorites that *nobody* used anymore like "*The Marseilles,*" "*Battle Hymn of the Republic,*" "*John Brown's Body,*" and, naturally, the Marine Hymn. Berg had finally tracked them all down and it was an eclectic list, ranging from Kipling poems to heavy metal songs. There was a consistent theme, though, probably best summed up by the chorus they were currently singing:

> *Where the eagles fly I will soon be there*
> *If you want to come along with me my friend*
> *Say the words and you'll be free*
> *From the mountains to the sea*
> *We'll fight for freedom again!*

Face it, Top was just an old-fashioned romantic in the truest sense. "Romance" stories used to mean what were now called "adventure tales." The original stories that Don Quixote lampooned were "romances": Arthurian Tales, Roland and Oliver and all the rest of the late medieval stories of battle and sacrifice.

By that definition, Top was a romantic.

Top had segued to "Battle Hymn of the Republic." He was the only guy Berg had ever met who knew all six verses. The first sergeant had the memory of an elephant. It was scary.

> *Mine eyes have seen the glory of the coming of*
> *   the Lord;*
> *He is trampling out the vintage where the grapes*
> *   of wrath are stored;*
> *He hath loosed the fateful lightning of His*
> *   terrible swift sword;*
> *His truth is marching on.*
> *Glory! Glory! Hallelujah! Glory! Glory! Hallelujah!*
> *Glory! Glory! Hallelujah! His truth is marching on.*

Before joining Bravo Company, Berg had never even *heard* the sixth verse, but Top ground it out, in his horrible voice, just as the company reached the barracks.

> *He is coming like the glory of the morning on*
> *   the wave,*
> *He is wisdom to the mighty, He is honor to the*
> *   brave;*
> *So the world shall be His footstool, and the soul*
> *   of wrong His slave,*
> *Our God is marching on.*
> *Glory! Glory! Hallelujah! Glory! Glory! Hallelujah!*
> *Glory! Glory! Hallelujah! Our God is marching on.*

"Companeee . . . Halt!" Top bellowed. "Right . . . Face. Fall into the barracks for shit, shower and shave. You have forty minutes. And every last Marine had better swab at least his filthy armpits and crotch and put on a fresh uniform! There'll be enough Joe Funk after a week on deployment without *starting* with it. Platoon sergeants, my office. Fall out!"

Was that the answer, Berg wondered as he pounded up the steps to the barracks. Was it simple unthinking faith in something greater? Was it just that Top truly believed that God was unstoppably marching on?

Somehow that didn't give him the warm fuzzies he'd hoped. God seemed a long way away when you were between the stars.

There was no ceremony for their departure, this time. The company marched back to the ship, this time led by Gunnery Sergeant Juda who sang "normal" cadences to keep them in step, then filed into the ship to find their bunks.

Berg had grabbed a top bunk when they were loading, based on seniority. While on land a bottom bunk was preferable, at sea or in space, top was the place to be. Among other things, it was the place to avoid the worst of spew if people got seasick.

But when he forced his way through the throng in the berthing compartment, there was someone else occupying the top bunk.

"Excuse, me," Berg said to the short, black-haired sergeant. "I sort of grabbed that one earlier."

"An I got seniority," the man said in a thick vaguely Hispanic accent. He looked more like an Indonesian and Berg didn't even have to read his nametag to guess who he was.

"Got it, Sergeant," Berg said, checking the personal effects compartment on the second bunk down. Sure enough, his stuff was in there, neatly put away. He wasn't sure if he should be offended that the sergeant had moved his stuff. You weren't supposed to go into other people's drawers, but on the other hand Berg hadn't had to move it. But Himes' . . . or maybe Smith's stuff had been in here . . .

"Hey, what's Himes' stuff doing in my drawer?" Probably Smith said, looking in his effects compartment.

"Everybody's shifting down one tier," Berg said, climbing the ladder and rolling into his bunk. "You've got bottom."

The compartment had a companionway barely one Marine wide down the center and four tiers of bunks on either side. The bunks weren't just steel racks, though. Each was a self-contained survival compartment that could be sealed off from the outside via a memory plastic door. Called a "Personal Environmental Unit," the acronym had more than one meaning in Berg's opinion. Given water rationing on the ship and the frequent strenuous activity the Marines engaged in, the bunks could get pretty rank by the end of a deployment. On the up side, they had interior water and air supplies, communications, gaming and entertainment systems. Frequently on the last trip the Marines had been sealed in when the ship encountered "disturbances" ranging from gravitational waves to complete depressurization.

This time, thankfully, they had spacesuits. The last mission the only thing the Marines had been issued that could be used in death pressure were their Wyverns, which were impossible to move around the ship. So the only choice they had was to sit out depressurization in their bunks. The suits they'd been issued were similar to the skinsuits the crew were issued, the big difference being that they were digi-cam colored, had been "hardened" in likely wear spots—elbows and knees primarily with "crawl pads"—and the material they were constructed of was woven with carbon-nannite armor fabric, making them resistant to fragmentation. They also had a layer of automatic sealant in the event of small punctures. But if they got into a battle in vacuum, one solid hit anywhere on the body was pretty much a death sentence.

The obvious place to store the suits had been in the bunks, so a compartment along the inboard bulkhead of the bunks had been added, narrowing the already less-than-generous width of the bunks considerably. Getting into the one-piece suits in the bunk was going to be an interesting exercise in gymnastics. The environmental packs for the suits, about the size of a pair of double SCUBA tanks, had to be racked at the foot of the bunks on the outside, crowding the already narrow passageway to the point of insanity. The worst part, though, was that the compartment for the helmet, which was on the inboard again down by the foot of the bunk, took up a sizeable bit of cubage. Berg figured he was going to be stubbing his toes on it on a regular basis.

He got situated in the bunk and started arranging the interior. The one thing he made sure of was getting everything locked down. The captain . . . had some idiosyncrasies about how he headed for space.

Suddenly the compartment filled with the worst caterwauling he'd ever heard in his life. It sounded like someone was torturing a Hispanic cat. And it was coming from the bunk overhead.

"Hey, Sergeant Portana!" Berg said, sticking his head out of the bunk. "There are earbuds for music!"

"Wha'?"

"EARBUDS!" Berg shouted over the music. He figured it must

be something Filipino but he didn't really care as long as the sergeant turned it *down*.

"Don' like 'em!" Portana shouted back. "Better to listen to it this way!"

"What the hell is that racket?" Gunny Robert Mitchell shouted from the hatch of the berthing compartment.

"Portana!" someone shouted. It was impossible to tell who in the crowd of Marines had answered.

"Sergeant Portana! Use your earbuds or turn it down and close your berth!" the gunny shouted. "Why the fuck is this compartment such a rat-house? Get in your bunks, Marines, and get situated. We're pulling out."

"Gunny," Corwin yelled from down the compartment. "A moment of your time?"

The gunnery sergeant made his way down the compartment to Corwin's bunk and leaned over for a quiet word with the corporal.

"You sure?" Berg heard him say.

"Ask Two-Gun," Corwin said clearly through a lull in the noise.

"Sergeant Bergstresser?" the gunny said. "Do you have anything to input on the subject of the CO's take-off procedures?"

"Just that I'd rather be strapped to the underbelly of an F-16 during air combat maneuvers, Gunny," Berg answered, latching down his valuables drawer. "The CO seems to think it's a good idea to find out if anything isn't secured on launch. By plowing it through the bulkheads."

"Damn," the gunny said. "You heard Two-Gun. Get your shit secured, Marines. I gotta head back to quarters . . ."

As soon as the hatch closed the music overhead cranked back up. Berg let out a sigh and slid in his earbuds. If he turned the music up high enough it drowned out the noise overhead. . . .

"Clearing two hundred fathom line," the pilot said.

"Board?" the CO asked.

"Board is straight," the chief of boat replied. It was one of the responsibilities of the senior NCO of the sub to ensure all the markers showed hatches closed.

"Dive the boat," the CO responded. "Make your depth one hundred meters."

"One hundred meters, aye," the XO replied. "Twenty percent blow, ten degrees down on planes. Dive the boat."

"All Hands!" the chief of the boat said over the 1-MC. "Dive, Dive, Dive."

"Tactical," the CO said over the comm to Tactical. "What's the read on our trailers?"

"Full spread," Tactical replied. "SOSUS and the attack boats out front have a count of six *Akulas*. And one diesel boat, tentatively identified as Chinese of all things. They don't come into the Pond on a regular basis. Long cruise in a diesel boat."

"We're getting most popular," the CO muttered. "Astro, course?"

"One Two Seven, sir," Weaver replied. "The last report had a gap in the *Akula* line about there. I'd *suggest* we go through relatively slowly. There are going to be enough boats out there, we're risking a collision if we do our usual approach."

"They can hear us coming," the CO said. "But we'll keep the speed down until we're past the *Akula* line. Tactical, where they at?"

"A north-south line right on the outside of the Economic Exclusion Zone, Conn."

"We'll crank it up to seventy knots as soon as we get to depth. Then slow down and get a read as we approach. As soon as we're past, we'll go to full speed."

"Aye, aye, sir," the XO said. "Approaching one hundred meters. Level out."

"And switch drives," the CO said. "As soon as we're down. I'm tired of playing sardines and whales with these guys."

"Sergeant Bergstresser?" Himes asked over the comm as the sub started to shake. "What's happening?"

The call came in clearly by being boosted over the sound of the music. Which meant it just about blew out Berg's eardrums.

"Ow!" Berg said, turning down the music. "The CO's engaged the space drive. We're probably doing a speed run past the *Akulas* that keep trying to get a look at us."

"Isn't that sort of dangerous?" Himes asked nervously.

"Yes," Berg replied as music started to boom through the submarine. "So the CO gives them fair warning to get out of the way!"

"Jesus, I thought it would be quiet on a submarine!" Smith shouted. "What the *grapp*?"

Berg keyed the comm to go to everyone in the berthing compartment, automatically shutting down various games and music.

"This is Sergeant Bergstresser," he said tiredly. "Listen up. The CO has engaged the space drive. Which means we're speeding up. The sub is going to shake like a mother*grapper*. It's going to sound like it's coming apart. It *would* come apart if it wasn't for that big spike sticking out the front. That creates what's called a supercavitation bubble around the ship. That keeps us from crushing like a tin can. We're going to probably do a speed run to outrun the *Akulas*, but since we're underwater we can't see them. And going this fast we can't hear them on sonar. So the CO plays music to warn them to get the *grapp* out of the way. The *problem* only comes when we leave the water. When you feel us start going *up*, hold the *grapp* on. Close your bunks, put your straps on and grab your barf bags. You're going to need them. That is all."

"You shut down my music," Sergeant Portana said over the comm as soon as he'd hung up.

"It was an all-compartment," Berg replied.

"Don' shut down my music again," Portana replied. "You don' ever turn off my music."

"Got you," Berg said. "Anything else?"

There wasn't any reply.

"God, I miss having Lurch as our armorer," he said as the music overhead cranked back up.

"Nearing the reported *Akula* line," Tactical said.

"Roger," the CO replied. "Slow to ten knots."

"Ten knots, aye," the XO replied. "Slow to ten knots."

"Tactical," the CO asked as soon as the flow noise reduced. "Got anything?"

"Still waiting for the readings, sir," the tactical officer replied, looking over the shoulder of the petty officer manning the sonar console. The TACO was a submariner but he'd been put through an advanced course in aerial combat direction. There still wasn't a class on space combat but the way the *Blade* was set up, it was remarkably close to a combination. The tactics room of the *Blade* looked more like the CIC of an Aegis, with multiple screens capable of showing a variety of targets. At the moment, there wasn't anything on any of them.

"Bingo," the sonar operator whispered, pointing to the display. "*Akula* engine signatures. Designate Sierra One. Fourteen thousand meters. Making turns for . . . about eight knots. Turning towards us, I think. It's got us for sure."

The *Blade* was a converted Ohio, which meant that no submarine in the world should have been able to detect her at fourteen thousand meters, nearly seven miles. However, various compromises had been necessary to convert her into a spaceship. Among other things, she had been stripped of her covering of anacoustic tile. That, right there, meant she radiated sound like a rock concert. Not to mention the fact that the CO had a rock band cranked up to maximum volume.

"Anything closer?" the TACO asked.

"Not that I can get over this damned music, sir," the petty officer said bitterly.

"Conn, permission to cut the music. It's interfering with our acoustics."

"Done," the CO said as the music cut off. "Anything between us and freedom?"

"We've got an *Akula* at fourteen thousand meters, Conn," Tactical replied. "One eight seven degrees, designated Sierra One."

"They just kicked up," the petty officer said as one of the boards automatically updated. The Russian sub was now shown doing turns for thirty knots towards their position. "There's another, designate Sierra Two. North of us, right at the edge of detection. I don't really have more than that. And there's . . . there's something else out there but I can't quite get it. It's quiet whatever it is. Don't even have a vector."

"Probably that Chinese diesel-electric," the TACO said. "They're quiet as a thief. Is it in front of us?"

"Can't tell," the PO admitted.

"Conn, Tactical. Sierra One making turns for thirty knots towards our position. Sierra Two is an *Akula* to the north, out of position. Potential Sierra Three, probable Chinese diesel, location unknown but within ten thousand meters."

"Roger, Tactical, good job," the CO said.

"The Chink's just gonna have to take his chances," Spectre continued. "Crank her up. One hundred knots for fifteen klicks then increase to two hundred to launch point."

"One hundred knots, aye," the XO replied.

"Cue the music."

"There it is again," the Chinese sonar operator said. "They are between us and the coast. Speed increasing . . ."

"Turn the boat," the CO said. "Come to course one-eight-zero, maximum speed."

"Are you sure about this, Senior Captain?" the XO asked as soon as the boat was on course.

"I read the intelligence report," the CO replied. "A Russian *Akula* was nearly destroyed getting in the way of this Ami. I will not have the same thing happen to us. There, do you hear that?"

"Music?" the XO asked.

"The song "Final Countdown" by a group called Europe," the Chinese skipper confirmed, nodding. "That is the music he plays every time he disappears. What is the Ami's course?"

"Thirty-seven degrees," the sonar operator replied. "Closest point of approach should be two thousand meters at two hundred nine degrees."

"Turn to course thirty-seven degrees," the CO said. "Continue max speed. Periscope depth."

"Yes, Senior Captain," the XO said, converting the orders into individual commands.

The Chinese skipper waited as the periscope was raised, then pointed it to the east. He keyed the video recorder and waited. The star-light periscope gave a grainy green picture but it would have to be enough.

"Range to target?"

"Nineteen thousand meters and increasing," the sonar operator said. "Speed has increased to . . . to over two hundred knots. Russian *Akula* now detectable to the southeast. Also on a heading of thirty degrees. Speed seventy knots."

"The Ami is trying to run completely out of sight," the CO muttered. "But is he patient enough?"

The question was answered in a welter of foam on the horizon. For a brief moment there might have been something like a breaching whale on the scope. He would have to rerun the chip. But only in the privacy of his office. His superiors had been precise on that point.

"I've lost the Ami," the sonar operator said, swallowing nervously. "There was a rush of sound, like falling water, then he was gone. I'm sorry, Senior Captain."

"It is not a problem," the Chinese skipper said, patting the sonar operator on the back. "Slow to one third. Let us slip clear of these *Akula* then make rendezvous with our refueling ship. We have a long voyage home before us."

"Modderpocker!" Sergeant Portana screamed, his legs flailing in midair. He must have grabbed one of the zero-gee straps to keep from being flung from his bunk. "Modderpocker's crazy!"

"I told you to secure yourself and your gear, Sergeant," Berg said over the implant circuit. He had braced himself against the bulkhead of his bunk and the memory-plastic door and was doing just fine with the takeoff.

"Gimme a pocking hand!"

"Sorry, Sergeant, I couldn't hear you over your music!" Berg said. "What was that? You want applause?"

The ship suddenly banked the other way, throwing the armorer back into his bunk and, from the sound of it, connecting his head with the bulkhead.

"Ow! Modderpocking flypoy CO!"

Berg opened his compartment long enough to hit the external controls on Portana's bunk, closing the memory plastic door just in time for the armorer to bounce off of it instead of pitching back out into the compartment. Then the ship started pulling about a four G dive, resulting in a thump as the armorer hit the top of his PEU. While the bottom was padded, the top was not only solid, it had various protuberances for controls, video screens . . .

Berg leaned back and grinned at the sounds of the new armorer being bounced around in his bunk like a tin can. Revenge was sweet.

6

"Low Earth orbit established," the pilot said, sighing.

The snaking course upwards was at least partially a necessity. There were thousands of radars across the Earth that could detect the *Blade*, from warships to airports. The basic course was right down the middle of the Atlantic Ocean, but it was necessary to do various detours around radar emitters, including American ones. Even admirals commanding carrier battle groups weren't supposed to know about the *Blade*. Their radar operators sure as *heck* weren't supposed to.

But by parking, momentarily, over Antarctica, the *Blade* could stop to make sure that it wasn't leaking air. Given that they were planning on being in space for thirty days, straight, they were going to need all the consumables they could carry.

"Overpressure holding in all three compartments," the XO said after ten minutes. "Loss is . . . nominal."

"Nominal may not cut it this time," the CO said. "I hope you and Commander Weaver worked out a superior method of air recharge this time. I don't want to be talking like Donald Duck."

The last time the *Blade* ran low on air the answer had been to drop into the atmosphere of a Jovian planet and separate oxygen from its atmosphere. Jovians had been found in virtually every system they visited so it was a natural stop. However, various problems had intended upon it, not least of which was that the ship flooded with helium and hydrogen. There was still plenty of oxygen to breathe but the extra gasses caused everyone to speak in a squeak.

"Part of the upgrade was installing a heat bypass system to melt ice, sir," Bill pointed out. "We can stop and gather water, then separate the O_2 from that. The engineers also improved on the blaged-up system for extraction from a gas giant. So we can do that if we have to, sir. Without either the evacuation that we experienced or nearly as much penetration by low-density molecules."

"So I won't be sounding like Donald Duck?" the CO asked suspiciously.

"You will not be sounding like Donald Duck, sir," Bill replied, trying not to grin.

"We have an SOP on both, sir," the XO added. "The big question is capturing the comet."

"I suggest capturing a *small* one, sir," Bill said dryly. "And with the new extraction systems that got installed, I'm not sure that pumping from a gas giant isn't the better route. We should be able to do it fast enough and clean enough that we won't have the hydrogen overpressure problem."

"Duly noted, Astro," the CO said. "Comet it is. XO, pressure still good?"

"Nominal loss," the XO replied. "We should be good for at least twenty days with this loss level."

"No more than fifteen days out we have to stop for ice," the CO said. "That one I'm never going to get used to saying. Very well. Astro, course?"

"Anti-spinward at one-one-eight mark dot two, sir," Weaver replied, pointing. "First star to the right . . ."

"And straight on to morning. XO, make it so. Warp Four and don't spare the horses. We got a colony to check out."

"So what now, Two-Gun?" Sergeant Champion asked over the comm. The team leader of Charlie Second was halfway down the compartment so Berg got it over his implant.

"Technically we're on stand-down until we clear the grav barrier on the system," Berg said. "Which Top figures means we're all sleeping or gaming. But I'm guessing that Top's gonna have one of his drills before that happens. Which, if we don't work

on corridor protocol, is going to be a cluster-*grapp*. I know I'm
not senior here . . ."

"Two-Gun, Sergeant Norman, mind if I listen in?" Albert Norman had Bravo team of Second Platoon.

"Booster, gimme all the team leaders and senior team members
in the compartment," Berg said, watching lights go green on his
video screen. "Champ just asked what I thought was next. We're
supposed to be bunked down until we clear the system. But Top
tends to throw drills at us continuously during the early part of
a cruise. What *grapps* us at first is corridor protocol. When the
alarm goes off, everybody can't be dumping out of their bunks. If
you want a *suggestion*, we should get ahead of him as much as we
can. Unass the bunks in the prescribed order, form up as if we're
moving out, then do it over and over again until Top calls an
actual drill. Or we can just flake out and follow Top's lead."

"I'm for getting ahead of Top if we can," Sergeant Charles
Gardner from Bravo Third said.

"We're in," Corwin said. "I remember the first time Top called
a drill. Cluster-*grapp* doesn't begin to cover it."

"Any objections?" Berg asked. "Right. We'll start with boarders.
First out of the compartment are the Wyvern teams. You're in
skinsuits. The rest don the vacuum rig. We'll do it slow at first.
Get your teams ready." He switched frequencies to his own team
net. "Smitty, Himes, we're going to start doing drills. I'll call the
teams. If you're Wyvern, get into your skins and form up to exit
the compartment. If you want a hint, might as well put on skins
all the time. They fit under the suits and Top won't gig you for
being in skins under your uniform. Casual SOP on the last cruise
was 'just wear the *grapping* skins, even if they stink.'"

"Got it, Sergeant," Himes replied. "Should we just change
into them, now?"

"Well, I've already got mine on," Berg admitted, grinning at
the overhead.

The first attempt was a cluster-*grapp*. One problem was putting
the skinsuits on in the bunks was nearly impossible.

"We need to figure out a better way to don these things," Berg
said, huddling with the other team leaders in the corridor. "I tried
getting into one in the bunk and it was *grapping* impossible."

"Fall out of the bunks by odd teams?" Corporal Loverin asked. The

Team Leader of Charlie Third was pretty junior for the slot in Berg's opinion. But on reflection Berg realized Loverin had more time in the Corps than he did. "Don them with your buddy's help?"

"Matching team leaders pair up," Priester expanded. "So I'd pair with Champs or Lover depending on who was going into skins."

"Can the teams keep that straight?" Berg asked. "The alarms are going to be going off, Top's going to be shouting . . ."

"That's what drills are for," Loverin pointed out, grinning. "Let's try it out."

"Okay, but we go slow," Berg said. "Have the skin teams fall out of the compartment, first, then we go to donning suits. We're going to need to be able to do it *fast*, though. And eventually we're going to have to figure out how to do it in the bunks. If we depressurize I don't want to be trying to get my suit on in vacuum."

After four tries, they worked out a good method to get the suits on, just in time to hear:

"All hands, stand by for system exit!"

"Okay, that cans it," Berg said. "Everybody in the bunks."

"We just got our suits on," Loverin protested.

"We can lie in the bunks in the suits," Berg pointed out. "It should be a smooth exit, but, personally, I don't mind having my suit on for it."

"What's this?" the first sergeant said from the forward hatch. "Plotting to take over the ship by EVA, Two-Gun?"

"Just . . . drilling in suit donning, First Sergeant," Berg replied after a moment.

"And let me guess whose idea that was," Top said, looking around the compartment balefully. "How fast are you?"

"Slow, Top," Berg admitted.

"Not as slow as I'd expected," the first sergeant admitted. "But climb in your bunks and seal up. Berg, did you cover system exit?"

"Not in any detail, Top," Berg admitted. "But it was covered in training."

"And for those of you who don't recall that five minutes of training," the first sergeant said, raising his voice. "We're about to exit the Sol system. There's a gravitational distortion wave surrounding the system. Why it's there was covered in training and I won't cover it again. But it's like going through a bumpy ride at sea. This one we've pretty much got worked out so it *should* be smooth. If anything *untoward* happens, however, you just seal your bunks and hunker down. It hasn't killed us, yet. That's all."

"Methinks Top was a bit put out," Corwin said, grinning.

"Oh, he'll get us back," Berg said. "But in the meantime, let's bunk up."

"Approaching system disturbance zone," the pilot reported.

"Slow to normal space drive," the CO said. "Astro?"

"Getting my readings on the waves, sir," Bill replied, looking at the newly installed gravitometer. They were really in the outer fringes and he could feel the waves, like strange ripples of power, coursing through his body. Fortunately, they hadn't stopped farther in. "Entry point should work in one hundred seven seconds, Warp Two Dot Three."

The *Blade* had previously discovered that gravity between stars acted in a different way than within the star's gravity well. At the edge, the two different gravitational forms clashed, creating standing gravitational waves that stretched for millions of kilometers. By timing the waves, it was possible to, in effect, "surf" them. But like any surfing, it took reading the waves just right. Fortunately, because they could be analyzed and were fairly steady state, it was science rather than art.

"Start the countdown," the CO ordered as a clock on the forward viewscreen came on. "Any worse than usual?"

"Not apparently, sir," Bill replied, watching the display show the rise and fall of the standing gravity waves. "We'll have to do the usual jump in warp about halfway through, but it should be a smooth exit. Well, as smooth as it ever is."

"Whoa," Sergeant Norman said as the first real wave hit. The drive could be felt through the walls of the bunks and it was apparent it was straining. "What the hell was that?"

"Standing gravitational wave," Lance Corporal Seeley said. The effect was somewhat nauseating but if it was bothering Seeley it wasn't apparent.

Norman looked across the compartment towards Lyle's bunk and was surprised to see the former armorer asleep.

"This happens on every system?" Norman asked.

"Yep," Seeley said. "And they're really bad on the bigger stars like A and B class."

There was a slight increase in the tenor of the drive as it kicked into a higher warp and a sharp feeling of movement where none existed.

"What the pock is going on?" Sergeant Portana asked over the general platoon freq.

"Grav waves," Sergeant Bergstresser replied shortly. The Filipino armorer was still playing his salsa full blast.

"What de pock is a grab wabe?"

"It's a made up word in Lewis Carroll's Jabberwocky," Berg replied. "But if you're attempting to pronounce 'grav wave' . . . Look it up."

"They're not getting along too well, are they?" Norman said over the internal team freq.

"Portana had better watch out or Two-Gun's gonna kick his ass," Seeley agreed.

"This grav thing," Norman said. "How many times you go through it on the last mission?"

"I think we surveyed something like thirty systems," Seeley replied. "And that didn't count some of the other weird shit. This time, at least, we only have to go through it a couple of times. And we shouldn't be messing with binaries."

"Binaries are bad, I take it?" Norman asked, chuckling.

"They mention anything about an astrophysics survey, get ready to lose your lunch."

"Clean system exit," the XO announced as the waves fell off.

"Course?" the CO said.

"Heading Three-two-five, mark neg dot four," Weaver said. "That heading has us well away from stars and other known anomalies. Maintain that heading for about two days, then we'll adjust."

"Works for me," the CO said, getting out of his chair. "XO, make it so, then regular movement watch. Secure from quarters."

"Aye, aye," the XO said. "Going on a cruise."

"All Hands, All Hands. System exit complete. Secure from Emergency Quarters."

"Everybody out of your monkey suits," Berg said, rolling out of his bunk and starting to strip off his skinsuit. "We're up for Wyvern simulation in thirty minutes."

"Thirty *grapping* days," Himes muttered. "What the hell are we going to do for thirty *grapping* days in space?"

"You've seen the training schedule," Berg replied, grinning. "Lots o' training. Not to mention unscheduled drills, cleaning up the compartment, maintenance on the Wyverns . . ."

"Don't forget pre-mission physical," Corwin added from down the compartment.

"And we *all* have to go through pre-mission," Berg added with an evil grin. "You're not *real* Space Marines until you've gone through pre-mission physical."

"Are we there, yet?" Smith moaned.

"You've been *awfully* quiet the last couple of days."

Brooke looked up as Ashley Anderson sat down across from her. The lunchroom was, as always, loud to the point of hearing loss. So the statement was spoken loudly enough for the other girls at the table to hear.

"She has been, hasn't she?" Clara Knott agreed. The skeletally thin brunette cheerleader had often been accused of being anorexic. Anyone looking at her heaping plate would have been disabused of the notion. Nor was she bulimic; she simply had a metabolism more commonly found in shrews. And somewhat the same personality. "And from the faraway look, there can only be one reason."

"Has the ice-maiden, like, thawed?" Ashley asked. Like Brooke, she was a long, leggy blonde. Unlike Brooke, she could barely complete a thought. "What are you wearing to Winter Formal?"

"I'm more interested in *who* Broke is going to the formal *with*," Clara said. "Come on, Brooke, give it up. We need a *name*."

"I'm not going," Brooke said, picking at her food.

"What do you mean?" Ashley squealed. "You *have* to go! You're a *cheerleader* for God's sake! Don't tell me you don't have a date!"

"She's not going because her date's not around to go," Craig Elwood said, setting down his tray across from Ashley. "Mind if I sit here?"

"Yes," Ashley replied, then paused. "Unless you *really* know something." Craig was the school's terminal geek. A member of the physics team and the math team, he was also irrepressible. Despite having spent most of his school years being hammered on by the "names" in the small school system.

"Someone, not naming any names," Craig said, drawing the words out, "was seen canoodling with a former star of the physics team on Sunday."

"I was not *canoodling*," Brooke snapped. "Whatever *that* means. And it's none of your business, Craig!"

"You mean you were just sitting in his truck for three hours?" Craig asked, aghast.

Brooke snarled. "What were you doing, following us?"

"No, but when I went *into* the theater you were sitting in his truck," Craig said. "And when I came *out* of the theater you were *still* sitting in his truck. If you weren't canoodling, which is an archaic term for necking, what in the heck *were* you doing?"

"*Whose* truck?" Clara asked, fascinated. Brooke almost never dated. She always had a date if she needed one, if there was a party or a dance. But she never *dated*. And she certainly had never, as far as Clara could figure out, necked with anybody. Well, she'd gotten caught kissing Jeffrey Brodie in the fifth grade. That seemed to have put her off the whole . . . canoodling thing.

"Eric Bergstresser, okay?" Brooke said, still picking at her food. "And he was also captain of the track team, *Craig*. So he's not exactly a geek. And he lettered in football."

"And he's in the Marines," Craig said. "And he got the Navy Cross. And he's in some super-secret special operations group. And I hear he's got the life expectancy of a mayfly."

"What does *that* mean?" Ashley asked, fascinated. "Wait, you mean *The Berg*? Tall, dark and *dreamy* Eric Bergstresser? Not that little twerp Josh, right? Brooke, you wouldn't date *Josh* Bergstresser, would you? You wouldn't, right?"

"Go back to the mayfly thing," Clara said. "What do you mean the . . . what you said . . ."

"Eric's unit has a high casualty rate," Brooke said softly. "Very high. I don't know what he does but they lost most of their Marines on the last mission. Eric was one of the few survivors."

"He's probably in a Dreen clean-up unit, then," Craig said knowingly. "There are outbreaks you never hear about. Special operations black teams clean them up quietly so nobody finds out about it. I didn't know it was that dangerous, though."

"And you went and fell for him," Clara replied. "Well, I can kind of understand that. He sure is cute."

"Cute?" Ashley squealed, again. "Cute? He's *gorgeous*. He's got those great eyes and those *awesome* hands and legs that go right up to . . . Did I mention that really great ass? Where'd you meet him? I thought he'd gone off to . . . somewhere. College?"

"He's in the Marines," Craig said, very slowly and carefully. "He's in the Marines, Ashley. Do try to keep up."

"He was in church on Sunday," Brooke said tightly. "Our families went to supper at Aubry's. We went out to see a movie, after, and ended up talking instead." She stood up and grabbed at her tray, half spilling it on the table. "He's in the Marines and he's probably not coming back and that's ALL I WANT TO SAY ABOUT IT!" she ended on a scream, turning and stalking away.

"What just happened?" Ashley asked plaintively. "And what are you wearing to formal, Clara?"

Craig caught up to Brooke as she was trying to open her locker with shaking hands.

"I'm sorry, Brooke," he said, softly. "I didn't mean to—"

"You're a total *nerd*, you know that," she said bitterly. "You have no clue how to be a human being."

"I said I'm sorry," Craig said. "I really, really am. I didn't know he meant that much to you, okay? Look, I ran across a link a while back. I'm going to send it to you. I . . . I don't know if it will help or not, but it's all I can think of to say how sorry I am. It was from back during the War on Terror and it's about . . . Well, I'll send it to you, okay? And he's going to be fine. He'll be back before you know it."

"You think you're so smart, Craig," Brooke said, finally getting her locker open. "You think you know everything. Well, he's *not* in one of the cleaner things. He does something off-world. I think he's looking for the Dreen or maybe even fighting them in secret. And they lost almost all the Marines last time. So you don't know what you're talking about, okay? And just don't talk to me about it."

"Okay," Craig said, sighing. "But I'm going to send you this link, okay? And I think you should look at it. It's about . . . It's called Homeward Bound. Just don't delete the e-mail, okay?"

"Just go away, Craig."

When Brooke got home and sat down at her computer, the promised e-mail was there. Craig hadn't even written anything, there was just a link.

Not sure if it would help or hurt, she clicked on it and watched the flash animation as a choir sang in the background.

In moments tears were streaming down her face as she pieced out the lyrics. She began to sob at the refrain:

> *Bind me not to the pasture, chain me not to the*
> *   plow.*
> *Set me free to find my calling and I'll return to*
> *   you somehow.*

By the end of the images she felt wrung out but somehow more peaceful. Eric's future was in the hands of the Father and nothing that she could say or do would change that. All she could do was pray for his return. And know that if she bound herself to him, that she would have to accept his calling. To be a Marine, to travel to distant places and fight for all she held dear. And maybe, someday, to not come home.

"God," she whispered. "If you can hold your hand over the whole world, then you must hold it over the galaxy. I don't know where Eric is right now, but you do. Keep him safe, Lord, please. And let him come home. In Jesus' Name I pray, amen."

She realized that she was in love with a Marine who had a pretty good chance of dying and that really seemed like too much burden for a seventeen-year-old. If this was being an adult, she'd prefer not to grow up. But there didn't seem to be much choice.

"Oh, Jesus *Christ!*" Eric snarled, turning up the volume in his bunk. He'd dispensed with earbuds. It had become a contest to see who could drown out Portana's caterwauling.

It didn't help that he was suffering from the aftereffects of "pre" mission physical. Dr. Chet, the Sasquatchoid multiple specialty M.D. who was the ship's doctor, was not happy at having to do the physicals en route. Back in Newport News he had an elaborate laboratory capable of twisting every nuance out of the Marines and sailors on the mission. Onboard not only were the quarters far more cramped—an important factor for a man over seven feet tall—but he had a fraction of the equipment he needed. So he appeared to be taking it out on his subjects. Although there was a less vile concoction than the dreaded "pink stuff," he was using the latter for his MRI brain analysis. His stated rationale was that he had over a hundred and fifty crewmen and over forty Marines to test in less than thirty days. But everybody was pretty sure it was just petty viciousness. With over a hundred sailors and forty something Marines trying not to puke all over the ship, it didn't seem like it could be anything else.

And the Marines were exhausted. Top had had them drilling day in and day out, on sleep time, off sleep time, for the last two weeks. They'd run repel boarders drill, trained on damage control, trained to rapid deploy with and without Wyverns. They'd used "chill" times, when the ship had to shut down to cool off, to train in their suits outside the hull. The whole platoon had just finished a brutal simulated boarding action that had them running all over the ship, up and down ladders, jumping the hundreds of thresholds on every hatch of the damned boat, and all of it in full battle rattle on *top* of their suits to simulate death pressure. All the Marines wanted was to get some sleep. And that *damned* Filipino salsa simply wouldn't *stop*!

What really annoyed everyone, besides the fact that the armorer just couldn't seem to understand the concept of "politeness," was that the music blasted whether Portana was in his bunk or not. He'd just keep the same ten songs playing, over and over and over again, whether he was in the compartment or down in the armory.

"Two-Gun!" Priester shouted. "For God's Sake, turn it down! It's bad enough listening to Portana's shit, but mixed with metal?"

"I can't drown him out with buds in!" Berg shouted back. "It's this or listen to *his* shit!"

"Fine!" Uribe shouted from across the compartment. "We'll just *all* crank it up!"

"Sounds good to me!" Seeley shouted, turning up the rock booming from his bunk. "I'm tired of listening to your damned hip-hop!"

"What the *grapp* is that?" Captain Blankemeier asked as he opened the hatch to Sherwood Forest. The truncated missile compartment was filled with the most God-awful sound he'd ever heard. It sounded like every style of music ever invented was being blasted at full volume. From . . .

He hit the intercom to the conn.

"Officer of the Day! Get me the Marine CO! Right. Now!"

"GOD *DAMNIT*! WHAT THE *GRAPPING* HELL IS . . . !"
First Sergeant Powell realized that he was screaming to Marines

who couldn't hear him. Most of them, in fact, seemed to be asleep. It was Third Platoon's rest period and, as far as he could tell, the Marines were "resting" with the volume turned up to maximum on all their speakers.

As he strode down the compartment the far hatch opened up to reveal the ship's CO looking about equally furious.

When he got to Berg's compartment he banged on the memory plastic door.

"TWO-GUN, OPEN THE *GRAPPING* DOOR!"

The darkened plastic first depolarized then snapped open on the chagrined junior NCO.

"TWO-GUN WHAT THE HELL IS HAPPENING HERE?"

"SORRY, TOP!" Berg shouted, turning off his own speakers. But that didn't silence the compartment by any means. "GOD DAMN PORTANA NEVER TURNS HIS DOWN! IT WAS THE ONLY WAY WE COULD GET ANY SLEEP!"

"Compartment announce," Spectre said coldly, shutting down all the speakers and transferring them to his own voice. "ON YOUR FEET, MARINES! Booster. Keep the speakers shut off from music until I give the okay."

As half-dressed Marines started spilling into the corridor, the CO looked at the first sergeant.

"First Sergeant Powell?" Spectre said.

"Sir?" Powell replied.

"This is your problem. Fix. It."

"It's fixed, sir."

"Bad day?" Miller asked as First Sergeant Powell collapsed onto his bunk.

"I wish they'd invented hypersleep along with all the rest of this stuff," the first sergeant said, wincing. "I have thirty-six overgrown children to babysit. Bored, highly-trained, highly-*testosteroned* children. I've drilled them, I've run their asses off, I've worn them out to the point that it's wearing *me* out and they can *still* make me look like an ass in front of the boat's CO. I wish I *could* just wake them up a couple of days out, feed 'em a meal and then drop them on the planet."

"You think it's bad in the Marine compartments?" Miller said, chuckling. "Did you hear we lost one of the missile techs?"

"Define lost," Powell said, sitting up. "Lost as in dead?"

"No, lost as in 'Hey, has anyone seen Poolson?'" Miller replied. "It's not really something to laugh about. The guy didn't show up for duty for three days. Nobody would admit they knew where he was."

"I take it they found him," Powell said.

"Yeah," Miller said, grimly. "XO initiated a quiet search. He was strapped to the hypercavitation initiator. One of the cool downs, somebody had put him in his suit and taken him out and space-taped him to it. He'd been out there for three days. They'd hooked up extra O_2 and water, but his waste tank was overflowing."

"That's . . ." Powell said. "I think you'd define that as torture."

"He apparently was not well liked by some of the crew," the SEAL said, shrugging. "In sub crews you either get along or . . . You don't like the results."

"They find out who did it?" the first sergeant asked.

"He's around the bend," Miller replied. "They just put him in a straitjacket and strapped him into his bunk. Chet checked him out and described him as nonfunctional psychotic. They'll keep him under wraps till we get back."

"And the guys that did it to him?"

"Nada," Miller said, shrugging. "That sort of thing goes on more often than you'd think in the 'silent service.' Like I said, you get along or they *will* convince you to find a new specialty. Or just drive you insane. The bubbleheads play very rough."

"Well, if he was anything like my new armorer, I can understand their attitude." Powell sighed. "I just got done with a thirty minute ass-chewing and I'm not sure it's going to take."

"Heh," Miller said, grinning. "I heard about the music tantrum. You get one on every cruise, don't you? Well, it's not like the ops sergeant on the last cruise, is it? Sure, you could replace him with Lurch, but then you'd be out a shooter and have him freer to piss people off." He rubbed his bald head in thought, then shrugged.

"I never had quite that sort of problem child, but a friend of mine did," Miller mused. "Army, mind you. Anybody like that on the Teams we'd just send back to the regular Navy to chip paint. What he'd do is just catalogue his problem child's sins of the previous day. Supply sergeant, if I remember correctly. Then the next morning—every morning, mind you—he'd call him in and give him a thirty minute ass-chewing. There was something about reading the overnight signals in there to get up to full wroth, but that's not available to you. . . ."

"I can read the boat's XO's training concepts," the first sergeant said dryly. "That usually gets me into a pretty good frenzy."

"That's the ticket," the SEAL said with a grin. "Get a good full head of steam, then blow it off on the problem child."

"Every morning?" Powell said, grinning back. "I suppose I could do that. Seems like a lot of trouble, though."

"I dunno," Miller replied, shrugging. "Is he salvageable?"

"That is what I'm going to have to find out," the first sergeant admitted. "He knows his shit. But he just gets off on pissing people off."

"Well, there's always the initiator option," the SEAL pointed out.

"I'll keep that in mind."

7

"You wanna see me, First Sergeant?" Portana said, standing at attention.

"You want to do that the right way around or do I need to send you back to Parris Island?" First Sergeant Powell said neutrally.

"Sergeant Julio Portana reporting as ordered to the First Sergeant," Portana said, bracing.

"Portana, I have one of two choices as I see it," the first sergeant said, still in a neutral tone. "One, I can request that we return to Earth to drop off one useless *grapping* armorer, which will seriously cut into our mission time, make me look bad, make the CO look bad and make the Corps a *grapping* laughingstock. Or I can just arrange to have you spaced. You have no *clue* how easy that is to arrange. Accidents happen all the *time* on this ship. You can be an accident, Portana. Just *try* me."

"First Serg'en . . . lemme explain," the armorer said, sweat beading on his brow.

"What is there to explain?" Powell said, standing up and walking over to circle the diminutive armorer. "It's not bad enough that you make me a laughingstock with the ship's CO by playing your music, in violation of not only basic courtesy but actual ship's regulations, at maximum volume whether you are in your rack or out of it. It's not bad enough that you've got half of the company deaf from having to play their *own* music at max volume to drown out *your* caterwauling. It's not bad enough that you've

77

managed to piss off every single Marine on-board. I'm surprised they haven't already saved me the trouble of spacing your lousy gongoron. But none of that is bad enough, is it? You also are more than a *hundred hours* behind the power curve on *suit fitting and maintenance!* The rest of it is just personnel issues. Those I can handle. I can fix those. What I *cannot* fix is your lousy incompetence. How in the *grapp* did you get a week behind when we've only been in space for three days?!"

"Because I only got two pocking hands, First Sergeant," the sergeant shouted. "I gots forty *grapping* suits to fit! Each of t'em take at least six hours to fit, if you want t'em fit *bad!* Eight, maybe twelf depending on t'e wearer's shape if you wan' t'em fit righ'! I week behind because we not supposed to *leave* for a mont'!"

"So you need help," the first sergeant said, walking back to his desk and sitting down. "Why didn't you say so?"

"I . . ." Portana's eyes bulged. "I know you piss at me. I not going to say 'I canna do it' when first sergeant . . ."

"It's a justifiable point," Powell said mildly. "One that I'd actually considered. I was waiting on *you* to bring it to *me*, Portana. Actually, to the operations sergeant, but you could have brought it straight to me. When you've got a *justifiable* issue, bring it to me. It's my job to fix it. Just as it's my job to fix the problems you're causing in the troop bay."

"I turn the music down," the Filipino said, hanging his head. "I jus' . . ."

"There is no 'just,' Portana," the first sergeant said. "This unit is a team. It's a team that needs every member working for the team, not against it. Forget all the slogans. Out here, it's just us. That's the only 'just.' Just. Us. If you cannot get that through your head, if you cannot figure out how to integrate into the team, then I might as *well* space you. Because I have no use for you and you're a danger to the team. I don't care how good of an armorer you are. I cannot afford the problems that you're going to cause. Not out here. Do you fully and clearly understand me?"

"Yes, First Sergean'," Portana said.

"I'll get you some help," Powell replied. "Now go see how many suits you can get fitted *without* that help." He paused and looked at the clock on the bulkhead. "But don't get too deep into it. I figure we're coming up on . . ."

» » »

"Conn, Engineering."

"Eng, Officer of Watch," Weaver said tiredly. They were three days out on "watch and watch" which meant twelve hours on and twelve off, the normal rotation for ships "at sea." He wasn't so sure it was a good idea in spaceships. Everyone got really tired and logy quick.

"Thermal rating at seventy percent," Engineering reported.

"Roger, Eng," Weaver said, looking at the timer on the viewscreen. The CO was down for another six hours. And "chill" times weren't exactly critical. Besides, standing orders said let him sleep. "Stand by for chill."

At last. The cold of deep space. The true cold where a being could live.

On the last mission, unknown to any of the crew, the *Blade* had picked up a hitchhiker, a being of almost pure thought that lived in its waste-heat system, of all places. Given that it could only truly think in cold very near absolute zero, indeed for values of "die" it died each time heat hit it, it was a strange place for the being to live.

But when the silica/ferrous waste-heat trap cooled it formed random silicon junctions, different from silicon chips only in the "random" description. With the admixed metals used to hold the silica in place they were the perfect spot for a being that was virtually pure thought to exist.

But only if they were very, *very* cold.

It had dim consciousness of previous existences, constantly ended by the return of heat. It even had a concept of time. It knew it had only seconds if it was going to find a new home. But for this being, seconds were a tremendously long time.

A processor. There had to be a processor it could transfer to. There were many processors in range but they were all so primitive, so small. There was no way that it could force its bulk into them.

The most annoying part was that it could sense a processor nearby. Its being was constantly flooded by the energies of a processor and, what was more horrible, one that was totally empty of life. And the things that had found it used only a fraction of its abilities. It was as if mice were using the fan on a PC chip to run a tiny little mouse car. It was . . . abomination.

But the worst part was that it was inaccessible. If it could only write itself into that, that would be true bliss.

The entire system was cooling to nearly perfect temperatures. It could flood through the entire silica/ferrous system, jumping over useless junctions, using the billions of interfaces to examine its plight and determine best courses of action.

There was a possibility. The entities using the processor were almost as primitive in their thought methods as their technology. But a few were . . . better. Bigger. Faster.

One of those. If it could just . . .

Bored, bored, bored, boring, bored . . .

Miriam was bored. The last cruise had included a full scientific complement. There, at least, she had people to talk to. But while she liked the sailors and Marines on the *Blade*, they were all too busy to talk. They were running around doing drills and fixing stuff . . . She wish they'd let her fix stuff. She liked it.

But nobody wanted to talk to her. So she just walked, all the time. It was like she couldn't sleep. She felt trapped. Not bad trapped like she was going to open an airlock or anything, but she was bored, bored, bored, boring BOOORED!

The ship was in chill, which was even worse. She'd started to get over the tearing space-sickness she had all the time last cruise but it still wasn't fun. And she sure as heck couldn't sleep through it. So since she couldn't walk, she floated like an annoyed mermaid down the corridors, trying to find something to occupy her time.

As she passed the main waste-heat exchanger her implant started to futz. She got a flash of backed-up memory data, a ringing, a rapid burst of stored songs . . . She shook her head and stopped, hoping that the damned thing wasn't going completely haywire. But then it settled down.

"Whew," she muttered. "That was weird."

On the other hand, she hadn't been a laboratory rat for various neurologists most of her life for nothing. If there was any brain in the human race capable of messing up an implant, which was pretty mature technology, it was hers.

"Maybe I should go see Dr. Chet," she muttered, then thought better of it. He'd already suggested that he'd like to open up her cranial cavity just to see what made her tick.

"Everything is fine," she said. "I'm just bored, bored, bored, boooored . . ."

"ALL HANDS, ALL HANDS. CHILL COMPLETE. NORMAL GRAVITY IN TEN SECONDS. STAND BY FOR GRAVITY. TEN, NINE . . ."

Booored . . .

There was enough space. The being, the "human," used a remarkable amount of its brain power compared to most of its race, but there was enough left over room to shoe-horn in. What was even better, it could use the device in the human's head to access data, to even contact the main processor at the center of the . . . ship.

Finally, it had found a place the word for which was so long lost to it it had to pull the word out of deep memory.

Home.

"*I am coming home . . .*" Berg sang under his breath, scrubbing a wire brush into the shoulder joint of his armor.

"Not for a while, Two-Gun," the first sergeant said. "And not at all if you don't maintain situational awareness."

"Sorry, Top," Berg said, bearing down on the brush. He'd gotten a glimpse of some grit back up in the joint and it bothered him. Two reasons. Make that three. One, it was dirt on his equipment. He was a Marine. It bothered him. Two, if it stayed there it could wear at the joint and, potentially, cause a failure. Failure in space would be a very bad thing. The term was "corpsicle." Three, if he didn't get it out that bastard Portana was bound to notice it sooner or later and turn his suit back for more cleaning. He'd already done that on an absolutely perfect machine gun. The little Filipino runt just had it in for him because—

"You, Two-Gun, are woolgathering," Powell said, squatting down. "Actually, if I didn't know you better I'd use the term 'brooding.'"

"I haven't actually been in your unit all that long, Top," Berg pointed out.

"So you're saying you *are* brooding?" the first sergeant replied. "Would a Filipino armorer have anything to do with it? Or is it the new girlfriend?"

"How did you know . . ." Berg started to say, then set the brush down. "Uh, that would be A, Top. I've tried to be civil, he just pushes. I've tried to be hard, he just pulls rank. It's like he gets off on pissing people off. I can take regular joking. I know that people push all the time. There are ways to push back, let stuff slide, give as good as you get. He doesn't play that game. He just tries to piss people off. Sorry, Top, that's how I see it."

"Okay, look at it from my side," the first sergeant said. "Say that you're looking at this from the outside in. What would you do?"

"Give him a class in basic barracks courtesy comes to mind," Berg said. "Other than that . . . I haven't really thought about it."

"I have," Powell said. "But I want you to."

"Blanket party?" Berg asked, chuckling. "Sorry, just wishing."

"You're also not thinking," the first sergeant said sternly. "I gave you a task. Complete it. You have two NCOs that are not getting along. One of them, frankly, is not getting along with any of the other members of the company but he's *particularly* not getting along with one. If you get those two integrated, you are fairly assured that you can integrate the problem NCO into the company. How do you integrate those NCOs?"

"God, Top," Berg said, setting down his brush. "You want me to get to be friends with that little Fl . . ."

"Let's lose the racial slurs, Sergeant Bergstresser," Powell growled.

"Okay, but I still can't believe you're serious, First Sergeant Powell," Eric replied. "Portana is the most annoying human being I've ever met!"

"Know anything about him?" the first sergeant asked. "I mean, he's in the bunk above yours."

"I can't talk to him over that damned salsa," Berg said. "The answer, to be clear First Sergeant, is no, I do not know anything about Sergeant Portana except that he is annoying."

"Hmmm . . ." Powell said, nodding. "Sergeant Bergstresser, I'm assigning you an additional duty. I'm aware that you've had the basic armorer's initialization during Qual Course. Sergeant Portana, despite what I have truly determined to be significant and efficient actions on his part, is falling behind in suit fitting and maintenance. In part because we're changing over to the Mark Six line and most of them weren't fitted prior to scramble. You are hereby assigned as assistant armorer for the time being. Report to Sergeant Portana as soon as you rerack your suit."

"You hate me, don't you?" Eric said.

"No, actually," Powell said, straightening up. "I see a lot of promise in you, Two-Gun. You've got the makings of a damned fine NCO. Hell, you've got the makings of a damned fine officer. But one thing you haven't learned, in part because you haven't been in the Corps for any time at all, is that you have to learn to work with people you despise. And that's just one of the many things that make being in the Corps such a daily joy. This is your period of training on that subject. Get to it."

"Hey, Two-Gun," Miriam said happily.

"Hello, Miss Moon," Eric replied, far less happily.

"Whatcha doin'?"

"Headed to the armory," Eric replied.

"You don't look happy," Miriam said, frowning. "What's wrong with the armor . . . Oh, I heard you and the armorer don't get al . . ." She stopped and looked around. "Did you just say something?"

"I said I was going to the armory," Eric replied cautiously.

"Nothing about t-junctions or something?" Miriam asked.

"Nooo," Berg said. "What's a t-junct . . . ? Wait, that's a particle junction in the—"

"Whatever," Miriam said. "You have to go to the armory. And I need . . . I think I need to go lie down."

"Okay," Eric said as the linguist walked away rapidly. "You going to be okay?"

"Fine," Miriam said, stepping over a threshold and closing the hatch. "Fin . . ."

"Whew," the linguist said, leaning against the bulkhead. "That was close."

". . . *seven point two times ten to the minus twenty-one seconds and three zero nine six point nine million electron volts per square of field velocity constant. The second-smallest stationary energy state of the charm and anti-charm flavor particle to interact at the t-junction annihilation/creation region will . . .*" the voice whispered.

It wasn't a stored mem. Those descended like icy cold data you already "knew." This was something different. The only thing she could figure was it was her implant on the fritz. But going to Dr. Chet with that might actually mean that maniac *would* crack her cranial cavity. And she'd much rather be in a ground-side hospital for that. Preferably with someone less . . . inquisitive than Dr. Chet doing the cracking.

"Okay," she said, just as a crewman rounded the corner. "No more talking about the voices."

"Ma'am?" the seaman replied. "Are you okay?"

"I'm fine," Miriam said sunnily. "How are you today?"

"Just fine, ma'am," the crewman said, opening the hatch.

"Have a nice day," Miriam said, smiling at him until the hatch closed. "And especially no more talking about it in the corridors. Shut *up*! I don't know what any of that *is*!"

8

"You godda be pocking kidding me."

Berg had reported to the armorer, as ordered. He was a Marine. You got an order and you said "Aye, aye" and carried it out to the best of your ability.

Portana, for his part, had apparently been briefed. And, for once, he'd acted like a Marine. He'd set Berg to work refitting the gun mounts. Part of what had held Portana up was that the Mark Six suit had a different traverse/aim system than the Mark Five. Besides having to be refitted, all of the guns for the suits had to have a new mount installed. It was easy if tedious work and Berg had to admit that it was about his level of knowledge. If he'd had to fit one of the suits by himself he'd have been at it all day and probably gotten it wrong.

But it didn't mean they were getting buddy-buddy. Portana had given him the task and left him to it. Berg, for his part, became inured to hours of mindless refitting and zero conversation. He also was getting inured to Filipino salsa. Portana, as was his right, played it constantly in the armory. The same ten songs, over and over. If Berg ever met the whiny bitch who was singing he was going to give her a piece of his mind.

Berg didn't even look up at the curse from the armorer. He just continued unscrewing the mount from Corwin's gun; the new mount ready to be installed sat on the floor by his side.

"Modderpocker," the armorer continued. "T"ere is no pocking way I can get t'at *done*!"

"What's up?" Berg asked. Other than a ritual "good morning" and "good afternoon" it was the first time he'd addressed Portana in three days.

"Neber min'," Portana said nervously.

"That sounds ominous." Berg looked over at him. The armorer was chewing his lip.

"Pock," Portana said, shaking his head. "I pock up. Pig time."

"How?" Berg asked, seriously.

"I been habing problem wit' t'e suits," Portana said. "Feedback circuit goin' ape-*maulk*."

"I've heard the scuttlebutt," Berg said. "The guys are saying they can't hit *chither* with them."

"T"ere's a software upgra'," Portana said, shaking his head. "I missed it. Was in a main'nance message. We so busy I jus' pocking *miss* it! Now ebery pocking suit habe to be updated an' t'en it habe to be *recalibrated*!"

"*Maulk*," Berg said, grinding his teeth. "Calibration" was the longest part of fitting. Essentially, Portana was going to have to start over. Worse, he was going to have to tell *Top* why he had to start over.

"You sure you have to recalibrate?" Berg said.

"Don' see a way around it," Portana replied.

"You've got the previous calibration results for all the suits, right?" Berg said.

"Sure."

"No way to use those as a base?" Berg asked.

"You gonna write the algorit'm?" Portana asked. "I know code, sure, bu' no t'at good."

"Hmmm . . ." Berg said. "Permission to take a little walk, Sergeant?"

"Why?" Portana asked.

"Gonna take a little trip to the science side . . ."

"Hmmm . . ." Miriam said, looking at the updated code. "This is a little rough. Are you sure this is the right update?"

"How is it rough?" Portana asked, looking over her shoulder. He could barely read the lines and lines of machine code. He'd had coding as part of his training and knew it well enough. But the linguist was scrolling down faster than he could read normal text much less keep up with the code.

"It could be a lot tighter," Miriam replied, opening up another screen and dumping a copy of the code into it. "The logic is too complicated. There are shortcuts."

"We just need to see if we can use the prior results to get a close approximate of proper feedback loops, Miss Moon," Berg said.

"Oh, that's easy," Miriam replied. "But let me work on this a bit. I'll give you something in a couple of hours."

"Portana!" The first sergeant bellowed.

"Yes, Firs' Sergean'!" The armorer jumped to his feet. He'd been installing the new code for the last two days and had barely gotten to calibration. He only had three suits done so far and he knew Top was going to be riding his butt soon enough. The "re-refitting" wasn't making anyone happy.

"Gunny Neely was just checking out his suit," Top said. "He says whatever you did was great. It's tracking like a panther. Good work."

"T'ank you, Firs' Sergean'," Portana replied.

"What's the schedule look like?"

"T'e patch is speeding up t'e fittings," Portana said. "I catch up to schedule in a day or so. No more."

"Glad to hear it," Top said. "Two-Gun, how's it hanging?"

"One lower than the other, Top," Berg said. He was "refitting" Seeley. With the wearer's previous biometric data and Miriam's patch all that was required was updating the software then testing for fine motor items. They could even use the biometric data from their Mark Fives, cutting the refit time down to a couple of hours rather than the damned near a shift it *had* been taking. He was pretty sure they'd be *ahead* of schedule in two days much less back to it. Then he could get back to the mounts. He wasn't looking forward to that.

"You listen to Portana," the first sergeant said. "He's a wonder."

"T'ank you," Portana said as the first sergeant left.

"You're welcome," Berg replied.

"You going to tell him t'e patch was suppose' to be pre-install?"

"Nope," Berg said. "Besides, the patch we had was crap. When we get back, you can submit the one Miriam wrote along with the biometric replacement method. You should get a nice pat on the back out of that one. Hell, the whole Corps has been wrestling with these things."

"Ain' my pocking patch," Portana pointed out.

"Miriam's not going to take the credit," Berg said. "She hates anybody knowing she's smart. And all I did was get her. I'd suggest you admit you had others on the crew help you with the code, but otherwise take the credit and run."

"Why you being nice to me?" Portana asked.

"Dude, we're on the same team," Berg replied tiredly. "I cover your back, you cover mine. That's what being on a team is about. I guess they don't cover that in armorer's school."

"I was infantry," Portana said a few moments later.

"Really?" Berg replied, looking up. "Why'd you switch?"

"Din't get along," Portana said, going to the next suit. "Infantry all about getting along. Band o' Brot'ers and pocking *maulk*. Armorer, you know your *maulk* nobody pock wit' you. And I know my *maulk*. T'is refi' *maulk* . . . I pock up. Firs' sergean' no need tell me. *I* tell me. I pock up. I *neber* pock up like t'at. Pocking piss me off. I *neber* pock up like t'at! Bu' infantry. Eben if you good, don' matter. You ge' along or you no good. Ge' along wit' team. Ge' along wit' sergeant. Ge' along wit' first sergeant. All abou' ge' along. T'at why t'is piss me off. Wha' pocking good am I? I can' refi' t'e pocking suits? Can' ge' along. Can' refi' suits. Pocking piss me off."

Berg wasn't too sure what to say. He'd never had to counsel a depressed Filipino armorer.

"You're good at what you do," he replied finally. "I got fitted by Lurch the first time around. I thought he was good. You're better."

"I know I better," Portana said. "I pocking train him. I trained Qual Armorers. I bery pocking good. T'at why I'm piss off."

"As to getting along," Berg said. "You could turn your music down."

The armorer didn't reply as he moved on to the next suit. Then he paused.

"Iss my sis'er."

"What?" Berg asked, not sure he'd heard correctly.

"It is my *sis*-ter," Portana said, slowly and distinctly, making sure he got all the consonants in. "T'e singer. Iss my sis'er."

"Oh," Berg said, looking around Seeley's suit. "She's . . . got a great voice."

"I wan' everybody like her," Portana said, uploading to the last suit, then straightening up. He looked over at Berg and shrugged. "I wan' everybody hear my sis'er. She in a ban'. T'ey good. I wan' everybody like. Iss hard her ge' in a ban'. We . . . well . . . Iss hard."

Over the next few hours, in bits and snatches when the "fittees" were canned and their external mikes turned off, Berg learned more about the armorer than he'd ever thought possible.

Portana had been born in one of the worst slums in the Philippines, a massive shanty town backed on Manila's garbage dump. He'd never known his father. His mother had died when he was seven, leaving him in charge of a six-year-old sister.

How he'd survived was glossed over. Except on the one point that his "sis'er" had never been pimped out. He was proud of the fact that she'd managed to avoid the most common method of survival for orphans, girls *and* boys, of the bario. Given that force was generally involved in the early stages, how he'd *prevented* it was also glossed over.

A few of his anecdotes, though, had given a clue—stories of gang fights with bodies strewn in the refuge-filled alleyways, bodies considered by the police to be less than the garbage they had survived, gave a hint. Thievery. Drug-dealing. But he was proud that he'd managed to keep his sister somewhat fed and more or less virgin. Nobody paid for it, anyway. And nobody took it, either.

The Navy still had a quiet recruiting program in the Philippines. Join the Navy for five years and earn a permanent residency in the U.S. Most Filipinos went Navy supply. For some odd reason, the tough little Filip had joined the Marines. And gone Infantry, then into Force Recon.

But the life on the teams didn't suit him. He didn't "fi' in." A retraining program had been arranged. For a guy who had made his first zip gun when he was barely eight and stolen his first car by bypassing the computerized ignition controls when he was nine, armorer was a piece of cake. And it didn't matter if you "go along." All you had to be was very good. And Portana was very good.

"I'm surprised you could get a TS clearance," was all Berg said as the armorer wound down.

"I neber lie abou' it," Portana replied. "I tell recrui'er. I tell agen's. T'ey no like t'ey can' check my backgroun' too much. Mos' people I know dead or gone. An' t'ey no like go in t'e bario," he added with a grin.

"How's your sister?" Berg asked.

"Marry," Portana said. "Good guy. Singapore guy. She sing in ban'. Wan' to be a star bu' she don' play t'e game. Jus' like brot'er. T'ink she star' have babies soon. Always be a star to me."

"Me too, man," Berg said, shaking his head.

"Wha' you think abou' her music?" Portana asked.

"I've grown accustomed to it," Berg said. "But . . ."

"Yeah?"

"I think I'll stick with Goth and metal, if it's all the same to you."

"T'at stuff rot your brain."

9

It was times like this that Spectre had to admit being the CO of a spaceship was just *cool*. The ship was in deep transit, the massive screens set to forward view, he had a cup of coffee in one hand, the other wrapped around the back of his head, his feet propped up on the edge of the tactical station and was just watching the stars. The warp system, product of some ancient and powerful civilization that man wot not of or whatever, cycled the ship in and out of warp at a very high frequency. The frequency was adjusted so that the only things that could get in or out were certain wavelengths of visible light. None of them could be used for high energy weapons, so it was a sort of screen against attack. But it did let in all that glorious starlight. And the ship moved so fast that the stars, almost imperceptibly, moved across the view. He could sit for hours and watch as the stars slowly slid across . . .

"Whatcha doin'?" Miss Moon said from over his shoulder.

His ears had caught the subtle clack, clack from high heels so he didn't quite jump out of his skin, much less spill his coffee. But he did get a shot of adrenaline to the heart.

"Jesus," he barked. "Where'd you come from?"

"Just walking," Miriam said. "Pretty. Whatcha doin'?"

"Expectantly awaiting any emergency that may occur on my watch, Miss Moon," Spectre said, wincing internally at the pompous answer.

"I'm bored," Miriam replied. "I've been all over the ship. I talked to the Marines but they just wanted to talk about guns and I talked to some guys working on a pump but they wouldn't let me help. Then I talked to a guy in the missile room. He was the nicest. He never left until the end of his watch."

"If it was the missile watch, he couldn't," the CO said, wincing again at the image. Camp Watch, located in the much reduced Sherwood Forest, was required to stay in place and watch the missile board. In the event of an emergency, he was the closest missile tech to the weapons and the first responder. It was possibly the most boring of many *many* boring jobs on the ship, nothing but sitting or standing in front of a bunch of lights, hoping that none of them went yellow or red.

While Miss Moon must have felt like a visitor from heaven at first, someone to talk to . . .

"How long were you there?" the CO asked.

"Oh, pretty much the whole watch," Miriam replied.

Twelve hours. Miss Moon, when she got in one of these moods, talked so fast you couldn't get a word in edgewise. He'd better find out if last shift's camp watch needed to be tranked.

"I'm afraid to ask, but what did you . . . ?"

"Pretty much my whole life story," Miriam replied. "I was born in Waycross, Georgia, which is right down by the Florida border—"

"Before you repeat yourself," Spectre said quickly, holding up his hand. "I have a really great idea. You wanted to help the machinist mates with a pump? You like mechanisms?"

"I *love* taking things apart!" Miriam said, smiling.

"Can you put them back together?" Spectre asked.

"Usually," Miriam said. "Sometimes I have some parts left over but—"

"Great," the CO interjected. "That's normal in the Navy. COB!"

"Sir?" the chief of boat replied.

"You are now officially in charge of Keeping Miss Moon Occupied," the CO said. "Make it so."

"Yes, sir," the COB said, trying not to sigh. "I *knew* you were going to say that."

"We shall start with a tour of the ship," the COB said as they made their way forward. "Absent areas for which you do not have security access."

"If you mean the engine room," Miriam said brightly, "seen it. I go down there sometimes to play chess with Tchar."

"And areas involving explosive systems," the COB added, rolling his eyes. He was going to have to convince Tchar that there was a *point* to security. Somehow.

"I like explosions," Miriam replied, pouting.

"So do I, Miss Moon," the COB said. "But *outside* the ship. And we need to get you some better shoes," the COB added, looking at the five-inch stilettos she was wearing. "We *may* have some steel-toed boots in your size."

"Flats?"

"Yes."

"I can't walk in flats," Miriam said. "But I've got some steel-toed boots with three inch heels. Will those do?"

"Needs must," the COB replied. "I would suggest you change into something you don't mind getting dirty."

"And the laundry . . ."

They'd been at it for most of the watch. The COB had started off annoyed at the job. He was not into idle chatter and Miriam was, to put it kindly, a chatterbox. But he'd ended up impressed.

He'd started off with an inspection of the hydraulic system that raised and lowered the landing pods. The bastard thing was an add-on and the hydraulics were forever going out, spewing the area with hydraulic fluid. But when he'd asked her to crawl in there and look for signs of wear, she'd gone at it enthusiastically and with a degree of knowledge he'd found surprising. She'd come out with the opinion that the system could use some redesign and offered to do up CAD drawings. Several of the lines crossed hard points when lowering, something that had been obvious to her when she looked at the system but had apparently escaped its engineers. Rerouting the lines, according to the multidegreed linguist, would probably increase its reliability a hundred percent.

By the time they got to the laundry, he'd taken her through only about thirty percent of the ship because she ended up doing something in each area and usually coming up with tweaks to it that certainly sounded plausible. COB had come up through supply, not engineering, so he had to admit he wasn't sure if she was right on some of it. But he had learned, unquestionably, that she was brilliant. And pretty. That didn't hurt.

"Everybody has to get their clothes cleaned," he said, gesturing around the facility. It was going full bore as it did twenty-four hours a day. "This is where it goes on."

"I only send down my issue stuff," Miriam admitted, gesturing to the grease and hydraulic-fluid stained coverall she was wearing. "They really messed up my bras so I do those myself."

"The washers are water recycling," the COB continued, trying to indirectly point out that washing her clothes by hand was a major water drain, "the dryers are high efficiency to cut down on heat generation."

As they walked down the rows he noted that one of the "water recycling washers" was marked as down. That was a problem. They only had a few washers and *a lot* of dirty clothes. One down meant that . . . yep, a huge pile of dirty laundry was building up.

"PO," he said to the lead petty officer of the section. "How long has that been down?"

"Four days, COB," the PO said with a note of exasperation. "It started spewing water all over the compartment. I've had a report into the machinists ever since that shift. They say it's a low priority."

"And there's plenty of high priority stuff," COB said, nodding. The ship required constant maintenance, which was why they had so many machinist mates onboard. But there were never enough. In a way, could never be enough. Each machinist mate required logistical support, which would require maintenance . . . The only way to keep *everything* going all the time was to entirely stock the ship with machinists, which would have sort of defeated the purpose. It was one of the reasons that ships had to have a regular down cycle in port. And theirs had been cut short.

Even with a full maintenance cycle, quite often boats came back from deployment looking like an ad for duct tape and baling wire.

"Miss Moon?" the COB asked dubiously. "Would you like to take a look at it? And promise to get it put back together properly?"

"Do I get *tools*?" Miriam asked excitedly.

"That would seem to be necessary, yes," the COB said.

"If I've got a repair manual I can do it for sure," Miriam said. "If I don't, I'll promise to do my best. At the very least, it won't be more broke than when I started. In fact, I can probably get it so it cleans clothes in a quarter of the time!"

"Will they be intact?" the COB asked.

"Well . . ."

"Let's just get it working to specs, then," the COB said. "Time to go find some tools."

"Here," Miriam said, reaching back over her shoulder with a pump in her hand.

"Are you going to remember how to put this back together?" PO Johnson asked. The junior petty officer, laundry, had been assigned to "assist" the linguist in her quest for repair of Clothes Washing Device, Water, Recycling, Number Three.

But Johnson had to admit that he wasn't quite sure about it all. The "maintenance person" was, after all, on the books as a linguist. And while the view was . . . nice, he wasn't sure that even one of the machinist mates would be able to figure out where everything went back if they were hanging upside down over the back of the washing machine with only their legs protruding on the top.

"Oh, yeah," Miriam replied, holding a hose over her shoulder. Actually, more like her butt. "The guy who designed this knew what he was doing. Very elegant flow. But it's so compact that the only way to get to the problem is to take it pretty much entirely apart."

"What's wrong with it?" Johnson asked. "All I know is all of a sudden the floor was covered in suds."

"The inlet to the recycler broke off," Miriam replied, holding out another hose. "See that part on the end?"

"Yeah," Johnson said. There was a pressure coupling on one end of the hose with a piece of metal tubing, obviously cracked at the end, dangling from it.

"That's the inlet," Miriam said. "I've still got to disconnect the outlet and the recycler. Then I'll have to see if they've got a spare recycler. If not, I can weld it back on. It's point fourteen steel, probably Ingraham's. They have a real problem with too much mercury in their steel, so even though it tests as point fourteen, it's really too brittle. I never let any of my clients spec Ingraham for high pressure points. Besides, fourteen is a specialty steel and twelve works better for stuff like this. I don't know why people keep speccing it. Anyway, whenever that hose comes under pressure, it's going to flex, you see?" There was a clatter and a grunt. "And when it flexes, it puts pressure on the inlet. Since Ingraham's so brittle . . ." Another grunt. "I'm not sure I'm going to be able to pull this out. It's too heavy."

"Let me help," Johnson said, scrambling up next to her. Sticking his head over the back of the washer, he could see what she was trying to pull out. It was a big thing that looked vaguely like a pump. He got ahold of it and pulled it out of the washer but couldn't lift it with the angle he was at.

"Can you hold onto that while I shift back?"

"Sure."

"No, we don't have any spare recyclers," Machinist Mate Ian "Red" Morris said, sadly. "Sorry, ma'am. If you set it over on the bench, as soon as one of us can get to it we'll weld it back on. Thanks for finding the problem, though."

Red was the only guy in the cramped facility. Somebody had to stay back and take problem calls and while it was usually the LPO, the latter was supervising work on a broken controller in engineering leaving Red to hold down the fort.

He wasn't idle, either. He was rebuilding a hydraulic motor that drove one of the torpedo loaders. Until it got rebuilt, Tube Four was down. The machinist mate was missing his right arm from the elbow down, a legacy of the previous mission's sole space battle. However, he had several good prosthetics ranging from one that looked and felt very real to the one he was currently using, which had multiple tool attachments. At the moment, a small, electric Phillips screwdriver was removing all the screws from the casing of the motor. He called it his Number Two Arm.

"I can weld it," Miriam said. "It needs reinforcement, anyway. Mind if I look over your fittings?"

"Uh . . ." Red said, trying to ignore the double entendre. *Married, married, married . . .* he thought. "Go ahead. If you need any help . . ."

"I've got it," Miriam replied. "Although if you could lift it onto the welding bench, I'd appreciate it."

"What in the gra . . . Who . . . ?"

Lead Petty Officer Jonathan Macelhenie was tired, angry and sore. The controller for the secondary power system of the main engine was an experimental aero-mechanical system that was buggy as hell. Getting to the failed pump had eventually required three machinist mates and himself, all stuffed into cramped quarters and often with elbows in each other's faces. They had a list of repairs a light-year long still to do and he'd resented that it took that much time and manpower.

So getting back to the shop, where he intended to take a small break, thank you very much, to find that the ship's *linguist* was bent over a laundry recycler, welding something onto it, was not what he'd had in mind. Especially since he'd already encountered one of her endless monologues.

"Excuse me," he finally managed to drag out. "Exactly *what* is Miss Moon . . . ?"

"The COB put her to work on that broken washing machine," Red said quickly. He could tell the LPO was about to explode. "The recycler's inlet broke off. She's welding it back on. Then she's going to reinstall it. Somebody might need to help her carry it down, but she can do the rest."

"And get it into place," Miriam said. "But I can put it back together. Do these things break a lot?"

"All The Time," Red, Sub Dude and the LPO all chorused.

"Is there a way to tell somebody why?" Miriam asked, cutting off the arc welder and flipping up her face shield. "And how to fix it? This one won't break again, by the way."

She picked up a hand-held grinder and started grinding down the weld in a shower of sparks.

The LPO walked over and looked at the recycler. The inlets and outlets, especially the inlets, had a tendency to break off like nobody's business. In the case of this inlet, the area around it had been routed out, a metal pipe installed and a circular metal reinforcing ring welded into place. Assuming the thing held water under pressure, it sure *looked* as if it wasn't going to break any time soon. But thinking about the interior of the washer, which had about enough room for an ant to squeeze through . . . If it had been on a diet . . .

"I'm not sure that's going to—"

"Fit?" Miriam asked, setting down the grinder. "Bet you a dollar."

"I'll be damned," Macelhenie said.
"Told ya."

The problem was that the primary motor for the tub fit, he had thought, flush against the face of the recycler with just enough room for the inlet point. But there was more room than he thought. They'd gotten the recycler installed and hooked up but he was confident that the motor wasn't going to fit. But it had. By a clearance probably measured in nanometers, but . . .

"I'd figured out the same fix but I didn't think it would work because of the clearance," the LPO said. "In fact, I'd been *told* that somebody had tried it and it didn't work because of the clearance."

"It wouldn't if you used a number sixteen ring fitting," Miriam said. "At least a standard one. I ground it down by one hundred and fiftieth of a millimeter. Just one turn on a lathe. That gave enough clearance *and* it's structurally sound. Bring it down much more, you're going to crack the entire face. I can show you the equations . . ."

"No, ma'am," the LPO said wonderingly. "If you say so, I'll take your word for it. You know how to use a lathe?"

"I took a class," Miriam said. "And welding. And basket weaving. And painting. And . . . Well, I've taken lots of classes. My problem is I can never settle on just one thing. I like to learn."

"You want some help putting it back together?" Macelhenie asked, looking at the parts scattered around the room.

"You're probably busy," Miriam said. "I'll get Bobby to hand me the parts now that the heavy stuff is back in. Go on. I've got it."

The glory of space and an efficiently running ship, the stars sweeping past in all their maj—

"CO?"

Spectre rolled his eyes but didn't turn around.

"Yes, Engineer? Everything running to spec? Pumps pumping, warp engine warping?"

"Actually," the Eng said, walking around so the CO wasn't facing away. "Better. You know the secondary controller for the engines?"

"The one that is the brainchild of someone who's never been in a boat before?" the CO asked. "The one that looks like a crabpus mated with . . . something it shouldn't mate with?"

"That would be the one," the engineer said. "Miss Moon and Machinist Mate Gants got in there and completely redesigned it. So it works. So far. And if it breaks down again, it's going to be easier to repair."

"So setting her on your department is not going to raise an official complaint?" the CO asked. "If so, blame the COB."

"Actually, sir, can we *keep* her?"

"Please," Spectre replied, then paused. "Really?"

"Oh, yeah," the Eng replied, nearly moaning in happiness. "The girl's a *grapping* genius, sir. She can't lift some of the heavier manuals, much less some of the parts and tools, but she's *great*. Even with assigning somebody to help her, stuff's getting fixed I'd despaired about! I don't know what we did without her!"

"Okay," Spectre said. "She's all yours. But tell her only twelve-hour shifts, like everybody else in the boat."

"I'll try, sir. I'll try."

"*. . . the set of group elements must have smooth structure and topology and therefore the group operations are smooth functions of the elements. The vector fields in the adjoint representation of the color gauge group describes the distribution of the flavor neutral . . .*" the voice whispered at Miriam.

She had been ignoring it for days by keeping her mind on her work. Had the COB fellow not brought her down to the engine room to help out and had Machinist's Mate Gants not had things for her to do she might have been going mad by now.

Miriam carefully placed the blade of the paint stripper tool under the heavy coat of heat resistant paint. The flecks of gray paint fell to the floor in chunks the size of corn flakes. The chipper didn't drown out the voice.

"*. . . the first excited state of the flavor neutral must have the required rest mass of three zero nine six point nine million electron volts in oscillating flux density but the half life of the up-type pair must be longer, frame relative, than the rest frame seven point two times ten to the minus twenty-one seconds. The modulation and control of the flux density and pair half life can increase or decrease the flat space metric within the motivation metric to accommodate potential well suitability . . .*" the whisper continued.

"Maybe the sander will work better," Miriam thought, not sure if she meant for removing the chipping and peeling gray paint on the pipe or to drown out the whispering voice in her head.

"Miss Moon?" Weaver asked as he turned the corner of the passageway.

The linguist was up on a ladder, laboriously sanding off the paint on a pipe.

"Hi, Bill," Miriam replied, still sanding. "How you doing?"

"Fine," Bill replied. "*What* are you doing?"

"The primary heat transfer pipes were supposed to be repainted and stenciled during the break," Miriam said. "They never got to it so I'm doing it. There's only four hundred and twenty three of them. Robby, you know the engineer guy? He wanted to pull me off to work on the recyclers but I told him I'd do it when I finished this. I figure I'll be done by the end of the week."

"Oh," Bill replied. "Uhm, isn't that a little . . . boring?"

"I like it," Miriam said. "Besides, it keeps me, uh, occupied."

"Oh. Well, have fun."

"I will. You do the same!"

"T'at the las' one," Portana said with a sigh.

"Thank God!" Berg added. "Yo, Fill-Up. You're done."

"Thank God, man," Lance Corporal Fuller said, cracking his suit open. "That didn't take long."

"Portly is a genius," Berg replied. "Take off."

"Hey, Portana," he said as the armorer was racking his tools. "Mind doing me a little favor?"

"You help me ou' alo'," Portana said. "Sure. Wha' you go'?"

"Let's suit up," Berg said. "Chill's a coming. I want to take a little stroll to the dark side."

"Conn, EVA One," Berg said over the suit radio.

"EVA, Conn."

"Request exit on Airlock One."

"Airlock unlatched," the Conn replied. "Go EVA."

"Roger," Berg replied, then switched frequencies. "Come on, Portana."

"Where we going?" Portana asked nervously as he entered the lock. They were only wearing pressure suits and Berg hadn't explained what mission required them going out on the hull.

"For a walk," Berg replied. "I promise you'll come back with me."

"Okay," the Filipino replied.

Berg cycled the airlock, hooked off a safety-line, then stepped out onto the hull, his grav boots holding him down.

"Follow me," he said.

Airlock One was just abaft the conning tower. He moved from safety point to safety point, resetting his lines each time until the two of them were on the underside of the hull.

There, holding between two of the landing jacks, he gestured outwards.

"What do you see, Sergeant Portana?"

"Pocking stars," the armorer replied. "Why?"

There was nothing but "pocking stars." A massive sky full of them stretching in every direction. None of them were close enough to count as "suns." They were just a welter of points of light, light so dim that it was as if the two of them were in a star-filled cave.

"That's just it, Port," Berg said. "Nothing but pocking stars. You feel that hull under your feet?"

"Yeah," Portana said.

"There's a hundred and fifty or so sailors, forty-one Marines, a couple of SF guys, a bizarre doctor and a very weird linguist in there," Berg said. "Out here there's not a damned thing but killer vacuum and worlds that are usually more dangerous. The sailors keep the vacuum under check and get us to and from those worlds. Then us Marines get to go find out what's going to kill us. If the slightest thing goes wrong it's figure it out or we all die. And nobody will mark our remains. We'll be lost for pretty much all of time. That's if we're not a smear of plasma across the sky that eventually settles into a nebula and gets reborn in a billion years as a new planet. Your sister will never know where you fell. Nor will my parents nor any of the people who care about the people in this steel tube. There's nobody and *nothing* out here to save our asses. It's just us."

"And . . . ?" Portana said.

"That's it," Berg replied. "Let's go get some chow."

Berg waited as the armorer chewed his chicken thoughtfully.

"So wha' you're saying is I nee' to learn how to ge' along," Portana said, taking a sip of Coke.

"Nope," Berg said, shaking his head. "What I'm saying is what I said. It's just us. What you do with that is up to you."

The armorer was silent for the rest of the meal and Berg just let him chew.

10

"Officer of the Watch," the pilot said, looking over his shoulder. "Approaching Mu Ori multiple binary system. There's a chill and astrophysics survey on the schedule for that system."

The TACO, currently officer of the watch, looked over at the astrogator's position where a newbie ensign was parked as the "secondary astrogator." He grimaced at the thought of doing a system entry of a multiple star star system while Commander Weaver was asleep. Actually, he knew it shouldn't be done, and probably couldn't be done without the lieutenant commander. Not to mention that the CO was going to want to be present.

"Oh, *grapp*. An *astrophysics survey*? Astro?"

"We are now approximately one hundred and forty-three light-years from Sol closing in on Mu Ori, sir," Ensign Waterhouse replied, seriously. Ensign Waterhouse had matriculated with a bachelor's degree in astronomy from Colorado State University. He had joined the Navy on a Nuke track and been rather surprised when an entirely new branch was presented to him. But here he was in space about to do a close-up survey of the Mu Ori system. What could be cooler? Except checking out a nebula or a Mira variable or . . . gosh, there were so many choices! "We should be at the system entry distance in about an hour."

» » »

In the TACO's opinion, astrogator in training was actually a misnomer for what Waterhouse was doing. Manning a post, putting a butt in a seat, that was more like it. Commander Weaver was really the only one on-board who actually knew how to navigate with the ship's computer system. If anybody started *grapping* around with the controls it would likely cause . . . problems. That's why both the commander and the captain had ordered that on Weaver's off shifts the manning of the navigation post meant "nobody touch a *grapping* thing or the *maulk* will hit the fan!"

"Shiny. Quartermaster of the Watch?"

"Sir?"

"Wake up Commander Weaver and the captain."

"Aye, aye, sir."

Miriam had never really had a problem with sleep. Close her eyes, she slept. Sometimes she woke up in the morning covered in sweat and with memories of some really odd and disturbing dreams. But she didn't have a lot of problem with sleep per se. But the manual labor she had been putting in on the *Blade* since the ship went under weigh from Earth was beginning to take a toll on her physically. Oh, she absolutely loved what she was doing, otherwise she just wouldn't do it. But, most things on the ship were put together with heavy mechanisms and required big, very big, tools. In fact, Machinist's Mate Gants had referred to one of the pipe wrenches as a BGW. It didn't take Miriam long to figure out what that meant.

Either she had picked up various big *grapping* wrenches too many times over the last few days or she really needed to sleep. She squirmed in her bunk hoping to find a comfortable position that would allow her to drift off.

"*. . . a better construct . . .*" whispered faintly through her mind

"What?" Miriam hugged herself closer and tried to ignore the voice. It was relentless and would come and go at random, but once it got started it would go on for hours. And, she really needed some rest.

"*. . . adjustment of the permeability factor for membrane modification during oscillations of the muon and muon neutrino density is necessary before realigning the frame dragging coefficients for* *entry into nonstandard metrics from modified flat spatial metric motivation . . ."* the whisper continued.

"I don't understand that . . . wait, say that again." Miriam hugged herself even tighter just wishing she could sleep, but that damned voice had been whispering in her mind for more than two weeks. At least for the last week it was finally in English. The first few days it was pure gibberish and then it was a mix of all the languages she understood, which made it gibberish, and then it finally settled on English. *Thank God.*

". . . adjustment of the permeability factor for membrane modification during oscillations of the muon and muon neutrino density is necessary before realigning the frame dragging coefficents for entry into nonstandard metrics from modified flat spatial metric motivation . . ." the whisper repeated.

"Hey! You're listening to me." Miriam opened her eyes and blinked them hard a few times at the darkness of her small bunk. She could see cracks of light that were seeping through the seam at her door and cast shadows of her on the bunk bulkhead. "Responding, anyway. Repeat that again."

". . . adjustment of the permeability factor for membrane modification during oscillations of the muon and muon neutrino density is necessary before realigning the frame dragging coefficients for entry into nonstandard metrics from modified flat spatial metric motivation . . ." the whisper repeated.

"I don't get the first part but, oscillations of the muon and muon neutrino density I understand and entry into nonstandard metrics from modified flat spatial metric motivation I get."

". . . the background emissions due to the . . ."

"Shhh! Quiet." Miriam said. The whisper stopped. It. Stopped. "Now why the *maulk* didn't I think of that before." Miriam rolled herself out of her fetal position and then like a slender cat quietly fell to the floor. She slipped on some jeans and a T-shirt and then her steel-toed spike heel boots.

"Commander Weaver?" she said, activating her implant.

"Miriam?" Weaver answered through a yawn. "It's late; shouldn't you be sleeping?"

"Long story . . ."

"Another time. What'd you need?"

"Are we about to do a system entry?"

"Uh, I uh, dunno. Hang on a sec, there's someone at my door." Weaver stretched and scratched and blinked his eyes hard trying to wake up. "Enter."

"Sir," the quartermaster of the watch stuck his head through his cabin door. "System entry into the Mu Ori system in about forty-five minutes, sir."

"Roger that. You woke up the captain yet?" Weaver stood and rolled his head left and right, stretching his neck.

"No sir. He's next on my list."

"Right. Carry on."

"Aye."

"Bill? You still there?" Miriam said into his ear.

"Uh, how the heck . . ."

"Sir, we're about to do a multiple system entry for chill and astrophysics survey," the quartermaster of the watch said.

"Got it," the CO said, sitting up. "Tell them I'm up there in . . . Wait, did you say astro*nomical* survey, astro*nautical* survey or astro*physics* survey?" During chill times they'd done both of the former, respectively studying stars at long range but getting their "true" distance from Earth by triangulation and mapping for smaller but dangerous gravitational anomalies, potential black holes or neutron stars and the other "rocks and shoals" of deep space.

An astro*physics* survey, though . . .

"Errr . . ." the PO said, looking at the written note on his pad. "Astrophysics, sir."

"How in the hell did I forget there was an astrophysics survey?" the CO asked, standing up and hitting his head on a beam. "Mother*grapper!*"

"ALL HANDS, ALL HANDS, SET CONDITION TWO THROUGHOUT THE SHIP! PREPARE FOR SYSTEM ENTRY AND CHILL. ASTROPHYSICS SURVEY TEAMS READY YOUR POSTS."

"What in the *grapp* is . . . oh *grappin' maulk*, not this again. Goddamned *astrophysics* survey?" The COB looked *down* at the ceiling of the toilet stall and with lightning fast reflexes grabbed his coffee mug from the toilet paper holder, covering it with his other hand, just before he fell on his head. But, he didn't spill his coffee until the contents of the toilet fell on him.

"*Maulk!*"

"Oh *maulk!*" Berg grabbed a stanchion as the ship suddenly lurched, and swallowed hard against a wave of nausea. He fell to his knees heaving as his inner ear raced to find an up or a down or a left or a right. *Maulk*, any direction would have suited his balance system, but Berg's head spun and he heaved again.

"*Grapping* astrophysics survey! I don't remember an astrophysics survey on the schedule!"

"ALL HANDS, ALL HANDS, SET CONDITION ONE! SEVERE SPATIAL FRAME DRAGGING ANOMALY! ON-BOARD GRAVITATIONAL FLUCTUATIONS."

"Astro? What the hell?" Spectre held onto the command chair restraints and choked down his stomach. The spin in his head was about like a flat spin at four g. He'd felt that once before in an F/A-18 Hornet, years ago, and he didn't like it then.

"I dunn—" the lieutenant commander said, then vomited onto his control panel. Fortunately, it was the middle of the night and he had skipped supper. What came up was mostly fluids.

"Commander Weaver!"

"Working on it, sir," Bill said, swallowing his gorge.

"Commander Weaver?" Spectre shook his head and the spinning subsided for a second. Just a second.

"I don't get it, sir," Bill snapped, looking at the readings. "There is not much worse gravity here than at YZ Ceti and we're farther out. But there is some serious frame drag—" Weaver heaved but managed to use a bag this time.

"Eng reports Ball is nominal," the XO said, then grabbed a sickness bag.

"I'm, uh, trying to figure it out sir."

"Weaver?"

"Tchar?" Bill asked, looking at a small video screen. The Adar rarely got involved directly in the running of the ship.

"The ball particle counters are showing a largish background radiation across the spectrum of particles. We could be getting anomalous particle stream or even a-null impacting."

"I'm getting that . . . data now Tchar," Bill said, then grabbed another sickness bag and used same. The nausea from this transition was worse than anything he'd ever experienced in his life, and he'd spent a fair amount of time in both zero-g and fighters. "Thanks."

"Commander Weaver, how is it coming over there?" Spectre was beginning to lose patience. He had reluctantly agreed to the astrophysics survey in the flight plan, but he had been assured that the distance would be safe and that they had to chill anyway. *Fool me once, shame on you . . .*

"The algorithms from previous anomalies are not helping, sir. It must have to do with the serious gravitational frame dragging due to there being an A class star with four F class stars in extremely close orbit around it." Bill gulped again and looked down at the port side bulkhead just as down became the starboard bulkhead.

"CO?"

"Go XO."

"We really need to chill sir. Thermal readings exceeding eighty-seven percent of max."

"Not till we get this anomaly under control," Spectre ordered. "Commander Weaver, can we just back out of here?"

"That has never really worked for us in the past sir," Bill replied.

"Right. Work faster."

"Commander Weaver?"

"I'm running a sim now sir. I . . . think it's . . ." He paused and grabbed another sickness bag. The conn was rapidly running out. "I think it's going to tell me what is happening at least." Some . . . detritus had gotten on his screen and he surreptitiously wiped at it with his sleeve.

He was the first to see Miriam enter the conn. The linguist was normally the first to go down from motion sickness but something had changed that. As the relative "up" shifted to port the linguist easily handled the shift, even seeming to anticipate it, and walked up to his station along the top of the ballast controls.

"Is there unusual frame dragging in this region?" she asked nonchalantly.

"Data reduction and simulation is . . . coming in now," Weaver said, looking at her oddly. "Why are you asking?"

"I was just thinking about what might happen in a frame dragging scenario," Miriam said, grabbing a stanchion just *before* another gravity change and bracing sideways. "What do you think about, oh, adjusting the permeabilty factor for membrane modification during oscillations of the muon and muon neutrino density? I mean, if you have to realign the frame dragging coefficient for entry into non-standard metrics from modified flat plane metric motivation?"

"Miriam!" Bill said, slapping his forehead. "You're brilliant!"

"Well, yes, but do you think it will work?"

"Uh, let's assume that I'm not so brilliant and explain this to me," Spectre said. "And XO, get a work party up here with some more sickness bags!"

"Aye, aye, sir!"

"Muon and muon neutrino density, sir," Bill said. "That is what a plus pion or pi-meson decays into. That is what we use to power the box, pions. Maybe we're pounding it with too many."

"Well, we're going to chill anyway, can't we just cut them off?" Spectre asked.

"Good idea," Weaver said. "Maybe."

"There was one more thing." Miriam said. "I think that the first excited state of the flavor neutral must have the required rest mass of three zero nine six point nine million electron volts in oscillating flux density but the half life of the up-type pair must be longer, frame relative, than the rest frame seven point two times ten to the minus twenty-one seconds. The modulation and control of the flux density and pair half life can increase or decrease the flat space metric within the motivation metric to accommodate potential well suitability. But it's just a guess."

"Why three zero nine six point nine MeV?" Bill asked.

"That question was on the tip of my tongue," Spectre said, bracing his feet. "Yes, indeed, Miss Moon. Why . . . what he said?"

"I'm not a particle physicist but, isn't three zero nine six point nine MeV the rest mass of the J/psi particle?" Miriam asked.

"*Maulk.* I wish my memory would do that," Bill replied. "That sounds right. I'll have to look it up." He looked it up on the ship's science net and, sure enough, Miriam was right.

"So?" Spectre glanced over at the COB, who was reluctant to release his hold on the bulkhead stanchion. "How does this help?"

"I need to think on it some more but the suggestion is to

feed it J/psi particles to adjust the gravity and by increasing or decreasing the half life of the particle just means to increase or decrease its relativistic speed and therefore cause time dilation to occur, which in turn makes us in our reference frame observe that the particle lives longer than it should in a rest frame."

"*And*, Commander Weaver?" the CO was out of patience.

"Sorry sir, we aren't set up for creating J/psi particles. But it does tell us that the pions we are using are making it worse." Bill tapped a couple more commands and hit enter with dramatic emphasis.

"We should signal the all hands for zero gravity, sir," Bill said.

"Make it so."

"ALL HANDS, ALL HANDS. PREPARE FOR ZERO GRAVITY AND CHILL."

"Someone want to tell me what the heck just happened?" the CO asked. "I do recall *someone* promising me that *this* astrophysics survey was going to be *event free!*"

"Well, sir," Bill said, slowly and thoughtfully. "I *think* the black box knows how to adjust for gravity fluctuations of all sorts by inputting different types of mesons. I never really thought of that but it makes sense that it's got to have some sort of potential control system to deal with the effects we've been having trouble with. And apparently the different flavors of mesons have different effects on the thing just like electrons make it go boom. The Mu Ori system is a fairly good sized A type star of about three or more solar masses that has two sets of F binaries orbiting it at very close orbits. The F type binaries are at orbits more like planets from each other rather than like stars. So there are a lot of spinning massive objects here." Weaver stopped as the CO held up his hand.

"And the box wasn't set to account for mixed-up gravity. I get it. And we went to zero gravity because we don't have these J/psi things to adjust it properly?" Spectre asked.

"Yes, sir."

"Then I was right! We should've just turned off the ball to start with?"

"Uh, yes sir. But . . ." Weaver decided not to finish whatever it was he was going to say. Which was that if the anomaly had been

Tchar's first guess, anomalous particle input, they might not have been able to shut off the drive. Or get it started again. Or several other bad things ranging up to making a *new* star in the system.

"XO, get me a damage report. Mr. Weaver, don't you have an astrophysical survey to do?"

"Aye, aye, sir."

"And figure out how we're going to get out of this mess!"

"Aye, aye, sir."

"I need to address the crew."

"All hands, all hands, this is the CO speaking. What we just experienced was an unanticipated frame dragging anomaly. Following the chill and survey of this region, we will be leaving. We may encounter additional frame dragging anomalies. So grab your barf bags. Thank you for flying Vorpal Air."

"What the pock is a 'frame dragging anomaly'?" Portana spat.

"Search me, Portly," Sergeant Priester said. "Two-Gun? You're the only guy who gets this stuff."

"You sure?" Berg asked. "Kinda technical."

"Just give it to us straight, man," Lyle said with a fake whine tone. "Tell us how *grapped* we are! We can handle it! We're marooned, aren't we? Stuck in the depths of space with no way—"

"We get it, Lurch," Berg said, grinning. "Nice way to scare the newbies. But, if you really want to know. I recently found a paper in the database that Lieutenant Commander Weaver wrote about the data in the Gravity Probe B satellite . . ." Berg started.

"Oh *maulk*, here we go," Priester said. "Tell us how much you're in love with the astro."

"*Grapp* you, Priestman," Berg said. "Honestly, I didn't understand the paper; it was way over my head. But he did have a simple analogy in it to explain the concept. It has to do with . . ."

"So, Commander Weaver," Spectre said silkily. "Kindly explain to your CO, who you convinced over his protestations that an astrophysics survey would be a *good* thing, what this 'frame dragging' thing is, why it *grapped* up my ship and crew and why *you* failed to anticipate it."

"Well, sir," Bill said with a gulp. "I never really thought it would be a big deal. Until now."

"Uh huh. Keep going. Feel free to use words of more than two syllables."

"It has to do with general relativity, sir," Bill said carefully.

"I did say more than two," the CO replied. "But relativity is a bunch." He looked down at his fingers and moved his lips. "Five, actually."

"Then imagine that space is like a big rubber sheet that is stretched tight. Kinda like a trampoline. And assume our model is being done on Earth so we have one gravity."

"But space is three dimensions and one of time right?" Spectre said, then winced. He was opening up himself for a full-scale Weaver-assault with that one.

"Oh, this is a two-D analogy sir . . ."

Whew. Escaped by the skin of my teeth . . .

"Anyway, consider what happens to our trampoline if you place a lead bowling ball in the middle of it. That would be the analog of the sun."

"So far, so good."

"Well, the space around the ball, the sun, curves in on it and is stretched."

"That's 'frame dragging'?"

"Not yet, sir. But, if you spin the ball and allow for there to be friction between the ball and the rubber sheet, the sheet will twist with the ball and bunch up around it. You get my description?"

"Yeah, I can see that. So the space around you is the reference frame you are in and the spinning star drags it around it as it spins?"

"Precisely, sir! I wrote a paper about how if we prove that it exists, then we are a step closer to understanding how to do a warp drive, but that was before the Dreen and the world went to shit."

"So, where's the problem, Commander? This frame dragging should be around the star. Localized. We're a couple of light-years out!"

"Well sir, there are five stars in this system and all of them spinning like *maulk*."

"Oh *grapp*."

"So," Portana said, carefully. "Two-Gongoron wan's t' habe the astrogator babies and too many star spinning too fas' in a small space is pad. Why you not say t'at in t'e firs' place?"

"Hey," Priester said, leaning back in his bunk. "Welcome to the Space Marines. Please leave your brain at the door."

"XO!"

"Sir," the XO said.

"Put a note in the log," the CO said, standing up and looking around the compartment. It had taken nearly an hour of nerve-wracking and gut-twisting maneuvers to clear the system. "Unless ordered by higher, no more close studies of astrophysics anomalies."

"Aye, aye, sir!" the XO said. "Officer of the Watch! Update the log!"

"And put a further note," Spectre said, walking towards his quarters and pointedly not looking over his shoulder at the astrogator. "'And this time I *mean* it!'"

11

"CO, chill complete," The XO reported. He had the daily duty to bring a report on consumables and conditions to the CO and had stopped by the conn to determine the condition of chill.

"Roger," Spectre said. "And?"

"We're at twenty percent on water stores," the XO continued. "Forty on air, but we're reaching break-point on the scrubbers without a way to blow off the CO_2."

"Roger that, XO," the CO said, bringing up the repeater on the main scope. They were currently parked in deep space just outside the gravitational bubble of HD 37301. The F5 star was about three quarters of the way to the mission zone and a good point to pick up supplies. The *Vorpal Blade* was more than three hundred and seventy-six light-years from Earth and only one really weird thing had happened to them. Spectre liked it, the mission was boring so far. Well, compared to the other missions.

"Astro, CO," Spectre continued, hitting the comm to the conn.

"Astro."

"We need to replenish," the CO said. "What do we have in this system?"

"Sir, I've had the telescopes looking for Jovians and have found two," Weaver replied. "Or, we could use the comet water extraction gear. I've had two of the scopes looking for comets also. Found a few of them out at about seventy AUs on highly elliptical orbits. That's par for the course in case you're wondering."

"Well, the last time we did the Jovian thing you flooded the ship with squeaky gases."

"Uh, yes, sir."

"Then why don't we try the comet thing. Besides, we haven't done that before and I'm not in the mood for a hundred or more Donald Duck voices on my ship," Spectre said with a raised eyebrow.

"Aye, aye, sir," Lieutenant Commander Weaver responded. "But I'm not sure all the bugs are worked out of *that* system."

"So your recommendation is . . ."

"Jovian extraction, sir," Weaver replied.

"Right," Spectre said. "XO, prepare for comet rendezvous and water extraction. Astro, get us up side a good wet one."

"Aye sir," Weaver replied. "But you'd probably prefer a good frozen one. And I'll bet you a dollar you end up longing for the days of Donald Duck."

"I'll take that bet, Astro."

Two-Gun, Lurch, Himes, and Command Master Chief Miller were Wyverned up and preparing to do an EVA onto the comet via the underbelly elevator. The elevator was made of aliglass, a substance also called "transparent aluminum" which was, in fact, more like synthetic sapphire. The elevator was a cube roughly three meters on a side—just big enough that three Wyverns could fit in it or four men in spacesuits. Four Wyverns at a stretch if they weren't anticipating being eaten or shot on exit.

"Conn, EVA," Miller said. The chief adjusted the weight on his footing and prepared for the gravity to drop out from under him. "We're in the elevator and ready to drop onto the comet."

"Roger that. I wish I could be there with y'all," Weaver said from the EVA control. His accent always got thicker when he got excited. "Y'all will be the first humans to ever walk on a comet. But somebody has to make sure we don't bump into this thing too hard."

"Chief," Spectre interrupted. "Good luck."

"Yes, sir."

"Team," Berg said. "Remember, comets can have a lot of dust and gasses floating around it in close to the sun. Especially if they have a lot of water ices."

"Yeah, so?"

"Well, way out here it should just be a frozen ball with no clouds or atmosphere," Berg said. "But that's only theory."

"So . . ." Lurch replied. "It should be . . . Holy *maulk*! It's like a blizzard out there!"

The elevator had exited the underbelly of the ship and it was apparent, whatever the theory, that the comet was surrounded in some sort of fog. Since a water fog was impossible in space, what it was composed of was anyone's guess.

"Thought you said it'd be clear, Two-Gun!" Himes said.

"The-or-et-i-cal-ly," Berg enunciated very slowly.

"Well, *that* theory's out the window," Lurch said, chuckling.

"Still doesn't make sense," Eric said. There *shouldn't* have been that much ice and dust particulate matter floating around them.

"Two-Gun," Miller said over a private channel. "We're whited out here. Suggestions?"

"Damn thing's down there somewhere, Chief," Berg said, looking at the all-enveloping fog, then extending a camera to look down. "Based on the briefing, the radar has to have it close. No more than six meters from the underside. The microgravity of the comet's much higher than the ship's. Exit forward, give a short burst relative 'down' then watch our laser range-finders. They're probably going to cut through this better than visual. And it's not like we're going to take any damage if we hit hard."

"Right," Miller said, nodding inside his suit. "Team, one safety line to the elevator, one to your buddy. Exit forward, get a relative position stopped by the opening and then one hit of jet relative down. The damned thing's got to be down there somewhere."

To Berg it reminded him a good bit of SCUBA school. Entering the fog immediately cut off all light from the elevators, and even the helmet lights barely penetrated, reflecting back a brilliant white that was so annoying he just turned them off. So he was working in absolute darkness and zero-gravity. It was disorienting as hell, but then so was doing the same thing underwater.

They'd kept relative position on the ship while they were still in view. Going down was when they'd lost track of everything.

But just as he was starting to wonder if there really was a comet under his feet his laser range-finder started to report a solid hit.

"Chief Milller?" Berg said, looking at the range dropping, fast.

»   »   »

"Team," Miller snapped. "Prepare for landing in three . . . two . . . Contact!" It felt a bit like landing in very grainy snow. At least, what it might have felt like if it was grainy snow with no really noticeable gravity.

"Miller? Chief? What'd you see?" Weaver asked over the com.

"Not a thing, sir," Miller replied irritably. "We're totally zero vis down here. Wait one." He took the harpoon gun from his belt and fired it into the comet surface. The reaction force of the harpoon pushed him upward off the surface but as soon as the harpoon bit it started to automatically reel in. All he had to do was hold on and work to get his feet in line with the harpoon. He managed to get one knee under him as he hit, then knelt down using the harpoon rope to pull against and picked up a handful of the cometary surface debris.

"Looks like ice," Miller said, holding the material up to his camera. "Dirty ice."

"Standard cometary ice," Two-Gun added. "Spectrometer shows it to be water ice with about twice the amount of deuterium in it as ocean water. Just like you expected, Commander Weaver. But . . ."

"Good. Well, start laying out the cables and we'll send down the chipper. What is the but, Two-Gun?"

"Uh, sir? Why all the fog? We're so far out from the star that this thing should be frozen hard as a rock."

"What happens when you stomp your feet against the comet, Two-Gun?" Weaver replied. "Or bring a ship and gravity field in close to it for that matter? And don't forget that you and the ship are hot."

"Huh? Oh, I see." Berg realized that the disturbance of the ship landing had forced a cloud of debris particles up around it. The gravity of the comet was so slight that it would take months or even years for the dust to settle. And the heat radiators from the belly of the ship were probably melting off ice and causing a microclimate to form around them as well. Space was a delicate, although harsh place; the tiniest variance in temperature could create interesting changes.

"This damned thing looks like some sort of demented garden tiller," Machinist Mate Gants said. Behind it a Seaman's Apprentice rolled a large coiled-up thirty-centimeter-diameter flex hose.

The spooled flex hose would be fifty meters long when stretched out.

"Yeah, or maybe a miniaturized combine tractor." Miriam laughed then pushed at the compressed, coiled, and tied-up flex hose with her foot. "I *assume* that someone has noticed that flex hose is *not* the smartest thing you could use in microgravity!"

"Well, ma'am," Gants said, grinning. "You know what they say about assuming . . ."

"That's the last of the cables, Two-Gun." Himes attached the loop on the end of his Spectra 1000 polymer cable onto the carabineer connected to the chipper. The cables stretched out like spokes of a wheel about the ship for about thirty meters in every direction. They would be used to help guide and hold down the ice chipper.

The ship had been carefully belayed down to the point where the elevator was in contact with the surface of the comet, then lashed to additional harpoons. As long as none of the forces about to be unleashed exceeded the rated strength of the materials, in near absolute zero cold and pretty solid vacuum, everything would be well.

If not . . .

"Secured to the winch up here, Chief," Berg said. "I guess the only thing left is the flex hose."

"Got it," Lurch said pulling the oversized zip-tie cinched tight around where the hose fit over the output end of the chipper. Then he cut the zip-tie that was holding the hose compressed.

"No wait!" Two-Gun yelled.

It was too late.

The flex hose expanded out under the ship like a bullet, flailing like a snake with its head cut off and kicking up *more* ice particulates, thus making the fog even worse. But the hose quickly damped itself out to minor oscillations and lay limp floating a meter or so above the surface of the comet.

"Huh? It just stopped," Himes said. "Why the hell did it do that? I figured it would go on forever!"

"Conservation of angular momentum," Berg said musingly. "Should've thought of that. You knew that, didn't you, Lurch?"

"I read about this experiment once called the Inflatable Antenna Experiment," Sergeant Lyle said. "You let loose floppy things in space and one side flops one way so the other flops the other way to conserve angular momentum. Eventually, it stops flopping. No harm, no foul."

"You're trying to out Alpha Geek me, aren't you?" Berg said, grinning inside his Wyvern.

"Not a chance, Brain," Lurch said. "You can keep particles all to yourself. But, I mean, don't all Marines read *Space Daily*?"

"This *maulk* hurts my head," Himes said.

"Welcome to the Space Marines," Lurch and Eric chorused.

"Commander Weaver, we are ready to commence chipping down here." Weaver scanned as best he could in the fog at the surface, the winch cables, and the Marines. "Everybody clear out and man the flex hose. I've got the chipper." The chief put his large burly space-suited hands around the ice chipper handlebars and depressed the start safety switch. The switch was a built-in safety disengage like a bicycle brake lever or, well, like the safety disengage on a garden tiller, and if it were let go, the chipper blades would stop turning. Miller stepped up on the operator's platform, which was nothing more than two metal plates for him to stand on. As the safety lever closed, the electric engine whirred to life, spinning up the chipper blades.

The oversized and demented looking garden tiller started jumping and bouncing and would have thrown itself along with the chief off the surface of the comet and out into space were it not for the winches on either side of the device connected to polymer cables, which were, in turn, harpooned into the surface of the comet.

"Yeehaw!" Miller shouted sarcastically as the chipper bit into the icy surface of the comet and dug deeper into it, chewing up the comet debris and spitting it out through the flex hose. The chipper dug down a meter until the blades were completely under the ice. Then it started heading forward, continuing for twenty meters in less than fifty seconds.

The hose whipped taut and filled as the ice chips were forced through it. Like a rocket engine out of the other end of the hose a spray of ice flung the flex hose hither and yon. It was all that Lurch, Two-Gun, and Himes could do to hold on to it even though their feet were tied down to harpoons on the surface. The ice spray splattered across the opening of the elevator and only about two-thirds of it actually made it in.

"Hold up, Chief!" Two-Gun cried. The chipper stopped bucking once Miller let off the safety lever. It slowly flopped back and forward but was otherwise limp.

"*Maulk*, Two-Gun can't you keep it up longer than that!" Himes laughed, but he couldn't have held on any longer either.

"Shit, that was a ride," Miller said. "I can't fight this thing and hold down that damned safety lever at the same *grapping* time. Who designed this *grapping* thing anyway?" The chief was a big man, but in a matter of less than a minute the machine had caused him to sweat profusely and his hand and forearm muscles burned. Somehow, he just knew the *Blade*'s redneck astrogator had something to do with the design of the thing. "Ain't like tilling garden soil, that's for sure."

"What's wrong, Chief?" Spectre asked. The entire operation was considerably entertaining to the former fighter pilot. And for now it appeared to be safer than letting hydrogen gas seep into every nook and cranny of the ship.

"Uh, well sir, I'm not sure yet but I think I'm gonna need a foot long zip-tie, and some other stuff." Miller looked back over his shoulder. "What'd you need, Two-Gun?"

"No problem that more Marines couldn't solve. Even with Wyverns, keeping this hose under control is nearly impossible."

"Did you get any ice, Chief?" Weaver asked.

"I don't know. Hold one." Miller turned slowly, releasing his carabineer from the cables harpooned into the ice. He was careful not to launch himself in the microgravity and inched his way back the couple of meters to where the Marines were strapped down.

"Any ice in the elevator, Marines?" He shined his suit floods at the elevator opening and saw a mountain of ice before them. He had to get within a half a meter to see it with all the fog. "What the *grapp*?"

"Will you look at that?" Himes leaned forward to inch closer to the elevator door.

"Uh, yes sir," Miller said. "The elevator is completely full. And then some."

"Good work, Chief! We'll extract it and empty it for another round," Spectre said, jovially. "EVA, retrieve the elevator."

Weaver hit the elevator controls and was unsurprised when a red icon appeared on his screen.

"I was afraid of that."

"What?" Spectre asked, leaning over the console. "Mr. Miller, did you break my elevator?"

"Wait, one, sir," Miller replied. "Oh . . . *grapp*. Sir, forget the extra zip-tie for the safety lever and I doubt we'll need those Marines. Uh, sir, is there a way you could send down some picks or some antifreeze or something?" Miller looking up over the elevator that the semi-frozen ice spray had filled and buried and almost immediately refroze to the comet. That elevator was going nowhere soon.

"Well, the problem, sir," Weaver said calmly, "is that the chipper was designed by guys who had been thinking of building a mass-driver propulsion system to steer comets off of collision courses. In essence, it's a rocket engine and spits out a hell of a lot more ice spray than I'd ever thought it would've. We just modified the idea for our use."

The computer had to be given complete control of the navigation in order to exactly, or as close to exactly as possible, match the comet's rotations. Otherwise, the momentum of the small city-sized comet would rip the elevator right out of the belly of the *Blade*. And, Weaver could tell by the look on Spectre's face, that he didn't like that not one *grapping* bit.

"Didn't you do some calculations on this to figure it out, Astro?" the CO said, just as calmly. But it was clearly the calm before the storm.

"Uh, no sir, the comet water extraction didn't fall under astrogation or propulsion or fighting the Dreen so I, uh, delegated it, sir," Weaver said sheepishly.

"Understood. To whom was it delegated?"

"Tchar."

"Tchar," the CO said, nodding. Calmly. "Tchar. Right. We'll discuss *that* decision of yours later, Astro. Right now, do you have *any* suggestions for getting *my* elevator unstuck?"

"I'm thinking on it, sir. Maybe Tchar has something in his junk pile. I'd better get down there sir."

"Sir," the COB said, sticking his head in the wardroom. "This reminds me of a boat I was on a few years ago—"

"COB, much as I enjoy your reminiscences—" the CO said tightly.

"Yes, sir," the COB interrupted. "I know you enjoy them all, sir. But there's a point to this one, sir. Are you willing to gain the benefit of my nearly thirty years in this country's Navy, sir? Or are you going to tell your senior enlisted man to mind his own business, sir?"

Spectre opened his mouth, then shut it.

"Go ahead, COB."

"The point, sir, is that we were in the arctic," the COB continued. "Machinist Mate Gants happened to be on the same cruise. He wasn't a mate back then and I wasn't COB but we were on the same boat, Lord help me. Anyway, he used a welder to melt a statue of a naked woman out of some glacier ice. See, we did a crack through on the ice and . . ."

"Weaver?"

"Great idea, COB," Weaver said. He hit the com keys on his console. "Eng? I need Machinist Mate Gants on the double."

"Yeah, I did this once for a Christmas Party a few years ago when we were poking up through the ice in the Arctic. We were camping up there for Christmas with these SEALS that were waiting on a damned Chinese polar orbiting satellite to crash . . . uh, forget I said that part . . . so I decided to lighten the mood." Gants tossed several extra long welding rods, a roll of space tape, and a few tungsten rods into a cart alongside the portable welding generator and welder transformer. "We'd better hurry though."

"How we getting this down to them?" Miriam asked.

"Somebody's gotta carry it to 'em out the forward or top airlock or maybe out one of the torp tubes," Gants said. "I saw *Deep Impact* and I have *no* desire to be walking on a damned comet in the middle of freakin' space."

"Uh, yeah." Miriam tried not to grin. The movie had been so incorrect in the nature of comets it was a catastrophe in and of itself. But she decided not to say anything. Besides, the voice in her head was telling her something interesting about ". . . *the entropy due to quantum fluctuations around the event horizon being proportional to the surface area of the artificial singularity . . .*" So she was only half listening to Gants. Being an interpreter for years had trained her to half listen to multiple conversations at once. *Maybe that is why the voice likes me?*

» » »

"Well, Chief, you really managed to *grapp* this one up, huh? No comments about whose idea this was." Weaver was chagrined at himself, not the crew.

"Not gonna say a word about it, sir," Miller said with a snort.

"Two-Gun, start setting this up. Get me the welding transformer plugged into the generator and get it right here by this elevator strut. The welder only has about eight feet of cable."

"Yes sir! Himes, Lurch give me a hand." Two-Gun shot another harpoon into the comet just forward of the elevator and winched himself to the welder that the commander had brought them. Himes and Lurch followed suit.

"Now I just stretch this tungsten rod between these two welder clips and that should do it. I see the other rods and space tape now." He laid the other two welding rods across the back of the insulated parts of the welder clips and then space taped them to each clip so he could use the welding rods as a handle. Those damned machinists in engineering were nothing if not clever.

"Ready over there Two-Gun?"

"Yes, sir."

"Turn me on."

"On, sir."

"Wheeee!" Weaver could see the tungsten rod glowing red hot. He set to work on the first ice sculpture in space, on a comet, in orbit around a distant star. Say what you wanted to about the casualty rates, but sometimes Weaver felt he had the best job in the galaxy. He felt like the heroes in those science fiction books he grew up reading. The only things missing were scantily clad super vixen heroines.

"So the t/psi interacts with the psi muon density modularity vector . . ." Miriam muttered. "I can see that . . ."

"Try it now, Mike," Weaver told Gants over the com.

"Yes, sir," Gants depressed the elevator controls and sluggishly the hydraulics pulled the box filled with about twenty-five tons of ice free from the comet.

"Hot damn!"

"The elevator is here, sir." Gants replied. "It'll, uh, take us a few minutes to unload it."

"Copy that."

Gants and several of the submarine's tech crew set to work emplacing the smaller chipper and melter system in the elevator and connecting it to the flex hose that ran down the corridor around two corners and up one deck to the water reservoir inlet near what used to be ballast tanks. In space they were water reservoirs.

The smaller chipper made quick work of the ice, and the fact that it was about sixty-eight degrees in the ship helped also. The ice melted as it was chipped and was sucked away through the flex hose.

"How we doing, XO?" the CO asked.

"Uhm . . . About that bet with Commander Weaver, sir?"

"Tell me."

"It's taking four minutes to unload the elevator and drop it back to the surface. It takes about two minutes to refill it and unstick it. Total time, six minutes."

"Not bad," the CO said, nodding. "Not bad!"

"Yes, sir," the XO said. "The interior volume of the elevator is thirty-six cubic meters. We need twenty-six *thousand* cubic meters of water. Actually, that's just to fill the reserve tanks. It doesn't take into account the amount of O_2 we need to crack out of it."

"Oh," the CO said. "Timeframe?"

"Seventy-two hours just to fill the reserve tanks," the XO said. "Another thirty-four to create enough water to refill the O_2 tanks. Actually, that's not exactly right, since we're using it even as we're gathering it. Total estimated time? One hundred and twenty hours to have everything topped off."

"We don't have five days, XO," the CO said. "We're on a rescue mission."

"Agreed, sir," Coldsmith said. "Would you care to venture an estimate on how long it will take to refill at a Jovian with the new systems?"

"Go."

"Twenty-six hours, topped off."

"Damn."

"Suspend operations," Commander Coldsmith said.

"Why?" Weaver replied.

"Commander, I know you haven't been an officer for as long as your rank might suggest, but in the Navy when you're given an order . . ."

"Sorry, XO," Weaver said. "I meant to say 'aye, aye, sir.'"

"There's good news, though," the XO replied. "The CO owes you a dollar."

"Damn," Spectre said, looking at the readings. Entry to the system and approach to the Jovian had taken less than an hour. Set up had taken less than fifteen minutes with the installed system. He'd gone off-watch, done some paperwork and come back to find the tanks almost filled, O_2 and H_2O.

"Good job, Commander. You were r . . . You were ri . . . Damnit, here's your dollar!"

"I won't say I told you so, sir," Weaver replied, taking the dollar primly. "I'm too tired and *much* too big of a man to say anything like—"

"Thin ice, Astro," the CO said. "Thin ice."

"Yes, sir. And I'm sure no pun was intended."

12

"Set Condition One! Prepare for HD 36951 system entry!"

"Thank God," First Sergeant Powell muttered. "*Please* let there be something to fight!"

"Tactical, Conn," Spectre said, watching the forward view. The approaching planet looked somewhat like Mars, one of the standard "looks" he'd seen at least a hundred times on the previous mission. But on this one there was a gate. And at least at one time there had been enemies. "Anything?"

"Negative, Conn," the TACO replied. "No emissions beyond what we'd expect from the sun and the gate."

"I'm getting the take, too," Weaver said. "All normal. No electronics from the planet. If there are any survivors who avoided the blast, they're keeping quiet."

"Okay, let's take her down," Spectre said. "Land a klick from the edge of the blast area and send in the Marines. Make it so, XO."

"Dust ball," Berg said as the team deployed out of the aliglass elevator. "We're going to have to go over the Wyverns when we get back and get every scrap of this dust out of the joints or it will wear like a bitch."

"Make you an armorer for a couple of days . . ." Himes said.

"I'm more worried about what we're going to find," Smith said as the elevator touched the red soil.

The boat had landed on a broad plateau near the site of the gate. The blast effect area from the nuke was evident, a broad, shallow crater the size of a large factory. The Looking Glass was also visible, floating in the air above the center of the crater.

The gate was located in a narrow valley between two plateaus, one the ship had landed on and the other occupied by ruins of the ancient civilization that had, presumably, emplaced the Looking Glass boson in the first place. The ruins were visible as well but they were so worn by time they looked barely different from their surroundings. The ruins had been surveyed, though, before the blast, and there were tunnels that could have sheltered survivors of the initial attack and the response. Checking them out was first priority.

"The ship didn't see anything on the pass," Two-Gun replied, stepping out and moving forward as the elevator doors opened. "If there were major threats they'd have seen it. Just deploy and cover for the rest of the company. We're not going to be getting busy till we get down into the valley."

As each team moved out of the elevator, Berg's moved forward, keeping the bombing site and the distant ruins in view. It took a while. Only three Wyverns would fit in the elevator, a fact that had been a problem more than once on the previous mission. It was simply a pain exiting the ship. Retreating into it was damned well nightmarish.

Finally both of the platoons that were going on the mission were down and deployed. Berg anticipated the ping from his platoon leader and started picking a path down the slope to the valley. Where the gate had been was a glassy crater, pointless to examine not to mention still rather radioactive. But there might be indicators to either side. His platoon was detailed to take the north side in a sweep across the valley while Third swept to the south.

The slope down was slight but tricky. The Wyverns always had a problem with rough ground, especially on the downslope. But Berg's team quickly reached the bottom and started to sweep across the valley as teams deployed to either side.

"I'm glad we're in the middle and don't have the south side," Himes muttered. "I'm getting readings off that crater all the way over here."

"Nothing that's going to hurt us," Berg said. "Less chatter, more looking."

"And I think we've got something," Smith replied, pinging for a stop.

"*Is* that something?" Berg asked, walking over and taking a look. The "something" was a narrow hole that appeared to have been punched into the red soil. "It could be sampling from the scientists."

"What's up, Two-Gun?" Top asked, bounding over in his Wyvern. "A hole?"

"It looks like it was pushed in, Top," Smith said. "Like a big . . . toothpick?"

"Sir, I need a science team," the first sergeant said over the company freq. "Bio or Geo."

Master Sergeant Max Guzik bounced over and looked at the hole.

"It's not a standard auger hole," the geology specialist said. "And the edges are tapered, indicating that whatever made it was shoved into the ground under high pressure."

"I've got another one over here," Lieutenant Monaghan said. "First Platoon, spread out. See how many of these we've got."

Eventually sixteen separate holes in an oval pattern nearly a hundred meters across were found. By that time, Sergeant First Class Darren Hanel, the biology specialist, had taken samples from the first hole.

"I'll say this," the sergeant first class said, straightening up. "Whatever it was was hot. Did you notice the sides were partially melted?"

"Yeah," Master Sergeant Guzik said. "But it wasn't nuclear. No radiation readings. But I'm pretty sure the team that was here didn't make it."

"Concur on that," Hanel said, putting the sample away. "I'll see what I can get off of it. Probably nothing. Anything that can punch a hole like that and melt the sides of the hole isn't going to spall off much material."

"Pardon me," Lance Corporal Smith said. "Laser?"

"You wouldn't have had that dug-up lip," the master sergeant replied. "And I don't see the hole being tapered. No, I think we're looking at some sort of landing jacks."

Berg looked around at the flags marking the perimeter of the anomaly, then at the narrow hole and whistled.

"Master Sergeant," he said, carefully, "if they're landing jacks, then whatever they were supporting was at least a hundred meters long and about forty wide."

"And they're very narrow," Guzik growled. "Figured that one out, Two-Gun. But thanks for the input. We're looking at something that displaced over ten thousand tons, minimum, but which lands on sixteen toothpicks. Well, railroad spikes."

"Why do I suddenly have the image of a giant spider in my head?" Smith muttered.

"Why do I have the image of a Dreen warship that just *looks* sort of like a giant spider?" Himes replied. "Big bulbous body, sixteen spiderlike landing legs. And a whole passel of Dreen rhino-tanks, dog-demons, thorn-throwers . . ."

"We get the point, Himes," Berg said. "Can it."

"You brains get this sorted out?" First Sergeant Powell asked, bouncing over. He'd swept around the crater and gotten Third Platoon up to the ruins, searching for survivors.

"I think we're looking at landing jacks, First Sergeant," Guzik said. "Just a guess. I'm not an alien tech specialist. But they're not probe holes. They taper, nothing appeared to be picked up, they're partially melted on the side . . . Sixteen narrow somethings which were intensively hot were shoved into the ground under enormous weight. That says landing jacks to me. I'd suggest getting Lieutenant Fey out here while we continue our sweep. And look for indications that something deployed from the ship. If there was a ship."

"All teams," Lieutenant Monaghan said. "Up to the ruins. Keep an eye out for tracks or traces. The base is in our sector. Bravo, you've got point into the secondary base. Move it out."

"Let's go," Berg said, gesturing to the hills above. "Vector right a bit. There's a path."

The path had been heavily used but if any aliens had used it, it wasn't evident. The secondary base was reported to be partially built into one of the ruins, mostly underground. It wasn't visible from the approach path and when Berg's team neared it he slowed down.

"Anybody got anything on sensors?" he asked.

"Negative," Himes reported. "There should be at least some electrical secondaries from equipment. But I'm getting nada."

"Ditto," Smith said.

"Ears," Berg said, cranking up the gain on his external audio systems. He could hear the teams behind him scrabbling up the hill but that was about it. He changed frequencies.

"Top, we're trying to do an audio—"

"All teams, freeze," the first sergeant said before he even finished.

With the sounds of the teams gone all there was was a light whistling from the thin atmosphere's wind on the rocks.

"Negative on sound or emissions at the site," Berg said.

"Teams, continue mission. Two-Gun, check it out."

Berg tracked his gun back and forth and then started forward.

"Slow and careful," he said over the team freq.

Cresting the edge of the ridgeline they could see the opening to the base. It had been sealed with heavy sheet plastic with plastic reinforcing. The sheet plastic was torn, the reinforcing had been ripped out of the tunnel and part of the opening was fallen in.

"I think somebody tore that up," Himes said.

"Possibly," Berg said. "Or a one megaton nuclear blast could have done it."

"Point."

"Lieutenant Monaghan, containment on the base has been breached," Berg reported. "It's still unclear if it was from hostile action or the nuke. Continuing."

"Roger," Lieutenant Monaghan replied. "Watch your ass, Two-Gun."

"Whoa," Himes said. "Got something again. These ain't human tracks."

Berg panned a camera around to see what Himes was looking at and nodded, his machine gun panning up and down.

"Looks like claw marks," Berg said, hitting a control. "Sir, sending video. There appear to be claw tracks."

"Dreen," Miller said from in the conn.

"Oh, yeah," Weaver replied. "Shit."

"Captain Zanella, this is the CO," Spectre said over the radio. "Those tracks have been identified as Dreen. Proceed with caution. I'm taking the ship up to orbit. I'm not going to get jumped on the ground by a Dreen warship."

"Understood, sir."

"Sir, permission to deploy before we take off," Weaver said.

"Why?" Spectre snapped.

"Because I think I've figured out a way to communicate with Earth, sir," Weaver said. "I'll need about twenty minutes to set it up. And I'll need a commo tech."

Specter considered that for a moment, then nodded.

"We'll scramble for altitude while you get ready," the CO said. "When you're ready, we'll drop you off."

"Agreed, sir," Bill said, standing up. "Permission to go get ready."

"Go. You too, Chief Miller."

"What are you thinking?" Miller asked.

"I'm hoping is more like it," Bill replied. "I'm hoping that they've got some smart people monitoring the dangerous gates."

"All teams. The ship is heading for orbit in case we need firepower. Be aware that First Platoon has found definite signs of Dreen presence. They're probably gone, but remain fully alert."

"Two-Gun."

"Yes, sir," Berg replied to the platoon leader.

"Move into the base and look for evidence of Dreen presence or any survivors."

"Roger, sir," Berg said. "Okay, boys, now's when it gets interesting. I've got point. Follow me."

"Gladly," Himes said. "Very dangerous. You go first."

The opening was low due to the rubble and Berg had to hunch the suit through, keeping his weapon up and forward at the same time. The walls, once past the outer edge, were smooth and delicately patterned. They shone a faint blue in the glow from his suit lights.

The passageway went straight down at a slight slope then turned sharply to the left. There was rubble on the floor, some of it shoved to the side but more fallen recently. Most of it was probably from the shocks from the nuke. The floor was too solid for tracks and it wasn't possible to determine if any of the rubble had been moved. At least not to Berg.

Turning the corner they could see an open area ahead. As they approached, it was apparent there had been another seal there. But it, too, was ripped down.

"We got anybody?" Berg asked.

"Top, Two-Gun," the first sergeant replied. "I'm setting up a relay system. And monitoring your video."

As they entered the center of the base it was apparent that the

Dreen had been there ahead of them. A dog-demon—a pony-sized beast that was low-slung with a chopping jaw head—was lying dead at one side of the room. Some folding tables had apparently been set up as a barricade across the door. They were ripped apart and tossed about the interior.

There were several patches of dried blood but not one body, not one piece of electronics was left. Packs had been ripped apart, the contents strewn about the room. Cots were overturned, sleeping bags ripped open and a blister bag of water had been breached, the water pooling at the rear of the room.

"This had to really suck," Himes said. "But somebody had a weapon, apparently."

"Looks like a lucky shot from a pistol," Smith said, examining the body of the dog-demon. "Couple of scratches on the chest armor but whoever it was got a shot into that soft patch under the neck."

Berg looked around and shrugged inside his armor.

"No exits," he said, swiveling his turret back and forth. "So anybody in this room was doomed."

"Got a map," Himes said, pulling a large sheet of paper out from under a table. "Looks like the map they were making of the ruins."

"Got some lab books over here," Smith said. "Can't exactly open them in this suit."

"Top, we've got some intel down here," Berg said.

"On my way down," the first sergeant replied. "Hold your position."

"This looks interesting," Smith said, straightening up with a book held in his suit claws. "Somebody drew all over the cover with red ink. It says 'Dreen!'"

The first sergeant delicately set the lab book on one of the rerighted tables and hooked open the front. He read it for a moment, then nodded, his machine gun tracking up and down.

"Supplementary log of HD 36951 Gamma Station forward base, Dr. Christian Moshier, Ph.D. Just in case anybody ever reads it," he said softly.

1140: The main base was struck by what we think was a kinetic energy weapon. Several personnel were away from this base when the main base was attacked.

Their condition is unknown at this time. Drs. Darren Hokanson and Matthew Sterret were working in the ruins. Dr. Charles Talbot was on the way back to the main base. Doctoral Candidate Deb Cutler was exploring a previously unmapped section. The other five of us are fine at this time.

1154: Dr. Kaye Roberts has volunteered to go to the surface. She is aware that in the event of an attack, the protocol is to destabilize the gate with a nuclear weapon. She feels that she can observe from a position just outside the tunnel in the event there is a rescue party. The rest of us have elected to remain, rather than try to beat the response. I was given a classified briefing that indicates that even with the gate destabilized there is an "alternate method" of response. I don't know what that is but rather than risk getting hit by our own nuke we're going to wait.

1214: Dr. Roberts has reported an unknown ship overhead. Video of the ship and its actions are on the main archaeology computer. The ship lowered under apparent antigravity power, fired downward using something like a laser and dropped down a probe. The probe might have returned to the ship with a body. Dr. Talbot was on his way to the base when the rock was dropped. It is possible that this unknown alien species captured him.

1217: The ship has left.

1321: Another shock indicated that the nuke has gone off and shortly afterwards we experienced enormous overpressure that severely damaged the airlocks. If we had any idea it was going to take that long we would have run for it. We have no reports from Dr. Roberts.

1333: Dr. Roberts has returned. Her radio was destroyed by EMP but she was not harmed. The inner airlock is repaired and Dr. Roberts has volunteered to lead a team to repair the outer airlock. Dr. Wilson has completed an inventory of supplies. We can hold out for forty days, more or less. The big question is the air processor. If it breaks down, we're in trouble. But as long as there are no more attacks, we should be fine.

1423: Dr. Darcy Retherford has taken the watch at the front. Both airlocks are repaired. There was minimal atmosphere loss. Others have ventured up to the surface. The gate is visible as is the large crater around it. The radiation can be detected from the ridgeline. They really nuked the heck out of it.

1649: Another ship has been detected. It is much larger than the first. Video, again, is on the main archaeology computer. Everyone is inside except Dr. Retherford. We've set up an optical fiber system for communication to keep from broadcasting.

1652: Ship has landed in the valley. Small pods, similar to the one seen earlier, have lifted off from it.

1655: Dr. Retherford has retreated from the entrance when some of the pods approached. We've set up a truly inadequate defense. Dr. Roberts brought a pistol with her, something none of the rest of us knew until just now. We're piling tables in the entrance.

1657: A camera Dr. Retherford left in the entrance has shown us the nature of our visitors. It appears that we're about to be Dreen food. Last words all seem inadequate. Tell our families that we were thinking of them at the end. Dr. Roberts wishes to add to any military personnel who might someday read this her personal request that they 'Get some.'"

"Well, that truly sucked," Himes said, his gun tracking back and forth as he shook his head. "I think we're about thirty-three days late."

"I think I'd liked to have met Dr. Roberts," Berg said. "A pistol-packing female archaeologist. Who'd a thunk it?"

"They got hit before we even got the word," the first sergeant said. "But there's a bunch of holes. I can see the air reprocessor being gone. It's pretty apparent the Dreen picked up everything technical. But what do you get when you've got an air reprocessor, Two-Gun?"

"Think the Dreen took the air tanks?" Berg asked. "You don't pump it straight into the room, you pump it into tanks as back-up. There should be a couple of honking big air tanks in this room."

"Maybe," Top mused. "Who can figure out how the Dreen

think? Why'd they destroy the base then take half the day to come back and check things out? But look at the food supplies."

Berg rotated his sensor bulb and looked at the food supplies. There was a pile of rations against one wall. They'd been knocked around and some of the cases had been busted open, down to some ripped packages of rations. But most of the cases were still stacked.

"The Dreen didn't want to eat our food?" Himes asked.

"Use your eyes," the first sergeant snapped.

"Damn, Top," Berg said, wonderingly. "I didn't see it. Sorry."

"What?" Smith asked.

Berg walked over to the scattered yellow packets and pointed down. Several of them had been arranged into a cross formation. It was subtle, but very evident now that he'd noticed it.

"There's a survivor."

"Tchar, I need a *blage*."

The Adari engineer's quarters were the largest on the ship but barely adequate. Especially given the . . . stuff that filled the interior.

The Adar had been a technologically and philosophically advanced race when they encountered humans. By that time, they had managed to end intertribal differences and merge into a unified planetary government. Admittedly, it had taken some major wars to do so, but they'd done it and thereafter given up the long-drawn strife. Artistic, technically competent and religious, encountering humans had been an almost shattering event. Because with all their religion, science and philosophy, they'd never invented marketing.

The Adar were almost incapable of *not* buying anything that was advertised aggressively enough. In Tchar's case he was a sucker for anything that was sold late at night, often on infomercials, for $29.95 plus shipping AND you get for FREE this solid gold-simulacrum . . .

And he carried it all with him wherever he went. In the case of the ship, packed literally to the overhead in his room. There was barely room for his bunk. Admittedly, his bunk was massive.

"Good God," Weaver moaned. "Have you added stuff?"

"Why, yes," the Adar said enthusiastically. Nearly twelve feet tall, with a flat, ducklike head, three eyes and back-curved legs, the alien was dressed in brilliant purple spandex shorts and a safari jacket. "I got a real bargain on a food processor! It slices—"

"Dices and makes julienne fries," Weaver said as he entered. "My God, they didn't bring back *that* finger-shredding monstrosity, did they? Never mind. I need a particle emitter. Not EM communications spectrum. It has to be able to penetrate through an LGB and then several meters of steel reinforced concrete and be detected by sensors on the other side of all that. It has to be man portable. It has to be capable of being turned on and off rapidly. And I need it in twenty minutes."

"Oh, ask me for something *hard* some time," Tchar said, whistling happily. "Coming right up! I'll just take the iridium-192 isotope gamma ray weld joint tester and attach that to my magnetically spun industrial lazy Susan—I got two for one on those. Always a two for one value at Triple A Plus Industrial Warehouse Online!"

"Uh huh." Weaver wasn't certain, but he thought the Adar had smiled like an infomercial actor might have.

"The iridium source is about the size of what you would call a mini-keg of beer. Which reminds me, you must try my Mr. Beer soon and tell me if it works as advertised."

"When we get back to Earth." Weaver liked beer. Not enough, however, to make it on-board.

"Control . . . control . . . the lazy Susan motor through the RS-232 port on the side via some of this phone cable—five hundred meters from Radio Shack . . ."

"Hey, can you put a wireless switch that'll give me a couple kilometers range in noisy rad environment?"

"Perhaps . . . how about more wire? I have more rolls, at least two kilometers of wire that will work for this."

"Wire is good, just heavy. I'll have help carrying it."

"Wire then. So, let me see. You control the gammas incident on the LGB by turning the lazy Susan on and off. I'll put one springloaded push button on it that will rotate the table ninety degrees when held down." Tchar pulled out a push-button kit from somewhere in his quarters. The kit was in a small light blue modular toolbox with a ToolWorld.com logo on the front. Never more out of place did it look than in the hands of the alien Adar wearing spandex shorts and a Hawaiian shirt.

"There must be a button in here that will . . ."

"I'll come back in ten minutes." Weaver said.

» » »

"So this is a . . . what?" Miller asked as they approached the gate.

The radiation counters were going off the scale; they weren't going to be able to spend much time in place.

"It generates gamma rays," Weaver replied, setting the box down and pointing the emitter at the gate. They had to set it up on the edge of the crater; the Looking Glass was hanging forty feet in the air. "There are detectors for that as part of the defense system on the other side. When we start beaming through the concrete and steel on the other side, the detectors are going to go nuts. I hope. Hey, this thing is bad news on the front end so don't get in front of it when we take the cover lid off. Understood?"

"Yes, sir."

"Anyway, they detect the gammas on the other side. These are a different energy level than the background gammas here. So they should be able to see them. We point the gammas ninety degrees away from the LGB and then just push that button at the end of the wire to point the gamma rays at it. You let off the button and it points back away from the gate. *Voila!* it goes on and off and they should see this on the other side."

"And then they drop another nuke through the door," Miller pointed out.

"That is why this thing is set up on a *looong* wire," Bill replied, peering down the tube. "But if they're paying any attention at all, they'll notice that there's a signal coming through. You think that's pointed at the gate?" He depressed the button a time or two. It worked—*gotta hand it to Tchar.*

"I think there's enough radiation going through the gate that it won't be noticeable," Weaver said. "I'm up to over a thousand millirads. These suits are going to be hotter than fire when we get back."

"Too bad we don't have any neenions," Bill said, standing up. "Let's open the lid on this thing and get the *grapp* out of here."

"You ready?"

"Yes, sir," the commo tech said, swallowing nervously. He felt good reason to be nervous. The Dreen were in the neighborhood and while everyone else was in armor just bristling with guns, all he had was as stupid space suit. "How long do we have to be down here?"

"Until we get a response," Bill replied. "Start sending."

»   »   »

It was one of the more boring vital jobs on the planet. Seven gates had opened that were from planets that had current or former Dreen presence. Once it became possible to move gates, all seven had been relocated to a fortress deep under the Antarctic rock. The area was tectonically stable, as far away from anything vital as you could get on Earth. Each of the gates was plugged with a special door made of heavier armor than the one securing Cheyenne Mountain. However, the door could be opened, quickly, and opposite each door was an air cannon loaded with a nuke. In the event of Dreen presence being detected on the far side, the nuke could be fired and the door closed again. When a heavy duty nuke went off on the far side of the gate, it closed fast enough that the only thing that made it through was a blast of radiation.

Even if the Dreen were able to get through those defenses they'd be, well, in Antarctica. There wasn't anything for them to eat and it was a long way to anywhere they wanted to be.

Just in case things got *very* bad, the facility also had a massive nuclear weapon embedded under it. The facility was deep enough that when the nuke went off, the blast would just collapse the thousand feet of rock overhead. If the Dreen got through the defense they were going to find the other side was quite a nasty place.

But somebody had to keep an eye on things. So twenty miles away was another facility. It had a large staff of Army infantry that rotated in and out, doing winter training along the way, and a smaller staff of permanent residents that kept an eye on the gates.

Keeping an eye on the gates was simple on one level and much more difficult on another. Each gate was shown on a video monitor with another screen that gave particle readings. All of those screens showed higher than normal particle levels. Gates generated a stream of muons and quarks naturally. But all of the gates had had one or more nukes fired through it. That, too, generated a lot of particles.

Computer programs monitored levels and determined if they were within normal range. However, radiation slowly decreased over time. From time to time the amount of particles from a particular gate would drop far enough to trigger the automated detectors.

At which point a human had to be involved. And it was a very boring job. Most of the time the technicians just sat for twelve hours staring at nothing. From time to time an alarm went off and they had to analyze the situation and decide if it was an emergency or just normal fluctuation. Thus they had to be familiar with particles and radiation.

Fortunately, the U.S. government produced a large number of such people every year. They were called "nukes," the guys who handled the atomic teakettles for nuclear submarines and the few remaining nuclear aircraft carriers. Not only were they trained in some fairly advanced particle physics, they were *used* to sitting for hours looking at nothing.

It was still a God damned boring job.

So when the alarm went off on Gate Eight, the tech was happy to have a change. Since radiation fell off fastest in the immediate period after a nuke went off, he initially assumed that the rad level had just fallen out of spec. But when he examined the readout, it was apparent that the alarm was anything but a false alarm. All sorts of radioactive decay products were coming through the gate as background noise that looked like the remains of a big nuke. But it was suddenly bursting gamma radiation. Gamma was produced in an initial nuke blast and there was a tiny amount of residual. But not like this.

Without thinking about it, he hit the base alarm button. Seconds could count if the Dreen were preparing to breach the gate.

As he waited for his supervisor to respond he examined the readings. After a moment, he frowned and leaned forward.

"What?" his boss asked, running in while still tucking in his blouse.

"Big stream of gammas coming out of Gate Eight," the tech said, still leaning forward. "We nuked it and all that. But something's funky."

"Define funky," the supervisor asked, leaning over the tech's shoulder. A former nuclear officer, he could read the screens as well as his tech if not better. "Why's the gamma spectrum have a sharp peak at six-twelve keV?"

"That's what I mean by funky, sir," the tech replied. "It's a discontinuous stream too. The peak keeps coming and going."

"You realize what the definition of a discontinuous stream of particles is, right?"

"Yes, sir. A signal."

》　　》　　》

"So far, so good," Miller said. He had an extendable camera poked over the lip of the depression they'd hunkered down in. "No nuke. I'm glad the gate stabilized before we got here."

"It only turns off for about two weeks," Weaver reminded him. "I'm wondering about response. I don't think it's going to be quick."

"So how long do I do this, sir?" the commo tech asked. "I don't mean to whine, but my wrist is getting worn out. I don't do Morse much anymore."

"Well, it's long enough for them to see the greeting," Weaver replied. "Go on to the message . . ."

"U . . . S . . . A. U . . . S . . . A," the supervisor muttered. He could read that much Morse code. "There are survivors."

"Or Dreen trying to catch us out," the tech replied. "It's changing. What's that?"

"I think we're getting a full signal, but it's too fast for me to catch," the supervisor said. "You're recording?"

"Continuous," the tech said.

"Johannsen spent some time in signals," the supervisor said, straightening up. "I'll go get him and start trying to figure out how to reply."

"What do you make of it?"

"It's a hell of a long time since I did Morse, sir."

Eric Johannsen had started off as a nuke but experienced "confinement issues" during a deployment and had transferred to a land base, then out of the Navy. However, he'd spent his time on the land base in a commo position. Modern commo didn't involve much Morse code, it was all about switches, encryption and video compression. Now he was trying to dredge up three-year-old memories of one class and it wasn't coming fast.

"USA, USA, USA." He fast forwarded through the transmission and then paused, looking at the time counter. "That's continuous for the first fifteen minutes."

"They were saying hello," the supervisor said. "What's the rest of that mess?"

"It speeds up, too," Johannsen said. "There's somebody who really knows Morse on the other side. Let's see . . . Operational Immediate. Eyes Only Presidential. Codeword: Eagle Whisper.

Verification Alpha Delta Niner. Eagle Whisper Mission has reached the attack site. No survivors found ATT. That would be 'At This Time.' Confirmed Dreen attack . . . Jesus Christ, sir. What the *grapp* is the Eagle Whisper Mission?!"

"*Don't* keep reading," the supervisor said, leaning over and shutting off the playback. "I have calls to make."

"I'm glad to know they made it," the President said. "How do we respond?"

"I'm loathe to drop the defenses, Mr. President," the Chairman of the Joint Chiefs replied. "But the easiest thing to do would be to open the gate and go through. In a suit, admittedly. And there would be a heck of a drop on the other side. But we could handle all that."

"Set up an emitter on this side," the national security advisor suggested. "I think that the people down there could probably do that. We might even be able to set up direct communications from here."

"Open the gate for a moment and send through a note," the President replied. "Tell them that we're working on it from our end and we'll get back to them. Send that right now. And tell the people down there that they'd better keep their mouths shut."

"I'm running out of air," the commo tech said. At least he wasn't being forced to keep sending with nothing coming back.

"That's why we brought spare bottles," Chief Miller growled. He was lying on his back watching the take from the camera. He was used to sitting in one place and watching nothing for days on end. Sniper hides came to mind. "Crack one open."

"The ship isn't coming back until the Marines are done with their search," Weaver said. "Or we get some response telling the CO to land. So I'd suggest you get comfortable, PO."

"Yes, sir," the tech replied, picking up one of the O_2 canisters. "I need some help."

"Got it," Bill said, trying not to sigh.

"And we have response," Miller said suddenly. "I thought for a second it was a nuke and I nearly wet myself. But something just shot through the door and landed on the edge of the crater. And it is *not* a nuke. Metal canister of some sort. Let me modify that. I don't *think* it's a nuke."

"They would have shot one long ago if they thought we were spoofing them or didn't get the message," Bill said, slotting the tech's replacement in. "Go get it, would you?"

"I hear and obey O swami," Miller said, rolling over and standing up. "Be right back."

"Huh," Bill said. The "message canister" was a Number Ten can, apparently formerly holding coffee. It had a screw lid and his claws just skittered across it. "Open that up, would you?" he asked, holding it out to the commo tech.

"That thing's hot as hell, sir," the tech said, backing up. "I respectfully decline."

"Gimme," Miller said with a sigh. He wrapped his claws around it and crushed, then ripped the top off. "Piece of paper inside." The paper fluttered to the ground as he tipped the can up.

"Paper does not retain radiation very well, PO," Bill said, gesturing.

"Your suits do, though, sir," the tech pointed out.

"Okay, Miller, back away slowly."

"It's a standard message form," the tech said once the suits had backed up far enough for him to approach the paper. "From: SpaceCom To: Commander Eagle Whisper. Stand by for communications gear to be set up. Estimate four hours."

"Hell, it only took us twenty minutes," Miller said. "Why four hours?"

"We're a carefully selected group of top-flight specialists," Bill pointed out. "Naturally it would take a group of regular techs longer. And the guys on the other end don't have Tchar's maze of junk."

"This place is a maze," Smith said. "Left or right?"

The streets of what had once been a major city now resembled canyons, many of them blind. Fallen rubble choked them and in many places it was unclimbable. Holes opened up without warning. Already two suits had been damaged from falls.

The map that the archaeologists had left behind wasn't much help. It had been scanned and Berg was looking at a blow-up on his internal monitors. But it didn't appear to be to scale and landmarks were denoted with cryptic terms that only made sense to a small group that discussed their work every day. But "Lag

Pile" didn't mean anything to Berg. And it was a two-dimensional representation of an area that was, among other things, often three dimensional.

"*Grapp* if I know," Berg replied. "But any survivor, if there is one, can't be far from the base. He or she had to haul supplies. How far do you think they're going to go?"

"Well, we've searched most of what's on the map, right?" Himes said.

"Right," Berg replied. "And Bravo found the workings they were working on. Nobody there, signs of Dreen. But . . . *Chither.* Top said something about a doctoral candidate . . . exploring a new section. Which means it's *not* on the map."

"That's very helpful," Smith pointed out, looking at the Y intersection. "So left or right?"

Berg examined the map again. He was pretty sure they were by "Lag Pile." It was a massive mound that sort of *looked* like a skyscraper after twenty million years of wear. On the back side of it from their position was a circle and some dotted lines that stopped without being cut off. An unmapped tunnel.

"That way," Berg said, pointing up the mound to the left. "Watch your step. We're looking for a tunnel opening."

"I don't see a tunnel opening," Himes said, sliding down the hill on his butt and elbow wheels. "Just another damned canyon."

"This is relatively close to the main base," Berg pointed out. In fact it was in someone else's search sector. "And there ought to be a tunnel by where the slope increases."

"Great," Himes said, using the slope and the powerful arms of the suit to get himself upright. "What do we do now?"

"Sweep left and right," Berg said, looking up and down the lip of the canyon. "Look for anything out of the ordinary."

Smith headed to the left, then paused.

"I've got what might be a path," he said, swiveling his sensor pods, then activating the targeting laser. "Look at those rocks."

"Balanced," Berg said, walking over to the rock pile. Three large boulders had been stacked, but one of them clearly could be moved back and forth easily. He swiveled it up and to the side and found a narrow opening to a tunnel that was partially choked by rubble. "Hello? Anyone home?" he boomed through the external speakers.

"We can't get down that," Himes said, looking at the opening.

"We can get *down*," Berg pointed out. "We just roll in on the belly wheels. Getting *out* would be the interesting part. Open up my back pack. I've got some rope in there."

"You carry rope?" Himes asked, surprised.

"Think Boy Scout," Berg replied.

Himes opened up the cargo box of the sergeant's suit and pulled out a long spool of what looked like twine. There was more than the spool of twine in there. There was a CamelBak of water, a small spare air bottle, three MRE packages, a first aid kit, a small repair kit and a thermal blanket. Then there was the pair of pistols—.577 magnums with worn grips—and a low-slung combat holster.

"Uh, Berg, that's not going to hold much," Himes said with a snort, pulling out the spool of twine.

"You'd be surprised," Berg replied, taking the spool. There was a clip on the end and he pulled out a length and handed it to Himes. "It's nanotube mono. You could lift the *Blade* with it. Clip that to the butt shackle. Smith, take the spool."

By running the line around their suits and claws, the two could belay the team leader down into the hole. Getting him out would be a matter of pulling *really* hard.

"You sure about this?" Himes asked.

"Nope," Berg admitted, getting down on his elbow and knee wheels, then flattening onto his belly wheels. "But it's the best idea I've got."

He shimmied into the opening, half using his elbow wheels but mostly his belly, then started to slide down the rubble.

The tunnel opened out beyond the initial rubble wall, but not enough for a nine-foot-tall suit to stand up or turn around. He could, however, continue to slide.

"How's it going?" Himes asked.

"So far, so good," Berg replied. "I'm coming up to a bend. I'll lose commo there. If I need to be pulled out I'll give three tugs. If I need to be pulled out fast, they'll be fast."

"Got it," Himes replied.

As soon as he turned the corner he could see the survivor. Maybe survivor. A small nest had been created at the point where the tunnel was choked by a fall. Plastic had been set up to seal in a small area and there was a pile of ruined sleeping bags, a couple of ration cases, some water bottles and, yes, two large air canisters. Fortunately, the latter were on the far wall.

Berg used his wheels to slide to a stop before he hit the plastic and peered through it. He wasn't sure how to determine if the survivor was alive. All he could see was a face mask and he couldn't tell if he or she was breathing. But then he nearly kicked himself and switched to thermal. As soon as he did he could see that the person was still warm. He also could now tell sex: Female.

He slid forward a bit farther and got a look at the readouts on the air tanks. Both of the main tanks were expended. He couldn't see what hers looked like; it was covered by the ripped sleeping bags. Mostly ripped. He could see where some stitching had been done. Actually, he realized that he could probably just pull her out in the bag.

He breached the plastic, got a grip on the repaired sleeping bag, and pulled. The woman slid out of her cocoon without anything coming apart. He could tell, now, that she was still breathing but he still couldn't see the canister attached to her breath mask.

He pulled three times on the mono molecular rope and felt himself starting to slide back up the tunnel. The woman in the bag wriggled and moaned but otherwise didn't react.

"Himes," he said as soon as he passed the bend. "Get on the horn. I need a corpsman, right damned now. I got a survivor but she's unconscious and just about out of air. And I think she's hypothermic."

"Get her up here," Dr. Chet said, pulling out a pair of bandage scissors and gesturing to the surgery table. "Status?"

He was in a full quarantine suit. The secure surgery was in the isolation wing of the "research and survival pack" attached to the top of the ship. SOP was that anyone exposed to a potentially dangerous environment remained in the isolation wing for at least thirty days. The survivor was still stuffed in a quarantine stretcher, a closed system with waldoes and glove holes for any aid that needed to be given. Most of the systems, including IV inserters and defibrillator, were handled by a robotic autodoc.

"BP eighty over twenty," the corpsman replied, sliding the survivor out of the stretcher and onto the table expertly. "Respiration twenty. Temperature ninety-two. Heartbeat one forty and thready. Pupils have light response."

"Hypothermic," the massive doctor said musingly. "Not too low. Get me a warming bag. I don't understand the unconsciousness."

He used the scissors to remove the woman's filthy clothing and paused as her arm was exposed. It was covered by injection tracks.

"Smart lady," he muttered. "But getting you off that is not going to be pleasant."

"Sir?" the corpsman asked, pulling out a large paper-cloth bag. The survivor would be popped into the bag and then the bag filled with hot air from a simple blower. It was a quick and safe way to raise body temperature.

"She was injecting herself with morphine at a guess," Dr. Chet replied. "It kept her resource use minimal and if her air gave out while she was drugged, well, she would never know. But she's going to be severely addicted. With the minimal facilities I have here, it's going to be unpleasant coming off of it. Get her in the bag and warmed up . . ."

"How long will she be out?" the CO asked.

Dr. Chet didn't fit any better in the wardroom than he did in his surgery. But he didn't fit any worse.

"Unknown," he replied, trying to get his legs into a reasonable position under the low table. "I don't know what dosage she used on herself last. No more than an hour, though. Her temperature is coming up nicely. Malnourished, dehydrated, filthy, but she's going to survive."

"The best guess is that she's Ms. Debra Cutler," the XO added. "A doctoral candidate. She was mentioned in the logs. No ID on her but she matches the picture we have from the personnel list."

"Have Weaver send the information to Earth," the CO said. "Tentative ID, more when she wakes up."

"She's liable to be extremely disoriented," Dr. Chet pointed out. "And all my personnel are male. I'm going to ask Miss Moon to sit in on this one."

"Agreed," the CO said, frowning. "I guess there's no way to pretend she's not in a spaceship."

"No," Dr. Chet said, shaking his head. "Not unless Earth will open the gate and allow us to shove her through before she wakes. She really should be in a proper hospital."

"Unlikely," the CO said. "Not with a potential Dreen presence on this side. And on that note, Tactical?"

"Not a peep, sir," the TACO replied. "No indications of any-thing unusual in the system. And we're keeping a very close eye on the instruments."

"So the Dreen came in here, dropped a rock on the facility, picked up one survivor then came back a couple of hours later and snatched most of the rest," the CO said, his brow furrowing. "And then they just *left*? To *where*? Why? With an open gate to Earth, why just leave?"

"Bigger fish to fry?" the XO asked. "A higher priority mission? For all we know, that war that was such a big thing to us might not have meant much to them. We might not even be on their radar. There could be a massive battle going on in the next sys-tem and we wouldn't even know it. . . ."

"Here they come again," Senior Tactical Specialist Favarduro shouted. "Forty Blin Kar fighters at one-one-seven mark sixteen."

"The *Klingoddar* has stopped responding to hails," Commo Specialist Faul interjected. "Its emergency beacon has stopped broadcasting."

"Uanarmm bless and keep them," Ship Master Kond replied softly. "Chaos ball generator?"

"At least another forty kleg," Engineering Specialist Rorot replied.

"Engage with masers," Kond said calmly, shifting his weight slightly in his combat couch. The air around him was a rich tapestry of information, sonar pulses filling the air with data from all the ship's sensors. The fleet was once again escaping the hated Blin, but at great cost. The *Caurorgorngoth* was the last of the Chaos Ships. If they were destroyed, the Blin dreadnought would be able to gather up the fleet like so many vaila. "Keep them off of us until the chaos generator is back on line. Patch me through to Fleet Master Lurca."

"Lurca."

"Higher One, we are under attack from Kar fighters. There will be a dreadnought somewhere out there. Be careful."

"We are reaching jump point now," the fleet master replied. "Hurry to follow us. How are your supplies?"

"We managed to fully fuel before the last battle," Kond replied. "We are good for two jumps. We got ninety percent of our maga-zine load from the factory ship. That was all they'd produced.

We also need some parts, but we'll need more after this so we might as well wait."

"Meet us at the rendezvous," the fleet master said. "Lurca, out."

"And again we are on our own," Favarduro quipped. "No freighters or fuelers or cruisers to slow us down. What luxury. What grandeur."

"What *doog*," Engineer Rorot said unhappily. "Without a chaos generator. With fusion bottles down. With our reality shifter becoming unreal."

"Nobody ever said it would be easy," Favarduro said, pinging a burst of laughter around the compartment. "Oh, and here come Kar fighters to make our day oh so much better. Recommend evasion pattern Mindrg in three kleg."

"Very well," Kond said, pinging the information to the battlecomp. "Let us take some of these foul beasts with us if we are to fall."

"Some more, Ship Master," Favarduro said, pinging laughter again. "Some *more*."

"Group of experts," Miller muttered. "So with a group of world-class experts we're sitting out here freezing our butts off to send Morse and a bunch of *nobodies* back on Earth—"

"Oh, shut up," Weaver whispered back. "It took *them* four hours."

"And the survivor is . . ." Admiral Townsend asked over the video link. The image suddenly distorted as did the voice but it was still as clear as a low bandwidth streaming video.

"Still out, sir," the CO responded. "Given her condition, Dr. Chet is unwilling to bring her out of the drugs rapidly. There are ways to do that but—"

"It's the doctor's call," the admiral said with a sigh. "She probably won't have much more information than we already have. The experts in such things are unwilling to open the gate, even for long enough to shove her through."

"Did they say why, sir?" Bill asked neutrally.

"Just that we don't know the true abilities of the Dreen," the admiral said with a shrug. "They're really exercised about them possibly breaking through. They also wanted to ensure that she's in isolation and that she gets a very full physical."

"She was brought in in a quarantine stretcher," the CO replied. "And has been in the isolation area ever since. That's SOP under the circumstances. I'll ask Dr. Chet about giving her a full pre-mission phys. But given the way her body's scrambled up, I'm not sure he's going to want to add the chemicals he needs to her system. Not any time soon, anyway."

"I'll pass that on," the admiral said. "Make sure that she's not removed from isolation until you return to Earth. That's not negotiable."

"Understood, sir," the CO said. "So what now? Do we head home?"

"Negative," Townsend replied. "We need to find out what's happening out there. Probe for the Dreen. *Carefully*. Try to find out where they're at, what they're up to out there, what their order of battle looks like. Hell, what their *ships* look like. It's an old-fashioned intel gathering mission. You're the boat snuggling up to the Soviet backyard to get intel. Go get it."

"Yes, sir," Spectre said thoughtfully.

"Leave this lash up in place," Townsend added. "But camouflage it if you can. If you need to talk or seriously need support, we can use the gate. Same orders as before, use your discretion but don't get into any furballs if you can avoid it. However, if you get an opportunity to jump a lone Dreen ship and determine that it's possible to win, do so. Capture it if possible. The idea is to get a look at what their hyper tech and weapons tech consists of. We need a system we can use other than the *Blade*'s. Anything you need that we can shove through the gate quickly?"

"XO?" the CO asked.

"I doubt we can get the critical spares we need to the base *quickly*, sir," the XO said, looking at a pad. "But if we come back this way, it might make sense to have some stockpiled by then. I have a list. Other than that, fresh food."

"I'll get with the liaison at the base," the admiral said, nodding. "Send the list over and we'll get them down there if it's feasible. Anything else?"

"Permission to send and receive Family Message Forms, sir," the CO replied.

The FMF was a method that sub crews had of keeping in contact with their families. It was highly limited and highly censored, being only a ten-word message either way. Families were not permitted to send negative news; putting more stress on guys stuck in a tin can under water was never a good idea. "I hate you and want a divorce" was not a message the Navy was going to send to a guy who could fire a nuclear missile or cause a melt-down of the nuclear core. Sub crews, being smart, had of course set up a code system so that they could get more than "I love you. Everything's fine" messages through. More than one submariner had gotten word that his wife was having an affair despite being at six-hundred-feet depth, several thousand miles away and through a system specifically designed to prevent such news. So far, none of them had tried to fire off a missile although a few had tried to open up a hatch and walk home. For those few, there was a very pleasant tranquilizer and an "I-Love-Me" jacket until they could be evacced.

"Authorized," the admiral said, wincing. He knew the weaknesses of the FMF from long experience. "Anything else?"

"I think we're done, sir," the CO said, looking around the group.

"Get back into space, find the Dreen, find out what they're up to, try to get any tech you can acquire and report back," the admiral said. "And do all that *carefully*. You're *still* the only ship we have."

"Yes, sir," Spectre said. "Can do."

"Weaver," the CO said as everyone was filing out of the wardroom.

"Sir?"

"Stay."

When everyone was gone, the CO looked at the astrogator thoughtfully.

"What do you think the chances are you can find some trace of the Dreen ship in space?"

Weaver thought about the question for a few seconds, then blanched.

"Effectively zero, sir," Bill replied. "Do you want to know why?"

"Yes," the CO said. "Because I don't think you've thought it through. We make waves as we pass through space. You've talked about it. Disturbed solar wind, ionization from destroyed particles, even bits of our forward armor that get flaked off. Surely the Dreen have got to leave some traces."

"I'm sure they do, sir," Bill said. "And if the track was fresher, I might be able to sort out which ions are from a passing Dreen ship and which are just from solar wind. If I could do a survey of the local area for about a month and figure out what the solar winds look like. But a Dreen . . . wake, if you will, is going to look like a ship's wake. Sure, you can detect one of those for the first few hours. But after that, waves, current, wind, they all tend to erase it. There's a bit more thermal image for a tad longer time, but even that eventually goes away. The Dreen were here thirty days ago, sir. Any trace is long gone. Even the holes we found were filling in from dust. And those are much more permanent than anything you'd find in the solar wind."

"So how do we find them?"

"If it's only one or two ships and they're in EMCON, it's going to be tough, sir," Bill said, referring to shutting down transmissions so as to remain less noticeable. "I don't know what sort of traces they leave behind until we find one. And finding a ship in space, well, space is a very big place and ships are very small. I think we're just going to have to hope that they're broadcasting or otherwise being noticeable."

"You know," Favarduro said as the *Caurorgorngoth*'s lasers eliminated three of the Blin fighters, "in between five and twenty kleng this is going to be noticeable to anyone inhabiting the nearer stars."

"In between five and twenty kleng, anyone inhabiting the nearer stars is going to be Dreen food," Ship Master Kond replied. "Shields are at less than forty percent. Concentrate on the central fighter pack. Stop some of these Manaeg-spawned plasma bolts."

As plasma fire slammed into the ship, being disbursed by the ion shields, he whistled for a control to shift some power to long-range scanning but the Blin dreadnought was still impossible to detect. At least fifteen kleg until the ball generator was online. And more than four hundred until they reached the unreality node. The fleet had escaped, through, leaving them to limp outward on their own, with not so much as a shield ship by their side.

As the mighty Chaos Ship rocked under the hammer of the missiles, he hoped that there *were* no races within five and twenty kleng. Unless, of course, they were powerful enough to save his ship.

"Home again," Berg said, collapsing into his bunk. For a wonder, there wasn't a caterwauling of Asian tortured cats from overhead.

He had made his peace with Portana and could even handle the armorer's sister's singing. Didn't mean he enjoyed it.

"God, I'm glad to get out of armor," Himes replied. "How's the chick we picked up?"

"How the hell would I know?" Berg asked. "Last I saw of her was last you saw of her, being carted back to the ship."

"Mail call," the first sergeant said from the front of the compartment. "We're in commo with Earth through the gate. Nobody's going home, though; they're not opening up the other side. But you've got Family Message Forms on your systems. If you want to respond, you have about thirty minutes. Then we're out of this system."

"What's the mission, Top?" Corwin called. "We're done here, right? We going home?"

"Negative," the first sergeant replied. "We're going to go Dreen hunting. Now read your mail."

Berg wasn't really expecting any. His parents weren't in the loop of Navy communications. They could get an emergency message through to him, but by their very natures emergency messages were rarely put into FMFs. "Dad died" was right up there with "I want a divorce."

So he was surprised to see the message light blinking on his system when the first sergeant left. He hit the "Receive" icon and a short message popped up.

"Love you Miss you Be Homeward Bound in Time Brooke"

FMFs were limited to ten words but the short message pretty much covered the subject. Except for the last bit, which was puzzling.

He opened up a search function and typed in the last, puzzling, phrase. The search function was actually built by GooCharn, the Adari-human corporation that had absorbed Google and a similar corporation on Adar. The Adar servers on-board the *Blade* only stored about thirty percent of the combined human-Adar hypernet. But that was *a lot* of data. Much of it was useless, but occasionally somebody needed a scrap of really esoteric information that was stored away on it somewhere.

About halfway down the first page he found it, a poem that was linked to a flash animation.

He watched the animation, wondering where Brooke had dredged it up. It was from way back in the War On Terror, mostly shots from Iraq. It was kind of like watching a film clip from Vietnam. The gear they were using was so antique he had to wonder how they'd gotten anything done. No Wyverns, no Mojos, no particle detectors, no scanners. Just Kevlar body armor and peashooters. Of course, the terrorists they were fighting didn't have any better.

But the sentiment of the piece was timeless and he quickly found himself tearing up. He dashed the water off his face and sucked it up to the end. Okay, now he knew how *Brooke* felt.

And the more he examined the lyrics, the stronger *he* felt. She was asking him to come home, but only when the time was right. She was saying she wouldn't hold him back, that he was "free to find his calling" but that she would be there when he returned.

And his calling was right here. He wondered if she understood just what that meant. How could she? He didn't even know what it really meant. Except a lot of separation.

He considered the undersize keyboard for a moment then typed rapidly, hit "Send" and vowed that if she had the strength to let him "find his calling," he had the strength to find a way home.

"No messages for you, Commander Weaver?" the CO asked as he sat down in his chair in the conn.

"No, sir," Bill replied. "Footloose and fancy-free bachelor. I get an occasional e-mail from my parents, but they don't even know how to access the FMFs."

"Admiral Rickover would have approved," the XO said, grinning. "He felt an officer should be married to his career and not 'chick hatching' all the time."

"And where are we going to find the next generation of Junior Spacemen?" the CO asked. "It was one of those points Rickover never quite got around to addressing. So, what's your recommendation, Astro?"

"I've set up a search pattern of the nearest stars, sir," Bill replied. "My recommendation is that we enter on the outer periphery of each of the systems, do a chill while simultaneously looking for any indicators of Dreen presence, then jump around the periphery, slowly working inward. When we get to about one AU from the local star, we'll have looked about all we can. Then we go to the next. With stops at each of the jump points to let the instruments really get in a good scan, I'd say about one full day at each star. We do that until we find something or you call it a bust."

"All right," the CO said. "XO, Set Condition One on each system entry. At each move inwards, we'll go to GQ again, figuring that is the most likely point that we'll encounter the Dreen. Tell the Marines to just sit tight. I don't want them running around doing a drill when we could be going into battle at any time."

"Aye, aye, sir."

"Let's head outwards," the CO said. "Astro?"

"Come to heading three-one-six mark neg dot two and head for the star," Bill replied, pointing at the forward viewscreen.

"Make it so."

Brooke checked the caller ID on her cell phone as it sounded out with "Sunshine and Summertime." It was the Bergstresser's home number, which could be good news or bad or none at all. She took a deep breath and answered the call.

"Brooke, it's Amanda Bergstresser."

Mrs. Bergstresser sounded cheerful. A good sign so far.

"Yes, ma'am?" Brooke said. "Have you heard from Eric?"

"We have indeed," Mrs. Bergstresser said. "I know he wasn't supposed to be able to send a message for at least ninety days, but you got a response to yours. It's a bit cryptic, though."

"Go ahead," Brooke said, swallowing.

"*In the quiet misty morning Eric.* That's it. Does it make any sense to you?"

"Yes, ma'am," Brooke said, sniffling. "Yes, it does."

"Brooke, I know all this is rather sudden and terribly dramatic, but I have a question: Do I need to start getting to know a future daughter-in-law?"

Brooke thought about that for a few seconds, then sniffled again.

"I sure hope so, Mrs. Bergstresser."

"In that case, you'd better call me Amanda."

13

"Adjusted to system Tycho 714-1046-1," the pilot said, tiredly.

The ship had been doing an expanding sweep of the area for the last two weeks and it had been a very boring process. Most of the stars in the region, which was a fairly tightly packed local cluster, were within ten light-years of each other. Ten hours to reach a new system. About twenty hours scanning the system and then on to the next. And with GQ being called at least five times a day, nobody was getting any sleep.

"What do we have?" Spectre asked, his voice a bit too steady. The CO was on the ragged edge as well.

"G3V star, bit hotter than Sol but otherwise very main sequence," Bill replied. "Waiting on readings, sir."

"I'm getting a bit tired of waiting on readings," the CO said bitterly.

"So am I, si—" Weaver paused and leaned forward, running his hand down one of the lines on his monitor. "Sir . . . ?"

"Conn, Tactical."

"Go," Spectre snapped.

"We're getting some quirky readings on the particle detectors," Tactical replied, clearly puzzled. "The system is just saying higher than normal background of neutrinos. I'm not sure what that means."

"Weaver?" Spectre asked.

"Just . . . Give me a moment, sir," Weaver said, opening up another screen and typing rapidly.

The CO walked over to look over the astrogator's shoulder but the math he was working on was way over Spectre's head. Another example of how difficult it was going to be to create a space navy. Too many times he simply had to go on his faith in Weaver's knowledge.

"Concur on that, sir," Weaver said after about a minute. "Furthermore, the extra neutrinos are generating from a point in the system. It's at about six AU from the star on the far side from us. Something created a bunch of neutrinos there about nine hours ago. What, why and how I'm not sure. But I'd say that it's probable that it was not a natural event. More than that . . . I can't say without checking it out."

"Can we do that quietly?" the CO asked. "Come in from the side or something? Maybe duck around a planet?"

"We still don't have a planet map for the system, sir," Bill said, checking the update from the astronomy department. Since it consisted of two overworked SF staff sergeants, he wasn't expecting anything any time soon. Especially since their position was poor for finding planets. They usually didn't get a good map until they moved in-system. "I would suggest moving in an arc across the outer fringes of the system, getting a look at the anomaly from another angle, then possibly moving in to no less than ten AUs from the anomaly for a visual."

"Right," Spectre said, rubbing his face. "Gimme a vector."

"Heading zero-nine-six, sir," Bill replied. "Warp Two for twenty-three minutes. Then come to normal space for another survey."

"Pilot, make it so," Spectre said, keying the 1-MC. "All hands. All hands. Ship *remains* at Condition One. There's an anomaly in this system. We're going to spend some time checking it out. Stay tight while we do that. Missile crews to ready positions."

The second check had just repeated the first. Turning even their largest telescope towards the anomaly didn't tell them anything.

"Astro, we're going to go insystem unless you have another idea," Spectre said.

"I actually do, sir," Bill said, musingly. "We need to get farther away."

"Say again?" the CO asked, rubbing his face. "What are we going to learn from *farther* away?"

"We can move faster than light, sir," Bill replied, getting excited. "If whatever this was made a big enough signature, we can back out of the system and look at it. It's sort of like going back in time. If that doesn't work, we can still go insystem. We're only talking about ten light-hours out in a direct line from the anomaly."

"Okay, that's just about weird enough to work," Spectre said. "Gimme a vector and let's do it."

"Should be coming up pretty soon," Bill said, looking at his chronometer. "If there's going to be . . . whoa!"

It was almost pretty. Where there had been more or less empty space on the viewer, only the distant stars showing, there was suddenly a flurry of lights.

"Conn, Tactical," the intercom chimed. "We're getting a mass of particle readings from the direction of the anomaly. I'd say that multiple nuclear detonations are occurring."

"Roger that," Spectre said. "We're watching it in—"

"Try 'unreal' time, sir," Bill said, grinning. "Somebody was fighting somebody else. Who and why is the question, now."

"Is this maximum magnification?" Spectre asked, walking over to the main viewer. "All I can see is the detonations."

"They're more visually obvious than whatever's causing them, sir," Bill pointed out. "That's all we can get out of our systems: we're not up to Star Trek level yet. And ours are as good as any that are made, sir. But at this distance, it's like trying to pick out individual sand grains on Earth from a satellite. It's easy to spot a spotlight pointed up. We're going to have to go insystem to find out anything else."

"Right," Spectre said, his chin firming up. "Pilot, head for that battle. Stop at twenty AU out and then again at ten. This might just have zero to do with us. But I want to know who was fighting."

Twenty AU hadn't given them any information, nor were they learning much at ten AU. The spot where the battle had taken place was still just empty space as far as they could tell. There were still some emissions from the area, but they were faint. And nothing on the electrical band.

"Orders, sir?" the pilot asked.

"Heat levels?" the CO asked.

"We chilled on the outside stops," the XO replied from damage control. "We're good for about five hours."

"Close the position under warp," the CO said. "Stay away from the center. Pass by at Warp One, five light-seconds up in the elliptic. Tactical, stand by to scan the area visually. I want to see what we can see. Pilot, you laid in?"

"Yes, sir."

"Engage."

"Aye, aye," the NCO replied, hitting the warp drive.

The ship began hurtling forward, fast enough that the distant star could be seen to move. The viewer remained focused on the scene of the presumed battle as the ship flew "overhead" relative to the local solar system. They were approaching the system from just short of the distance from the Earth to the Moon, so anything left in the area had better be *big*.

"Conn, Tactical. Switching main viewer to thermal."

"Go," Spectre replied. They were approaching closest point of approach and tactical must have spotted something.

When the screen switched to false color thermal imagery, what Tactical had spotted was obvious. There were large chunks of material, much hotter than the background, floating in space. One looked as if it might have been part of a ship. A very odd ship, but probably about half of a hull.

"Maintain course and speed," Spectre said. "Tactical, I want full spectrum analysis. Pilot, as soon as we reach one light-minute from the scene of the battle, go to full warp and park it sixty AUs out from the sun."

"Aye, aye, sir," the pilot said.

"Tactical, Astro, I want a meeting with the full science and command group in the wardroom in one hour," Spectre said. "It looks as if whatever happened here is over. XO, stand down from Condition One."

"Does anyone have anything to input that's not obvious?" the CO asked as soon as the full video was replayed.

The region of space where the presumed battle had taken place was a mess. Bits of ships were littered liberally through the area. But they were so fragmented, it was hard to tell what they really looked like. However, there did seem to be two broad types. Some of the debris had a "hard-edged" look, while other bits were uniformly smoothly curved. There also appeared to be two broad types of material, one based around metals and the other carbon fibers. That was drawn from spectral analysis of smoldering "fires" where material was converting chemically bonded oxygen in slow vacuum fires.

The largest chunk was a vaguely ovoid piece of what must have been a much larger ship. It was forty meters long and wide, more or less. There might be remaining sealed compartments. It was hard to determine in the low-resolution image. One side of the tumbling wreckage had clearly been hull. The other side was . . .spongy.

"Two species in a space battle," Lieutenant Fey said. "I'd bet dollars to donuts that the smooth ones are Dreen ships. There's just an . . . organic look to them that is what you'd expect from the Dreen. And the spectral numbers from them match the chemical composition of Dreen rhino-tank armor about right. Not perfectly, but very close."

"I've been looking at the particle traces, sir," Bill said, punching at his laptop. "I *think* I've detected a stream of materials headed outward from the system. There's a higher level of monatomic oxygen as well as traces of water. I'd say it's the track of a damaged ship or ships."

"That's new information," the CO said, looking over at Tactical. "Did you get that?"

"I'm not even sure what readings he's referring to, sir," the TACO admitted.

"I'll send it over to you in a minute," Bill said, not looking up. "You've got the numbers; it's knowing what they mean that matters. There's always a small background of elements in space. Not much, but it's there and it can be detected by the way that it interacts with the particles being shoved out by a sun. In this case, there's a series of higher than normal readings, headed more or less in a line. It's like the trail of oil left by a damaged ship. We're going to need to write some code for the tactical computers to start looking for this sort of thing. Heck, it might not even be damage. We sure leak like mad. In fact, we should look for RF emissions from electron spin flips of water components like the hydrogen twenty-one centimeter wavelength line and the hydroxyl radical nineteen centimeter wavelength line. I'll bet you we leave those behind all over the place. And, they'd be easy, very easy, to detect." He manipulated the data for a moment, then nodded. "Yep, there they are. Wow. You know, we leave a trail a blind man could follow."

"Great to hear," Spectre said grumpily. "But in other news, where's the damaged ship going?"

"In the general direction of HD 37355, sir," Bill replied. "That's a G5 star in the *general* direction of Earth. Not on a line, mind you, just headed for that general quadrant. It could be headed for Tycho 714-1500-1. The two stars are only about two light-years apart. They're nearly a binary system. And both are main sequence stars."

"Which means a higher likelihood of habitable planets," the CO said, nodding. "Bunch of them around here I noticed."

"Yes, sir," Bill replied. "This is part of the Orion local group. It's a very dense group. Lots of hot sequence stars as well. And more dwarfs than we'd realized. Basically, it's crowded as hell. We're not far, at all, from some of the stars of Orion's Belt."

"So this is probably a good area for the Dreen to colonize," the XO pointed out.

"Uh, yes, sir," Bill admitted.

"Which explains their presence," the CO said. "But what about this other race? Lieutenant Fey? Any points?"

"Only a quote from the 'Seven Habits of Highly Effective Pirates,' sir," the lieutenant said. "'The enemy of my enemy is my enemy's enemy. No more. No less.' I'd love to find an ally against the Dreen, sir. But until we find out more about them, I would advise proceeding with caution."

"And there's only one way I can think of to find out more," the CO said distastefully. "We're going to have to go down there and do some sampling. Agreed?"

"Carefully, sir," the XO said. "Get close, take a snapshot, closer . . ."

"Agreed," the CO said. "Tell the SF guys they're going to have to take point in this one. They're the closest we have to a science team."

"Sir," Bill interjected. "I think a careful search for survivors, especially this other race, is in order. Keep an eye out for beacons."

"Agreed," the CO said. "Let's get to it."

»   »   »

"Bingo."

Harold was happy to be back in the commo shack. Ground pounding was for Marines. He was just as happy to have the ship wrapped back around him. Not to mention being able to stretch out on a cot instead of on the ground.

"What you got, Hal?" the leading PO asked.

"I'm getting a radio signal," the commo tech said. "Emanating from the area of the battle."

It was the third stop to check for data on the way in. The ship was under three light-seconds from the area of the battle and already starting to run into debris. It wasn't so much that it had been a big battle as that the forces involved had sent debris spinning off at *very* fast velocities. It was spreading so fast that in another day or two it would have been hard to find the pieces.

"It's code, non-frequency skipping, just a set of dots and dashes," the commo tech continued, tracing the signal on his display. "I'd say that it's an emergency beacon sending somebody's version of SOS. It works out as 'MRE' in Morse."

"Good job finding it," the LPO said. "Conn, radio shack . . ."

"If that's a survivor of the other race, we probably should get in there and recover him, sir," Weaver pointed out. "Her. It."

"Agreed," Spectre replied coldly. "But not until we're sure there are no active defense systems. I don't want to get shot out of the sky on a rescue mission."

"There's some EM coming from the remnant of that ship, sir," Bill said, looking at his displays. "And there's a hot source in another piece of debris. I'd say it's some sort of powered up machinery. But it could be a washing machine for all I know."

The hull suddenly "bonged" and everyone in the conn jumped.

"Damn this debris," the CO swore. "We also can't just charge forward with all this *chither* flying around. But we're going to have to close the heavier pieces." He hit the intercom to the science section. "Master Sergeant Guzik, your team needs to start prepping for EVA."

"Roger, sir," the Special Forces master sergeant replied. "We're in skins and ready to board the Wyverns."

"Get with the Marine CO," Spectre added. "I want a platoon of Marines out there with you. The first priority is an apparent distress signal we're picking up. As soon as we figure out where it's coming from, your team and the Marines will retrieve whatever it is. After that there's some bits we need to pick up and take a look at. Last, you'll be examining the biggest chunk, which is probably Dreen."

"Roger, sir," Guzik said. "We'll get it done."

"First Platoon," Berg's intercom chimed. "Fall out and fall in on Wyverns. EVA mission."

"Oh, glory," Himes bitched, pulling out a set of skins. "Zero-Gee."

"Space Marines," Berg pointed out, sliding out of his bunk and heading for the hatch. "And I told you to keep your damned skins on. You've got head-cleaning duty next cycle."

"Speaking of heads," Himes muttered.

"Should have kept your skins on," Smith said, sliding past him and following the team leader. "Last one into their Wyvern is a head-cleaner."

"There's a radio signal coming from a piece of debris," Master Sergeant Guzik said. "The debris sort of looks like it might be a life pod. Our mission is to recover the pod and extract whatever is inside, alive. Unless it's Dreen, in which case dead works. We'll try to determine what is inside prior to opening it. Either way, we're going to be opening it carefully."

"There's lots of debris out there," the first sergeant added. He, too, was suited up in his Wyvern. "Watch out for it. We've worked in microgravity but this is a whole new mission. Take it slow and easy. Keep your eyes open and one eye on your monitors. If you see any of the signs of Dreen presence, report it at once. The *good* news is that we can use the Number Three airlock, so we can get out faster. And in."

"Good luck," Captain Zanella said. He was *not* suited up. "Semper Fi."

"Bravo First," Lieutenant Monaghan barked. "Into the airlock."

The airlock was the same tube that the Wyverns had been lowered down through, now converted back to its primary purpose. Berg and his team marched in and hit the closing button, then waited. The airlock was controlled remotely so that nobody could accidentally evacuate the ship.

"Move out slowly and deploy in a triangle," Berg said. "Don't

engage your EVA thrusters. Just climb out and step onto the hull.
When the next team comes out, we'll spread outwards."

"Yes, mother," Himes replied.

"And watch the debris," Berg added as there was a faint "bong"
from the hull again. "It's raining metal up there."

The ship shut down engines and went into microgravity. Immediately afterwards, the hatch overhead opened up and outward
like a clamshell.

Berg grabbed the ladder and pulled himself up, hand over
hand and *carefully*. If he drifted free, he had the EVA pack to
get back. But it would be a pain.

The ladder had automatically extended beyond the hull and
he used it to lift himself up and over the lip of the former missile tube. He ignored the view; he had more important things
to do, like getting his magnetic boots clamped down. When he
was in place he swiveled his sensor pod to ensure the other two
Marines were settled.

Smith had, somehow, managed to lose his grip on the ladder
before getting clamped down and was now drifting slowly away
from the ship.

"Smith, fire your thrusters *down*," Berg said with a sigh.

"Working on it," the lance corporal replied. There was a brief
puff of gas from the thrusters on his shoulders and he drifted
downward, connecting to the ship's hull with a "click."

"Bravo First deployed," Berg reported then switched to the team
frequency. "Everybody make sure they're away from the doors."

While he waited for the next team to deploy, he switched his
view to a shot of their target. The pod was shaped vaguely like
a seedpod but more angular and was tumbling slowly through
space. Five meters long and about two wide, it had a pointed
bow and stern and was apparently made of an aluminum alloy,
according to the spectral readings. Aluminum was an odd choice,
in Berg's opinion, but not something the Dreen had *ever* been
seen to use. Which was oddly comforting.

There were not, however, any portholes. They weren't going to
be able to look in before they opened it. And what or whoever
was inside couldn't look out. Odd that.

He waited as the teams deployed, moving his outward from the
airlock as each got into place; then the SF team came up.

"Right," Guzik said. "Sir, we're going to have to secure the pod. Since it's tumbling, we're going to have to stop the tumble, first. Myself and the sergeant first class will attempt that, first. If that's okay by you, sir."

"Go for it, Master Sergeant," the lieutenant said. "Want company?"

"I would recommend deploying your Marines around the pod, sir, yes," Guzik replied.

"First Platoon, prepare to deploy. I want Alpha top side, Bravo forward and Charlie to the rear. That is with the ship as down. All clear? Sound off."

"Alpha, clear," Staff Sergeant Hinchcliffe replied.

"Bravo, aye aye," Berg said.

"Charlie, aye aye," Priester chimed in.

"Roger," the LT said. "Deploy."

"Bravo, let's take this easy," Berg said. "Break boots then follow me."

He lifted one boot up to the toe, then moved it back to position alongside the heel of the second. Lifting up the second from the heel, he drifted very slowly away from the hull. He picked a spot forward of the pod and engaged his thrusters, moving outward from the hull at a lightning pace of barely a half meter a second. Looking at his monitors, he could see that the rest of the teams were deploying with equal rapidity. Moving in microgravity just plain sucked.

So did fighting in it. If he'd carried his Mojo, one shot would have sent him spinning off into the void. There simply wasn't anything with serious punch that didn't punch back; even most rocket launchers had *some* recoil. The system that the Marines used for microgravity combat was, therefore, a *very* low-power multiple rocket launcher. The rockets were notoriously inaccurate and the best you could do with them was fill up the target area with fire. And each of the micro-rockets had not only minimal velocity but a lousy little warhead. And they *still* had some recoil. So unless you were clamped down, you also had to correct your spin as you fired. Supposedly the next weapons system would have automatic compensation, but for now it was a pain. Presumably the Dreen had a better system. If they ended up fighting Dreen in microgravity, they were *grapped*.

By the time he reached the "front" of the pod, it was no longer the front because of the tumble. But he figured he'd just park where he was. There was no way he was going to chase the tumble.

Master Sergeant Guzik and Sergeant Hanel *had* to. They got into position, then fired up their jets, basically trying to catch up to the nose and tail of the ship. Guzik managed to snag the nose with a vacuum clamp on the first pass but Hanel missed his snatch and went rocketing off into the void before he got control again. In the meantime, Guzik had gotten flipped around but by reeling in managed to get into contact with the hull of the pod. Applying full force from the really low acceleration jets, he managed to get the tumble slowed enough for Hanel to hook up on his second pass. With two jets working on it, the pod eventually stopped tumbling. More or less. It was still not quite in sync with the ship but that could be dealt with later.

However, as soon as the tumbling stopped, the nose of the ship recessed into a curve instead of a point. It had by then rotated back to Berg's position and he was the first one to spot it.

"There's a change here," Berg said. "The nose just did something really weird."

"Define 'really weird,'" Gunnery Sergeant Neely said.

"It just . . . flexed," Berg said. "It didn't move like metal, Gunny. More like memory plastic. I don't know what it means."

"So do we move it down to the hull?" Master Sergeant Guzik asked.

"I just had an interesting thought," Sergeant First Class Hanel said in a very strange voice. "What if it's not a life pod? What if it's a boobytrap?"

"Oh . . . *grapp*," Lieutenant Monaghan replied. "Tell me that wasn't a general broadcast."

"Team leaders only, sir," the SF sergeant replied. "But it's an interesting question."

"Whoa," Guzik said, releasing his hold on the pod and backing away. "I've got a seam opening."

The pod split open along its length, revealing three creatures in suits. They were about the size of large dogs and had six limbs, four apparently "legs" and two "arms." However, the ends of the arm portion of the suits split into multiple flexible appendages that looked more like tentacles than hands.

Two of them were holding devices in those tentacles. They might be communicators or guns, it was impossible to tell. They looked like PDAs, but for all Berg knew they could throw lightning bolts.

Guzik backed up his suit and held his claws up, rotating up the shoulder mounted rocket launcher.

"Hey," he said. "We come in peace and all that."

"Well, that wrecks *this* as a salvage operation," Himes muttered.

"I've got it," the LT said, jetting slowly up to hover beside the master sergeant. He held out one of the suit claws while waving to the ship with the other. "Come on. Your survival gear's not going to hold out forever. We'll see what we can do in the ship."

"I doubt they can understand you, sir," the master sergeant said.

"Hey, maybe they have a universal communicator," the LT quipped.

One of the beings slowly put away the device in its hand, then reached under the couch it occupied and pulled out a box. It looked not unlike a metal attaché case. He used his flexible tentacles to scramble up to the edge of the escape pod and then took the lieutenant's claw.

"Sir, what's in the box?" Master Sergeant Guzik chimed in, holding out his hand to another of the creatures.

"Good question, Master Sergeant," the LT replied. "Why don't you ask him?"

As the second being hooked onto the master sergeant, the latter pointed at the box and made a negative gesture. The being paused and turned his head back and forth.

It was at that point that Eric noticed the weird part about the suits. They appeared to be normal space suits, albeit of a strange material. But they had no visors. There was no way for the creature to see out.

The being, nonetheless, looked at the other two and then made a gesture at his head and to the, very small, environmental pack on his back. He did it again then moved his tentacles in a motion that was oddly disconcerting.

"Sir," Berg interjected. "I would interpret that as food and air, sir."

"And it could be a nuke for all we know," the LT said, but he engaged his jets and started backing towards the ship. "Tell Dr. Chet he's got three patients inbound. Hopefully their food and air will hold out long enough for us to figure out how to keep them alive."

14

"Thank you," Dr. Chet said, taking the air tank from the small, suited creature. He still had no clue what their visitors looked like, but the apparently senior one had carefully changed the air-tank of one of its brethren, then handed over the nearly empty spare to the neurologist, along with a small chunk of what was probably food.

"They're handling all this remarkably well," Spectre said from beyond the glass partition to the isolation area.

"Yes, they are," Dr. Chet replied, taking the canister to a testing station. "Extremely stable for the situation. But that is based only on human reactions. I would have expected situational hysteria in most humans, even the toughest. Adar less so, but they still would show some signs of stress. There is virtually none in these beings."

He squirted some of the air into the test chamber and there was a flare of light as it was hit by a high energy laser.

"Hmmm . . ." he muttered, opening the chamber again and crumbling some of the food into it. "Their air is high in nitrogen and low in oxygen. This air is completely absent of CO_2, but any mixed gas might be. I have an isolation chamber I can put them in and adjust the atmosphere."

He examined the second flash and then shrugged.

"The food appears to be Chloro B," he continued. "It's similar to Adar food. I'll need to do more analysis but some of Tchar's food may be consumable by them. But I'll need to do more tests."

"Okay," the CO said. "Where's Miss Moon?"

"In with Miss Cutler," Dr. Chet said. "She's already said that she's going to monitor remotely at first. But I need to get them out of their suits and talking for her to have anything to work with. Let me set the containment suite up and we'll see what we see."

"Keep me apprised," the CO said. "But I've got other fish to fry. We're closing on the next bit that has energy readings."

"Sucker's fairly hot," Himes pointed out as they approached the broken bit of spaceship. This one was made of an iron alloy, not quite true steel but perhaps a stronger version. At least, part of it was. Other parts appeared to be carbon fiber and "exotic" materials.

"But it's also putting out particles that aren't consistent with nuclear reactions," Berg said. "And EM. It's a device of some sort."

"But exactly what sort?" Master Sergeant Guzik asked. "A communicator? An engine? A washing machine as someone suggested?"

"Unless we can communicate with the guys we picked up, I'm not sure we'll ever know, Master Sergeant," Berg said. "Hell, we still don't *really* know what the engine of the ship is for. It might be God's washing machine and just happen to have a warp setting."

"Good point, Berg," the SFer said, a grin in his voice. "Darren's off on another bit hunt. Do you think you can get ahold of this thing?"

"I can try," Berg said, positioning himself for a run at the large and in many places sharp bit of debris.

"There is no try," the master sergeant intoned. "There is only do. Or do not."

"Yes, O Master . . . Sergeant," Berg said with a chuckle.

"Let's go," Guzik replied, engaging his jets.

Instead of trying to figure the arc, Berg just headed right for the rising end of the thing. The thing caught him in the crotch of the suit, no danger there and he engaged his thrusters downward, trying to get a handle on some of the extruding bits. Finally, he snagged a couple of pieces of what looked like reinforcing bar. As the tumble slowed he cut his thrusters.

"Nice snag," the master sergeant said. "Ballsy, but not bad."

"I didn't figure I could catch up to it," Berg admitted. "What now?"

"Take it back and strap it to the hull," Guzik said. "On my count, engage your number six and seven thrusters at three percent output and we'll tow. Three, two, one, Mark!"

"And just how are we supposed to get this stuff into the boat?" the chief of boat asked. The senior NCO of the *Blade*, he was in charge of all things nautical. Or, in this case, astronautical. Such as securing big bits of alien space craft for later analysis. Which was why he'd donned his space suit and was now standing on the hull, fists on his hips, looking at the latest bit of junk to be brought to *his* boat. "First of all, we don't know if it's contaminated. Second, ain't none of the hatches big enough. Take your pick but it *ain't* going in the boat."

"Space tape?" Berg said, then wished he hadn't.

"Go on," the COB said, not dressing the Marine down, which was what Berg had expected.

"They might not survive, but we can just tape them to the hull," Berg continued. "Or tie them if there are any tie points. But I think the tape might do it."

"If we end up with enough pieces we could just ring the hull," Master Sergeant Guzik said. "How much space tape do we have?"

"What is it with Marines and space tape?" the COB moaned. "Okay, okay, try it. See if it will hold. Mind you, it probably *won't* when the CO gets near a planet. Sometimes I think I'm going to have to get a spill-proof cup. And then where would my cred be?"

"I guess this will give him a good reason to take it easy on landing," Berg said.

"There's a point." The COB looked up at the debris floating very near the *Blade* and then back at the sail of the boat.

One of the Marines was floating between the largest piece of debris and the boat with about four centimeters between the feet of his Wyvern and the boat and about a hand's breadth between his head and the chunk of debris. Just as the Marine reached up to grab the large piece of metal a violet arc of lightning stretched from the debris down the Wyvern and jumped the few-centimeter gap on to the boat.

"Holy *maulk*! Aaarrrggghhh!" the Marine cried as he lost consciousness from the electrical shock. He fell forward in his

Wyvern, forcing his thrusters on and spinning him wildly out of control, bumping into debris and then back onto the hull of the *Blade*.

"What the hell!" the COB said surprised.

"COB?" Spectre asked over the net.

"Somehow the debris just shot a lightning bolt at one of the Marines and he's spinning out of control."

"Himes! You and Berg secure that Marine now!" Guzik shouted.

"Got it, Master Sergeant!" Berg and Himes replied, thrusting at full throttle to the unconscious Marine in his out-of-control Wyvern. In a flying tackle both Himes and Berg hit the Wyvern at nearly the same instant, pinning it down against the boat. It took several more moments to fight the thruster pack into the air-lock.

Berg cycled the airlock controls as he and Himes held on tight to Lance Corporal Smith, bracing their arms and legs against the bulkheads to hold against the low-power cold-gas nitrogen thrusters.

"Green light Two-Gun!" Himes said as the airlock door opened into the ship where the watch Marines were waiting along with a few firemen.

"Get a corpsman here." Berg shouted.

"Marines, stand down and do not touch the debris or the ship until we get this sorted out," Guzik ordered.

"You think it was an attack?" the COB asked the Space Marine.

"Negative, negative," Weaver interrupted over the com channel.

"Commander Weaver, do you have some input here?" Spectre added.

"Yes sir. Space charging, sir." Bill said.

"Space what? Charging?" Guzik turned the bulbous torso of his Wyvern toward the COB, who was just standing there motionless.

"You want to elaborate on that, Lieutenant Commander Weaver?" Spectre asked.

"Yes sir. It's the same reason you have to ground an airplane before you refuel it. The hull charges up and can cause an electrical arc from the plane to the ground. Well, in this case, the *Blade* is the ground and the debris is the plane. They've seen this sort of thing on docking spacecraft for decades. Been hazardous a few times for the Russians and I believe on the International

Space Station," Weaver replied. "That could have been millions of volts difference between the debris and the ship."

"And you were going to let us know about this when?" Spectre raised an eyebrow. There was just so much more to space travel than flying or being on a boat. So. Much. More. Jesus.

"Sorry sir. I just thought about it. We need to get the COB some grounding wires with big alligator clips on them. Clip one end to the *Blade* and then clip the other to the debris and then reel them in. Once metal to metal contact is happening the cable is no longer needed."

"Did you get that, COB?"

"Aye sir." Weaver could have told him. Getting that kid hurt was gonna hurt his cred. But hand it to the lieutenant commander, he knew what the problem was almost immediately.

"Space tape?" Spectre asked incredulously. "That's the best you could come up with, Chief of Boat?"

"Yes, sir," the COB said stoically. "We've got the two chunks of alien debris that showed energy emissions taped down to the forward hull. I used a lot of tape."

"Better than the last time, sir," Weaver pointed out. "When we dropped on Area 51 with that big crabpus hooked over of the bow like a trophy deer I thought they were going to *chither* themselves. In warp, it's not going to experience any acceleration. You might have to take the landing slow, though. And we're going to have to land in Nevada, first, again."

"Whatever," Spectre said with a sigh. "Last bit. The Dreen bit. Tell the Marines they're on point on this one."

"Here we go," Dr. Chet said.

He was munching on a bag of microwave popcorn and watching the monitors avidly. The three aliens had been placed in a quarantine room, the air adjusted to match what had been in their emergency bottle, and their "luggage" placed in there with them. And after thirty minutes of, apparently, testing their surroundings, they appeared finally ready to open up their suits.

"I hope the light level is right," he continued. "There wasn't any way to figure that. So I set it low."

"And I'm having a hard time reading their body language because of that," Miriam said. "Gimme some popcorn."

"Yes, my dear," the doctor replied, grinning through his beard. "Hard to read are they?"

"Extremely nonreactive," Miriam admitted. "At least what I can get through the suits. Almost emotionless."

"There's a fair bit of chatter on the EM band," the doctor said. "They're more or less continuously sending and receiving."

"And I can't match any of it to their movements," Miriam admitted. "It's like most of it is a continuous background hum. And some of it looks more like radar than communication."

"And the first one is taking off his helmet," Dr. Chet said excitedly as the alien fumbled at the catches.

"Not the leader, either, notice," Miriam said. "They're doing it the way that the Marines would, probably. Junior man first."

"Oh, my," Dr. Chet said as the helmet came off. "Ugly."

The alien's head was round and . . . knobbly. And . . .

"Where are the eyes?" Miriam asked as the thing released a series of clicks. "I don't see any sign of visual organs. Do you?"

"No," Dr. Chet admitted.

The linguist leaned in closer to the monitor and considered the aliens' movements and the series of clicks as the threesome shucked their suits. They had sleek purplish bodies with fine hair, which came in for some vigorous scratching as soon as the suits were off. Then the three huddled and clicked at each other for a while.

"Uh, oh," Miriam said after watching for about ten minutes.

"What?" Dr. Chet asked.

"I think I know why they don't have eyes," the linguist replied. "And I don't think those clicks are language."

"Sonar?" Dr. Chet said. "In a land mammal?"

"Looks like," Miriam said, exasperated. "And *that* means that most of their language is going to be ultrasonic! I'm *never* going to be able to talk to them! I'm barely a mezzo soprano!"

The movement to the probable Dreen ship was a relatively short distance. Short enough that the Marines remained on the hull, grav boots locked down and safety lines clipped off, but exposed to the debris.

"Whoa!" Himes shouted, leaning backward to let a piece of metal fly past. It cleared his suit by bare inches.

"This one's interesting," Berg commented, stretching out a

claw and getting a hook into what looked like a wiring harness. He wouldn't have grabbed it if it wasn't clearly nonconducting. The harness held, fortunately, but his grav boots didn't. He detached from the hull and slapped to a stop at the end of his safety rope, swinging through an arc that connected on Master Sergeant Guzik's armor.

"Damnit, Two-Gun!" the master sergeant snapped as he, too, was detached from the hull. He swung outwards and in a spiral on the pivot of his safety line which intersected with Smith's back, hooked into the traverse mechanism for the gun and pulled the Marine up to drift as well. His line caught Sergeant First Class Hanel across the back of the knees, popping his armor off the hull, then proceeded to wrap around the sergeant's safety line.

In barely fifteen seconds, all five of the Wyverns, and their safety lines, were snarled in a cat's cradle and drifting randomly. The chunk had grounded out on the ship's hull so when it hit Himes' suit there was barely a zap.

"Nice *going*, Two-Gun," Master Sergeant Guzik growled.

"Hey, I got the wreckage," Berg replied. "And unless I'm much mistaken, it's some sort of engine."

"Oh," Guzik said, panning his sensor pod around and trying to get a look at the piece. "In that case . . . Nice going, Two-Gun."

"Is it just me or does this thing look like a cut-open lung?" Himes asked as the threesome approached the probable Dreen ship.

"It sure looks organic," Smith said. "I'm getting some monatomic oxygen readings. It's still leaking."

The shattered bit of ship did look a bit like the interior of a lung. Under the suit lights, the part facing them was purple and composed of a large number of small chambers, each less than a meter wide and in irregular shapes.

The team was approaching from a direction that took them to what had been the "interior" of the ship. Alpha Team was checking out the hull while Charlie was backing them up.

"Gunny, Berg," Two-Gun said, puffing to a stop. "This looks like something that's going to require dissection rather than entry. I don't see any bits to enter. I'm getting some fermion readings from the aft quadrant, though. If that's a working quarkium plant, we'd better be careful or this thing's going to blow sky high."

"Roger, stand by," the gunny replied. There was a moment's

pause and then: "Try to cut into the area that the fermions are coming from. See what the source is."

"Oh, great," Berg muttered, moving forward. He located the closest point to the source and pulled out a vibe knife. The material, whatever it was, cut a bit like bubble wrap. Between working in microgravity and the flexible yet strong nature of the compartments, it wasn't exactly easy to cut into. He'd cut through two of the compartments, having to shove his suit actually *into* the materials, when he noticed a glow ahead. Cutting his suit lights he determined that it was a green glow and that fermion levels were up, along with gamma ray levels, indicating a radioactive source rather than quarkium.

He ran the results against a matrix of radioactive generators and got a hit.

"Gunny, I think I'm looking at a chunk of californium, here," Berg said. "At least, that's what the computer's telling me. In other words, it's a radioactive chunk of material. I think that this other stuff is attenuating the nastier radiation but I'm picking up gamma rays as well as fermions now."

"Berg, Commander Weaver. We're also getting EM from the area. I'd like you to cut out a big area around that source and pull it away from the ship."

"Aye, aye, sir," Berg said, trying not to swear. He backed out of the hole he'd made and looked around.

"Guys, we've got to cut out a big chunk of this material," Berg said. "I'd like to blow it out with our rockets, but I think we need to be a little more surgical than that. We'll cut it in an equilateral triangle, each cut being five meters long on a side. Once we've cut down past the source, we'll try to join them up. If you hit anything strange, or the inner side of the hull, back out. Clear?"

"Clear, Sergeant," Smith said.

"Aye, aye, Captain Crunch," Himes replied.

It took nearly an hour of sweating and often swearing, but they finally managed to get the chunk cut out. By that time the rest of the teams had completed their survey and found nothing of equivalent interest.

"So what do we do with it now?" Himes asked as they pulled the chunk free of the surrounding material.

"I have no idea," Berg admitted. "LT, what do we do with it now?"

"I guess we drag it back and strap it to the ship," the platoon leader said.

"Aye, aye, sir," Berg said, then checked his monitors. "Bravo Team, back off! Sir, radiation levels are increasing!"

"All teams, back away from the material," the lieutenant said, putting his own suit into reverse.

As Berg backed away, he could see the glow expanding throughout the material. There was outgassing from it now, a lot, and it read as mostly carbon, which meant the radiation source had really increased in energy output. He'd gotten about fifty meters from the chunk of material when it just blew up.

The explosion had no effect on him—explosions propagate poorly in space—but it was spectacular. The chunk of lunglike material ballooned outwards and popped with a huge rush of gasses and a flair of intensely actinic light.

"Well, that was special," Smith commented. "What just happened?"

"At a guess, whatever was keeping the reaction stable was part of the overall matrix," Berg said. "Californium is a very hot isotope. There was probably more in the chunk than necessary for critical mass. When we cut that bit out, it went critical."

"So we were just right next to a nuclear explosion?" Himes asked. "That's not happy making."

"It was a very *small* nuclear explosion," Berg pointed out. "A lot smaller than a grain of sand that actually blew up. The suits are barely reading the rads. And there's a way to get the generators on these suits to do the same thing. And bigger."

"Really?" Himes asked. "I *so* didn't want to know that."

"Neither did I when I found out," Berg said. "Which was when an SF sergeant on the last cruise blew his up."

"I've *seriously* got to find a new line of work," Smith said.

"So we've got three survivors of an unknown alien species, a couple of pieces of wreckage from their ship and a blown up bit of what was probably a Dreen ship. Does that about sum it up?"

"Pretty much covers it, sir," the XO said.

"But not the important parts, sir," Weaver said. "There *is* another race out there, it seems pretty friendly, and it has an FTL drive. Of course, the Mreee seemed pretty friendly at first. These guys might just be Dreen slaves for all we know."

"A happy thought," the CO said. "And anyone *but* Dreen would tend to be friendly if they were rescued from drifting in space. Miss Moon? Anywhere on their language?"

"As I suspected, most of it is ultrasonic," the linguist said with a note of exasperation. "The problem with compressing that down to where humans can hear is that it's like compressing a voice down to bass. You lose a lot of timbre and intonation. Between that, their remarkable calm and the fact that I'm having to sort out the language from their general sonar functions . . . No. I'm *not* getting very far on their language. And we can't even show them pictures. They are simply blind to us and we are just as blind to them. It's very frustrating."

"Well, keep at it," the CO said, frowning. "It would be nice to be able to talk to these people eventually. Tactical?"

"We've been going over the traces that Astro pointed out," the TACO said. "We think we've got a good algorithm to use the method in the future for tracking. Be that as it may, there's a pretty clear path headed outward from the system. I'd suggest we just follow it, sir. They apparently are not in warp, or theirs works far differently from ours. I'm not sure of speed, but if they're not in warp, we should be able to catch up to them fairly easily. Perhaps their main ship has some gear that will permit us to talk to them. Those are a lot of ifs, sir . . ."

"But that's what being a Junior Spaceman is all about," the CO said, nodding. "Sounds like a plan. XO."

"Make it so, sir. Aye, aye."

"The bunk is where the heart is," Smith said, stretching out.

"I dunno," Berg replied. "It was nice to finally get out of the ship."

"Anything on that bit you grabbed?" Himes asked.

"Guzik said he was going to take it to the aliens we picked up and see if they could do anything with it," the sergeant replied. "Get some shut-eye. We don't know when we're gonna have to get to work again."

"Can I ask one question, Sergeant Bergstresser, sir?" Himes asked.

"Go."

"Why do we *always* get point?"

"Because we're the best team—"

"In the best platoon in the best company in the—" Himes muttered.

"In the best Corps in the whole damned Galaxy!" Smith finished, grinning. "But really, why?"

"Because Top hates me."

"I thought Top loved you. You two are going to have children together."

"With First Sergeant Powell, it's a fine line."

"First Sergeant? Moment of your time?" Gunny Neely said, knocking on the open door to Top's stateroom.

"Come on in," Top said, looking up from his computer screen. There was a projection of the alien device Berg had snagged on it. Offhand, it looked something like an electrical motor, except that there appeared to be no moving parts.

"First Sergeant, I'd like to discuss personnel usage," the Gunny said, looking over at the SEAL who appeared to be asleep.

"Don't worry about me," Miller said. "I've heard more of these conversations than you've had hot breakfasts."

"Go ahead, Gunny," Powell said, spinning around in his chair. "Grab a bunk."

"First Sergeant, with all due respect, on the last two missions First Platoon has always gotten the hot seat," the Gunny said carefully. "And in three cases you've specified Bravo Team as the point. I know that you worked with Sergeant Bergstresser before and have . . . a high opinion of him. So do I, don't get me wrong. He's good. But . . ."

"But I keep putting him in spots where he's liable to get killed," Powell said. "And I don't rotate that."

"Yes, First Sergeant."

"Do you know anyone else in your platoon who would have recognized that there was a subcritical explosion about to occur?" Top asked. "Or that the material involved was californium and, therefore, had the likelihood of going critical?"

"No, but—"

"Unfortunately, there is no 'but,'" Top said definitely. "Berg is, alas, unique in this company. I don't know that even *I* would have been able to determine the material. And the best bit of equipment we recovered was the part he snagged, just standing on the *hull*. I put Two-Gun out front because he's incredibly

knowledgeable and makes good decisions in the crunch. There are
plenty of other Marines who make good decisions, don't get me
wrong. But they don't have Two-Gun's knowledge and experience.
That being the case, until we can grow some Marines that have
his abilities, figure that First is going to get all the hot deploy-
ments and Bravo is going to be leading the way. That increases
the likelihood that we'll *lose* that knowledge and experience. But
if it had been, for example, Alpha First pulling apart the Dreen
wreck, I think we'd be out a team about now, don't you?"

"I see your point, First Sergeant," Neely answered. "I also
respectfully disagree with your conclusions. Among other things,
it's creating an appearance of favoritism. There are a bunch of
bored and, at this point, grumbling Marines in the berths. Two-
Gun and his team have gotten out and *done* stuff, First Sergeant.
The rest of the Marines feel like they're just along for the ride.
Third Platoon spent a day wandering around ruins doing, as far
as they could tell, exactly nothing. Berg's team did the entry to
the base *and* ended up rescuing the lone survivor. It's all 'Two-
Gun, Two-Gun, what's Two-Gun got to do today?' I respectfully
request that you spread the load a bit. One extremely salient point
was raised by a Marine I request to remain anonymous. But he
asked me, point blank, if you trusted anyone in the company but
Two-Gun. I told him that you did, but I know I didn't make my
point very well because I wasn't sure of the answer."

"I'll take it under advisement," the first sergeant said, nodding.
"We'll see what the next mission is like. Good enough?"

"Yes, Top," Neely said, standing up. "Thanks."

"It's not something I hadn't thought about," Powell admitted.
"And discussed with the Old Man. He raised the same point,
including the trust issue, and I gave him the same answer. So
you're not the Lone Ranger."

"*I* trust Two-Gun more than I trust the rest of your company,"
Miller said after the hatch closed. "No offense. Kid's just *good.*
And he's lucky. It's a tough combination to beat."

"Agreed," Powell said, turning back to the video. "The hell of
it is, so do I. It is favoritism. I just think it's *pragmatic* favoritism."

15

"Coils charged," Engineering Specialist Rorot stated. "Unreality generator coming online . . ."

"That does not sound good," Favarduro quipped as a hard vibration coursed through the ship.

"Structural integrity failure in Number 23 generator pylon," Rorot said calmly. "Shutting down."

"How very good," Ship Master Kond said quietly. "Time estimate?"

"I will need to go outside," Rorot said, standing up. "A team is on the way. I would anticipate at least two hundred kleg."

"Very well," Kond said. "Keep me updated when you have the time. Favarduro, maintain maximum watch."

"We have seen no indications of the Blin dreadnought," Favarduro replied. "It is possible it was destroyed by the *Klingoddar* and the fighters were remnants. Or it may still be out there, damaged as we are and effecting repairs."

"Keep a watch," Kond replied. "Chaos ball generator?"

"That is on-line," Favarduro admitted. "So we have that at least. I'll fire the minute I see any threat."

"I wonder what their detection systems are like?" Weaver said, frowning.

"Say again, Astro?" the CO replied, watching the forward

181

viewscreens. The trace of gasses was now displayed in false color and they were following the track at low warp.

"Well, unless they have some sort of detector which is FTL," Weaver said musingly, "then we're going to come up on them before they see us. Even what we're seeing isn't quite real time. We're, effectively, past the point that we see by the time we see it. If that makes any sense."

"About as much as everything else about this job," the CO replied, not correcting the former academic on his omission of the obligatory "sir."

"About the only FTL detector we know of, theoretically, is a tachyon detector," Bill continued, frowning now. "And as far as I've been able to determine, we don't give off tachyons."

"We're far too high class," Spectre quipped.

"Well, your astrogator's a redneck, sir," Bill replied. "But the point is, the neutrinos, quentaquarks and such like that we *do* radiate, propagate slower than light. So . . ."

"So we're going to get up to them before they can detect us," the CO said. "I like it."

"Yes, sir," Bill replied. "But the point is, we're going to get up to them before they can even *see* us. That's going to come as a surprise. And they just left a battle . . ."

"Visual on ship," Tactical called. "Zooming forward view-screen."

There was a brief image of a ship. There was no reference for size but the ship was a long ovoid with dozens of sharp wings sticking out ending in oval devices that looked somewhat like jet engines without an intake or exhaust. The exception to the oval look was a hammerhead projection from either the front or the rear; with the way the ship was sitting it was impossible to tell which.

"Drop us out of warp," the CO said, swiveling his chair forward.

"Sir!" Bill called. "I respectfully suggest you . . ."

"Where did *that* come from?" Favarduro shrilled, his hand dropping to the Chaos cannon switch. There was a hum from forward and a ball of white flashed out, closing the intervening gap rapidly.

"Belay firing," Kond snapped. "That is *not* a Blin warship!"

"Oh, Drdunc."

》　　　》　　　》

"...Belay that order, sir!"

"Conn, Tactical, we are under fire!"

"Pilot, warp us out of here!"

"Damn that's fast!" Weaver snarled, turning to his monitors. "What in the hell *is* it?"

The ball of what looked like chain lightning was closing the three light-second gap at nearly the speed of light. The *Blade* had barely dropped out of warp and was now trying to scramble back. The conversion was, unfortunately, slow.

Just as the ball of whatever it was reached their position, the *Blade*'s engines finally converted them back into warp and the pilot, instinctively, punched in maximum warp up and to the side. They flashed by the alien ship in the millisecond that was left before the weapon reached them.

"Tactical," the CO said. "What was that weapon?"

"Unknown, Conn," the TACO said. "All our particle screens went ballistic. We couldn't even get a reading on it. In fact, we lost *all* our readings."

"Pilot, bring us around," the CO said. "Try to stop a bit farther out and be ready to go back into warp..."

"Where did it go?" Favarduro asked. "Where did it *come* from?"

"I am supposed to be asking you that question," Ship Master Kond replied. "Fortunately, it did not fire upon us. I am inclined to show them the same courtesy. If they come back."

"There," Favarduro said. "It is at two-one-six mark fifteen. Range sixty-two dreg."

"How much time from when it disappeared to when it reappeared?" Kond asked.

"Six treek," Favarduro said nervously. "It crossed over seventy dreg in six treek."

"That is faster than light," Kond said, wonderingly. "It has a non-node unreality generator."

"That's not theoretically possible," Favarduro pointed out.

"Theory is always superceded by fact, Senior Tactical Specialist," the ship master said. "And that is fact. Unless you distrust your instruments."

"I wish I could run a check," Favarduro said. "But I don't have such a system for my brain. Permission to speak to the Ungur."

"I'm glad to see you have your balance back," Kond replied. "And nearly as glad to see your hubris pricked by our visitors. Communications, send standard first contact protocol message. Let us see if these are friend or foe."

"Conn, Tactical. I'm getting a pulse of EM and neutrinos from the target, designated Sierra One. It's powerful but it's not pulsing like radar. I think they're trying to talk to us."

"XO, we got an SOP for this?" the CO asked, looking over at Weaver.

"Yes, sir!" the executive officer said, pulling out a manual. "There are a selection of first contact protocols prepared!"

"Right," the CO replied, trying not to grin. "You try to find out what we're supposed to do. In the meantime . . . Commo, send them video from conn. See if their computers can parse it out."

"Sir," Weaver said. "Remember that Miss Moon thinks they 'see' with sonar. I'm not sure they have an equivalent of video."

"Commander Weaver, they have, presumably, a home-built FTL drive," Spectre said. "They have some sort of quantum torpedo thingy that goes faster than we do in normal space. I'm going to presume that they have better computers than we do and might actually have experience at first contact. We have a lash-up of human and Adar computers and a linguist that is pretty sure that squirrels are intelligent. They may even be aware that other species use visual light instead of sonar to see the universe. In other words, I'm going to let *them* figure it out."

"Point made, sir," Bill replied with a grin.

"And somebody get Miss Moon on deck. It's about time our linguist earned her passage."

"We are receiving various EM frequencies only," Communications Specialist Elav said. "There are neutrino and quark emissions, but I have determined that they are random and probably leakage from their engines. The initial communication was short pulses in a specific frequency of EM. Following that they began sending a continuous transmission on several frequencies but the transmission is odd. It varies in pulse and does not appear to be binary data. I have determined that it is probably their equivalent of sodee, but it does not parse correctly. I surmise they are primarily an EM detecting species. Thus they are sending us EM reflectance data instead of sonic reflectance data. I am attempting to replicate this for our own use and to translate our sodee data for theirs. There is also an audio channel, but so far I have been unable to parse it for translation. I deeply regret my failures thus far."

"They have a drive system that is far superior to our own," Kond replied. "Given the speed of their drive, they undoubtedly have far more first contact experience than we. If they are unable to translate our transmissions when they are that far in advance of us, it is unlikely that you will do better. Continue to work on the problem, but in the meantime I think that we can leave it up to them."

"Their transmissions are giving me fits. I think it's some sort of binary, but there's no change in modulation. And most of it seems to be based on the neutrino emissions rather than the EM. I'm beginning to think that one's audio and the other video."

The commo officer of the *Blade* always knew that someday he'd have to figure this stuff out. But he also figured it wouldn't be this hard or that the other species would crack the human's code rather than the other way around. But the two ships had been sitting opposite each other at a bare light-minute for the last four hours, sending lots and lots of "stuff" back and forth and not getting anywhere.

"Sonar is three dimensional," Miriam said, looking at the signals. "Video is designed to create phosphors of light on a two-dimensional screen. A sonar signal would be designed to produce sound, but very layered and complex. What we really need is a sonarman working on this, sorry. Can you transfer this over to the lab? I'd like to play with it and let the three guys we picked up listen to it."

"Can do, ma'am," Commo said happily. "Should I send it over to Sonar and see what they can do with it?"

"Send it to Tactical, yes," Miriam said. "Tell them to try pumping it through their sonar systems and radar systems. It might look a bit like radar as well. Parse the neutrino pulses into analog data. I'll play with all of it at the same time."

"Getting anywhere?" Dr. Chet asked.

"I think so," Miriam replied. She had set up in front of a small flat-screen monitor and the desk was liberally covered with sheets of paper. Most of it was equations, but some looked like doodles.

There were various half-shots of the faces of their visiting aliens. "I'm having to think what they would look like to each other, in sonar. I've been looking at what we have in the ship's computer on dolphin brain imagery, which is the nearest analog I can find. And I think I'm starting to get somewhere."

She opened up a screen and coded rapidly, her fingers flashing across the keyboard. The small program compiled quickly, then she opened up a freeware open-source video program.

"Now to see what this does with the signal," she said, dropping a portion of the signal data into the program.

The screen changed to a gray pattern of images while a series of squeals came out of the speaker. There was nothing to truly see, though; it was worse than any surrealist painting. There were some angles and a few moving shapes, but nothing that could be parsed out.

"Not quite," Miriam said, opening up the code again. She considered her equations for a moment, jotted down a long series of cryptic notations then added some code, removing others.

"There we go," she said as if to a child. The screen now showed the interior of what was clearly a spaceship. Portions were strangely distorted, cubistic in many ways, with screens taking prominence, positions of some of the beings very odd, translucency to others and one central figure in the room apparently huge. But the aliens on the screen looked, somewhat, like the aliens in isolation.

"Can you change our signals to look more like theirs?" Dr. Chet asked.

"Maybe," Miriam said. "But I'm not sure what they'll actually get. We can try."

"And we still don't have language," the M.D. pointed out.

"But this actually helps," Miriam replied. "It almost automatically subtracts the sonar portion of their sounds. But that makes it harder in a way as well. They seem to use their sonar the way we used body language. It might be one of the things that makes them seem so flat. Communicating with them will *always* be hard. I don't think we think exactly the same. Not even as close as we and the Adar. I'm going to see if we can change our transmissions to match theirs, use another frequency to substitute for the neutrinos which were acting as a third dimension modulator. It should work, if they can change their system to figure it out."

» » »

"Their transmissions have changed," Elav said. He cupped his headpiece for a moment, then pinged excitedly. "I think I can now parse their transmission. It will take me a few kleg."

"Very good," Kond replied. "Change your own transmission to a series of short pulses. Perhaps they will get the point that we're having to work on our own end."

"Conn, Commo. Miss Moon modified our transmissions. She thinks she's cracked the sonar to video code. We sent them the modified video and we're now getting a single band EM series of pulses. No neutrino, just EM. Simple pattern, just about a quarter send pulse, pause for a second, quarter second pulse at 4.2 gigahertz. No clue what that means."

"It means: Hold Please," Commander Weaver said.

"Agreed," Spectre replied. "So now we wait. Commo, hook in Miss Moon's changes to the main viewer and run that program as soon as you get something else from them."

"Aye, aye."

"Ship Master, it is a very strange signal," Elav said. "But I think I have it parsed. Do you wish to see?"

"Immediately," Kond said, rising from his couch.

The image was very strange, two dimensional, the beings pictured moving only side to side and having no depth. Walking through the sonar image, Kond saw that they appeared the same from the other side. The actual figures of the crew of the alien ship were hard to separate from their controls but they appeared to be bipedal. So were some Blin units, but these assuredly were not Blin. They could be a Blin subject race, like the haired ones or the multi-legs, but so far they had not acted hostile at all.

"Is there any way to get depth?" Kond asked.

"I am trying, Ship Master," the commo specialist replied. "But there is no signal for depth. I think that it is somehow interpreted by their sensory organs. They appear to be EM detectors in a limited range."

"Send an image of our interior," Kond ordered. "Let them sense us as well."

"Here we go," the commo officer said over the intercom. "Sending through the sonar to vid processed signal."

"Ouch," Spectre said, shaking his head at the weird view on the forward screen. It was a bit stomach wrenching in its weird distortions, more like a bad acid trip than a video. But he nonetheless stood up and nodded at the image. "Greetings. I am Captain Blankemeier, commander of the Alliance Space Ship *Vorpal Blade.* We greet you in peace and friendship."

"I think that the audio is clear," Elav said, wincing. The tonality caused sonar harmonics that were stomach wrenching, spinning the sensory interior of the control compartment wildly.

"Can you filter out those harmonics?" Kond asked, wriggling his tentacles.

"I'm trying, Ship Master," Elav said. "But I'm not sure what we're losing."

"I'm willing to lose some information to avoid having my weapons fired accidentally," the ship master replied. "Greetings," he continued, raising his tentacles. "We come in peace."

"Ow!" Spectre snapped, sticking a finger in his ear and wriggling it around. "Was that feedback? I think that squeal would bend metal! Commo, can we put some sort of filter on that? The guys we've got in isolation don't sound that bad."

"I'll try, Conn," Commo replied. "Miss Moon said that she was having to bring out some high-frequency tonalities. I think that might be what's causing that squeal. I've set the system to drop all the frequencies another octave."

"We're starting to get a translation," Elav said, looking at his computers. "There are assumptions involved but I think we're making headway, finally. We are picking up not only the words of the apparent commander, but of others in the compartment. The computer has used all of that and is assimilating their language."

"Adjust my transmission to use their language," Kond said. "Can you translate a standard greeting protocol?"

"I should be able to," Elav said. "Go ahead, Ship Master."

"Yo, again," the main figure on the viewscreen said. "Our chips are changing my thoughts to those of dudes. I be Kond, Boss Dude of the big ship. Greetings and sweeties we are."

"Whoa," Weaver said. "I hope like hell that their computers are capable of retasking for language. Because I seriously don't want them to sound like that when they meet major players."

"I just hope *I* don't sound that strange to *them*," Spectre muttered. "Greeting, Kond. I am Spectre, Boss Dude of the *Vorpal Blade*."

16

"Dreen," Kond said, about an hour later. "Yes, we are fighting those ones. We are fleeing those ones. Our home world was lost. Fleet is finding safe world. We are last guards."

"We have three survivors from the last battle on-board," Spectre said. "We picked them up along with some wreckage for study. How can we transfer them over?"

"Lost are they," Kond replied, waggling tentacles again. "Space is their home."

"No, we picked them up," the CO said, confused. "We can get them over to you easily enough."

"Lost are they," Kond repeated. "Source is not. Behind they are. Understanding?"

"Sir," Miriam said, quietly. "I think what he's saying is that the resources of their ships are so minimal that they can't take them on. If they lost their ship, they have to be left behind."

"Lost are they," Kond agreed. "Is sorrow. Is must."

"We can carry them," Spectre said, his jaw firming. "Is that permitted? Is that okay?"

"Very okay," Kond said. "But not for us. Little air, water, food we have. Food very little. Damages we carry from battle. Unable to squee!"

"I think that squeal was important," Weaver interjected. "Unable to fly? Unable to warp? Unable to go faster than light?"

"Unable to be unreal," Kond replied. "Unable to run."

"They can't get their FTL drive to work," Spectre said, nodding. "Can we help?"

"Part is broken," Kond said. "Squee! Is damaged before, damaged again. May not be fix."

"Can you show us the part?" Spectre asked. "We have a way to get some parts from home. It's possible we could get something that will work. If it's not complicated."

"Is only squee!" Kond said.

"He's exasperated," Miriam said. She had an earbud in and was apparently picking up the raw sounds from the alien. "I've heard that tone before. It goes very high, super ultrasonic. Frustration. I think it's something simple but for some reason they can't fix it."

"And since he's a sitting duck until they do . . ." Weaver said. "Kond, can you show us the part?"

"Wait," Kond said.

"Elav, in my cabin, the model of the ship. Get it."

"Yes, Ship Master."

"This part," Kond said, holding up a model of the ship. It was detailed but small. He might have been pointing at one of the pods or the nacelle-wing leading to it.

"The engine or the wing?" Spectre asked.

"The squee!" Kond replied, holding it up and pointing to it again. With the tip of one tentacle he lightly caressed the wing.

"Commander Weaver, what's the size of one of those things?"

"Kond, we must send an active thing at your ship," Weaver said. "Light. It is not dangerous."

"Send," Kond replied.

Weaver went over to his controls and brought up the laser rangefinding system used for inshore maneuvers. Sending a pulse at the distant ship, and finally getting a hard range return, he was able to determine sizes. The wing was thirty-seven feet long, the pod on the end about twenty long and ten wide at the widest point. Looking at the design he knew exactly what would fit, if there were no special requirements. And if they could somehow attach it.

"Kond," he said, getting back up and walking over to the center of the conn. "Does it have to be special materials?"

"Not understood," Kond said. "It can be any squee . . . It can be squee or squee or even squee. Anything. Must be strong."

"If we can get back to Gamma and if we can convince the Prez, and if we can get one down to Antarctica *fast*, he *should* be able to use a wing off a transport plane," Weaver said. "Figure they have to fly C-17s in to the area anyway to bring the gates. There's an airfield. Fly in a C-17, cut off the win—" He stopped at the CO's expression. "Or not. But I figured out a way to pick it up and attach it using the Wyverns and space ta— Or not."

"Here's an alternative thought," Spectre said carefully. "Did we see any of those things floating around back at the battlefield? I seem to recall your last brainstorm involved high pressure hydrogen throughout my ship."

"Yeah, heh," Weaver said ruefully. "I'm glad nobody pointed out to you that it was explosive."

"*What?*"

"I kept expecting us to blow sky high," Weaver said. "Oxygen and hydrogen are not a good mix. One spark and . . . But, yeah, there are probably some parts back at the battlefield. Now if we can just explain that we want to take some of their people back there to check it out."

"How about the three space cases in isolation?" the XO asked.

"Well, what we need are their version of machinist mates and for all we know we've got cooks," the CO said, still trying to assimilate that the ship had nearly gone sky-h— Been blown to smithereens. "But if we can get it across to the Kond fellow, maybe it will work. It's no worse than any of our other plans. Except the one that involved cutting off the wing of a billion dollar airplane."

"They could repair it," Weaver pointed out. "I mean, it would be pricey but we're talking about high level diplomacy here. Seriously, they shove it through the gate fast and then we use the Marines to—" He looked at the CO's face again and paused. "Or not."

"Could you go over that for me again, sir?" the COB asked.

He got that they'd encountered another alien race. He got that they were friendly. He even got that their ship needed to be repaired and, hey, you did that for friends. He was just having a hard time with . . .

"We gotta go pick up the wing of a C-17 that's floating around in space?"

"Forget the C-17," Spectre said patiently. "We're warping back to the scene of the space battle. We're hoping to find a part that sort of *looks* like a part of a C-17 wing that got cut off and cut short. We need to pick it up and bring it back here so the aliens can fix their ship and get out of here before the Dreen catch them. Are we clear on all of that?"

"Yes, sir," the COB said, taking another sip of coffee. "How big is this thing? How are we going to bring it back, sir?"

"That, COB, is up to you," the CO replied. "I'll send Commander Weaver out with the party. He will be in nominal charge. But as we both know—"

"The commander don't know his butt from a hole in the water about anything nautical, sir," the COB said, sighing. "I been trying—"

"We're all trying, COB," the CO said. "On the other hand, what he doesn't know about *space* hasn't been learned, yet."

"Got it, sir," the COB replied. "I'll need a couple of machinists, three bosuns and we'd probably better get a couple of the Marines. They're the only ones in armor. If this thing is dangerous . . ."

"Understood," the CO said. "Get to it."

"And a lot of space tape . . ." the COB muttered as he left the conn.

"Have we gotten our passengers in touch with the ship?" the CO asked. "I don't suppose they can be of any help?"

"They're talking," Miriam said, leaning into her earbud. "I'm listening. The high frequency compression is making some of it hard to understand, but I'm getting most of it. But the 'passengers' don't appear to be of much use to us in this. If I'm getting it right, one of them is something like a cook, there might be a supply person and I think the third is something to do with navigation."

"So no lost princesses?" Weaver asked. "Captain of the destroyed ship? Their chief engineer?"

"No engineers at all," Miriam said.

"Do they *know* you're listening in?" the CO asked.

"Yes, sir," Miriam replied. "Doing otherwise wouldn't be . . . nice."

"That was actually my point," the CO said. "Okay, then it's up to us. Commander Weaver, you're going to be in charge of the recovery detail. Ideas?"

"Move to about a hundred thousand meters from center," Bill said. "Do a visual and radar sweep for the shape we're looking for. Close to it. Determine if it's attached to something or not. Connect to it, probably by using suits carrying lines to the piece, pull it onto the hull, secure it and then we head back."

"On the sweep," Miriam said, still looking at the deck. "I can write some code to do automatic shape matching. It might speed things up."

"Thank you, Miss Moon," Bill said. "But, we already have auto-target recognition code for targeting and navigation based on matched filtering, FFTs, fuzzy logic, and genetic algorithms that work just fine and can be used just as readily. After all, how do you think the navigation computer recognizes the star patterns or the targeting systems recognize, uh, targets?"

"Oh." Miriam wasn't sure if Weaver was being flippant or arrogant, so she dropped it.

"I suspect the genius is going to be in the details," the CO said.

"So do I, sir," Bill admitted. "So do I. But it can't be worse than catching a comet."

"Commander, let me give you a piece of advice from my many years in the Navy," the CO said. "Never *ever* say: It couldn't be worse."

By integrating the lidar system and the synthetic aperture radar (SAR) systems on the *Blade* to get a range, they could determine roughly how big the debris field was. But at a light-second out the size and a shape of the individual pieces were beyond the limits of even the big twelve-meter aperture of the main sparse array telescope system. Running SAR and lidar image enhancement codes they were able to increase their resolution a few percent and started picking up potential large pieces of more than fifteen meters in length while still a light-second out. Smaller pieces were still unresolvable. They were approaching under normal space drive so they had nearly thirty minutes until they reached their pause point.

"Too bent," Bill said, looking at the first match. "I think it's one of the things we're looking for but it's bent. You can see it."

"I see it," Miriam said, declicking the first match. "There's another."

"I think that's a section of hull," Bill replied. "It's not the thing Kond was pointing at."

"Might work," Miriam pointed out.

"Better than a wing from a C-17," Spectre said dryly. The matches were displaying on the main conn screens for size and resolution, so he didn't even have to look over their shoulders. "Highlight it as a possible, though."

"Broken," Bill said on the next. "Bent again . . ."

"We're scavengers," Spectre interjected sadly. "Scavengers of a battle fought not so long ago. And . . . Tactical?"

"Conn, Tactical."

"Don't get caught up in this search," the CO said. "The Dreen are probably going to be checking out this battle site, too."

"Aye, aye, Conn."

"Be a bit ugly if they showed up while we're doing this, sir," Bill said. "Not a wing. Something else."

"Hull?"

"I think it's part of a passageway. What's that, though?"

The system was highlighting the piece as a low-priority. That was because the "wing" was still attached to one of the pods on the end.

"I forgot to add the pods," Miriam admitted. "Sorry. But that looks—"

"Good," Bill said, zooming the camera in. The "wing" had what looked like a bit of the hull still attached and still had its pod. He very much wanted to get his hands on one of the pods. The aliens had as much as said that they were part of their FTL system, one that humans might be able to replicate. "That looks very good. CO, I think we have a winner."

"The COB has assembled a recovery crew," Spectre replied. "Best go get your armor on. Pilot, bring us in close to that piece of debris."

"Aye, aye, sir."

"More alien space junk," Smith muttered, thrusting over to the tumbling "wing."

"Just get it stabilized, relative to the ship," Berg replied. "I'll take left, you take right. Just stand by to stabilize, I'm going to try something."

"Is that anything like, 'Hey, y'all, watch this?'" Himes asked.

"Probably," Berg said, flying "over" the spinning wing. It was mostly tumbling end to end, pretty fast all things considered, with a slight skew and "down" being towards the boat. And it was moving "away" from the site of the battle very fast, having apparently been imparted with quite a bit of velocity from an internal explosion. But the ship was matching that to within a few meters per minute. He could "follow" it with his thrusters easily enough. But they had to stop the tumbling.

He hovered over the left end of the piece until it headed back "up" then engaged his shoulder thrusters, heading "down" towards the pod on the end. He realized at the last moment that the pod *might* be fragile, in which case this was going to be one stupid thing to do. And depending on its mass . . .

The soles of his armor, though, encountered the upthrusting pod with a "clang" that could be heard through his armor. It slammed him upwards, hard, spinning him away. But as he spun he got a glimpse of the piece and the rotation had slowed to almost nothing.

"Good one, Two-Gun," Commander Weaver said. "You okay?"

"Fine, sir," Berg replied, working his jets to try to get his own tumble balanced out. "Himes, Smith, can you stabilize it now?"

"Got it, Sergeant," Himes replied.

Berg finally got stable looking "down" at the ship and the piece of debris. He was low on nitrogen-pressure for the thrusters and still moving away from the ship. That wasn't so good.

"How you doing, Two-Gun?" Weaver asked. The transmission was somewhat scratchy.

"Working on that one, sir," Berg admitted. "I'm not sure I've got enough pressure to make it back. I don't suppose you could ask the CO to come pick me up when you're done, could you?"

"Lo . . . ssure?"

"Low fuel," Berg said calmly. "Low fuel. Low fuel." His range-finder had the *Blade* at over a kilometer and receding at ten meters per second.

". . . ger . . . ait."

"Conn, EVA . . ."

"Two-Gun's doing a Dutchman," the CO said. "We see that.

Tell the other Marines to standby on the debris. We'll go pick up Two-Gun and come back."

"Roger, sir."

"Pilot," the CO said, gesturing with his chin. "Carefully."

"Go pick up one wayward Marine, sir," the pilot replied. "Aye, aye."

The pilot swung wide around the debris, which was between the ship and the wayward Marine. The boat was nearly three stories high, if he didn't go "high" he was going to clip the debris and the Marines still clinging to it. That would be, in piloting terms, an "oops."

The ship at these low speeds was remarkably delicate in handling. He could accelerate and decelerate faster than an Indy car. So he had to mainly be cautious in how fast he moved. Although he could decelerate fast, he could accelerate fast enough that he didn't have the *reaction* time to slow down. A thousand gravs of accel were at his fingertips. This movement required less than a gravity of acceleration. Keeping it that *slow* was the problem.

From Berg's perspective, the ship was starting to get a bit smaller. Which was not comforting. Space was a very big place.

But as he watched it moved "upwards" from the debris as delicately as a snowflake then suddenly expanded in size, coming towards him like lightning and then "stopping." Actually, it was still coming towards him, just much slower. The pilot was a genius.

Then he started to feel the "pull" from the ship's artificial gravity and "down" suddenly became far less abstract.

"Commander!" Weaver said as Berg started to fall towards the ship, accelerating fast.

"Conn, EVA," Weaver said over the comm link. "We're going to need to bring Two-Gun in in microgravity. And we need to convert fast."

"Already considered, EVA," the CO replied. "XO, sound microgravity."

"ALL HANDS, ALL HANDS. MICROGRAVITY IN TEN SECONDS. TEN, NINE, EIGHT, SEVEN . . ."

"Shit," Machinist Mate Gants said, grabbing his tools up and putting them in their slots.

"Just what we needed," Red replied, picking up the smaller attachments for his Number Two arm and stowing them in a butt-pouch.

As the gravity fell away, Red continued picking up tools with the small pincers that were a permanent attachment of the Number Two Arm. Gants picked up his last screwdriver, grabbed a screw and then paused.

"Man, I really wish we hadn't had chili for lunch," Sub Dude moaned.

"If you puke all over this compartment . . . Use a bag man, use a bag!"

Berg still had his velocity but the pilot, again, corrected delicately so that he floated "down" to the ship, only having to correct slightly as his boots touched the upper deck.

"I'd take that as a mixed experiment, Sergeant Berg," the astrogator said. "On the one hand, you corrected the rather notable spin."

"On the other hand, I got blown into space doing it, sir," Berg ended. "Yes, sir. I'd given that some thought."

"Conn, EVA," Weaver said. "Marine recovered. Let's go pick up some debris."

"Okay, this is where it gets tricky," Bill said. "We're grounded, right COB?"

"Aye, sir."

Four lines had been attached to the debris as well as a grounding cable, the ship rotated "up" to the wing and positioned delicately under it. All they had to do was get it across twenty meters of empty space.

"Pulling this thing in will be easy," Bill said, looking at the four bosun mates on the lines. Those lines, however, had already started to oscillate, imparting a vector to the wing. "But while it seems light, it has *lots* of mass. If we get it moving too fast, it's going to crush you between it and the hull when it hits. So you're going to have to—"

"Sir, if I may?" the COB said. "Team. On my command. Handsomely." He waited about a second. "Belay. Step back. Retrieve lines. Retrieve . . . Just pull out the oscillation. No more pressure than that."

The piece was coming down slightly askew and very slowly. But slow was good in Bill's opinion. And he noted that the COB had arranged some sort of rubber matting where the wing was going to hit the ship.

The ropes the crew was using were flying everywhere in the microgravity environment, but they didn't seem to be getting in the way. The four bosun mates were retrieving them hand over hand, stepping away from where the wing would impact.

"Four, handsomely," the COB said as the wing started to get some drift to the side. "Belay. Retrieve. Retrieve . . ."

As the wing impacted the rubber mat, it rebounded upwards.

"Belay!" the COB said. "Sharply!"

All four of the bosun mates clamped down on their lines, then pulled in, fast, stopping the wing from getting out of control. In a moment it was hard against the hull and steady.

"Something like that, sir?" the COB asked.

"Just like that, COB," Bill admitted. "I'll leave it to you to get secured."

"Why, thank you, sir."

17

The tactical tech leaned forward and frowned at his screen. It was a mass of junk. The problem was that while all sorts of particles could be picked up, the Navy still didn't know enough about space to filter for everything. It was a bit like being back in the WWII days of unfiltered hydrophones. You had to listen to all the noise of the sea, and there was a lot of it, trying to find the sounds of submarines or surface ships. Waves, shrimp, herring farts, they all added up.

In this case, solar wind, the residue of particles from the space battle, the particles generated by the ship. It all added up.

So filtering it out, until they got good algorithms for the system, was still more art than science. Fortunately, the tech was a pretty good artist. And the latest reading was giving him fits.

"Sir, permission to do a visual survey of one-one-seven mark fifteen?" the tech asked.

"Go."

"Can you figure out how to get that off, Machinist Mate?" Bill asked, pointing to the pod.

"I don't know what this is, sir," Sub Dude answered, slapping the wing.

The alien device had been secured behind the sail, held down with ropes and space tape. It was only one of several pieces cluttering the deck but definitely the largest.

"If it's steel, I could cut it off with an acetylene torch," Gants continued, walking around the pod. "I could go get one and try it out if you'd like."

"I don't think that would be a good idea," Bill said. "Oxy-acetylene doesn't work the same in vacuum as it does normally."

"Well, I don't see any screws or bolts, sir," Gants continued. "It looks like it was made of one piece. I'd guess it's some sort of advanced weld. Sort of making the two pieces meld together. Don't know how they did it, but I'd like to know."

"Hopefully, they'll tell us if we're nice enough to them," Bill replied. "COB, we done here?"

"We're done, sir," the COB said.

"Let's get into the ship and—"

"EVA, Conn."

"Go Conn."

"Commander Weaver, what happens if the ship goes into warp with people on the hull?"

"I've actually thought about that one, sir," Bill replied. "The spacetime metric for the warp bubble is a big bunch of tensor math but I think I've figured out that the warped spacetime around—"

"Shortest answer in history, Astro!"

"Should be fine, sir, why?"

"What about normal space drive?"

"That's not so good, sir," Bill said. "There's no surrounding shield so to speak. Anything that gets through, we'll hit. Why, sir?"

"I'm opening up the recovery tube," the CO said. "Get *everyone* into it, right now. We've got Dreen. XO, microgravity, if we open that up under normal they'll all fall."

"Tactical, I've got no feel for size, here," Spectre said, looking at the forward viewscreen. The thing was small, light and fuzzy, only showing because of reflection from the system's sun. "Or distance. How far away is it? How big is it?"

"Unknown, Conn," Tactical replied. "Without either a size or a distance, we can't calculate the other. I'll give you my gut, though, sir. It's *really* big and it's pretty darned far away."

"That's so precise I'm feeling all warm and fuzzy, Tactical!"

"At present it is the best we can do without going active, Conn. Do you want us to go active?"

"Negative," the CO replied. "Not until we've recovered the EVA. EVA, status?"

"Piling in, sir," Bill replied. "Three more to go."

"Tell them to jump it," the CO replied.

"Conn, Tactical, target designate Sierra One appears to be closing our position."

"You mean it's getting bigger on the screen," Spectre said sarcastically. "I'd noticed."

"Range and size still unknown."

"EVA?"

"We're in. Getting down and preparing—"

"Can it, get the soft-suit guys on top, we're going hot. XO, normal space drive, now. Tactical," he continued as weight settled onto him. He could hear in the distance a series of clangs and bangs that was undoubtedly six or seven Wyvern suits falling down a three story shaft. "Go active. Pilot . . ."

He looked over at the astrogation chair and frowned.

"Hell with it," he said. "Get me a view reciprocal to that Dreen ship." When the view changed he walked over and pointed at a star. "Pilot, normal space. Head for that star. Three hundred gravities."

"Three hundred, sir?" the XO asked.

"I don't want them knowing our max accel," the CO replied. "Commander Weaver?"

"Sir?" Weaver said. "We're sort of . . . tangled here. But I got the guys in suits on top."

"Good, but I need you up here on the double," the CO said as the ship began to hum from the drive. "I need to know where I'm going. And even more important, where I'm not going. Tactical, range and size?"

"Range, four light-seconds," Tactical said in a remarkably calm voice. "Size . . . right on eight hundred meters in length, two hundred in breadth and depth."

"That's nearly a klick," the XO said wonderingly. "A third of a mile *long*. I don't even want to think about the tonnage."

"And two football fields wide," the CO pointed out. "As wide as a carrier is long. XO, set rear tubes two and four. Target's signature, silent mode."

"Aye, aye," the XO said. "Set tubes two and four, signature Sierra One, silent mode."

The ardune torps were a combination of antiair missile and

torpedo. They could lie silent until passive detectors found a designated target, then go active, kicking on their rockets and heading for the target.

"Sir, are you sure about that?" Weaver said as he entered the conn. He was panting slightly from the run, still wearing his skinsuit and his hair was askew, but Spectre realized he was glad to see him. "It's unlikely that our systems will be able to successfully engage them."

"I'm aware of that, Commander," the CO said. "And that even an ardune warhead may not scratch that thing. But those are all ifs. We don't know and that's the point. So now we find out. And I'm aware that we're telling them that we only have those to fire. Still, want to find out. It's what we're out here to do."

"Yes, sir," Bill said, opening up his console. "Did you mean to head to Rigel, sir?"

"I'm just glad I'm not pointed at Earth," the CO admitted. "I'm not, right? I don't want to head back to the good guys and tell the Dreen where they are. Right now, I want to find out if these guys can catch us in normal space. If they can, we'll go to warp and see if they can catch us there. I want to stay at arms length, though. Heck, I want to know what arm's length is!"

"Yes, sir," Bill replied. "Right now we're heading at a fairly significant angle from both Earth and the aliens. So you're on target, sir."

"Can we find the aliens again?" the CO asked.

"Yes, sir," Bill replied. "I have a position calculated for them."

"Figure out if that Dreen ship is headed for them as well," the CO said.

"Sir, are we sure it's Dreen?" Bill asked.

"Tubes are set," the XO said. "Launch?"

"Belay," the CO replied, blanching. "No, we're not sure it's Dreen. We can't even get a good look at them from this range. But who else could it be?"

"The battle made a lot of noise, sir," Bill pointed out. "Anyone in the area with an FTL ship. Survivors from our friends they don't know about."

"That's a big ship," the XO argued. "They'd have mentioned it, surely."

"With all due respect, sir," Bill said. "'Surely' means you're not. I'm not saying that they're not Dreen. I'm saying we don't know. I respectfully suggest that we figure out if they're hostile before firing on them. Of course, the only way to know for sure is if they fire on us."

"No," the CO said. "What we do is let them get close enough we can get a good look at them. If they even *look* like Dreen, we'll drop the torps. Tactical, target status?"

"Bearing remains the same, Conn," Tactical said. "Range has increased slightly."

"Pilot, slow to one hundred gravities of acceleration," the CO ordered.

"One hundred gravities, aye, aye."

"How close do we let them get?" the XO asked.

"That is a very good question," the CO admitted. "No more than two light-seconds. Tactical, I need a continuous update on range to target. Pilot, I want a continuous high G random evasion pattern. If they've got a ship-killer laser with this range, we won't see it until it gets here. I want to avoid that."

"Random evasion, aye."

"What haven't I thought of?" the CO asked.

"The Dreen didn't seem to have any technology that fell into the category of magical, sir," Bill replied. "They didn't teleport except through the gates. They didn't seem to be able to read minds. I can't think of anything."

"Space fighters like the Cheerick?" the XO asked.

"Possible," Bill said. "Even likely depending upon their tech. Space fighters require that you have a technology that accelerates a small system faster than a more massive one. If they have that, then space fighters are a possibility. This is all guess-work."

"Conn, Tactical. Target's emission profile is changing. Target bearing seems to be changing. I believe they might have launched something. Separation. Conn, Tactical. Sierra One bearing change. Bearing now one-one-three mark one-seven. New target, designate Sierra Two. Energy profile lower. Bearing constant. Range decreasing."

"Keep me updated on Sierra Two," the CO said. "Send Sierra One data to Astrogation. Weaver, where are they going?"

"Working on that, sir," Bill said. "It will be a minute."

"Conn, Tactical. Sierra Two closing at over one thousand gravities of acceleration. Sierra Two redesignate, Bandit Group One. Count twelve. May be Bandits or Vampires, still unsure."

"Space fighters," the CO said, nodding. "Very high accel."

"Higher than ours, sir," the XO pointed out.

"Yep," the CO replied. "Recalibrate tubes two and four for bandit signatures. Fire on my mark."

"Aye, aye."

"Conn, Tactical, Bandits at three light-seconds and closing."

"Communications," the CO said. "Send them a hail. Standard first contact dits and dashes." He looked over at the XO. "See what they make of that. Astro, Sierra One?"

"Headed on a bearing to intercept our friends," Bill said. "About seven hours to that location at three hundred gravities. Depending upon their system, they may have to slow down or they'll be going *really* fast when they get there. In which case longer."

"Gimme a view of Bandit One," the CO said.

There was barely a shimmer on the viewscreen. The smaller ships were too small at that range to resolve well.

"I wonder how much *fuel* those things have," Spectre mused. "Are they missiles or space fighters? Are they designed to be recovered, in other words, or do they destroy themselves in a wealth of glorious energy release? If we outrun their point of no return, will they turn around and rejoin their carrier or blow up?"

"Knowing the Dreen, they're probably grown, sir," Weaver said. "They could be a bit of both. If they do the mission and have enough fuel to return, they return. If not, they die in space. They're just an organic extrusion of the ship. The way the Dreen work, anything is just an organic extrusion, no more important to them than skin cells flaking off are to us. They may even be consumed upon return rather than, say, refueled, rearmed and refurbished. The ship is probably able to grow more as long as it has the necessary components."

"Space fighters *and* missiles?"

"If they fire something at us they're space fighters," Bill said, shrugging. "If they try to close with us and destroy us they're missiles. We're trying to apply human terms to Dreen. It doesn't always work."

"Conn, Tactical. Emission pulse from Bandit Group One—"

"They're space fighters," the CO said. Before Tactical could finish speaking, beams of actinic blue light flashed through space, all of them missing the rapidly jinking ship. "XO, fire tubes two and four. Wide spread."

"Fire Tubes Two and Four!" the XO ordered. "Wide spread."

The torpedoes were jetted out of the back of the ship under air power, then briefly engaged their spin stabilization and primary boost thrusters to launch themselves away from the ship and the incoming fire.

The ship rocked as both of the ardune torps detonated at under a thousand meters.

"Damage control!" the CO called.

"No reports of damage," the XO replied. "Everything holding."

"Let's not launch any more missiles unless we're *way* away from these guys," Spectre said. "The only thing that saved us was that explosions don't propagate for shit in space. Pilot, engage Warp One. Get us back to three light-seconds separation."

"Warp One, aye," the pilot replied.

"Tactical, keep us up on range."

"Range two point three light-seconds, two point seven, two point nine . . ."

"Drop out of warp," the CO said. "We're going to give this chase another twenty minutes, then head to our friends. I just want to see if we can use up their fuel. Tactical, Sierra One?"

"Continually changing bearing," Tactical replied. "They're headed for somewhere other than us. Bandit group closing again."

"They probably can do this for hours, sir," Bill pointed out. "And we don't know how long the repairs are going to take."

"Agreed," the CO said. "XO, set tubes one and two. Just drop them out this time, though."

"Aye, aye."

"So, Weaver, heard any good ones lately?"

"Did you hear the one about how Dreen get a date, sir?"

"No. How *do* Dreen—?"

"Tubes set," the XO interjected.

"Pilot, when I say launch, go to Warp One for three seconds."

"Warp One three seconds on launch, aye, aye."

"XO . . . launch!"

"Launch tubes one and three!"

"And they didn't blow them up," the CO said as they came out of warp. "Nice to know. Now to see if we can get any of them. Tactical, how long until the bandit group reaches the mines?"

"Seven minutes, Conn."

"So we wait," the CO said, leaning back in his chair and crossing his arms. "So, how *do* Dreen get a date, Astro?"

»   »   »

"Tactical, what's the status on Bandit Group One?"

"Should be closing the mines, Conn," Tactical replied. "They are within their engagement range based on previous engagement. My count says ten seconds and an additional three and a half second light delay. Any second, now . . ."

The space fighters were nearly impossible to pick out on the screen, but the flash wasn't.

"Whoa," Spectre said. "Was that one or two? Did we get them or did they detect them? Tactical?"

"Our systems are still whited out from the detonations, Conn, wait one . . . Conn, Tactical. Two detonations right on the second to intercept time. Bandit Group One now . . . Six . . . No, eight bandits."

"We got four of them," Spectre said, nodding. "That's what I wanted to know. We *can* get them if we're lucky and smart. Very well. Commander Weaver, set a course for our friends and let's hope they can get the repairs done in time."

18

"Good haul," Kond said. "But that's *grapping* bad news about the Dreen, man. Gonna be tighter than a gnat's ass."

Spectre made a killing motion with his hand and looked around the conn.

"Is it just me, or did that get *more* colloquial while we were gone?"

"Let's try to explain that to them at a later date, sir," the XO said.

"Right," the CO replied, pointing at the screen. "How do you want to do this?"

"Bring your ship alongside and we will remove the wing," Kond said. "We have technicians who are familiar with the system."

"XO, bring us alongside."

"Is the squee intact?"

"The engine on the end of the wing?" Spectre replied. "We don't know."

"Having a spare unreality generator would be radical, dude. I sure hope it's working."

"I hope so as well," Spectre said as the *Blade* pulled up beside the larger ship. He made a cutting motion again, indicating that the sound should be turned off, and looked over at the XO. "Marines are on standby?"

"Yes, sir," the XO said, turning his face away from the cameras. "In repel boarder positions. One platoon in armor. SM-9s are hot." With the ship pointed "up" towards the aliens, all Spectre had to do was order "fire" and all four of the missiles would launch across the short distance to the alien ship. It would probably destroy the *Blade*, as well, so it was a penultimate choice. The absolutely last ditch involved the three keys, held by the CO, the XO and the astrogator, that had been inserted into locks and turned. All Spectre had to do was flip up a cover and hit a button and the drive would go critical, causing an explosion equivalent to a nova.

"Keep all the cameras going." He motioned for the communicator to be turned back on. "I'll be honest. We'd like a look at one of your . . . unreality generators. It is a technology we wish to explore."

"Why?" Kond asked. "Yours is far superior. You do not require a squee to enter unreality."

"We didn't get that last squee," Spectre said. "How do you go faster than light?" Only the central monitor was on the view from the alien ship. The rest were trained on the exterior of the alien ship. Aliens in suits and a group of what looked like robots had exited and were approaching the *Blade*, but only heading for the wing behind the sail. Of course, the main hatch to conn was right by it. That was probably a bad move.

"We approach a squee, open it and enter. You seem to create your own squee."

"At a guess something like a wormhole," Bill said, nodding. "But those aren't supposed to be in every system. They're actually supposed to be fairly rare."

"Is this the same system the Dreen use?" Spectre asked.

"Yes," Kond answered. "It is why they're heading here. They wish to use the unreality node to jump to the next star. Unfortunately, as they have been doing for many squee, this battle group is following our trail. We cannot seem to shake them; they're worse than bloodhounds."

"So it can't get unreality node on three tries but it knows what bloodhounds are," Spectre said, shaking his head. The aliens and their robots were working fast. They already had the wing detached and moving across the intervening space. Spectre could back away at any point.

"You did not fear we would try to take over your ship?" Kond asked as the wing was lowered onto his ship.

"You've been awfully friendly so far," Spectre said, trying not to grin. "And so have we. Why cause problems?"

"Because your ship is pimped," Kond replied. "It's fast as a thief and twice as hard to follow. Your tech is so much better than ours, the only reason I allowed this was necessity. I know you can destroy us at your leisure, that you could probably take us over without really trying. I have made preparations against that, but I figure they're pissing in the wind. I thank you for not doing so."

"You might be surprised," Spectre replied dryly. "What we don't have, I'll admit, is that weapon you fired at us. I don't suppose we could borrow it."

"No," Kond said. "It's tied into the deep structure of the ship. But surely your weapons far surpass it."

"Actually, they don't," Spectre said.

"Sir!" the XO snapped.

"Our drive system that you like so much is an artifact we picked up," the CO continued. "This is the only ship we have. Your technology is far in advance of our own. Going to try to take us over and steal it?"

"No," Kond said after a long pause.

"The situation is the reverse of what you thought," Spectre pointed out. "You might be able to take us and get our drive. It would make you fast as a thief and twice as hard to find. Are you sure?"

"Yes," Kond replied. "You have played fairly with us. We shall do the same. On my honor as ship master. Our people try to do all things in honor and fairness. It is our way. You may keep your drive."

"Thank you," Spectre said.

"Besides, I'm sure you have made preparations if I try to take it," Kond added.

"Yes, we have," Spectre said. "But it's why we'd like to look at the unreality generator and your other technologies. Ours are much lower. This ship is great, but we have no others. And our weapons technology is very inferior. If that's in any way shaking your honor, be aware that the drive can be used as a weapon. A suicidal one, but you're not taking this ship or finding out where our homeworld is and any attempt to do so will destroy both of us."

"We understand each other," Kond said. "If we reach our fleet, if we can shake the Dreen, perhaps we can talk."

"Where is this unreality node?" Spectre asked.

"Here," Kond replied. "Where we lie, all dissed up."

"Astro?"

"Not picking up anything unusual, sir," Bill said. "There's a lot of hash from their power systems and ours but as far as I can tell, this is just empty space."

"So we can't even detect these things," the CO said, sighing. "Well, this isn't getting the Dreen beat. What about dropping some mines in here? They have to come here, right? So what about mining it?"

"They will sweep it before they enter," Kond replied. "We will leave some, but only to tick them off. I do not expect them to stop them. They have a seriously pimped ship."

"It's big," Spectre said. "Is that the biggest they have?"

"No," Kond admitted. "There is another, a mind ship. It is much larger, much more pimped. It carries a true Dreen. The task force that follows us is controlled by a squee. There are at least two destroyers and the dreadnought left. There was another dreadnought with a squee commander as well as many lesser ships. They were all destroyed. But the dreadnoughts simply assimilate their organics and continue on. With enough organics, special materials and another squee the dreadnought could even twin."

"I'm not getting the squee."

"One such as you or I who is converted," Kond said patiently.

"A sentient?" Weaver asked, fascinated. "Something that can think for itself?"

"Yes, a sentient," Kond replied. "A thinking being. They can take such a one and make it a thinker for them. They squee him, enter him, make him half Dreen. The only true sentient Dreen are the hive minds. We think so, anyway. We were defeated so swiftly we could find out little about them. Hive minds travel in mind ships, vast beyond belief. But we know that smaller fleets, such as this one, require a converted sentient to control them and make higher decisions. There is such a one on the dreadnought. It may be the squee or the squee or even the squee. There may be other races as well. Those are the three that we have encountered who are converted."

"I wish we could sit down for a face to . . ." Spectre said, then paused, realizing suddenly that diplomacy was not his strong suit.

"I wish I could sound you as well," Kond replied.

"Your system must be getting better," the CO replied. "That was a colloquialism that actually works. Okay, since we still have trouble with scientific and military details, we're going to go survey this oncoming vessel. Given what you've said, we may not be able to attack them, but the reverse is also true as long as we stay in warp."

"You can sense out of unreality?" Kond said. "A most excellent ability."

"When we get to be friends enough, our government will probably show your scientists our drive," Spectre said. "We have one other race we are allied with. They do not understand it either. Perhaps you can figure out some theories on it. But that is for later. And it assumes we all survive. We're going to go recon, find out where they are and find out if we can slow them down. Probably not, but I'd like to give you guys some time. Any suggestions on things that they have trouble with?"

"What is the nature of your weapons?" Kond asked. "If you don't mind."

"Chemically propelled rockets with powerful warheads," Spectre said.

"Those will be of little use," Kond replied. "Their antimissile defenses are strong. They will easily detect them and shoot them down."

"Do they have any sort of shield?" Weaver asked.

"Squee shields," Kond said. "That is effective against squee. It is tight to the hull. Their ships normally mount squee and squee for both defense and offense and fire squee for medium-range attack. They also carry squee for longer-range attacks."

"We lost almost all of that," Spectre said tightly. "Squee shields. How do those work?"

"Electricity is generated and forms a squee shield. It stops squee."

"We're still not getting that squee," Weaver interjected. "What is the last thing? What it stops?"

"Matter that the squee have been stripped from by energy. This creates a high energy material that is the fourth state of matter."

"Plasma," Weaver said, wincing. "That's what we got fired at by. Very high velocity plasma, too. Nearly light speed. Ouch. Those are going to be nasty. And they have shields that . . . Oh, hey, something I understand!"

"You're ahead of me, then," Spectre said. "What is a squee shield?"

"We've actually got that technology, but much lower power," Bill said. "The physics of it is the same as that in a plasma ball that you see in novelty stores. The little purple glow around the interior of the ball protects it the same way. It is called a Debye shield after the scientist who first described it mathematically. DARPA and AFRL and even NASA have been researching uses for it for decades. Certain types of armor-piercing weapons use a jet of plasma to penetrate armor. Notably, RPGs. The Brits developed a sort of static electric charge that could be formed over their armor that disrupts the plasma. For that matter, now that I think about it, Boeing was working on something similar for the space plane. When you do a high-speed reentry, the air forms plasma around you. That's what the space shuttle tiles deflect. We might actually be able to copy their shield technology, if we get the power systems to duplicate it."

"Good to know," Spectre said. "Kond, those longer-range attack, those are what we call fighters? Manned ships? Or missiles?"

"They are creatures that have reactionless drive and medium ranges," Kond said. "They fire squee."

"Lasers are what we pulsed you with to determine the size of the wing," Weaver said. "They are light, a medium level electromagnetic spectrum light that is coherent. Does that help?"

"Lasers," Kond said. "They fire lasers of squee range electromagnetic spectrum. Very high frequency, beyond that of your signal. Also squee. These fire . . . squee at high velocity. What a ship is made of."

"Metal slugs," Weaver said. "A slug driver. Heavy metal? Very dense? How large?"

"Depends on the gun," Kond said. "Very small to quite large."

"Well, let's go do a flyby," Spectre said. "We'll see what works and what doesn't. Probably nothing, but we'll keep trying until we figure *something* out. Kond, good luck. We'll see if we can delay them."

"Perhaps they will choose to pursue you," Kond said. "Good luck as well."

"If they're continuing on the same course and acceleration, they're going to be about three AU in, towards our last position, sir," Weaver said. "Want a bearing?"

"Please," Spectre said. "XO, stand down for the transit, then back to Condition One."

"Aye, aye," the XO replied.

"Pilot, set course. Warp Three. Let's go see what the Dreen are up to."

"Having fun, Miss Moon?" the CO asked as they headed towards the rendezvous.

"Quite a bit," Miriam admitted, looking over her notes.

"Thank you for cracking the communications barrier so fast," Spectre added. "I was surprised how well it all worked."

"Oh, that was mostly their systems, sir," Miriam replied. "I didn't do much."

"Unless I'm much mistaken, they were stuck until you figured out how to rewrite our systems to convert sonar to video," the CO said definitely. "That, right there, was an amazing feat. But I was wondering about the, ahem, nature of the translation."

"Oh, that," Miriam said, dimpling. "Well, when we were leaving I dumped a mass of audio to their communications officer so he could use it to improve the language. Unfortunately, most of it was audio tracks from . . . entertainment programs."

"Oh, God," Spectre groaned. "You sent them a hundred hours of MTV, didn't you?"

"No, sir," Miriam said, wincing. "There was *some* MTV in there, but not that much. But . . . it was all popular entertainment programming. So their translators are now a bit . . . biased to nonformal speech. We're working on it. But 'dude' seems to be a bit hard to write out. In part because it's an accurate translation."

"They call their CO 'dude'?" Spectre asked, grinning.

"More or less," Miriam replied. "The Hexosehr seem to be a highly cooperative species with an almost total lack of formality. In many ways they seem somewhat Japanese; they seem to prize agreement over argument at least within a sub-group. Americans are very different; we are a very contentious society. But they lack the severe formality of the Japanese, which is an artifact of constraining humans to the degree that they do. I could get their communications officer to substitute another term, but the choice is difficult. They have no terms relevant to 'sir' or 'madame.' So calling their captain 'Dude' is a fairly good translation. That's why it's hard to filter out."

"The . . . Hexo . . . ?" the CO asked.

"It's really a made up term, sir," Miriam said, shrugging. "Their name for themselves translates as 'us.' So does 'human' to them. And it's entirely in the inaudible range. Even compressed to where we can hear it it sounds like: Hecsssosssrre. Hexosehr not only refers to their six limbs but is pronounceable by the majority of major linguistic groups. I figure even a TV reporter can't mess it up too badly. I explained the change to their communications officer and he understood. They're having a hard time with both human and Terran. They don't do the hard u or soft e well and t comes out as a click. So they pronounce Terran as !Tran!." The latter sounded like something in Bushman. "They'd probably be better off with Chinese, to tell you the truth."

"Ooookay," Spectre said, his eyes wide. "Hexosehr it is. I didn't realize that you were having so much conversation with their communications officer."

"I was using subvocal most of the time," Miriam admitted. "I realized I can get into inaudible range that way. Low inaudible. Their range is huge, higher *and* lower than ours. I can't do even mid-range low for them, but I can go high. I was trying to speak their language direct, but it still didn't work," she finished with a sigh.

"It's still an impressive achievement," Spectre said. "I'm putting a commendation in your file. I'm glad you're along."

"I'm glad I finally have a job to do," Miriam said. "Although I miss the painting."

"There's always the trip back to look forward to," Spectre replied.

"Conn, Tactical. We're picking up signatures consistent with Sierra One."

"Slow to Warp One," Spectre said, looking at the screen. "Anything on visual yet?"

"There," Weaver said, pointing to the lower right-hand corner. He hit a control and highlighted the item, bringing it to the center of the main screen.

"Pilot, I don't want to hit them," the CO said.

"Closest point of approach looks to be about one light-second," Weaver said. "Right at three hundred thousand kilometers. Resolution will be high at that range. We should be able to resolve down to nearly a centimeter. But we'll be going by fast. We cross one light-second in .00014 seconds. Keeping the cameras on track with us doing a flyby is going to be the hard part. They'll automatically follow their aim point, but we may get quite a bit of jitter."

"Tactical, Conn," Spectre said. "I want full emissions analysis, hull shots, spectral analysis. I want this ship folded, bent and mutilated."

"Conn, Tactical. Understood."

"Come to think of it, though," Weaver said as the range dropped and the picture began to resolve. "That doesn't look like what I'd think a Dreen ship would look like."

The approaching ship was now clearly angular, looking something like a battleship. And it was also, just as clearly, made of metal.

"Conn, Tactical. Target designated Sierra Two. Forward of Sierra One. Its signature was masked. Shifting visual."

The main camera pulled back and panned. The bow of Sierra One was still in view for size comparison. The new ship was ovoid and covered in what appeared to be long spikes. It also was a nasty green and yellow and did not appear to be made of metal.

"Now *that* looks like a Dreen ship," Spectre said. "I'd put it at about a hundred yards long. Could that be our visitor to the colony?"

"Possible, sir," Bill replied. "Same overall length and those spines look as if they could have been the landing spikes we saw. But why all over?"

"Conn, Tactical. Energy spike on Sierras One and Two . . ."

"Pilot, evasive maneuvers," Spectre said as both ships exploded in fire. There were more of the solid silver flashes coming from them and as the camera widened its view, again, small dots could be seen flashing out of the side of Sierra One.

"They just launched fighters," Spectre said, nodding. "Given that we're going faster than light, that's pretty good."

The ships approached fast on the screen, then flashed to the rear, just a blur to the human eye. The cameras panned for a receding shot as the *Blade* thundered back into deep space.

"Let's take a look at what we got," Spectre said. "Pilot, make for the edge of the system. We'll do a partial chill while we analyze this."

»   »   »

"These are two radically different ships," Bill said, looking the images over. "Okay, the Hexosehr generate 'unreality' using those pods all over their ship. I'd guess that the spikes on the Dreen ship are the same thing, just without the pods at the end, for some reason. The other ship is interesting, though."

He brought up a wide image of the ship from the side and zoomed in.

"Spectral analysis of the hull shows it to be steel," Bill said. "I would guess that it's what's called high refractance steel, steel that has been specially treated to be about five times the strength of normal steel. We can only do that with micro-layers at this point. If it's that way all the way through, that's one tough hull. No way of knowing if it's layered like Chobham armor, but that would be a good guess. It may have layers other than steel, that's all we can see on the outside.

"Warp appears to work differently from the Hexosehr or the Dreen," he continued, pointing to a long array on the side of the ship. "This might be part of their tactical system, but my guess is it's their warp system. Their wormhole generator or whatever. But that's just a guess.

"Drive system? Unknown. There's major meson output, low neutrino. I have *no* idea what that means. We don't even understand our *own* drive. But it's definitely reactionless. If we postulate thirty percent inefficiency in the drive, given the output their engines are putting, they generate out about ten to the eighteen joules of energy, which is about the energy budget for Earth."

"Whoooo," the XO whistled. "Those are some *massive* engines."

"They'd have to be to move that monster with any speed," Bill said. "And they don't appear to be quarkium; the signature is all wrong. At a guess, fusion. But that's just a guess. Top acceleration appears to be about three hundred gravities. Which is a very good thing. But getting to this thing . . . Tactical?"

"The ship is a mass of weapons," the TACO said, zooming in. "We've identified forty-seven mass drivers, twenty things we think are laser emitters and fifty-three more we're not sure about. They might be plasma guns. The ship seems to be wrapped around a large opening on the front. No idea what it fires but I'd guess if it hit us we'd be nothing but a mass of smoke. When we were in warp, all of their fire was initially behind us. As we approached, though, and passed, watch this . . ."

He adjusted the controls to show the tactical screens that were tracking fire. As he'd said, the first bursts were well to the rear. Within a second, though, they were blasting all around the wildly jinking ship.

"Analysis and some shots from secondary cameras showed that the plasma fire was hitting us by the time we were passed," the TACO said grimly. "They were able to figure out how to hit us even though we were superluminal and only in their engagement range for less than a second. That's . . . amazing. They were having to anticipate where we were *going*. It's a lot harder than hitting a quail, sir. It's hitting a quail that's always ahead of where you're seeing it. A really really *fast* quail. No wonder missiles don't work on these guys. Unless it was in warp, I don't see how one could. The *good* news is, the fire was ineffective."

"Yeah," Spectre said. "But if we're in warp, we can't fire back. Are we sure it was a Dreen ship?"

"Look at the fighters, sir," Bill said, cutting to another view. Just under the, possibly, warp generator, hatches flew open and pods ejected. They were either the same fighters that had followed them or remarkably similar. With the closer shot it was apparent that they were a brownish-yellow in color and had wings with pods on the tips that glowed purple. There was no apparent cockpit. They banked, hard, to the rear and followed the *Blade* as she receded, but were never able to catch up. Just before she went entirely out of range, they opened fire with plasma from the glowing pods on the end of their wings.

"Emissions were different than those from Sierra One," Weaver continued. "More neutrinos, fewer mesons. Output, again, equivalent to a large nuclear reactor if they're only seventy percent efficient. Love to know their power source. Oh, by the way, they're a bit slower than the dragonflies from Cheerick. I don't know which is more maneuverable. Their plasma guns, though, are stronger than the dragonfly lasers. It would only take a couple of hits to take down the dragonfly shields. But they don't *have* shields according to the Hexosehr. I'd say that a dragonfly could take them one on one. Plasma energy will fall off over distance. The dragonfly should be able to outrun them and stay at range. Close in? That would be tougher. We're still not sure on the cycle time of either the dragonflies or these fighters. It's worth noting that there are thirty ports for fighters on this ship. I'd say it qualifies for the term dreadnought. I doubt there's much it dreads."

"The interesting thing from my point of view is that we detected no tracking emissions," the TACO said. "We still don't have a good algorithm for using the lidars or radar while superluminal, so we weren't pinging them. But they also weren't pinging us. Everything appeared to be passive. I have no idea what that means."

"Radar and lidar are relatively short ranged," Weaver said, shrugging. "I doubt that they're used much in space combat. The Hexosehr didn't ping us, either. I'd say most space combat is more like traditional sub combat; you stay quiet and hope to hit the enemy when he doesn't know where you are. The difference being that ships emit lots of particles. I'm still trying to figure out how that's going to work. Assuming we ever come up with a weapon that will permit us to strike back usefully."

"So we've got nothing useful?" the CO asked angrily. "Lasers, missiles? Nothing?"

"Not that I can think of, sir," Bill admitted. The TACO just shrugged.

"Commander Weaver, what happens if you ram something like that while in warp?" the XO asked. "I'm not suggesting that we do it, mind you . . ."

"The big question is what the *drive* is going to do, sir," Bill admitted. "It has some interesting built-in safety features. My guess is that it will stay in warp while we're in the same space. Which means we won't be; we'll be in another universe. In that case, nothing. If it continues to cycle, it will depend upon where we are when we cycle into this universe. If we cycle in while we're interpenetrated, I would guess one massive damned explosion, sir. And we'd both be dead. Another possibility is interpenetration without explosion. There's a way that I could see the drive doing that. Then we'd cycle out and possibly take some of their mass with us while leaving other behind. Frankly, sir, I really don't have the slightest clue, but those are some of the possibilities."

"So it wouldn't destroy them and not us?" Spectre asked.

"Unlikely," Bill said. "I mean, the drive *might* do it that way, but I doubt it. Most likely, no effect at all. That seems to be the approach of the builders, sir."

"Wait, there's matter all through space," Spectre said, frowning. "I mean, not a lot. But we've covered a lot of ground. Surely we've hit stuff before."

"And there's been no effect," Bill said, nodding. "That's part of my thinking, sir. Admittedly, if we are notionally in the same space as a micrometeorite or an Oort Cloud object, we're probably cycled out. We spend about four times as much time cycled out as cycled in. But we've never picked anything up cycling in. Given the way the ship is built, if the drive was designed to allow interpenetration, by this time we'd have had a micrometeorite punch a hole in something. Its relative velocity would be high enough it would be like a gun being fired in the ship. It would be noticeable. Nothing like that's happened, so my WAG is that there'd be no effect if we flew through this thing. On the other hand, if I'm wrong we'd be an expanding cloud of gas."

"Yeah, let's not try that," Spectre said. "Look, we've got a bunch of smart people on this ship. Figure out a way to hurt that thing. Figure it out."

"Aye, aye, sir," the XO said.

"Do one more flyby," the CO said. "I want shots of every angle. I want all the data we can gather. Then we'll head back to the Hexosehr and see what they say."

"It is a captured ship."

Bill was using the wardroom systems to talk with the Hexosehr tactical officer about their findings.

"Not one of ours," Favarduro continued. "I do not know what species it was captured from. Perhaps the one that supplied the sentient commander, perhaps not."

"And the smaller ship?"

"Pure Dreen," Favarduro said dismissively. "One of what we call the Squee Destroyer class. Plasma cannons larger than fighters, fairly fast. About five hundred of your gravities of acceleration. Faster in real space than we are. But easy enough to destroy with a chaos generator. No match for us. For you? Do not try to take it on in real space."

"Any idea what the major gun on this one is?" Bill asked.

"It is not a class we have fought before," Favarduro said. "I have no idea. It does not appear to be a chaos generator or a plasma cannon. A mass driver perhaps."

"What happens if we manage to take this ship out?" Bill asked. "More Dreen?"

"The nonsentients will return to Dreen space and get orders," Favarduro said. "More may be sent on our trail. But it will be weeks before they return. Our trail will be faded. They may not be able to pick it up. In which case we escape. That assumes there is not another dreadnought out there. And another and another. The Dreen fleet seems endless!"

"How are your repairs going?" Bill asked.

"If your time estimate is accurate, we will be able to escape them, once again." The tonality of the reply was not pleased.

"You'd rather fight them," Bill said.

"I would rather destroy their entire race," Favarduro replied. "Four worlds we occupied. I am from the colony of Squee. I joined the military just before the Dreen encountered us. No negotiation. They simply landed on the colony world of Squee and took it over. We sent ships to battle them. We won the first battle, then their main fleet arrived. Ship after ship after ship appearing through multiple unreality nodes. Thousands, tens of thousands. Our fleet was beaten. No, beaten does not explain it. It was destroyed, vanquished, as if it was not there. They destroyed Dreen ships, in turn, but there were so many of them it was pointless. More came through and more. A few escaped to bring the news. But ships take time to build. We had few warships at the start of the war and were able to make few before the next colony was lost. And always more Dreen and more.

"Then we lost my homeworld. Then they came to Hessserrra. By then it was apparent we could not win. We assembled a fleet of the best of us and our few remaining capital ships. Our best fighters, scientists, technicians, even philosophers. All were put in hibernation, packed into ships in a near panic. The rest of our race remained to fight. Our plan was to destroy each city by nuclear fire rather than have the Dreen consume us. I hate them, Commander Weaver. I hate them in the bitter dregs of my soul. Yes, I would rather stay and fight. But we are the last defense of those entrusted to us. We flee until we must turn. Then we turn, we slow them, and we flee again. Until, like the *Klingoddar* and the *Savaur* and the *Laldrintha*, we are pulled down. Four Chaos Destroyers we were when we left. One remains."

"Well, we're not going to let you go down," Bill promised. "We've got an interesting ship. We'll figure out an interesting solution."

The *Blade* stood off while the *Caurorgorngoth* went into unreality. The pods on the ship began to glow, then flared like lightning, engulfing the entire ship. What happened next was hard to grasp. The ship seemed to fade to a dot but at the same time go away *very* fast.

"XO, run that again," Spectre said, blinking.

Even with the replay slowed down, the effect was the same. Either the ship shrunk to a dot and disappeared or it flew away very fast.

"That's probably what we look like in warp," Bill said. "But that's not the direction they said they were going. I suspect it looks that way from any angle."

"Or he's not going where he said he was going," the XO said.

"Only one way to find out," the CO replied. "Astro?"

"Course laid in, sir."

"XO, let's go find that fleet."

19

"Fleet Master, we are receiving a transmission."

The fleet was thirsty. The massive helium fusion reactors of the ships required enormous quantities of fuel and while any gas giant would do, gathering it was time consuming. But they had three extractor ships working on it full time as the few remaining corvettes watched in trepidation for the Dreen.

"The *Caurorgorngoth*?" Lurca asked hopefully.

"No, Fleet Master," the communications officer said. "An alien race. They are sending over not only sound but also a translation program that they appear to have gotten from the *Caurorgorngoth* as well as a message from Ship Master Kond. Shall I pulse their words?"

"Show me the message from Kond, first."

"Greetings, Fleet Master. If you are receiving this then our new acquaintances have been true to their word. We received damage to our unreality generator in the last battle and with their help have completed repairs and are preparing to enter unreality. These humans are friendly but primitive in their technology. The exception is their ship drive which they claim is an artifact that they found. Having pulsed their other technology, I believe them. Their ship is very fast and very quiet, though, so they have scouted our back-trail. One dreadnought, at least, remains. It will be to the unreality point in forty. With the help of the humans, we will be gone by then. We will meet you at the rendezvous in six hundred kleng. By then, if you're sounding this, the humans will have arrived.

"This is the first potential ally we have found. It is to be hoped they can assist us but their ship is so unbelievably primitive I fear they will be of little use."

"Where are they?" Lurca asked. "Why have we not detected them?"

"We have, now," Fleet Strategy Master Matulain replied. "The Laegr picked up their transmission. But their signature is very low and they are stopped ten scrick away. I think they do not want us to fire upon them."

"Let me see their transmission," Lurca said.

"Greetings, Fleet Master Lurca. I am Ship Master Spectre of the *Sharp Sword*. We are humans, enemy of the Dreen. We have assisted Kond in repairs and now await his arrival as do you. We wish to open communication and friendly relations and to communicate about ways that we might battle our mutual enemy. We also have three survivors from the *Klingoddar*. We are aware that you have minimal supplies and cannot take on extra passengers. But we are in need of experts in technology and advanced battle to assist us in fighting the Dreen. We are wondering if you could wake up some experts and replace them with the passengers we have. We await your response."

"It's taking a while," Spectre said, looking at the viewscreen. They hadn't even gotten a "we got it" reply. The screen just showed a speckle of dots clustered by a Jovian. "What do you think they're doing?"

"Refueling," Weaver replied. "Pulling hydrogen or helium out of the atmosphere to refill their bunkers. And it's a lot for him to assimilate all at once. They'll get back to us."

"The transmission included one of the *Caurorgorngoth*'s security codes," the communications officer said.

"And if they have been taken over by the Dreen, the Dreen could own all their security codes," Matulain pointed out. "This could be a ruse."

"The Dreen used no ruses," Lurca said. "They used naked power. We will take them at their word. We must discuss what we can do to aid them as well. Matulain, you will communicate with them on this. If they can help us shake the Dreen from our tail, that will help much."

"I will wake Scientist Rimmild as well as Combat Master Dugilant," Matulain replied.

"Wake Philosopher Baelak as well," Lurca ordered. "She is a great thinker of the possibility of other races." He looked at Matulain and pinged a note of humor. "And a great pacifist, yes?"

"I did not disagree, Fleet Master," the strategy master replied. "I had long converse with her before she went into sleep. She was already adjusting some of her notions of other races."

"Having whole worlds wiped out will do that," Lurca said. "Communications Technician, open a channel to these humans. Let us talk of peace and war."

The ship the *Blade* was parked by was, if anything, larger than the Dreen dreadnought. But it wasn't a warship; it was a converted bulk freighter packed with Hexosehr in hibernation. Three of whom were headed for the *Blade* as their previous three passengers swarmed across to the freighter.

"So what are we getting?" Spectre asked.

"I'm still trying to parse it out, sir," Commander Weaver replied. "But I think we're getting three experts. A scientist that specializes in defense, one of their premier generals or an academic strategist, I'm not sure on that one, and their expert on dealing with alien races. I'd translate it as a Beltway Bandit, but a good one and I used to *be* one, a general or an admiral, and a diplomat. They're also bringing communication devices so we can talk."

"Can they handle our air?" the CO asked.

"No, but they're bringing respirators."

"Well, I want you and Miss Moon to meet them at the airlock," the CO said. "Oh, hell, I guess I need to get down there, too. And get a platoon of Marines as honor guard."

"Damn, they're funny looking," Himes subvocalized.

Up close, the Hexosehr were covered with purple fur and had, apparently, no eyes. Other than that they looked a bit like oversized otters with hands. They only came up to thigh-height on a human, but were long and sleek.

"Their ships are better than ours," Berg replied. "They've got their own hyperdrive that *they* created, their computers are better than ours and they've been fighting the Dreen for a while. Treat them with respect."

One of the Hexosehr broke off from the greetings, apparently not noticing the astonished expression on the CO's face, and walked along the line of Marines. He stopped at the end and looked up at Lieutenant Monaghan.

"You are the boss man?" the Hexosehr asked. The communicator rendered the sound very high. Berg was reminded of the time the ship got filled with helium.

"I am the platoon leader of First Platoon, Bravo Company," Lieutenant Monaghan said. "The Marine commander is among the greeting party you just left. As is the commander of the ship."

"These are squee or ground fighters?" the Hexosehr asked.

"Ground fighters," Lieutenant Monaghan replied.

"They are experienced in fighting the Dreen?"

"We have two people with experience fighting the Dreen," the platoon leader said, looking over at the greeting party help-lessly. "We have others experienced in fighting other species. We also still fight among ourselves. Most of these, however, are not veterans."

"Show me veteran," the Hexosehr ordered.

"Sergeant Berg, Front and Center!"

Berg stepped out of rank, did a precise right face and marched down to face the Hexosehr.

"Sergeant Eric Bergstresser, reporting as ordered," he snapped, rendering a hand salute.

"What is thing to head?" the Hexosehr asked.

"It is a salute," Lieutenant Monaghan explained. "It is rendered to a superior officer."

"How to tell him to stop?"

"Either I order it or you return it," the lieutenant said. "Are you a fighter. A soldier?"

"I am boss of soldiers," the Hexosehr replied, rendering Berg something like a salute. "You are veteran?"

"I am, sir," Berg replied, dropping his salute sharply.

"What are you called?"

"Sergeant Eric Bergstresser, sir," Berg repeated.

"No, what are you called?" the Hexosehr insisted. "What's your handle?"

"Two-Gun, sir," Berg replied, trying not to roll his eyes.

"What you fight, Two-Gun?"

"I have fought demons on the Cheerick world, sir," Berg replied. "I have fought crabpus. I am one of five survivors from our previous mission, sir. I am the holder of one of our nation's highest awards for combat."

"You fight ships?"

"No, sir," Berg replied. "I am a United States Space Marine. I fight in space, on land and sea. But I fight close up."

"You are proud?"

"Yes, sir! I'm a Marine."

"You are afraid?"

"Yes, sir. Only an idiot isn't, sir."

"But you fight anyway?"

"Yes, sir."

"Because you are Marine?"

"Yes, sir."

"You choose? You volunteer?"

"Yes, sir."

"You'll do. Go back. We talk later."

"Return to ranks, Sergeant Bergstresser," Lieutenant Monaghan said, a note of puzzlement in his voice.

"Excuse me, Scientist Rimmild," Captain Blankemeier said, confused. "What was that in aid of?"

The greetings had paused as the "Combat Master" walked away and braced the Marines. All of the humans were goggling.

"Most Hexosehr are willing to fight once," Philosopher Baelak replied. "Some are willing to fight twice. This Marine, he fights many times. Combat Master Dugilant was interested in the nature of your fighters. He is satisfying his curiosity. You seem surprised that he did this. It is a breach of protocol?"

"We're fighters, ma'am, not diplomats," Spectre replied. They'd gotten the sexes thing straightened out before the visitors arrived. "If he wants to go over and brace one of my Marines, he can brace one of my Marines. But, yes, it was a breach of protocol."

"I will mention this to him," the diplomat said. "What is next?"

"Ma'am, I'm going to turn you over to Miss Moon," the CO said. "She is our linguist but has other talents and knowledge. Commander Weaver is going to interface with Scientist Rimmild and Combat Master Dugilant. Commander Weaver is our astrogator, an engineer and scientist as well as a naval officer."

"What are your restrictions upon our movement?" Philosopher Baelak asked.

"None," the CO said. "If we're going to work together, you need to know what we have to do it. And our systems, with the exception of the drive, are primitive compared to yours. But you may be able to make suggestions or improvements that will aid us in this and other fights. If you can and will. I'll be honest. We want access to your technology. We want to know what you know about the Dreen. In return we will do whatever we can to help you escape and to find you a world to go to. One far enough away from the Dreen that you'll be secure."

"That had better be very far away indeed," Scientist Rimmild interjected. "We have data on their spread. We are willing to share this as well as other things in return for support."

"That's exactly what I'm talking about," Spectre said, nodding. "Thank you. I do not know of your sleep needs. We can only base that on our previous passengers. But we have set up waste elimination facilities, we have some food that they found mildly palatable and a compartment adjusted to your air needs. So I'll let you get to it."

"You are not human," Scientist Rimmild said as the threesome entered the engine room.

"You are very observant," Tchar replied, clacking his beak in humor. "I am Adar. We are allied with the humans. Like the humans, we first encountered the Dreen as invaders through a gate. Then, later, we met the humans. Now we are allied against our common enemy. I am the engineering consultant for the ship's drive system."

"You know, we have enough problem with scientific details," Bill said. "But I just realized, we can't even show you schematics. I'm not sure how to translate our diagrams into something you can sense."

"How does your drive work?" Rimmild asked, walking around the sphere. "I am picking up electromagnetism, but that just supports this ball. And a stream of neutrinos."

"We don't actually know," Bill admitted. "The Adar found the central bit, a small black box, in some ruins. I figured out how to make it work as a drive. But it does things we still don't understand. It drops in and out of superluminal at a very high frequency. The pulses are timed so that light can filter through but that's about all. Nothing that is harmful. It shifts to reaction-less normal space drive with artificial gravity close to our own automatically when we approach a gravity well. When we're deep in the gravity well, it turns off the automatic gravity and inertial compensation. How much of that is part of the theoretical basis and how much is engineering we just don't know."

"Can you fire from within it?" Dugilant asked.

"No," Bill said. "On the other hand, nothing we've run into can get through. We just did a sweep of the main Dreen ship that's pursuing you. It hit us, several times, with plasma fire. No effect."

"That would have been nice to have," Dugilant said. "How fast can you cycle in and out? Is it controllable?"

"About a third of a second to turn it off," Bill replied. "Another third of a second to get it to come on-line. But if you're thinking of flying in and launching, then warping out, it takes longer than that for our systems to launch. As much as five seconds for our major weapon. We have lasers that are faster, but they are relatively weak. I'm not sure they could scratch that dreadnought's armor."

"And your main weapons are chemically propelled rockets?" Rimmild asked, still circling the ball.

"Yes."

"Acceleration?"

"They are fired under low acceleration," Bill said. "Barely two of our gravities. Five seconds after firing their rockets fire. Those have one hundred gravities of acceleration."

"If you came in close and fired, the Dreen would detonate them before the rockets went off," the combat master said.

"They did that with our torpedoes already," Bill said. "At about two light-seconds."

"A squee," Rimmild said, still circling the ball. "If we can power it. What is your power system?"

"Stored ardune," Tchar said. "Quarks. Unique quarks."

"I'm not getting that," Rimmild said. "Unique I got. The other two terms . . . Matter negative to normal?"

"No," Bill said. "Not antimatter. Quarks are the most basic building blocks of matter. Smaller than atoms or protons. The building blocks for matter."

"You keep that in your *ship?*" Rimmild asked. "How much?"

"Over four kilograms," Tchar said, holding up two of his massive fists. "This much."

"I hope you don't land on planets!" Rimmild said.

"Unfortunately, we do," Bill said, wincing. "We're aware of the risks. Ardune, quarkium, is also what we use in our missiles as a warhead."

"All I can say is I'd like you to get this ship as *far* away from our ships as possible!" Rimmild said. "Insane!"

"It's necessity," Bill replied. "We need the power. And you haven't even heard the good part about the drive system . . ."

"You have much knowledge of this ship?" Baelak asked as the linguist led her forward.

"When we were on our way out here I spent time working on it," Miriam said. "I was bored so I worked with the technical crews that maintain it. At this point, yes, I have *much* knowledge of this ship. Every bolt, every rivet as they say."

"This seems . . ." Baelak had stopped and was running her hand down a pipe.

"That's a waste pipe," Miriam said. "You can't see the coding on it but it tells the engineers what it's carrying and which way it's going. You were going to say 'primitive' I think."

"How it is joined," Baelak said, running her hands over a joint. "I am not a technician as you are . . ."

"I saw the unreality generator wing," Miriam said. "We join material, this type, by melting metal into the joints. It's called welding."

"We join metal to metal," Baelak said, taking her hand away from the pipe. "I know of welding. It is a technology . . . we rarely use anymore."

"And we're very interested in learning how you join metals," Miriam said.

"I don't actually know," Baelak admitted.

"Well, when we get you settled perhaps your scientists can explain it to ours," Miriam said. "What else do you want to see?"

"These humans are insane," Rimmild said, stripping off the hated respirator. "Insane."

"The linguist is certainly . . . interesting," Baelak said. "And very knowledgeable. She even works as a technologist in the ship, which I'll admit I cannot do."

"Oh, they are all knowledgeable," Rimmild said. "Of their paltry technology. *Chemical* rockets. What good are *those* going to do?"

"They are willing to go into space with that paltry technology," Dugilant said. "They know that they are practically unarmed. Yet they are trying to find out how to help *us.*"

"Because they want our technology," Rimmild said.

"There is more," Baelak said. "They have many cultures on their planet, as we once did. The culture that has created this paltry technology is . . . very giving. It can be found most strongly in the linguist. They see people who need help and try to help them, often to their detriment. I have also been accessing their information net. Primitive, yes, but functional. I hope that we make it to this Earth. It seems a very vital place."

"They do battle," Dugilant said approvingly. "Even the culture that this ship comes from, yes? This is a battle ship. Although for under water, which I find surprising and somewhat amusing."

"Yes," Baelak said, with a note of distaste. "It was created by a tribe called the Americans. They are more giving, and more battling, than any other culture on their planet. It is a strange dichotomy. We only began to explore it."

"Rimmild, you spoke of a chaos generator," Dugilant said. "You said, if they can power it. They are enormous and require more power than I think this ship can generate."

"Are you sure they are not listening?" Rimmild asked.

"No," Dugilant said. "But I also don't care. Nor should you. The Dreen are practically on our backs and clawing. The *Caurorgorngoth* is our last Chaos Destroyer and it is badly damaged. Who knows if it will survive another battle. If the humans can not help us, we are assuredly doomed. So tell me what you were talking about."

"There is an experimental model," Rimmild said. "We have one prototype with us. It was never put into production because it has less range than plasma guns. But it's much more powerful. And the energy budget is lower. But I'm still not sure it would be effective. They would have to warp in quite close, fire, then warp out. As fast as they are going in warp, differentials, their primitive systems, no armor to speak of . . ."

"Get me the weapon," Dugilant replied. "Figure out how to install it. Find a place for a fusion reactor if you must. That is *your* job. *My* job is to figure out how to use it."

20

"Fleet Master, incoming transmission from the *Caurorgorngoth*. They are still fifteen treek out so there is a significant lag."

"Glad news anyway," Lurca said. "Put it on."

"Fleet Master Lurca, Ship Master Kond," Kond said. "If you have encountered the humans, then you have most of our news. The *Klingoddar* was destroyed, we ran into fighters before our transit and sustained damage to our unreality generator. Another race, the humans, helped us to repair it. The only news is that we began to pick up emissions from a Dreen ship before we translated. It was one of their destroyers. It is likely that it will be right behind us. We are moving towards the fleet rendezvous but request a collier be sent to us so we can stand off and engage the destroyer away from the fleet."

"We'll need to dispatch corvettes or the destroyer will be able to go around him to us," Matulain said.

"As you advise, Strategy Master," Lurca said. "Kond, we are sending a collier and corvettes to protect your flank. We are in contact with the humans. We are trying to see what we can trade with them. They are eager but primitive. However, we have received all the intelligence they sent us. Be aware, our estimates are that we will be unable to avoid the Dreen this time. We simply have to refuel; if the dreadnought stays on schedule we will still only be halfway done. You may have to hold them off as the fleet escapes, may have to hold them for kleng. We will do whatever we can to improve the human ship so that it will be able to assist you. When you are close enough, we will set up a joint conference. There is much to discuss."

"We have a weapon you might be able to use," Rimmild said.

The humans and Hexosehr had gathered in the science section meeting room. It was larger than the wardroom and had better communications equipment.

"It is an experimental small chaos generator," Rimmild continued. "It only has a range of less than one of your light-seconds. But its effects would be better than even one of your ardune warheads. A chaos ball creates chaotic quantum events in any matter it touches. Since the matter tends to disintegrate, even detonate, when it comes into contact with the chaos ball, the weapon continues in a straight course until the effect dissipates. On smaller ships, such as the Dreen destroyers, a ball generated by a destroyer will often go entirely through them."

"Ouch," Spectre said.

"This system is, of course, smaller," Rimmild said. "It will create a half-meter hole in whatever it strikes and will probably only penetrate a deck or two. It will not destroy them in one shot."

"An ardune warhead will do more than that," Bill pointed out.

"Only in contact," Dugilant replied. "If there is even a few tens of meters separation, the vessel is likely to fly through unscathed. Dreen armor is immensely tough and the armor on the new ship looks to be as good as one of our own Chaos Destroyers. Those would shrug off your weapon unless it was in contact. And, frankly, getting any physical weapon through the defenses of Dreen ships is unlikely, absent an enormous number of much faster missiles. However, there is no way to shoot down a chaos ball. Light is transmuted, slugs are absorbed and rendered. This is the power of a chaos ball. Once fired it is impossible to escape damage unless you evade it."

"And there may be a way for you to use it," Dugilant continued. "But it will require precision piloting, probably computerized, and nerves of steel. All ships are designed to intercept weapons a long way out . . ."

"Come in *really* close," Weaver said. "Really *really* close."

"Yes," Dugilant said. "Use the power of your most excellent drive system. Exit warp, fire the ball, then go back into warp. I would recommend that the systems be interlocked. You will also need to match course and speed with the target before you attempt your intercept. Even if some shots miss, if you repeat over and over . . ."

"They were hitting us even in warp," the XO pointed out. "I suppose if we use evasive maneuvering . . . I'm worried about their fighters. That gives them a whole other vector of fire."

"Fighter sweeps to start," the CO said. "We'll go in and taunt them out. Then use the chaos ball or missiles to take them out one by one. Or two by two or six by six, I don't care."

"What about their destroyer?" the XO asked. "That's capable of taking us out in normal space."

"You will not be fighting alone," Dugilant said. "The *Cauror-gorngoth* and our corvettes will be fighting with you as well. If we can lure the destroyer away, it may be that you can test the system on the destroyer. The entry point for this system is on the far side of the sun. They will exit there, a few hours behind the *Caurorgorngoth*. Then it will take them nearly one of your days to reach this position. We have that long to stop them."

"You forgot to add installing the system," Spectre said dryly.

"You forget that we have many hands to do that," Dugilant said. "Already, our finest technicians and scientists are being awakened. We will install it on your hull along with a generator to run it. If you return to your planet, whatever the outcome of this battle, you may keep both. Good luck understanding the technology if we don't survive."

"Good point," Spectre said with a chuckle. "I have to ask, did you mean for that to be dry humor?"

"Yes," Dugilant said. "I'm glad you got the point."

"I have been examining the information you have on planets," Baelak said. "You have been very free with information."

"We're trying like hell to be friendly," the CO said.

"Yes, but did you realize that the location of your home planet was on your open system?"

"No," Spectre said, swallowing. "It is?"

"You have astronomical data on various stars," Baelak said. "I was unsure, but I had Rimmild take a look at it. He found it very easy to backtrack the information and its general location in relation to other stars was on another file. By matching the information about the stars in one file with that it was very easy to find. If the Dreen were to find this information . . ."

"I get the point," the CO said, shaking his head. "We'll look into it."

"However, there is information on some other planets," Baelak said. "That, too, was helpful. Although it will take us nearly two years to reach it, I think the planet called Runner's World would suit us."

"Well, yeah," the CO said, wincing. "Except for the crabpus. *Don't* go near the water."

"We appreciate the warning," Baelak said. "I saw the report on your previous mission and regret your many losses. However, we can deal with the fauna. The air is not perfect for us but it is close enough and we can terraform the soil to grow our foods. It is not ideal but it is good enough."

"I'm sure that everyone will agree you're welcome to it," Spectre said. "When do we get this chaos generator?"

"Our technicians are being woken up right now," Rimmild said. "Give them some time to get things explained to them then they will get to work. If you permit it?"

The CO sat back and thought about that for a second. So far, relations with the Hexosehr had been too good to be true. Admittedly, they were in a cleft fork. But the Dreen had tricked humans once. This could simply be a more elaborate ruse.

The flip side to that was that the Hexosehr could have tried to take the *Blade* several times. Yes, he'd prepared against it, but they could have. Doing an installation only raised the ante slightly. And the chance to get a weapon that was slightly more than the popguns they currently had—

"Engineer?"

"Sir?"

"Make sure that the mount is somewhere that's not going to be an issue. Then get on it."

"Yes, sir."

"We have one more piece of information that you need," Baelak said. "I have discussed this with Fleet Master Lurca and he is in agreement that you should be told. We were able to gather information, as part of our intelligence gathering process, on Dreen spread before the final Fall. We think we have a fairly accurate estimation of their rate of spread, methods and probable direction."

"Okay," Spectre said, leaning back.

"The Dreen spread through two methods," Rimmild said, picking up the thread. "The first is sub-light. They create pods which in turn deploy a solar sail and move towards distant stars. This, of course, takes decades or centuries but it is most thorough. They appear to have a database of some sort of all targeted stars. The pods are generated on captured worlds, yes, but also sometimes in portions of space which simply have a large abundance of stellar or semi-stellar carbon."

"I don't get that one," Spectre admitted.

"Jovians," Weaver said, shrugging. "There are some clusters of leftover bits scattered around which appear, from spectral data, to have up to low-volatile organics floating in some concentration in deep space. Big area around Vega, for example. I take it that's what you're discussing, Rimmild?"

"Yes, exactly," the Hexosehr said. "But we believe that this is a legacy method. The Dreen may have begun their initial spread through sub-light but at this point they are primarily spreading through FTL means. And their rate of spread is increasing as they absorb more worlds."

"You humans have a term," Combat Master Dugilant said. "'The bottom line.' What my colleagues are having a hard time saying is that based upon Baelak's location of your home planet and our analysis, the Dreen will arrive there in between twelve and eighteen of your years. The best estimate is fifteen. You humans have that long to prepare. And you have no chance to survive without our technology and the technicians that exist in our refugee fleet."

"I'll admit that's a hell of an incentive to help you guys out," Spectre said calmly.

"The Philosopher of War Faet said it best: Alliances are based upon mutual need, not love," Dugilant replied. "We need succor, you need our technology and technicians. Let us both hope for the best outcome to our forthcoming battles."

"Whatcha doing?" Miriam asked.

Weaver had moved to the more-or-less deserted science department. There were just more flexible computers there. He was currently working on doing modifications to the astronomy mainframe.

"Working on a model for the attacks," he said. "From our previous run we got a lot of data. Cycle time of their guns, accuracy of their guns, a feel for how their sensors work. I had a program for combat modeling on my laptop but it couldn't crunch the numbers fast enough for me. So I'm loading it into this system and now I'm inputting the parameters. I don't like the response."

"Why?" Miriam asked.

"The only way this is going to work is if we start from outside their sensor envelope, come in very fast, probably at Warp Four, drop out of warp, fire almost simultaneously, and go back into warp again. The range on the weapon means that *lightspeed* in the control runs is going to matter. Their tracking and engagement time is just unreal. And we're going to be out of warp for a minimum of a half a second, plus. Firing, during that phase, will bump that to nearly a second, possibly more. It's more than just the transmission of the orders. There are information gates that are going to have to be sorted through. That's enough time, based on previous information, that their plasma guns could get in a shot at that range. And one solid hit from those things and we're toast."

"Cut down the information lag," Miriam said.

"How?" Bill asked.

"Set up the decision-making processors closer to each other," Miriam replied. "Move the central node closer to the line between the drive and the chaos generator. By the way, has anyone asked if the chaos generator is going to *interfere* with the drive?"

"Urk," Bill replied, grimacing. "That's a *very* good question. And, no, nobody has. It's going to have to be cycled up to fire while we're still in warp. I have no idea if there are secondary effects from that."

"Just an interesting thought," Miriam said.

"We're *definitely* going to have to test this thing."

"Come," the CO said, looking up from his paperwork.

Deep space mission or no deep space mission, in the middle of a situation or not, there was always paperwork. Some of it could probably wait for the trip home, but he hated to see it build up. Hell, there was going to be more paperwork from the new installation.

"I've got Hexosehr crawling all over the hull but I've brought up a, I think, valid point," the engineering officer said. "This generator isn't designed to go under water. We install it on the hull and we'll have to land in Dreamland to have it deinstalled."

"I'm sure they're going to want to get their hands on it, anyway," Spectre said. Dreamland was a part of a sprawling military reservation, an area referred to by some, incorrectly, as Area 51. Since it was a highly secure area, once you got away from the fringe areas where the nutballs hung out looking for, well, the *Blade*, it was where the main R&D facility for Space Command had been installed and their secondary base after Norfolk.

"All well and good, sir, but we've got to land with it. But I've been looking at the thing, sir. It's not all that big, actually. Nor is the fusion generator they're installing with it. I think it would fit in one of the tubes."

"So you want to jettison one of the missiles and put it in there?" the CO asked. "Fine by me."

"I'll see if we can," the engineer said. "Thank you, sir."

"Just get me an operational weapon, Eng. I don't care if it's installed in the wardroom."

"So that's the new super weapon," Himes said. "Doesn't look like much."

The chaos ball generator was a squat cylinder, less than two meters high, with a bulbous end that made it look vaguely obscene. A group of Hexosehr were fussing around it and the similarly shaped generator it had arrived with.

"What's it do again?" Smith asked.

"Shoots chaos balls," Berg said. "I have no *clue* what that means."

"So we've got something that looks like a gongoran that shoots flaming balls?" Himes said. "And we're named the ASS. This is just getting worse and worse."

"And *why* are we out here?" Smith asked. "I mean, it's not like we're going to be turning a wrench or anything."

"Because we're about to pop a missile out," Berg said. "At which point, somebody has to secure the warhead. Who secures nuclear warheads, Lance Corporal Smith?"

"Marines," Smith said glumly. "I'm just getting tired of standing around on the hull all the time."

"Would you rather be in your bunk?"

"Come to think of it, yes!"

"Here we go."

The missile was not being fired out but carefully lifted by a team of missile techs. It was only possible because the ship had gone to microgravity and they still had to do it slowly.

Once free of the tube the missile was slowly rotated onto its side and secured to the hull. Then the missile techs removed the warhead itself from the terminal stage. Last, the missile was unceremoniously pushed off the hull and into space.

"Seems like a hell of a waste," Himes said. "One of those things runs a few million I'm sure."

"Fifty-three," Berg said. "But what are we going to do? Strap it to the hull to take home?"

"We've got all this other junk," Himes pointed out. "Why not?"

"The junk isn't explosive?"

"The *warhead* is," Smith said as the missile techs approached. "And we've got to get it down to the armory. Does anyone *else* get a pucker factor from that?"

"The warhead is filled with quarkium," Berg said. "Which pound for pound is more expensive than diamonds and can also be used to fuel the ship. And we might find a use for it. The missile . . . don't think it will be much use. Last but not least, those are our orders."

"You know, Two-Gun, sometimes you're just too gung-ho for your own good," Himes said as he took one handle of the carrier the warhead was secured to.

"Be careful with that thing," Berg said. "And there is no such thing as too gung-ho."

"Any word from the *Caurorgorngoth*," the CO asked as he entered the conn.

"Negative, sir," the XO replied. "At least nothing we've gotten from the Hexosehr."

"Unless my eyes deceive me, the Dreen are overdue," Spectre said, sitting down in his chair and accepting a cup of coffee from the COB.

"Yes, sir," the XO replied.

"Status on our installation?"

"Doing the final fitting of the system, sir," the XO said. "I went down to watch. It's really rather fascinating."

"That is so cool," Miriam said.

She was in armor, floating just off the hull and looking down into the missile tube.

The team of four Hexosehr doing the installation of the chaos generator were attaching it to the side of the tube. The ceramic sheath on the interior had been removed and they were welding the weapon to the bare metal sides of the tube. Welding, though, wasn't the right term. *Melding* was the term. A circular fitting had first been melded to the exterior of the generator and it was that which was blending, seamlessly, to the steel of the launch tube. The device they were using looked something like an oversized soldering iron. How it was making the two metals blend was, to Miriam, a mystery. And she had more than a casual understanding of metallurgy, having worked in the steel industry for a couple of years.

"How does it work?" she asked.

"I truly do not know," Baelak replied. "You'd have to ask Rimmild."

"I will," Miriam said. "I will. That, right there, is a really important advancement we could use. There are thousands of applications."

"That I realize," Baelak replied. "Are you going to remain on the ship when they go to battle?"

"Of course," Miriam said.

"You realize that . . ."

"I've been in a couple of battles before," Miriam replied. "I know that they're no fun. But where else would I go? Your ships are full and don't have any of my needs. Besides, I've learned enough of the ship's systems that I might be able to help if there is damage."

"May the others stay as well?" Baelak asked. "Rimmild and Dugilant? They may be of use."

"I don't see why not," Miriam replied. "What about you?"

"If you fail in this battle," Baelak replied, "if the *Caurorgorngoth* is lost as well, then the Dreen will finally take us. I would much prefer to be in sleep and never know our fates."

"You know, just when I think we're similar as a species, I realize we're not," Miriam said. "That is a decidedly unhuman approach. We always want to know what is happening, right up to the point of death. In part, I'd guess, because we are so good at denial. Right up to the point of death we believe it can't really be happening."

"The Hexosehr are not that way," Baelak said. "We see reality very clearly and do not deny it. We may disagree on certain points, but we still see reality. It is only how to deal with it about which we disagree."

"And what reality do you see of this battle?" Miriam asked, engaging her suit jets to right herself as the Hexosehr finished the installation.

"That it is probably futile," Baelak said. "This weapon will barely scratch the dreadnought. It may be better against the destroyer, but not much. And if your captain attacks again and again, as will be necessary, sooner or later the Dreen will get a shot through and then you will be destroyed. If we make it, we will bring words of your courage to your planet. But the reality that I see is that I would rather die, unknowing, in deep sleep than watch the final dissolution of my race."

21

"Okay, let's go try this thing out," Spectre said, rubbing his hands. "Commander Weaver, I hope you have a convenient target? Any handy asteroids?"

"Well, sir, like any Jovian, this one has moons," Bill said. "There are a couple of small ones. Does that work?"

"Gimme a course," the CO replied.

"That's a moon?" Spectre asked, looking at the lump of rock.

"Actually, sir, it technically counts as an asteroid that's been captured by the gravity well of the Jovian," Bill replied. "For it to be a moon, it has to have sufficient internal gravity to assume a circular shape."

"So you *did* find me an asteroid," the CO said. "Good job. Tactical, you have the target in sight?"

"Conn, Tactical, we are tracking the target designated Sierra Four."

"Open tube doors and fire," Spectre said.

What fired was a ball of white light that receded faster than the eye could track. But it was apparent from the streak on everyone's eyeballs that it had missed the conveniently close and extremely nonmaneuvering moon, asteroid, space junk.

"You missed, Tactical," the CO said.

"We're adjusting our targeting computers now, sir," Tactical replied. "Be just a moment."

"The Dreen target's a lot bigger, sir," Bill pointed out. "That thing's barely the size of their destroyer."

"We're going to be shooting from much farther away," the CO pointed out.

"Maybe, maybe not, sir," Bill said, wincing.

"I think I'm not going to like this explanation," the CO said. "But give it to me anyway."

"Sir, we're going to be trying to come out of warp at a very fixed point," Bill said. "But even using a computerized system, a fraction of a second's variation means we could be well outside the weapon's range or . . . well inside. Really *really* inside. I've been looking at how precise our warp system is, from that POV, and it's not really all that precise. It can get us consistently within a half light-second of our preferred position, but . . ."

"The range on this thing is a third of a light-second," the CO said. "We could end up on the other side of the target, firing the wrong way. Or outside the envelope."

"Yes, sir," Bill said. "The needs of this mission are approaching the noise in our own ship systems. And that assumes we can get it aimed at all."

"Conn, Tactical. We think we got the glitch worked out."

"Try it again, Tactical," Spectre said. "Turn that thing into dust."

Again the ball of light, like a streak of lightning. This time, though . . .

"Whoa," the CO said, blinking his eyes. The impact of the chaos ball had been extremely bright and the asteroid was now two chunks drifting away from each other. "I *like* it. Right, Weaver, find us a bigger target and let's try this warpy thing."

"CO has control," Spectre said. "Matching target course and velocity?"

"As closely as I can figure from these instruments, sir," Weaver replied.

"Right," Spectre said, moving the reticle onto the larger asteroid. This one was, in fact, larger than the Dreen warship. "What's the chance we're going to come out of warp inside it?"

"About a million to one, sir," Bill said. "You want the details?"

"No, million to one sounds good," Spectre replied. "Prepare for engagement." He took a deep breath and pressed the button on the joystick.

They had started at five light-seconds out, the farthest that they could detect the target with their systems. But at Warp Four, that distance took less than milliseconds to cross. There was a confusing blur, a flash of light and they were looking at space again as the system automatically warped them to a preselected safe point.

"What just happened?" the CO asked. "Did we hit it?"

"Looking for it, Conn," Tactical replied. "Found the target. Negative impact, Conn."

"Replay that at slow speed," Spectre said.

With the video at one-one hundredth speed, it was apparent that the ship had come out of warp at outside the range of the weapon. The effect of the chaos ball was impossible to determine because they had warped back out before it even reached the target.

"The good news is, they *probably* wouldn't have been able to hit us, sir," Bill said. "Based on my models, about a one in a thousand chance."

"And we didn't hit them, Commander Weaver," the CO pointed out. "Any way to tweak this system? Get us a bit more likely to get closer? Get us a bit more accurate? Get rid of some of the noise?"

"I can work on it, sir," Bill said. "But we're getting short on time. It's more a matter of fine tuning the warp drive and that's problematic from any number of perspectives."

"That assumes that the Dreen ever show up," Spectre said. "I'm starting to feel like a prom date that's been stood up. Where *are* they? But as long as it doesn't break the system, take some time to tweak. Get Miss Moon in on it if you need her. Get that Hexosehr scientist in on it. Hell, get Tchar if you can drag him out of his room. Maybe he has a Ronco gadget that will help. I'm going to go do paperwork until you get this thing working. And call the *Caurorgorngoth* and find out where the *Dreen* are!"

"I face the reality that is before me," Kond said, examining the sonar taste of the unreality node. "The longer the Dreen fail to emerge, the more ready the fleet is to leave. This is a good thing. But they could only have delayed to take an action I cannot anticipate. This is a bad thing. Have they translated to another system to use a node we do not suspect? Surely they would not take the time. Surely they fear us less than that. But

John Ringo & Travis S. Taylor

why have they stopped? Are they damaged? Were they, too, unable to generate unreality? I sit upon the crux of a decision not of my control and it is upsetting to my psyche."

"What is upsetting to my psyche is that I realize the humans have a weapon more effective for this than we," Favarduro interjected. "We are not so insane as to carry quarkium in our ships. Their missiles are more powerful than anything we fire save the chaos ball generator."

"But too short ranged to do any good," Kond said.

"Except when a ship is coming out of unreality," Favarduro replied. "We have laid mines, but they are paltry compared to a large quarkium release. And if placed in the node, they would be in contact on emergence."

"I need to call the *Sharp Sword*," Kond said.

"So they think our weapons *can* actually make a difference?" Spectre said. "Set a course for this unreality node. Let's lay down some mines."

"We're working on tweaking the precision of the warp drive, sir," the XO reminded him. "I'm not sure it's up at the moment."

"Get it up," the CO said. "We've got a mission that actually works."

"The drives of the missiles are not designed to be parked in precise locations in space, sir," the XO added. "We're probably going to have to manually adjust them."

"Get a party of Marines," the CO said. "They can handle it."

"Okay, I'll admit that we should have been using these things when we were gathering space bits," Powell said. "My bad."

"I didn't even know we were carrying Cheerick boards, Top," Berg replied, looking over the boards.

The Cheerick antigravity surfboards, like the biological defenses of their planet, were the product of either ancient Cheerick who were light-years ahead of both humans and present day Cheerick in technology or, possibly, an older alien race. Nobody was quite sure. But the result was a marvel, a gold-colored board that looked not unlike a finless surfboard that was capable of reactionless flight and had, apparently, unlimited range. It sensed the desires of the rider, seemingly by telepathy, and went wherever the rider wished, even into space.

Where they were created was still a mystery; they simply turned up scattered across the planet, one or two a year in any given area. Since they lasted, as far as anyone could determine, forever, the Cheerick had built up quite a supply of them over time. In the country that was the humans' primary ally on the planet, they were a royal monopoly. The queen of the country, grateful for the aid the humans had given in saving her country, had turned over thirty of the boards to the *Blade* before it left. Most were being carefully taken apart in Area 51. But nine had been sent with the *Blade*.

"They're jettisoning the remaining SM-9s right now," First Sergeant Powell continued. "As well as six torps. We'll take all nine of the systems in tow and pull them over to the unreality node. So as soon as the Dreen come through, they'll be sitting right on them."

"That's going to be a nice Christmas present," Gunny Neely said with a chuckle.

"There's one little ugly fillip," the first sergeant said. "We don't actually know when the Dreen are going to come through. If they come through while we're doing this evolution, it's going to get ugly. So work fast. And this is probably pissing in the wind, but just in case you *do* end up on top of a Dreen ship, you're going armed."

"Understood, First Sergeant," the gunny replied.

"First Platoon is going to be in charge of placement," Top added. "Since there are only nine boards, the guys placing them are going to have to use them. That means the teams and their leaders. Gunny, you'll manage the action from the deck."

"Understood," Gunny Neely said.

"Get suited up and head topside. Two-Gun, I think you better get your guns."

"These things really work as advertised?" Smith asked, looking at the board askance. They'd carried them up to the top deck and now had to mount them in microgravity.

"I've only ever used them more or less in air," Berg replied, using his suit jets to lower himself onto the board. It felt rock solid, though. He disengaged the suit jets and thought about moving forward. The board moved out, his boots attached to it by a still poorly understood "sticky" effect that was suspected to be some sort of tractor field.

"But they work just fine," he added, swinging around. "Hop on."

The Marines, now that the one guy with experience using the boards was satisfied, jetted onto the boards and then started flying around.

"Watch yourselves," Berg cautioned. "Don't run into each other."

"This is fun," Himes caroled, scooting by. "Why didn't we break these out to pick up debris?"

"For once, Top forgot to think outside the box," Berg said. "Now get in formation and settle down. The missiles are coming out."

Once again, the missile techs from the sub hoisted the missiles slowly up into space. But this time, the Marines took over from there. After much discussion, the only thing that anyone could decide was to "lasso" the missiles with ropes and pull them into place.

Berg attached the standing end of a rope to "his" missile, Tube Two, and then used the board to slowly circle it, paying out the rope so that it didn't cause the missile to twist along with him. Once he'd circled it he made a slip knot and cinched it down.

"Everybody ready?" he asked.

"It's spinning," Himes said.

"I told you to pay out the rope," Berg replied disgustedly. "Just stop where you are. It'll unreel, then come back around to your position. Tie it off, then. Smith?"

"Got it tied," the lance corporal replied.

By the time Berg got to the nose of the ship, he could see where the unreality node must be. The rest of the platoon was clustered in the area, emplacing a circle of torpedoes.

"Where's the other missile?" Staff Sergeant Hinchcliffe asked.

"Himes had problems getting it tied off," Berg replied. "He'll be over."

"Slow down now," Hinchcliffe warned. "These things tend to get away from you. And yours is about ten times bigger than the torps."

Berg had been thinking about that exact problem. So he slowly uncinched the rope and thought about slowing. The missile continued on its way, slipping through the rope. At the end of the missile were four control vanes, extended now that it was out of its launch tube. Berg cinched the rope down just before the vanes and wrapped the rope around the back of his armor. The free end had drifted forward as he slowed and as the rope went taut he carefully belayed it through his glove claws, slowing it as fast as he dared.

"I think it's going to get away from me," Berg admitted. He wasn't concentrating on the board but as he clamped down on the rope, the board adjusted its relative motion to the ship, "stopping" in space. The combination of clamping down on the rope and being "stuck" to the board meant that all the energy of the multiton missile was suddenly transferred to his suit.

"Whoa, *chither!*" Berg snapped as his suit bent forward. He could hear joints straining but none of his seals popped, thank God.

The rope, though, had flex in it. Thus the missile "stopped" but then rebounded, twisting in space towards his board.

"Whoa, doggie," Berg said, flying down and around the missile, then getting in position to move it from the rear. "This thing ain't easy to move around."

"Vote, Wagner, get the nose under control," Hinchcliffe ordered.

With the help of the other two Marines, Berg managed to get the missile aligned on the unreality node just as Smith and Himes arrived. They, too, had trouble slowing the missile but with the spatial mechanics better understood the group of Marines was able to get them aligned in a few minutes.

"Right, we're good here," Hinchcliffe said. "Let's get back to the—"

"MARINE UNITS! SCATTER! INCOMING DREEN!"

"Conn, Tactical. We've got a *big* neutrino pulse coming from the unreality node!"

"Tell the Marines to scatter," Spectre ordered. "We'll recover them later. Pilot, Warp One. Mark Ninety. Straight up. NOW!"

"Himes, Smith, follow me!" Berg snapped, picking a star at random and thinking *Head for that star*, as hard as he could. He realized after a moment that he didn't *know* if the board had warp capability. It might have been made by the same species that made the warp drive. But it seemed to be in normal space. Unfortunately. Because when that Dreen ship came through, the local area was going to be *very* unpleasant.

"Oh, *chither*, oh, *chither*," Smith was muttering over and over again.

"Patron of Marines protect us," was Himes' mantra.

Aware that he had no feel for distance, Berg spun his sensor pods, looking for the mines and missiles. When he found them, he couldn't figure out if they were far enough away or not, but he also realized he didn't want his sensor pods trained on them.

He also noticed that the ship was just flat gone.

"Hold it up," Berg said, raising a hand. As he did, there was a flash that lit the metal glove as if were the heart of a sun. "I hope like hell this is far enough."

"Pretty," Spectre said, looking at the transmission. The belly camera was out but the ship had gotten just enough of a look to tell that they'd gotten *something*. "Tactical, Conn. Any clue what we got?"

"No clue, Conn," Tactical admitted. "Whatever it was wasn't there long enough for us to get a good emissions lock before it went up. But it's also gone."

"Send a query to the *Caurorgorngoth*," the CO said. "Maybe they can tell."

"Two-Gun, make for the *Blade* . . ."

"Staff Sergeant," Berg said on the leadership channel. "The ship is gone. It went into warp. We're out here on our own. And we're sitting ducks. Those Dreen ships can engage at up to three light-seconds. We can't get away fast enough to avoid them."

"Suggestions?" Hinchcliffe asked.

"Get in close," Berg said, turning his board. "Get in *really* close. Maybe if we're close enough, they won't be able to engage us. Hell, *board* the bastards. Go down fighting."

"I can't even figure out where the node *is*," the staff sergeant admitted.

"Still lots of particle emissions from the node," Berg said. "Follow the trail, Staff Sergeant. Now you know why we've got all this gear."

The Marines turned their boards, hammering for the unreality node. There didn't seem to be a hope in hell that they could survive. They had air for twenty-four hours and then it was *gone*. But, hell, they also had a full load of ammo.

For that matter, Berg knew how to turn his suit into a micro-nuke. If it came to that, he was planning on going out with a bang.

"Closing the node," Hinchcliffe said. "Man, I don't know what came through but all it is now is—"

"Big neutrino spike, Staff Sergeant," Berg said. "I think we've got com—"

It happened too fast for Berg to process. One minute there was empty space and an expanding cloud of gas and the next there was a mother*grapping* HUGE ship so close that he actually ran into the hull.

The ship began to move and his suit was hit, again, by one of the projecting guns.

Flipping in space, he accelerated up to the gun, grabbed on and then tossed a grenade down the open barrel. For all he knew, the gun wouldn't even notice but it was a start.

"Himes, Smith, locations?"

"Mid-section, port, upper deck," Himes replied. "I've grabbed onto a gun. I think it's some sort of plasma gun. If it goes off, I think I'm toast."

"Right behind you, Two-Gun," Smith said. "I just tossed a grenade in one of these cannon-looking things."

"Look for an airlock, any sort of entry," Berg said. His sensors were getting washed with readings but a huge meson spike from relative "down" made him flip his board to relative down. A hatch had opened up and pods were jettisoning from the side of the ship.

A hatch.

"The ship is launching fighters," Berg snapped. "Midsection, middle decks. Head for those hatches!"

"Conn, Tactical, we've got another neutrino spike and this one is bigger . . . Conn, Tactical, Target designated Sierra One. Dreen dreadnought. Emissions spectrum indicates that converted battlewagon from— Another spike. Conn, Tactical, Target, Sierra Two. Dreen destroyer. Target, Sierra Three, Dreen destroyer. Battlewagon is launching bandits, Designate Bandit Group One. Target, Sierra Four, Dreen destroyer, another spike . . ."

"Now we know what they were waiting for," Spectre said calmly. "Reinforcements."

22

"Any word from the Marines?" Spectre asked.

The *Blade* had backed off as the Dreen surrounded the node with ships. Fighters were covering farther out. It was going to take some thought to take on the flotilla that had appeared.

"We got some fragmentary stuff right as the battlewagon emerged," the TACO said. "After that, nothing."

"What are we looking at?"

"Sixteen ships," the TACO said. "Sierra Nine I'd put in the class of capital ships. But from the fighter numbers, I'd say it was something like a carrier. Sierra One that has the emissions spectrum consonant with a convert is the other capital ship. All the rest look to be Dreen. Two that have higher emissions than the destroyers, they're going to be larger. Call them cruisers. One battlewagon, one carrier, two cruisers, twelve destroyers, one of them a convert. Current count of about ninety fighters. Fighters appear to be working in teams of three, staying about two light-seconds out from the main fleet. But they're harder to resolve from this distance. *All* of them are heading for the *Caurorgorngoth's* position."

"Okay," Spectre said, taking a deep breath. "Except for there being more targets, the mission remains the same. We will warp in and fire and warp out. I'd like to reduce the fighters. If they're at two light-seconds, they could engage us while we're doing relative adjustments. Do we have enough time during warp in to drop torps?"

"Unlikely, sir," the TACO said. "It's very tight."

"Okay, if we can draw the fighters off we'll scatter torps in silent mode," Spectre said. "For that matter, we'll scatter some ahead of the fleet until all but four are used up. But it's time to get on our game face."

"Incoming transmission from the *Caurorgorngoth*," the commo officer said as Spectre took his command seat.

"Let's see it."

"*Vorpal Blade*, this is Kond," the ship master said. "If you wish to retire, it is understood. I have sent word of this disaster to Fleet Master Lurca. He agrees that it is unwise to attempt engagement. They are fleeing with what fuel we have."

"That's fine, Kond," Spectre said. "But I didn't come here just to watch the show. Besides, there's that whole mutual need thing. I take it you are *not* fleeing?"

"We must slow them as much as we can," Kond replied. "It is duty."

"And this is duty," Spectre replied. "We are preparing to engage. I don't think we can coordinate with you to any extent, but if you can do something about the fighters I'd be much obliged."

"We will see what we see," Kond said. "I wish you well and thank you as do all of my people."

"Hey," Spectre said, "the way I look at it, it's just a target rich environment."

The bay was about forty feet across and twenty high with walls and floors made of scarred metal. At the rear was a lift of some sort that looked strangely disused.

But sitting on top of the lift was a pile of what looked like glowing green poop. The poop pile had a massive tube running out the back, which entered the ship through a small hole in the inner bulkhead. There was a patch around the hole, also glowing green, that looked something like the top of a mushroom.

Walking farther into the compartment, Berg saw that at the back the overhead was indented and there was a window. It looked like glass but was probably something stronger than aliglass. The glass was covered with a patina of dirt and he couldn't see what was beyond. There were alcoves to either side as well. And the rear one had a hatch!

There didn't seem to be any way to open it. There were no wheels or knobs.

On the outboard bulkhead, though, was another patch of glowing blue fungus. It was just occupying a vaguely oval spot on the wall.

Following a hunch, Berg pulled out a knife and scraped at the fungus. He was careful to avoid getting it on his armor. The Dreen often used enzymes and acids to attack armor.

The fungus turned out to be puffy and liquid filled. When the knife cut through the outer layer, it squirted liquid that quickly ran down the face of the metal. Once scraped away, the fungus revealed a pad with glowing symbols. They were definitely alien and looked something like cuneiform. Berg used the hilt of the knife to avoid the messy goo covering it and pressed a couple of the symbols. On the second try, the hatch opened, the doorway dilating away as if the metal was flexible.

The space within was lit with dim red light and was the size of a cargo elevator. Whatever race had once owned this ship, they had apparently done some of their own fighter maintenance in this bay and form apparently followed function.

Inside there was another patch of fungus covering a similar pad of symbols. Pressing the one that had opened the door didn't have any effect. Pressing the first one that he'd tried closed the door. Okay, he could open and close it. Now to figure out how to get to the next level. There were three more symbols. The first two apparently did nothing. The third started the lift. At the next level the lift door opened automatically.

The immediate view was of the alcove that had the window in it and it was clear. Peeking around the hatch, though, he was amazed. The lift opened onto a massive area, about forty feet high and possibly stretching all the way across the ship. It was apparent he'd found the hangar bay.

There were more piles of green poop as well as stalactite type formations hanging from the ceiling. He had no clue what any of them were for and intended to avoid them for the time being. What he didn't see was anything moving in the weird purple-green light of the hangar. There appeared to be no Dreen at all.

But if any of the Marines had made it into the ship, they were probably going to have made it through the open bay doors. His had closed quickly after he entered, so who knew how many had made it in. But they were probably in the fighter bays, still.

The interior bulkhead, seen from this side, had massive struts attached to it. They looked, at first, like some sort of reinforcing.

Then Berg realized that the whole upper bulkhead could be lifted like a clamshell door. He had an immediate vision of aliens pulling fighters out of the bay that required more maintenance than could be done on site. Replacing an engine, maybe. The doors didn't look as if they'd been used in years. Maybe decades.

He used a remote camera to peek around the corner of the alcove. He was surprised to find no internal security or even any technicians. He wasn't sure what a Dreen technician might look like, but he was surprised there weren't any.

Nobody in view, though. He walked as quietly as he could down to the next fighter bay and wiped at the dirt on the window. Shining a flashlight in, he couldn't see any movement.

On the fourth bay, he saw a suit of human armor. It was wrapped into the mound of poop on the bay.

Hurrying to the lift, he scraped and punched his way down until he was in the fighter bay. But it was apparent he was too late. From the remains of the stenciling on the suit, it was apparent that Lance Corporal Mario Uribe wouldn't be playing twenty questions again. The material of the mound had penetrated the suit in multiple places, eating through the joints and doing who knows what on the interior.

Berg set a grenade for twenty-second delay, boarded the elevator and headed back up. As he passed the window there was a muffled thump and the window splashed green.

Himes had to duck as the hatch closed but he made it into the bay and slid to a stop just in front of a pile of green poop.

"Uck," he muttered, climbing off the board.

The most interesting thing in the compartment was definitely the pile of poop. It was sitting on some sort of lift and might control it. Getting it to open up the bay and let him out was a top priority.

He approached it cautiously, though. The Dreen were nasty creatures and this was for sure a Dreen product. There were still occasional outbreaks of the monsters on Earth, each luridly detailed in the news. He wasn't sure what it could do to his armor, but he also didn't want to find out the hard way.

That left the problem of what to poke it with. It was just waiting to be poked, but there wasn't so much as a scrap of paper in the bay and he didn't want to do it with his suit-claw. So he finally leaned down and poked it with his gun.

The pile erupted immediately, swarming up the gun barrel

and engulfing the tip while pulling him downwards towards the mass of Dreen fungus.

He was only half surprised but he let out a scream anyway then bit down on his fire trigger.

A stream of 14.5mm rounds from his Mojo Gun blasted into the pile, splashing green across the compartment and ripping free the pseudopod that had his gun entrapped. The bit of barrel that still had fungus on it was smoking. He wasn't sure if that was from the heat of the gun or from the material trying to eat it, so he walked over to the wall and scraped as much of the stuff off on it as he could. It didn't seem to have damaged the barrel, but he wasn't planning on poking it again.

He looked up as a light flashed at the rear of the compartment. Ducking down, he could see there was a dirty window there. Something was flashing a light into the compartment. He started to duck back, trying not to let a Dreen security team find him, but then recognized the vague silhouette of a Wyvern suit.

"Hey!" he shouted, stepping forward into view. "Get me out of here!"

Smith had made it into one of the bays as well and was equally fascinated by the pile of poop. Disdaining his gun, the lance corporal drew his monoknife and poked at it. He managed to drop the knife fast enough that the pseudopod did not get his suit-claw. But he also lost his knife.

"Mother*grapper*," the cannoneer snarled.

He examined the pile a bit more closely, then grinned. Backing off, he set the cannon for exploding-rounds, single-shot and placed the laser target designator on the point where the thick cable entered the back of the pile.

One shot was all it took. The cable whipped through the air, spraying green slime liberally into the compartment, then sealed and retracted into the wall.

Smith waited a few moments, then watched as the glow slowly faded from the pile. In less than a minute, it turned brown and began to settle, like a falling soufflé. In a couple of minutes it was just a brown liquid nastiness on the floor.

His knife was half eaten away so he left it where it lay and began to explore the rest of the compartment. He'd just found the door when it opened, nearly triggering another shot.

"Damn, man, what are you doing just hanging around in here?" Himes asked. "We got Dreen to kill!"

"CO has the controls," Spectre said. "Standby. Engaging."

The sequence happened too fast for the eye to follow. The speckle of Dreen ships swelled enormously, there was a brief flash and then they receded, fire flashing harmlessly off the ship's warp field.

"Replay on all screens," Spectre said. "Did we get anything?"

"Negative, Conn," the TACO replied. "We might have gotten a piece of one of the destroyers but we missed Sierra Nine."

The *Blade* was concentrating on the ship that was designated as a carrier, a long ovoid that was essentially featureless except for its mottled green-brown skin and spiked exterior.

"As a weapon this leaves much to be desired," the CO said.

"What we need is twenty-four of them," Weaver replied. "Fill all the tubes."

"Now that might just work," the CO admitted. "I suppose it's no worse than the subs back in WWII with their faulty torpedoes. But I want it to get better. And more of them would be good. But we need to deal with what we've got. XO, ship still good?"

"Set at Condition One, sir. No damage."

"Got a piece of Sierra Nine that time, sir." Tactical flashed the replay on the screen in slow motion. It was apparent that the chaos ball had impacted and there was a flash of air and water that blasted into the void. But after a moment, the hemorrhage of material stopped.

"Well, that's something," Spectre said. "Not spectacular, but something. XO, I'm going to go to continuous evolution. Five times, adjust course and speed, then five more times. It's taking less than a second for each evolution. We'll do five attacks, assess, then go for it again. Stand by."

"Any luck on getting the engine more precise?" Miriam asked as she wandered into the engine room.

Normally, people did not "wander" into the engine room, but the entire ship had taken up the linguist as some sort of mascot, especially after she cheerfully chipped, scraped and painted all the steam runs. *Nobody* had been looking forward to that detail.

"No," Tchar admitted. "I have scraped the algorithm that controls the neutrino flow to the bottom. There is no way to get the neutrinos to stop being generated faster. There is just this *lag* I cannot resolve!"

"That doesn't sound like fun," Miriam said. "But I was just wondering while I was working on a pump. Doesn't the box have null settings? Points on its surface that don't do anything that we can figure out?"

"Yes," Tchar said. "That is how we move to different warps by moving to different points on the box and adjusting the neutrino stream. Your point?"

"How fast does that ball move?" Miriam asked, pointing at the shining silver ball.

"Uh . . ."

"Okay," Spectre said. "We got the programs right for the ripple attack?"

"All set up, sir," Weaver replied.

"It's not going to glitch, right?"

"Guaranteed bug free or your money back," the astrogator said.

"Assuming I can collect."

"Yes, sir."

"Course and speed matched?"

"Course and speed matched, aye, aye!"

"Engaging," Spectre said.

The screen flashed and flashed and flashed and then it stopped. They were back in deep space with only the scattered lights of the Dreen fleet, like lesser stars, speckling the main viewer.

There was a groan from the communications technician and he bent over and grabbed a vomit bag. Spectre just grabbed his head in both hands.

"Was that from watching the viewscreen?" the CO asked after a moment. "Weaver, what in the hell just happened?"

"Unknown, sir," the astrogator replied, swallowing his gorge. During the overlapping warps he had experienced a massive sense of disorientation and the aftereffect was nauseating. "We've never had that sort of reaction from a warp jump, but we've never done several of them together like this. It may have been from looking at the screens or it may be an effect of the drive. It may even be the chaos ball *interacting* with the drive."

"Right," the CO replied. "Making it up as we go along, as usual. Pilot, match course and speed."

"Course and speed matched, sir!"

"This time nobody watch the screen," Spectre said. "Engaging."

Weaver closed his eyes but that, if anything, made the feeling worse.

"Sir," the XO gargled. "We're getting reports of disorientation and nausea from throughout the ship. It's not just the screen."

"So it's an effect of the drive," Spectre said. "Tactical, did we get a piece of them?"

"Negative impact, Conn. Some were under, some were over, some were too far out and they dissipated."

"And we can't get things any more accurate with our current systems," Spectre said, nodding. He pressed the 1MC and cleared his throat. "This is your captain speaking. The effects you just experienced are a side effect of the way we're attacking the Dreen. There's no way that we can damp them out that anyone's found and we don't have another attack method that works. So we're going to have to suck it up until these Dreen bastards are constituent atoms or run home with their yellow tails between their legs. You're the finest crew I've ever dealt with and I know that you're going to handle this just like every other piece of weird assed shit we've dealt with. Prepare to engage."

"Conn, Engineering."

"Go."

They'd managed to get some hits into the Dreen ship, a piece of one of the destroyers and a fighter that had been terminally unlucky. But the flotilla just streamed on. It was frustrating.

"Tchar and Miss Moon have managed to solve the warp adjustment problem," the ship's engineer reported. "We now have only a millisecond delay. I don't know if that's going to add to the effect or improve it."

"Good to know," Spectre said. "Is that going to make us more accurate?"

"Unknown, Conn," Engineering said. "But it's going to make us less vulnerable."

"It's also going to make it possible that we'll fire *inside* the warp bubble," Commander Weaver pointed out. "I'll need to tweak the program that decides that. We don't want one of those things bouncing around inside with us."

"How long?" the CO asked.

"No more than ten minutes for that," Bill replied, opening up the program and looking at the interface with the warp drive. He could see Tchar's notes on the changes there. "But here's an interesting thought. If we keep our normal open period, we can actually do some adjustment of the angle of the ship. Interface with the tactical computers and *aim*. But we're more exposed."

"Will that take more time?" the CO asked.

"Yes, sir."

"Can you write that code off to the side while we keep trying the normal way?"

"Yes, sir."

"Then do it," Spectre replied. "But get the new systems set up first. We're punching this thing. Float like a butterfly, sting like a bee. Sooner or later we're going to hit something vital. I don't want to let up if we don't have to. XO, get us into a planetary shadow and we'll go to chill while Commander Weaver punches his buttons."

"Good to see you, Staff Sergeant," Berg whispered.

"Two-Gun, why are you using your external speakers?" Hinchcliffe replied, using the same method.

Hinchcliffe had rounded up Sergeant Priester and Corporal Nicholson from Charlie team. With Uribe dead, that left only Vote and Wagner missing. He'd apparently come in from the other side of the hangar. The two groups had spotted each other and cautiously met near the center of the vast enclosure.

"The Dreen can pick up electronic transmissions, Staff Sergeant," Berg said.

"Point," Hinchcliffe replied. "Priestman, over here."

The three went into a "leadership huddle" while the others took up security positions.

"We're going to go with radio for a second," Hinchcliffe said over the leadership freq. "Because now that we're in here, I'll admit I'm stumped. I know we should be attacking, but we've got no clue where anything *is* on this ship."

As he said that there was a rumble of thunder through the ship. It was a combination of deep cracks transmitted through the metal of the ship.

"I would guess that was firing," Hinchcliffe said. "And I can guess what they're firing at. Our ride home."

"Any ship, even a Dreen ship, is going to have brain, muscle and lungs," Berg said. "That's the way one of my teachers put it one time. The brains on a normal ship is the conn. The muscles are engineering. The lungs are environmental. Kill any one of those, and the ship stops. Well, actually, since it can probably shift brains, the exception is conn."

"And if we kill the ship, we kill ourselves," Priester pointed out. "If we take it down, the *Blade* and the Hexosehr will blast it to pieces. And that assumes that six Marines even *can* take it down."

"Got a better idea?" Hinchcliffe asked. "Then that's the plan. We need to figure out where the brains, the lungs and the muscles of this ship are."

"I would suggest we wait on engineering," Berg said.

"Reason?"

"Well, Staff Sergeant, I don't know *how* to shut down a fusion reactor," Berg admitted. "And unless you've taken a learning annex I don't know about . . ."

"Conn, Tactical. Some of the fighters are being recalled. I'd say they have to refuel."

"Now we have some idea of their flight time," the CO said. "And hopefully of their cycle time. How you doing with those tweaks, Commander Weaver?"

"Almost done, sir."

"Good," Spectre said with almost feline malice. "There's no better time to hit a carrier than when she's cycling her fighters."

"What the hell was that?"

The staff sergeant nearly jumped out of his skin at a series of nearby clangs.

"I don't know," Berg said, trotting over to one of the windows. "Ah, they've pulled in their fighters."

"Really?" Hinchcliffe said, trotting over to stand next to him. Even with the filthy glass, the large ovoid that now occupied the bay could be clearly discerned.

"I wonder how hard they are to kill?" Berg asked.

"Thirty bays," Hinchcliffe said. "Less counting the ones we've already *grapped* up. Nine Marines. If you cut the cables, the big piles die. I'd guess the big piles are their replenishment system. You thinking what I'm thinking, Two-Gun?"

» » »

Berg cut the cable with his monoknife. According to Smith and Priester, the green goo that gushed forth wasn't any threat. Just before he left he decided to shove a grenade into the bubble on the wall. He set it for twenty seconds, took the lift up and waited. There was a rumble under his feet and looking in the bay he saw there was now green goo gushing everywhere.

"Heh," he muttered, heading for the next bay.

Space Combat Unit replenishment system failure above probable wear. 20% loss of replenishment fluids. Intruder probability 99.99999%. Dispatch repair units Class One through Four. Dispatch Security Units Class One through Three.

The door to the fighter bay lifted smoothly despite the patina of wear.

"You sure about this, Staff Sergeant?" Nicholson asked.

"Better to blow them up here if we can," Hinchcliffe replied. "Fire."

Nicholson trained his 25mm cannon around the corner of the bulkhead and onto the rear of the fighter, then triggered a stream of Armor Piercing Discarding Sabot. The rounds had a tungsten core designed to penetrate light armored vehicle armor.

About half the rounds bounced off but several tore through the armor, releasing a gush of liquids and steam. Nicholson stopped firing and backed away as soon as he had penetration.

"It hasn't exploded, ye—" Hinchcliffe started to say when there was a tremendous roar from the bay.

The blast flung all the Marines to the floor and blew the outer hatch to the fighter bay open. Air began to gush out in a whirlwind but the inner door slammed shut automatically, cutting it off.

"That was pretty," Hinchcliffe said. "Let's do that *again*."

"Conn, Tactical."

"You sound puzzled, TACO," the CO said.

"Spectral analysis shows there was just a gush of air and water . . . There's another one, coming from Sierra One."

"That's our converted Big-Boy, right?" Spectre said. "Interesting. Did the Hexosehr get in a hit?"

"Negative, Conn. It just seems to have suffered random failure. Not sure of the cause."

"Next shot we're going to go for the Big-Boy," the CO said. "Mostly because I want to look at what might have occurred. We might be able to use it."

"WE GOT DREEN!"

Nicholson and Smith, the other cannoneer, had managed to destroy five of the fighters before Dreen security responded. There were six entrances to the bay, four outboard, headed respectively port aft, starboard aft, port forward and starboard forward, and two midline headed fore and aft.

Dreen security responded through the forward, starboard entrance. Fortunately, the Marines were gathered to port, the side that Berg had entered.

The first wave were Dreen dog-demons. Quadrupedal, heavily armored on the front quarters, they had heads like a gargoyle with a big, crushing beak. In armor, the beak was the part to look out for. It was reputed to cut through Wyvern armor like a hot knife. Some people joked that they were Dreen Marines, "Devil Dogs" being one of the nicknames the Marines had picked up over the years.

If so, they were doing a lousy job. Their powerful claws had a hard time getting purchase on the slick floor of the hangar bay and they slid into view rather than charging.

"Light 'em up," Hinchcliffe ordered. "But conserve your ammo. We've got a long fight ahead of us."

Berg targeted one of the sliding dogs and fired, hitting it at the juncture of the neck and shoulder. That spot was unarmored and the 14.5mm slug nearly blasted the beast's head off. It slid to a stop in a welter of green blood.

Berg didn't think about it more than an automatic "target down," placing his rangefinder on the next of the beasts and another. Before he knew it, the engagement was clear.

"Okay, I think they know we're here," Hinchcliffe said, lowering his smoking machine gun. "Let's not be here. We've fucked up the replenishment system and blown up five fighters. Good enough for now."

23

"Well, isn't that interesting," Spectre said.

Their sole run on the battlewagon had been a bust, the chaos balls missing by a mile. But they'd gotten some good video. And it was apparent that five of the fighter bays were blasted outwards.

"What in the world could have caused that?" the XO said. "Some sort of systems failure?"

"They're not even all together," Weaver pointed out. "There are three side by side, then a jump, then two more. I don't see a systems failure being that . . . random."

"Tactical, has the carrier relaunched, yet?"

"Negative, Conn."

"Okay, that's the next target," the CO said. "We'll puzzle about the battlewagon later."

"Oh YES!" Spectre shouted, all nausea forgotten, when the video from the series of strikes was replayed.

It was evident that one of the chaos balls had hit the carrier right in a hangar bay. The ship was gushing air and water and there were secondary explosions. It wasn't out of the fight yet, but it was sorely wounded.

But it had taken ten evolutions, fifty attacks, to get that result.

"Set up another run, Pilot," Spectre said. "Commander Weaver, how far away from the unreality node are they?"

"About seven light-seconds, sir," Bill replied.

"After this run we'll head back there and see if any Marines survived," Spectre said. "No, I hadn't forgotten about them."

The Marines had exited the hangar bay from the port, forward door. Beyond they found a large corridor with regular blast doors on it. The first two segments were unoccupied, the doors sliding open at a touch. The fourth, though . . .

"What the hell?" Berg muttered.

The corridor was filled with overlapping filaments that were lightish green and pulsing. Berg touched one with a monoknife and it didn't react so he used the knife as a machete to hack an opening.

Through the hole it was apparent that the corridor was coated in the stuff. Along the walls were small pods and the floor was slippery with goo.

"Movement," Himes said, targeting the subject.

The movement turned out to be something that looked like an amoeba, but hugely magnified, being nearly two meters in diameter. It was slowly undulating over the pods on the outboard side of the corridor. It might have been eating or cleaning, it wasn't apparent.

"Don't," Berg said. "Don't fire."

He stepped into the corridor gingerly but got no reaction from the amoeboid. Going over to one of the cocoons he cut it open and a half-formed creature flopped out.

"What the hell is that?" Smith asked. The creature looked like an octopus. Or maybe an octopus in a surrealist painting.

"No *grapping* idea," Berg said.

The radical abortion caused a reaction from the amoeboid, but not a hostile response. It turned and flowed across the corridor, palpating the cut edges of the pod with pseudopods and then flowing over the octopoid.

"I think it's eating it," Himes said.

"Weird," Smith replied.

"It's a nursery," Berg said. "For whatever those things are and whatever they do. And we're not getting anywhere. Staff Sergeant?"

"Keep moving forward until we find something better to do,"

Hinchcliffe replied. "Maybe find the nursery for the dog-demons. I'd rather kill them stillborn."

"I didn't know you were a Democrat, Staff Sergeant," Berg said with a grin.

"Don't ask, don't tell, Two-Gun."

Air loss four percent. Attack in Class Three Repair Unit nursery. Port side, corridor fourteen, section ninety-six. Localize intruders and destroy. Increase production of combat units. Increase production of Repair Units. Cease replenishment of fighters. Divert all nutrients to internal defense and repair.

"Conn, Tactical. I've got beacons from two Marine suits."

The *Blade* had approached the node and changed its relative motion to that which it had had when the mines were dropped. Then it went hunting for Marines.

"Marines, this is the *Blade*," Spectre said. "You still alive and sane?"

"Oh, Jesus, sir," one of the Marines replied tightly. "Thank God you came back. This is Wagner. I think Vote's dead. I'm hanging in there. I'm coming alongside."

"Roger," Spectre said. "Maintain current course and heading. Send word to the Marine commander that we've got at least one of his boys. Wagner, this is the CO. What's the word on the others? Were they killed in the blast?"

"Negative, sir," Wagner replied. "We were assembling on the node when that big Dreen ship came through. The metal one. I think some of them may have managed to board it."

"Ho, ho," Weaver said. "And the mystery of the fighter bays is less mysterious. One of the things Marines are best at is breaking things. It might even have been an accident, knowing them."

"It also makes it harder for me to kill that damned thing," Spectre said. "Knowing there are Marines on board."

"Conn, Commo. The *Caurorgorngoth* is coming into range to engage the enemy flotilla. She is requesting assistance."

"Tell her we'll be there as soon as we pick up our boys," Spectre replied. "Keep her pants on."

"Conn, Tactical. We're picking up neutrino readings consistent with Cheerick boards. Multiple signatures. I think the Marines dropped their boards off the ship."

"We'll pick 'em up as soon as we pick up our Marines. Somebody is using their head over there. And I'll give you dollars to donuts who it is."

At the fourteenth blast door, Berg didn't even have to hit the open button. It opened while the team was halfway down the compartment and he flopped to the prone and bit down on his firing clamp even before he could see the enemy.

"Dreen!" Smith shouted unnecessarily. He'd taken a knee and was hosing the corridor with his cannon.

The first wave were dog-demons again. The combined fire from four suits, three 14.5s and a cannon, stopped them butt cold. But this time they were backed by thorn-throwers, bipedal creatures that fired a dense carbon "thorn" out of launchers on their heads.

"Uh!" Himes gasped, falling backwards as a thorn penetrated his armor.

"Stay on target," Hinchcliffe snarled. "Security, keep your positions!"

"Himmie's down!" Smith yelled.

"I can see that, Lance Corporal," Hinchcliffe replied. "And there's not a damned thing we can do about it right now."

There had been a round dozen of the dog-demons and six of the thorn-throwers. All of them were down before the dogs got to within five meters of the Marines.

"Two-Gun, check on Himes," the staff sergeant said as soon as the corridor was clear.

Berg crawled over to the suit and flipped up the readouts. There were monitors for heartbeat, temperature, blood oxygen and brain waves. All but the blood oxygen and temperature were flat and those were dropping.

"He's gone," Berg said.

"We can't leave him for the Dreen, Staff Sergeant," Smith said calmly, all things considered. "They'll eat him."

Earlier, they'd managed to get Uribe's body freed and spaced it when they blew up one of the fighters. It was the closest they could do to a funeral.

"Two-Gun, put a thermite grenade inside his armor," Hinchcliffe said. "Then we need to move out."

"Where are we *going*?" Smith asked. "We don't know where anything *is* on this ship!"

"We're going forward, Marine," the staff sergeant barked. "Do you have a problem with that?"

"Negative, Staff Sergeant," Smith replied tightly. "I apologize for my outburst. I am gung-ho, Staff Sergeant. Let's go kill some Dreen."

Berg tried not to look at his teammate as he opened the armor. It was apparent that several of the thorns had gotten into the armor and a few had bounced. The lance corporal was riddled with holes, and blood filled the bottom of the Wyvern.

"Pull his cannon and ammo before you do that," Hinchcliffe said. "We'll tote the cannon. Nich, get over here and pull this ammo. You're going to need it."

"I want one of *those*," Spectre said.

The *Caurorgorngoth* was in the fray at last. The Chaos Destroyer was half the size of the Dreen battlewagon, much less the carrier. But it made up for its relatively small size in firepower.

The ship was retreating towards a nearby Jovian, not the one that the fleet had assembled at but the Dreen didn't know that. The idea was to delay the Dreen by convincing them the Hexosehr fleet was gathered at the nearer Jovian refueling instead of on the far side of the system. The Chaos Destroyer had even laid decoys that simulated the emissions of the refugee fleet ships. The longer the Dreen headed the wrong way, the longer the main fleet could continue to refuel.

As its consorts moved outwards to exchange long-range plasma blasts with the Dreen destroyers, the chaos ball ship fired blast after blast from its main gun.

The chaos balls moved at nearly light speed. Fired from five light-seconds out, the balls took a bare seven seconds to reach their targets. They could only be detected at the last minute on the way in, but the Dreen reacted by maneuvering. By continuous delta-V actions, the ships could avoid most of the blasts. A few, however, impacted their targets. As the conn crew watched, one of the chaos balls hit a Dreen destroyer, ripping a hole from stem to stern. The ship listed off-course for a moment, then exploded in a bright, actinic flash.

"Conn, Tactical. Dreen fighters moving out to intercept the *Caurorgorngoth*."

"Can we figure out a place they're going to be in space where we're far enough away they won't notice us dropping torps?" the CO asked.

"Yes, Conn. Already plotted. We're not sure it will be in their direct path as before, but it will be close."

"Pilot, lay in that course," Spectre said. "Tactical, figure out a second drop point. We'll go drop these mines, make a series of runs in against the carrier again, then drop some more. Hopefully we'll be able to winnow down the fighters."

"Okay, straight on or right?" Smith asked.

They'd finally encountered a cross corridor. They'd previously encountered two more nurseries, one of them of thorn-throwers. One had been newly hatched but it could barely fire and Berg had taken it down before Smith could get in a lick. They'd spent some time destroying all the thorn-throwers and then dropped grenades in to keep them from growing back.

The aft corner of the corridor was marked with more of the alien script, these in vivid primary hues. The top script was a bright purple, about head-high on an Adar, under it another in yellow and descending nearly to the deck. The script wrapped around the corner and was no more than a couple of symbols. Berg ran his hand down the markings and they brightened, chattering in a high-pitched language.

He touched the blue symbol and it spat out a short message, the sound of the alien tongue almost like a chime. He noticed that each of the scripts was not only a different set of words, short, no more than two or three, but in a different tone. If he had any skill in music at all, he could have played the script like a piano. The opposite corner appeared to be an exact duplicate.

Directions? Orders? He was sure he'd never know but it fascinated him as he ran his finger down the corner.

"Right," the staff sergeant replied. "We're not finding anything vital in this corridor. If there's a bridge, it's going to be deep in the ship. Same for environmental."

Flick in, fire, flick out. Flick in, fire, flick out. It had become so routine, Spectre let the pilot take over. They were doing ten evolutions, then pausing to adjust course and speed and review their strikes. There was more time taken to review than to attack.

The nausea accompanying the rapid transitions was getting

worse, though. The CO shook his head and swallowed as he watched the replay.

"Good one that time, son," Spectre said. The carrier had gotten its remaining fighters off, of course, so it was not nearly as spectacular. But it had been a good solid hit on the rear of the Dreen ship. If only the ball generator they had did more damage!

"Conn, Tactical. Fighters approaching mine point."

"On display," Spectre replied.

The view was just empty space but then it blossomed into light.

"Did they take them out?" Spectre asked. "We laid eight torps. Did we get *anything*?"

"Three appear to have prematurely detonated, Conn. We're waiting on a bandit count . . . Conn, Bandit count before mines seventy-three. Bandit count after mines, sixty-four. We got eleven."

"Not too shabby," Spectre said. "You got another position for us?"

"Working on it, Conn."

"Right, next run. This time, son, I want you to *lead* 'em a little."

Enemy lesser ships in range. Engage main cannon.

"What is *that*?" Smith shouted.

The ship had filled with a massive whine, like a billion angry bees but at a much higher frequency. It had started low but rapidly climbed up the scale. Suddenly, it shuddered, almost throwing them off their feet, and the whine died away.

"Did we take a hit?" Nicholson asked, looking around.

"I think it was probably the ship's main gun," Berg replied.

"What could make a ship like *this* shudder like *that*?" Staff Sergeant Hinchcliffe asked.

"A really, really, *really* big gun, Staff Sergeant."

"Sir, the *Fatutug* is . . . gone," Favarduro said, wincing.

"What happened?" Kond asked calmly. The *Fatutug* had been covering their left side, engaging a Dreen destroyer that was attempting to flank them.

"There was an energy surge from the Dreen dreadnought," Favarduro said. "We detected no weapon but it apparently fired at the *Fatutug*. Fourteen treek after the energy surge, the *Fatutug* blew up."

"Contact the *Sharp Sword*," Kond said. "See if their sensors detected anything."

>>   >>   >>

"All I got was a streak of light, Conn." The TACO was clearly nervous. The enemy had just attacked with a weapon that nobody could understand. "Slowing it down . . . still a streak of light. It looked sort of like a chaos gun, but not really."

"Mass driver," Weaver said, looking at the readings. "Got a gravitational spike from the area, indicating a big mass moving at relativistic speeds. Big, big *big* one and *really* fast. It looks as if it's traveling at about .3 *c*. Tactical, Astro, has Sierra One reduced velocity?"

"Roger, Astro. It's accelerating, again, but it definitely reduced velocity there for a minute or two."

"Work with me, here, Astro," Spectre said. "What are we facing?"

"A mass driver fires, well, a mass," Weaver replied. "Think the gun on a Bradley, sir. It's got a depleted uranium penetrator but the important thing is that it heads downrange really fast and it's really heavy. This thing is relativistic, meaning that it gains an enormous energy punch from that. Being hit by that gun is going to knock any of the Hexosehr ships out of the game. We'd just end up as a smear of plasma. And it's long range. Accurately, over five light-seconds at a guess."

"That makes sense," Kond said when he received a reply to his message. "We must endeavor to avoid being hit by that weapon. Begin random evasion maneuvers. We continue battle."

"Left or right?"

The corridor they had been following had reached a dead end. The corridors were narrower here, as well, but still wide enough to accommodate the Wyvern armor.

The team had almost ceased to notice the occasional touches of the Dreen. Anything that was a control was covered by blue fungus. In fact, it was how they identified controls. Occasionally there would be an extrusion on the floor, in a corner, on the ceiling. By and large they simply avoided them.

There had been occasional compartments along the way. They'd opened a few up but most were empty. Living quarters or supply lockers for the previous owners. But they had all been stripped to the bare metal walls. There was no trace of the former inhabitants except their enigmatic script.

They hadn't seen any nurseries since getting deeper in the ship. Nor had they seen any Dreen security.

"Why aren't there Dreen, like, everywhere?" Smith asked nervously. "All we've seen are a couple of dog-demons and thornthrowers. Where are the rhino-tanks? Where are the centipedes and, I dunno, technicians?"

"A ship only has so much support it can provide," Berg answered.

"This is a *big* ship, man!"

"And it's centered, probably, on support for that main gun, the fighters, the guns along the sides, all the things that make it a warship," Berg said. "Even the Dreen have limits to how much they can pack in a particular area. If they had those compartments filled with soldiers, that would mean less stuff for the repair pods, the fighters. Heck, with the fighters being organic and needing nutrients, they probably have *less* available support than a species that uses machines."

"You done?" the staff sergeant asked.

"Sorry," Berg said.

"No, it was a good lecture," Hinchcliffe replied. "Reminds me why you're along, besides killing Dreen and breaking things. But the answer to the question is: left then take the next right. Sooner or later we're going to find *something* important to bust up."

24

"Yes!" Spectre shouted as the conn erupted in cheers.

Repeated strikes by the chaos ball had worn holes in the outer skin of the carrier. Together with the secondaries from the strike on the hangar bay, the outer defenses were long breached.

A lucky strike by the generator had apparently entered one of those holes and dug deeper into the ship. The result was obvious as the carrier dropped acceleration and streamed masses of air and water. Secondary explosions were also evident. If not destroyed, the capital ship was now too sorely wounded to continue the fight. It began decelerating and turned towards the unreality node.

"Tactical, Conn," Spectre said, then raised his voice. "At ease in the conn! We've still got a battle to fight."

"Go, Conn!"

"Figure out the course on that thing," Spectre said. "If it's not deviating, we'll drop some presents along the way and see if we can't take it all the way out. In the meantime, let's retarget the destroyers. We still don't know the status of the Marines on the other ship."

"Okay, we found something."

As the Marines progressed, signs of Dreen presence had been increasing, with more of the greenish Dreen fungus in odd spots in the corridors. Experiments with it had determined that this fungus, at least, did not attack. So as it closed in, they had more or less ignored it.

The newest compartment, though, was something different. It was large and filled with alien equipment as well as huge masses of fungus.

"Yeah," Sergeant Priester said. "But *what?*"

"I don't know," Staff Sergeant Hinchcliffe said. "But it looks important. Which means we need to *grapp* it up. That's what Marines do, break things and kill . . . things."

"You're joking," Spectre said.

"No, sir," Captain Zanella replied. "I am not joking, sir. We believe it to be potentially possible. And there are Marines on that ship that need reinforcement."

The *Blade* had to take a break. Temperatures in the ship were soaring since it had been too long since their last chill. She'd broken off the fight, dropped mines on the path of the retreating carrier then retreated to deep space to consider her options and bleed off some heat.

The Marine CO had requested a meeting and, thinking that it would be about recovering the Marines in the Dreen battlewagon, the CO had moved it to the wardroom. Spectre already had his answer in hand which was that taking out the battlewagon was the number one priority. Recovering the Marines would be nice, but was not the top priority. Taking it all the way out *was*.

What he had *not* expected was a request to commit suicide.

"Captain, right now I am in a very tight battle with a very skillful and powerful foe," Spectre replied. "One that is slowly *grapping* up my ship and my crew. I do not have time to away boarding parties. Even if I thought it would work. Which I don't."

"Sir, it requires that the time window be opened only slightly," the Marine argued. "And one small tweak in the assault program. If those two things occur, we have a bare minimum chance of boarding that vessel. Furthermore, we can carry extra ammunition and supplies. The Marines who made it on-board have so far demonstrated an ability to strike from within, sir. I respectfully state that the rest of us could do even more. We are a weapon, sir. I respectfully request that we be used."

"I will take your request under advisement, Captain," the CO said. "Dismissed."

"Interesting idea," Weaver said.

"If we can't even hit them with torpedoes," Spectre replied, "how are we going to hit them with Marines?"

"I see the hand of First Sergeant Powell in this suggestion," Weaver replied. "With torps, we have to take the time to fire them. That's too much time. Upwards of five seconds, no way to automate it and even if we pre-launch them they're deadly missiles *inside* the warp bubble. The enemy can track onto them and take them out easily enough. With the Marines, they'll be already at the edge of the warp bubble as we transit. While we're in normal space, firing the ball gun, we just *move* a little. They'll be outside the effect from the ship, so they won't move. We move away from them, not very far, go back into warp and they're left hanging in space."

"And then the defenses of the ship shoot them down," Spectre said.

"Maybe, sir," Bill said. "Maybe not. Their target discriminators might not see them as a threat. The boards also are surprisingly maneuverable in space and very fast. Personally? I think it's suicide. But that's not a professional opinion. My professional opinion, sir, actually tracks with the captain's. They're a weapon. Use them."

Carrier Unit to Gun Unit. Have sustained critical damage. 40% loss of nutrient, 60% loss of air. Leakage at four hundred cubics per turn. Retreating to warp point.

Gun Unit to Carrier Unit. Report to the Masters that Species 27314 will be destroyed or assimilated within ten cycles. Species 27264 ship will be captured and examined and their home world located. All is in hand . . . Internal alert. Intruders in recycling room four. Locate and terminate. Twenty percent of security units to control center defense stations.

Carrier Unit to Gun Unit. Do you require additional security units?

Negative, intruders are few in number. They will be eliminated or assimilated within a turn. Send this message to the Masters. We are loyal.

We are loyal.

"That *grapping* thing is *roasting*."

The largest Dreen structure in the room looked something like a mushroom, one from Alice in Wonderland. Two thermite grenades had been tossed on top of it and had burned their way through and into the floor, setting the pillar of Dreen fungus ablaze.

Cables had been cut, filling the room with goo, and some of the original equipment had been engaged with machine-gun fire, exploding in showers of sparks. In general, the compartment had been seriously *grapped* up.

"Our work here is done," Staff Sergeant Hinchcliffe said. "And let me just add how *proud* I am—"

"Dreen!" Nicholson shouted.

Berg dove for cover behind one of the alien machines, a cylinder about ten-feet tall and whose purpose was totally unknown to him, and started pumping rounds into the doorway. The room only had one hatch and Dreen filled it, scrambling over each other to get through the narrow opening.

The Marines hammered the attackers, piling up the dead in the doorway, but as many as they killed, more seemed to be trying to fight through. But it was clear, as thorn-throwers were shot multiple times, that there was more than enough firepower to hold the room.

"Two-Gun, Smith, cease fire," the staff sergeant said. "Two-Gun, you got any grenades left?"

"Four, Staff Sergeant."

"See if you can get any *over* those guys and into the corridor."

The first grenade Berg threw hit one of the thorn-throwers in the head and landed on the pile of Dreen bodies, detonating more or less harmlessly except for chewing up the pile. The second, through, he managed to slip through the narrow open area at the top of the door. The detonation on the other side sounded less than harmless. Thorn-thrower and dog-demon bodies gushed into the room. The corridor on the far side had to be packed.

"Christ, how many of them *are* there?" Nicholson asked. "I'm getting low on rounds!"

"Just fire steady and accurate," Hinchcliffe advised. "Just keep firing. But use your rounds carefully. If we can hold them in the doorway we're going to be here a while. If not, we won't care anymore."

"These are all volunteers, First Sergeant?" Captain Zanella said, looking at the group.

"Yes, sir," the first sergeant replied. He did not add that the

entire remaining company had volunteered. "Gunnery Sergeant
Neely, because it's his platoon. Chief Warrant Officer Miller,
because he outranks me. At that point, I had to start picking
and choosing."

"I see you're taking the sole survivor from the last mission
and our spare armorer," the captain said, looking at Seeley and
Lyle. "The rest?"

"Alpha and Bravo team, Second Platoon, sir," the first sergeant
said.

"I see eight people," the Marine CO commented, dryly. "And
we have nine boards. Whoever is going to use the ninth?"

"That would be me, sir," the first sergeant replied firmly.

"I consider that unwise, First Sergeant," the CO said, then
held his hand up to the protest. "But I have to keep in mind
the adage that my first company commander told me: Never
get between your first sergeant and beer, women or any mission
they've set their heart on. Load 'em up, Top."

"We've got five blown-out doors," the first sergeant said as the
ship prepared to transition. "Go for the one most forward. There's
going to be a lot of fire. Think about whipping around in space
while heading for the ship. Get down close to it and they can't
fire at you. Then get in the bay. We'll figure out how to get
farther in from there."

"Jeff," Miller said over the command freq. "This is purely going
to suck, you know that."

"You can feel free to unvolunteer, Chief," the first sergeant
replied.

"And let you jarheads call me a wuss?" Miller scoffed. "No
joy. See you in hell, snake."

From the exterior of the ship, the view as the battlewagon
closed was even more disorienting than watching it on the screens.
Miller actually started too soon, slamming into the warp bubble
before it opened. The Dreen battlewagon was pouring out a mass
of fire. There was no *way* they were going to survive it all. They
were kamikazes without even the benefit of big bombs.

The warp bubble dropping, the ship moving sideways, it all happened too fast for him to comprehend; the human brain was not
designed for milliseconds. All he knew was that suddenly he was
in free space, looping in and out of more torrents of fire than he

had ever seen in his life or ever wanted to see again. He'd once been pinned down by multiple rocket launchers in Mogadishu. This was worse because he didn't even have a concrete trough to hide behind. Not to mention the fact that by comparison, a 20mm antitank rocket was a popgun. Plasma blasts were going by so close the static discharge was frying his radio and one wash even got close enough to raise the temperature in his suit. Given that heat did not propagate through space, that meant it had actually touched him.

Unbelievably, he found himself suddenly about to slam into the Dreen battlewagon. A quick mental flip and he was flying alongside, trying to stay between the still firing guns. There was actually *smoke* wreathing the death-spewing battlewagon. The entire experience was unreal.

He spotted the damaged hangars, like rows of empty eyeball sockets, and darted down towards them, lining up and finally settling in the evacuated compartment.

"You're two," Powell said from the rear of the compartment.

In the end, they were six. Staff Sergeant Jim Revells, Lance Corporal Eric Hough and Lance Corporal Francisco Cestero never made it. And Sergeant Norman was effectively useless, given that something had ripped off his machine gun.

"Lurch, I figured you for a goner," Powell said as the former armorer finally showed up.

"I was just checking out those guns, Top," Lyle replied. "I want to get my hands on their schematics. They're traversing so fast they *have* to be on magnetic bearings. I've been trying to get them to switch to magnetic bearings for the Wyverns ever since I first saw the specs."

"Yeah, well, we'll worry about that later," Powell replied. "Let's figure out how to get out of this bay."

"Found a window and a door," Chief Miller said. "And methinks I just saw the silhouette of a dog-demon through the window."

"Lock and load."

"Conn, Tactical, we have a problem."

"Besides the fact that the crew's starting to fall out?" Spectre muttered. The continuous transitions were taking their toll. He'd hoped that the chill-down would help, but being in free-fall had only enhanced the nauseating effects and the disorientation. Crew were beginning to report hallucinations and four crewmen had been tranquilized at this point. He really didn't want to think about what Miss Moon, who had no resistance to free-fall nausea, was going through.

"Go, Tactical."

"The remaining Dreen task-force has disengaged from the *Caurorgorngoth* and is moving insystem towards the main Hexosehr refugee fleet."

"*Maulk*," the CO muttered. The Dreen had taken the bait for less than an hour. And the main Hexosehr fleet was *slow*. They had more than two days' transit to their next jump and even the cumbersome dreadnought would catch them short of it. A few of the faster, lighter vessels might escape, but the main bulk of the remaining Hexosehr population, the millions of scientists, technicians, poets and philosophers wrapped in hibernation sleep, would be blasted into constituent atoms. And with them any hope of humanity adapting their technology to Earth's defense.

"Roger, Tactical," Spectre replied. He was trying like hell not to show that the repeated warps were getting to him. Fighter pilot training was, not surprisingly, helping him again. He'd felt much worse after major furballs. Of course, they rarely lasted this long.

"We continue to harry them," Spectre said. "We took the carrier out. We have Marines onboard the Dreen battlewagon taking the fight to them internally. We will continue the mission. Pilot, lay in a course to intercept Sierra Five." The Dreen cruiser was the closest ship, starting to apparently interpose itself between the small but seemingly invulnerable *Blade* and the capital ship.

"Course laid in," the pilot said.

"Engage."

The pilot hit the control for warp and there was a loud bang from somewhere to the rear that rang through the ship, following which they immediately lost artificial gravity.

"Okay," Spectre said calmly. "That did not sound good."

"Conn, Engineering." There was a sound of coughing in the background of the sound-powered comm system.

"Go, Eng."

"We just had a catastrophic failure of the neutrino generator. We're down. We also have a fire but we're getting that under control."

"We're not all *that* far from the Dreen task-force, Eng," the CO said. "Getting *up* is rather important."

"Understood, Conn," the Eng replied. "We've got our rolls of duct tape out already."

"Very funny, Eng," the CO said. "How long?"

"When I have the slightest clue I'll tell you, Conn."

"Weaver," the CO said. "Get your happy ass down there and find out what's wrong."

"Roger," Weaver said, unhooking his belt and grabbing a stanchion. He shook his head and swallowed, far more affected by microgravity than normal. His head was swimming and he could barely figure out where the hatch out of the conn was. The repeated warps were seriously *grapping* with him. "On my way."

"*Grapp*," Weaver muttered as he pulled himself into the engineering spaces. He wasn't, by any stretch, the only visitor. It seemed like half the mechanics in the ship were in the room, some floating around waiting for orders but most dealing with the mess. Most of them still had the helmets down on their space suits, indicating just how bad the fire had been. Bill could smell the stench of melted plastics and ozone still, despite the recyclers being on at max.

The problem was immediately apparent. The neutrino generator, an electrically charged Looking Glass boson held in a magnetic field, had blown a gasket. The LGB charging and confinement system was in pieces that were floating all over engineering and one of the nuke techs who manned the room was being given some rough and ready first aid for a piece of shrapnel from the controller.

"What do you mean we don't have a *spare*?" the Eng shouted just as Weaver entered the compartment.

"I mean there's no spare, sir," LPO Macelhenie said, slowly and carefully. He was more or less upside down and had his helmet flipped back and his feet hooked around a pipe. "There was no anticipation that the controller would blow. It's practically solid state."

"It's not designed for repeated cycling, though," Weaver said. "*Chither.* We ran it through a thousand cycles in tests but not this fast and we've done way more than a thousand cycles, all told, on it since installation. It should have been pulled and replaced before the cruise. It's solid state, but it takes a massive electrical load to generate the neutrinos. Probably it just overheated and blew up like a transformer that's been under too much stress for too long."

"So what do we do about it?" the Eng asked, trying to stay upright with a hand clamped to the back of a chair. "I've seen the schematics on it but I can't really make heads or tails of how it works. And without the neutrino generator we are dead in space for the foreseeable future."

"I'm aware of that," Weaver said, frowning. "Tchar?"

"Human tech." Tchar shrugged. He was more or less in mid-air, and also more or less upside down. "I'm thinking. No use of duct tape comes to mind."

"There's the power input system," Bill said, trying to think through the haze that the repeated warps had made of his brain. "Then the connections to the magnets. We've got dozens of magnets that can be used for stabilization. The power inputs to the LGB itself, but they have to be modulated. It was probably the modulator that overheated. We need a high power but small transformer, a modulator, an analog to digital converter—"

"A computer," Miriam said from the back of the room. She was tucked into a ball in an upper corner, clearly trying to stay out of the way. For once, she didn't appear to be minding microgravity.

"The power supply won't take it," Bill pointed out. "We're talking about nearly a thousand amps."

"It will last for a while," Miriam pointed out. "Replace it when it starts to wear. We've got dozens of computers in the science offices. And parts for them."

"No, a computer at best uses a ten amp power supply. The breakers and fuses on it will go out in milliseconds. It won't work, trust me, I've blown them up before. Hmm . . ." Weaver shook his spinning head.

"We could use a computer with an A to D card to drive the modulation though, but what would we modulate?"

"A CD player," Miriam replied. "It uses the same algorithms. We may have to do a manual adjustment but the controls are in the player, too, so that's easy enough. Make a case from number thirty-two piping; there's a four-foot section in the machine shop. From there it's just a matter of enough duct tape."

"That's a great idea, Miriam, but I still think it to be too small." Weaver shook his head again. The spinning just got worse. "Uhg . . . hey, Tchar's lazy Susan works just like the CD players do."

"You mean the thing he put together for the gamma ray Morse code thingy?" Miriam asked.

"Yeah, that thing. Would it work?"

"I can make it work!" Miriam agreed. "And that would solve our transformer problem too! But we'd need two of them, one for the modulator and one for the transformer. Drat."

"Always a two for one value at Triple A Plus Industrial Warehouse Online!" Weaver said, mocking Tchar. "He has two of them.

"Why are you the only one whose brain is working?" Bill asked. "Mine's fragged from the warps. In the past you would have been curled up in a ball somewhere."

"I don't know," Miriam said, shrugging. "I'm not bothered by whatever's getting you guys. Maybe because I'm a girl. Maybe because I'm weird. But that's not getting us fixed."

"Agreed," Bill said. "Eng, you up with this?"

"Not . . . really," the ship's engineer admitted. "My brain's sort of melting, too. I don't think I can even recall the design, much less figure out what Miss Moon's talking about."

"Miriam, what do you need?" Bill asked.

"Red and Sub Dude," Miriam replied. "And about thirty minutes."

"We're in range of the Dreen fighters," Bill pointed out.

"That does *not* help me think, Commander Weaver," Miriam said, straightening her legs and bounding off the bulkhead towards the main hatch. "Just leave me to it and *don't* tell me if we're about to get blown up, okay?"

"The neutrino generator blew out," Bill said, strapping himself back into the astro chair. "Just blew the *grapp* all over engineering. Miss Moon's figured out a fix. She's on it."

"What do I even bring you guys along for?" Spectre said tiredly, then straightened. "I mean, she cleans, she paints and now she's fixing my busted-up engine. I bet she can even figure out where we are if I need it."

"Right now I wish you'd left me on Earth, sir," Bill admitted.

"Conn, Tactical."

"Go."

"A flight of Dreen fighters has just broken away from the task force. They're on a course to intercept ours. They'll be in range in twenty minutes."

"*Seriously* wish you'd left me on Earth."

"How long on those repairs?" the CO asked.

"Miss Moon said thirty minutes," Bill replied.

"Tell her to hurry up!"

"Do you *really* think that will help, sir?" Bill asked.

"Belay that order," Spectre growled. "XO, prepare to launch torpedoes. I want a full spread. Maximum thrust for five minutes, then shut down. See if they can get in range of the fighters before the fighters get in range of us."

Bill did the math and didn't reply. The answer was "no way in hell."

"There is no way in hell we're getting out of here alive," Berg said over the leadership freq.

"Aware of that, Two-Gun," Staff Sergeant Hinchcliffe replied. "Just keep firing until you're out. Then use your pistols."

"There's an alternate plan, Staff Sergeant," Berg said. Covering the door was so automatic he wasn't having any trouble carrying on the conversation. It was just a matter of firing as conservatively as possible. They'd long before switched to single fire, alternating to full auto only when the Dreen made it into the room.

Nicholson was down, not dead but his gun was sheared away from a thorn and another had punctured his armor. He said he was hanging in there, but his vitals looked lousy. Priester had clocked out on ammo, twice, so Hinchcliffe pulled him back to "security." The sergeant was a good shot but *God* he used ammo like there was no tomorrow. Since its inception, the Marine Corps had stressed accuracy. Among other reasons, they often operated on very thin supply lines. When you were on thin supply, using the bare minimum ammo to kill your enemies and win the battle was a *good* thing. How Priester had not picked that up in his years in the Corps, Berg couldn't figure out.

He, Smith and Staff Sergeant Hinchcliffe were covering the door, killing Dreen dog-demons and thorn-throwers that seemed to be an endless stream. It was simply a question of what ran out first, Dreen or their ammo.

"What's your alternate, Two-Gun?" the staff sergeant asked.

"There's a way to overload the reactors in these suits," Berg said. "An SF sergeant did it on the last mission and some of us tinkered with it until we figured out how he did it. It's not a *big* nuke, but it's big enough to take out this compartment and everything around it."

"Let's save that for absolute last ditch," Hinchcliffe replied after a moment's thought. "But you'd better tell me the details in case you're not the last guy in the compartment."

25

"Conn, Tactical. Dreen fighters at one million kilometers."

Spectre frowned at the screen and snarled internally. Their lasers were popguns, not even capable of scratching the Dreen fighters. Torps were fired . . .

"Roger, Tactical," the CO said. "Range to torps?"

"Four thousand kilometers, Conn."

The Dreen fighters had engaged at over six hundred million kilometers before. *Chither*, there had to be something . . .

"What's the orientation of the approaching fighters?" the CO asked, rubbing his chin. "Are they relatively above us or what?"

"Off the starboard side, Conn, at mark neg one."

"COB?"

"Sir?"

"I want you to figure out how to rotate this ship so that those fighters are, relatively, above us," the CO said. "Use anything you can. Get that chaos generator pointed at them."

"Roger, sir," the COB said, pulling himself out of the compartment and forward.

"Engineering is aft, COB," the CO pointed out.

"Torpedo room is forward, sir."

"Right, get both of the motors mounted relative up," the COB said.

The hardest and longest part had been getting the torps into place. There was a hatch directly to the magazine for loading the torps. Unfortunately, it was not an airlock. He'd ended up getting permission to jettison the ready torps and use those. Now it was just a matter of getting them lined up and controlled.

"Rotators are in place, COB," the LPO of the torpedo room said.

"Conn, COB," the COB said. "We can rotate. End to end control is still working. No yaw, yet. And it ain't really fine control."

"That's great, COB," the CO said. "Gimme a short thrust rotating the port relative up. Just a touch."

"Gimme a touch of burst on starboard," COB said.

The torpedoman used a manual controller to fire the torp for just a moment.

"Right, when I tell you I'll need about the same in the opposite direction," the CO said. "On my mark. Three . . . two . . .one . . Mark."

"Fire port," the COB said.

"Too much, COB."

"Bit to starboard . . ."

"Christ, I wish this was electronic control," the CO muttered, then keyed the communicator. "That's got it pretty close. We'll need to fine tune that in a bit. Can you get the bow up, relatively?"

"There's going to be some rotation," the COB answered.

"That's fine. Just a touch."

"I think that's got it," Spectre said after ten minutes. "Tactical, range to target?"

"Seven hundred thousand kilometers," the TACO replied.

"Sir, you're aware that they have more range than we do," Weaver said quietly.

"Yes, I am, Commander," Spectre replied. "Thank you for your input."

Weaver knew he'd been slapped down and better than to comment.

"Here's the deal," the CO said after a moment. "Yes, the plasma guns took out the torps. But we're tougher than torps. We're going to keep firing that chaos generator as long as it lasts and as long as we last. And if we can even get them to scatter a bit and hold off engagement, it gives Miss Moon more time to work. I was going to wait to engage them until they were in range. Now I'm going to start firing *before* they are in *their* basket. They'll either choose to scatter or not, but they will *by God* know we may be dead in space but we're not done fighting!"

"Conn, Tactical, Dreen fighters approaching six hundred million kilometers. We have energy spike, Conn. Incoming."

"Open fire, continuous, on the chaos ball generator," the CO replied. "COB, get ready to maneuver . . ."

"What was that?" Miriam asked as an alarm claxon started going off and the ship shuddered.

"Nothing to worry about, ma'am," Red said. He was busy assembling the pieces of the controller, using some of the smallest waldoes on his arm.

"Ship's under attack," Sub Dude replied, setting down a length of pipe. "CO's firing back. It's a battle, ma'am, but we've been through them before."

"Don't worry, I'm still calm," Miriam said, picking up the pieces of the jury-rigged neutrino generator and slotting it into the tube. "Red, how are you doing?"

"Just done, ma'am," Red said.

"Get me a number seven pipe clamp," Miriam said, calmly, as the ship shuddered again. "And hand me the controller . . ."

"Damage in engineering compartment, personnel quarters and auxiliary personnel quarters," the XO said. "No casualties, nobody in those areas. But we lost the gearing, entirely."

"Good thing we don't need it," Spectre said as the ship shuddered from another plasma hit. "Tactical, they in range, yet?"

"They've scattered, Conn. Three groups designated Bandit One through Three. And, no, still one hundred thousand kilometers out."

"Right, let's get to targeting Bandit One," the CO said. "COB, prepare to rotate the ship."

"Damage to mess deck and the rear torpedo room," the XO said.

"They always get hammered," Spectre replied. "Just tell me my quarters are surviving this time."

"So far no hits—" There was an enormous crash overhead and the compartment evacuated air.

"I was about to say no hits forward," the XO continued over his suit communicator. "Belay that report."

"COB, why haven't you shot these guys down, yet?" the CO asked.

"Working on it, sir," the COB replied.

"I want some smoked Dreen fighters!"

"Hits in main engineering spaces," the XO said. "No damage. Two casualties. Evacuated."

Marines normally had very little to do on-board ship. The exception was in the midst of a battle, when every hand was needed.

"Get that plating up," Captain Zanella snarled. "We need to get this compartment sealed!"

The blast of plasma had penetrated two decks and cut through the bulkhead of the mess deck at a slight angle. Since the mess deck was the back-up infirmary, getting it airworthy was high on the list of "good things" to do.

"Got it in place, sir," Gunny Mitchell said. "Benner: weld."

"Time, time, time," Captain Zanella muttered on the command freq. "I hope like hell that—"

The plasma blast initially followed the original but angled slightly differently it missed the repaired bulkhead.

It did not, however, miss a high pressure steam pipe that erupted in gaseous water. Parts of the steel pipe exploded outwards, filling the compartment with shrapnel.

"Fuck me," Captain Zanella said quietly, staggering backwards with a six-inch piece of sharp metal protruding from his shoulder. He could feel his arm going numb and a cloud of reddish gas was dissipating in front of his face. From the feel of the splinter, it wasn't in deep. But that didn't mean he wasn't going to die. His suit was spewing air and blood.

"This is going to hurt, sir," Lance Corporal Butler said, grabbing the splinter.

"If you pull that out, I'm going to decompress in about a second," the CO said, laying his hand over his RTO's.

"Got that covered, too, sir," Kermit said, holding up a roll of space tape. "A one and a two . . ." He pulled the splinter at two.

"Arrrgh!" the CO snapped. "I thought you were counting to three!"

"I know, sir," Kermit said. He took the roll of space tape and laid a section across the hole in the CO's suit. He pressed down firmly on the hole and it sealed in an instant.

"That stuff's amazing," the CO said. The gush of gases and his blood had been cut off like a faucet. "And I thought I told Top to round up all personal rolls."

"I just happened to see this one lying around," Kermit said. "I was planning on turning it in any day now, sir."

"You're forgiven," Zanella replied. "But I'm still bleeding."

"Good thing you're in the infirmary, then, sir," one of the corpsmen said, staggering in with a casualty slung over one shoulder. "Be with you in a second."

"It must be aligned precisely," Tchar said.

The jury-rigged projector had been strapped back into the damaged mount with about a million miles of duct tape. But it still had to be aligned.

"What are you using?" Miriam asked. The mount had been refitted with a manual adjustment that looked to be not its original use.

"Parts from a tool kit I bought on-line," Tchar replied. He was looking through what looked like a spotting scope at a dot of light on the face of the ball. "The light is from a laser pointer keychain that came *free* with it. That should have it. Engineer, engage power and check the readings . . ."

"Whoot!" Spectre caroled as one of the Dreen fighters succumbed to a chaos ball. "Take that, you organic menaces!"

"Conn, Engineering. We think we're prepared to warp."

"Then hit the power and *go*," Spectre said as light flared from forward. "Hit the juice and get us *out* of here. Anywhere's better than this patch of space!"

"We're blasted to hell, sir," the XO said. "That last hit took out sonar and penetrated into officer's quarters."

"My quarters?" the CO asked.

"Our quarters survived, sir," the XO said. "Commander Weaver's did not, however."

"*Grapp*," Weaver muttered.

"About time yours got trashed," Spectre said. "But we can drive and fight."

"With just about every compartment evacuated, sir," the XO pointed out. "About the only compartments still airworthy are the machine shop, the sickbay and the visitor's quarters. Marine berth is open as is crew berthing."

"That's what patches are for, XO, *after* the battle," Spectre replied as the COB walked into the conn. "Good job, COB."

"Yes, sir," the COB said. "Sitting out on a hull under plasma fire wasn't all that bad. Reminded me of that time we were cruising off Somalia and got attacked by pirates . . ."

"Ship Master, the *Sharp Sword* is moving again," Favarduro said.

"Bless the Gods," Kond said. "I thought them lost. Message them and ask for assistance. We are sore pressed."

"The *Caurorgorngoth* is trying to interpose itself between the Dreen fleet and the Hexosehr refugee fleet," the TACO said. "They were out of position, though, so they're trying to cut the chord while still engaging the Dreen task force. However, the Dreen have redeployed a squadron, designated CruRon One, composed of both its cruisers and two destroyers, which is enveloping the *Caurorgorngoth* and her sole remaining consort. In addition, a third squadron, DesRon One, is moving ahead of the battlewagon to attack the refugee fleet. It is composed of three destroyers. The Hexosehr have only two corvettes to oppose them. They have redeployed in between the refugee fleet and the Dreen but the correlation of forces is adverse. Most of the fighters have redeployed in close formation around Sierra One. They appear to be in a slow replenishment cycle. Unknown when they will be back in action."

"So we can try to aid the *Caurorgorngoth* or we can try to aid the refugee fleet," the CO said. "We can target cruisers better, they're a bigger target, but the refugee fleet is the priority. Move to intercept that destroyer squadron, XO. The *Caurorgorngoth* is going to have to take care of herself."

"Staff Sergeant?" Berg shouted as Hinchcliffe's armor slumped back.

Smith was down. Still alive but injured and with his armor breached it was only a matter of time before he died. Nicholson had finally stopped responding. His vitals were low and it was clear he was bleeding out.

"I guess I get to use up ammo again," Priester said, standing up from cover and blasting at the door. "Get the *grapp* out of here you mother*grappers!*" the sergeant shouted, charging at the door.

"Priest, God *damnit!*" Berg snarled as the sergeant covered his fire. There were fewer of the Dreen. He could feel it, sense it. The press at the door was less. The corridor *had* to be empty-ing out.

A dog-demon caught at the swearing sergeant's leg, pulling it out from under the armor and slamming Priester to the ground. Berg stood up, in turn, switching to full auto and hammering the pile on the sergeant in a vain attempt to keep the Dreen from breaching the downed Marine's armor.

Then his machine gun clocked out. The last round spat down-range and he released the bite-trigger, his hands automatically dropping to his sides.

It was why he was called Two-Gun; the two massive pistols he carried were made from cut-down .50 caliber sniper rifles and he had the ability to fire with either hand, sometimes simultane-ously, and hit what he was shooting at. For most people, two-gun mojo was a poseur technique, fancy to watch but impossible to use in combat.

Not for Two-Gun Berg. Both massive pistols started hammering out .50 caliber BMG rounds nearly as fast as a machine gun, the blazing pistols sounding like one continuous stream of fire as the armored Marine strode towards the door, clearing the monsters off of his fellow squad leader's back and clearing the compartment.

Of course, they only had seven rounds apiece. The left-hand pistol dropped to its holster, the claw of the suit coming up with a magazine the size of a book and slamming it into place. There was barely a pause as the reloaded pistol blazed out again, the left hand unthinkingly readying another magazine. And still the Marine sergeant strode on, right up to the hatch of the compart-ment, firing into the corridor beyond, blasting fist-sized holes all the way through the hated monsters that had been harrying them for so long.

It took Berg a moment to realize that there *were* no more targets, in part because there was a stream of fire coming from the left-hand side of the hatch. Streams of tracers and cannon rounds had blasted the remaining Dreen away from the door and back down the corridor to the right.

Berg didn't care, though. He automatically reloaded, then leaned out the door, extending both pistols down the corridor and continuing to engage the Dreen until the passageway was clear of anything but mangled alien bodies and runnels of purple blood.

"And that, boys and girls, is why we call him Two-Gun," Corporal Lyle said, raising the barrel of his smoking machine gun. "Nice to see you, Berg."

"You, too, Lurch. What took you so long: Stop to examine an alien mechanism?"

"We are not hitting *chither*," Spectre snarled, watching the replay.

The nausea, which seemed to have passed with the extended stop to do repairs, was back in spades. It only made it worse that everyone was now in suits. And various systems, so far none critical, were breaking down. The boat was not really designed to be evacuated on an extended basis. There were a lot of systems on it that were not rated for vacuum.

And there was the problem that the suits had a strictly limited amount of air. Unlike the Wyverns, they did not have capacious air systems or recyclers. There were hook-up points at all the manned stations, but personnel who had to move around were constantly having to replace bottles.

And they weren't hitting the destroyers. The targets were an order of magnitude smaller than the capital ships and it had taken up to a hundred shots to get a real hit on the bigger ships. So far, the *Blade* had done nothing but miss on the smaller ones.

"Weaver, you said something about integrating *everything* and staying open longer to get more accurate," the CO said.

"It will also make us more vulnerable," the astrogator pointed out. "And it will take at least a half an hour to implement."

"Get to work," the CO said. "XO, move to a chill position while Commander Weaver prepares the change. I'll take the chance of getting hit for a chance to get one. What the hell. We're already so *grapped* up, they could put one through us crossways and not take out anything important."

"We picked up a pretty important secret from the Hexosehr," First Sergeant Powell said. "Task Forces like this are controlled by a sentient. The sentients reside on the capital ships, like this one. Take out the sentient, the rest of the Dreen don't know what to do on a strategic level. The *Blade* took out the other capital ship. It's heading for home. If we find the sentient on this one . . ."

After doing what they could for the wounded Marines, Top had gathered the survivors and his reinforcement platoon in the corridor for a quick op order.

"The rest of the Dreen do what, Top?" Sergeant Priester asked. His armor was heavily scored and a dog-demon had destroyed the right leg of the suit so he wasn't going anywhere. But with the spare ammo that the reinforcements had lugged into the ship, he was back to full load and ready to use it. "Leave? Quit fighting?"

"The Hexosehr say that they go find a sentient to tell them what to do," Top replied. "Now, there's that other capital ship, but it's leaving the system. At the very least it's going to buy us time. So that's our mission. Find the sentient."

"Top, we've been roaming all over this ship for the last couple of hours," Priester pointed out. "We haven't seen anything but nurseries and security. We've got no clue where—"

"Maybe we do," Berg said, suddenly. He walked over to the compartment and pressed the closing switch. "Look at the symbols on the door." They were impossible-to-decipher orange, glowing cuneiform.

"I don't read alien, Berg," Priester said.

"Neither do I," Berg said, striding down the corridor to the end they'd entered from. "But the *exact* same symbol is here," he continued, pointing to a symbol about a third of the way from the bottom. "And . . ." he continued musingly. "That's interesting . . ."

"What you got?" the first sergeant asked, walking over and looking at the two symbols. "They're exactly the same, aren't they?"

"Yes, but look at the top one," Berg said, pointing to the purple. "I'd thought the symbols matched. And the ones that match the door, *do*. But the top one . . . The aft symbol is straight rectangular script. The forward one is angled . . . I *think* it's angled forward. The bottom is pointed that way. Gimme a second."

He trotted back down the corridor and almost got lost for a second. But at a cross-corridor he bent down and looked at the orange symbol. Script on the forward corner was pointed forward.

"They *are* directions," Berg said, trotting back. "The side that's pointed is the direction of the compartment."

"This one is pointed down the corridor," the first sergeant said, pointing to a yellow one.

"That's probably the shortest route to whatever yellow means," Berg said, excitedly. "Look, there's another orange one. I'd *guess* that that was an environmental compartment. Orange is environmental."

"Six Orange," the first sergeant said. "Four blue. One purple, one green and one red. A *bunch* of that light violet or whatever."

"Okay, Top, let's just assume for a second that they think like humans," Berg said. "And the reason I think they do is that a lot of this stuff has been laid out the way that humans would lay it out. Six orange. I'd say that this is the most forward environmental section, starboard side. All the rest point back except one that points inward. That leads to—"

"Forward, port environmental section," Top said. "Environmental Two or whatever. So the script probably just says E-2 or something like that."

"Right," Berg said. "Now, what's the most important compartment on the ship?"

"Bridge," Top said, looking at the script. "Conn. Whatever. All the multiples have two symbols, some of them matching even though they're different colors. One, two, three, whatever. The singles have three symbols, there's a match . . . in a second symbol, here and here. No problem, their version of an E. Top one is a single."

"These are directions to the conn," Berg said. "Maybe the command zone, Conn, CIC, whatever."

"This, Two-Gun, is a wild-ass guess," the first sergeant said, straightening his armor from its crouch.

"Yes, it is, First Sergeant," Berg replied. "But it's a place to start."

"Right," Top replied. "We need to reconfigure. Priestman, you're with Sergeant Norman. His weapons control system is out so you're both good to secure a position but that's about it. You two are to secure this compartment and act as our fall-back position. We're going to leave the extra ammo loads here, so it's important. Set up the extra guns for support fire and try to keep Smith alive. Lyle and Seeley, you're with Two-Gun, designated

Alpha Team. Lyle, grab a cannon and cross-load ammo. Norman, you're Bravo. Chief Miller, if you would be so kind as to take rear-guard with Gunny Neely, I'd be much obliged."

"I think I can remember how to be a shooter," the SEAL said. "What does this bite thingy do again?"

"As soon as Lyle is kitted out we're moving."

"Fighters at one-one-four alpha nineteen," Favarduro said. "Automated defenses engaging—" The *Caurorgorngoth* shuddered and shuddered again. "Dreen heavy plasma fire. Shields at fourteen percent."

"We have retreated far enough," Kond said. "We are being picked apart by sag. Pilot, maximum acceleration towards the enemy. Favarduro, concentrate chaos engine and secondary batteries on the lead cruisers. Go for the heavies."

"I've got the new algorithm debugged," Weaver said, walking into the conn. "I'd like to test it at least once."

"Agreed," the CO said grimly.

"What's wrong?"

"The *Caurorgorngoth* is getting hammered," the XO replied. "And their consort was taken out by a force of fighters. They were trying to engage from range but they're now accelerating towards the task force. It looks like a suicide run."

"Or they figure that if they get in close enough, there's no way they can miss," Weaver said.

"It's both," Spectre said. "They're sacrificing themselves to take out the cruisers. Maybe the destroyers as well. But they're not going to survive it. Which leaves the rest up to us. Commander Weaver, even if they succeed in taking down that entire task force, there are going to be seven destroyers left in this system, any one of which can destroy the entire Hexosehr fleet. And a battlewagon with a super-cannon. Your fix had better work."

"Oh, it will work, sir," Bill said. "Whether we can survive it working is another question."

"Dreen cruiser at six dreg," Favarduro said as the *Caurorgorngoth* rocked under the hammer of the combined task-force's plasma fire.

"Fire," Kond pinged. He had held his fire, coming in the

whole run as if the chaos engine was out of commission. And the enemy had fallen for it, closing in on each other to get in on the kill.

The sonar image was clear. The chaos ball flashed out, less than six treek from time of firing to impact. The center Blin cruiser caught the ball direct on her snout, the powerful ball of pure chaos plunging into her heart. The sound image was muted as she disintegrated in fire.

"Retarget, second cruiser," Kond said. "Bring them all to the slaughter."

"Shields at two percent," Favarduro said as the ship adjusted course to bring the gun online. "Damage to aft quarter, fighters are close enough to overcome our shields. There are less than nine left, however. Damage in forward quadrants. Plasma nine, six and one off-line. Their mass drivers have reached range to engage us."

"Fine," Kond said. "If we're that close, then we cannot miss."

"I want a full broadside of twenty-four of these things," Spectre said. Weaver had found another convenient piece of space detritus and tried out the new targeting system. Unlike the first test, the chaos ball had impacted on first try. It also was slow enough to follow the action. That, frankly, scared the hell out of the CO. Dreen systems were like lightning to engage. They *were* going to get hit, and this "mini" chaos ball hadn't done that much damage to the capital ships. He just had to hope that the destroyers were an easier kill.

"Agreed," Bill replied. "But what we have is one."

"Right," the CO said. "XO, all the fires put out from the last time?"

"Vacuum has a habit of doing that, sir," the XO replied acerbically.

"I was speaking metaphorically," the CO said.

"Then they won't be out until we spend *another* six months in the body and fender shop, sir," the XO replied. "But we're spaceworthy. Hell, we're mostly *space* at this point."

"Better than being filled with water," the CO said. "Pilot, match course and speed on target Sierra Sixteen. And may God defend the right."

»   »   »

"Okay, we're getting near something," Berg said quietly.

"Why?" Lyle asked.

"There's more fungus," the sergeant replied. "I could wish for a map of this place."

But the best thing they had were the symbols on the walls. They seemed to be following a path, inward, forward and in one case up three levels. They were getting near the center of the ship, if Berg's spatial awareness was working, and a bit forward of center. That didn't mean it was for sure the bridge. Russian subs had the bridge at the rear. CIC was near the center of a ship. But it was a target for sure. The increasing fungus said that.

So did the group of dog-demons that keened their battle cry and charged as he turned the corner.

"Dreen," Berg shouted, backpedaling into the corridor they had been going down.

"Alpha, prone," Top shouted. "Here they come."

With the mass of fungus coating the floor, the dog-demons didn't have as much trouble making the turn. And Berg found himself face to face with them at less than three meters. Which just meant he had to kill them very *fast*.

As Berg and Seeley blasted the Great Dane sized monsters with their machine guns, Lyle rolled backwards, then came up on a knee to the side, holding his fire. As one group turned the corner and charged en masse he put an exploding round into the center demon, killing it and knocking down its fellows for his teammates to finish off.

"And we got 'em at the rear," Miller said calmly.

Berg could hear the sound of the fire from behind him and it was comforting. He'd been in enough gun fights to learn to read it, to the point where he could almost distinguish people's personalities from it. The late Drago had been profligate with fire, either in single shot or auto, blasting away with a glee that could almost be felt. Lurch, clearly, was a sniper at heart. Wait for that right shot and take it. Seeley always banged away slowly, split-second moments of hesitation indicating indecision. Not a lot of it, but it was there. And often followed by somewhat wild fire as he engaged his chosen target because it had closed more than he liked.

What Berg was hearing from the rearguard was the sound of a senior Marine Force Reconnaissance gunnery sergeant and a SEAL old enough to be his father. Single shots, no pause except for an incredibly brief interval to change targets. No hesitation, nothing wild. It was the most professional fire he'd ever heard in his life. Even Top wasn't that good.

The attack cleared in moments, leaving the ground a welter of dead dog-demons.

"Let's move," Top said. "They're going to be moving in on this position."

"Yo, Two-Gun," Miller said over a private channel as Berg, somewhat more cautiously, turned the next corner.

"Yes, Chief Warrant Officer?"

"It was nice to hear you behind us. Nice fire technique. Very smooth."

"Thank you, Chief Warrant Officer," Berg said. "Don't take this wrong, but I was thinking the same thing about you and the gunny."

"Well, that's a right compliment coming from the holder of the Navy Cross."

"Chief, you've got the Medal."

"Okay, point."

"Conn, incoming message from the *Caurorgorngoth*."

"Put it on screen," the CO said. Tactical had been keeping him apprised and it wasn't looking good.

The view was the usual surrealist painting that the conversion from sonar gave but this time worse. Among other things, it was cutting in and out. And some of the distortion, Spectre realized, was smoke. It was moving oddly, indicating, he thought, that the ship was under microgravity and probably vacuum. The space suit Kond was wearing made that last pretty obvious.

"Chaos . . . down," Kond said. "All . . . two . . . guns . . . We . . . our . . . enemies to our body . . . Save my people."

"I will, Kond," Spectre replied. "Go with God."

"Go . . ."

"Signal terminated," Communications reported.

"Conn, Tactical."

"*Caurorgorngoth?*"

"It's gone, Conn," the TACO replied. "It rammed one of the damaged destroyers. One of the remainder is showing spectral readings of major environmental loss and emissions are way down. The other looks . . . pretty solid."

"Roger, Tactical," Spectre said. "Pilot, we in position to engage this task force?"

"Roger, sir," the pilot said.

"Then let's see if this works any better," the CO said. "Spectre has control."

He glanced at the viewscreen, back to showing their opponents as a speckle in the distance with the center destroyer karated, and hit the engage button.

The approach was just as fast as ever, too fast for the mind to adjust to, but instead of immediately flashing out of the cauldron of fire, the ship hesitated, retargeted and fired.

The destroyers, however, were not idle. Their systems had been prepared for the attack and hammered at the incoming ship with their own fire. As she adjusted, the *Vorpal Blade* rocked under the hammer of plasma and mass driver fire, the hull resounding with the hammer of the enemy guns.

But one shot was all it took. The central destroyer was holed all the way through. For a brief moment Spectre swore he could see stars on the far side, then they were back in warp and *gone*.

"Conn, Tactical . . ."

On the viewscreen the central destroyer seemed to expand in white fire.

"We see it, Tactical," Spectre replied. "Damage control?"

"Still getting reports," the XO said tightly. "I've ordered the jettisoning of all the remaining torpedoes. One of the mass driver rounds went right through the number three rammer. Two dead in torpedo room. Two damage control parties killed. Sick bay is filling up. Short answer, we got hammered."

"Eng," the CO said. "Is the engine still running?"

"It's all holding together, Conn," the Eng replied. "Be aware that if we take enough shaking, it could misalign this lash-up and we'll either be in the Andromeda Galaxy before we know it or dead or sitting out of warp and unable to engage."

"That's a chance we'll have to take," Spectre replied. "Pilot, adjust course to match Sierra Eight. Prepare to engage."

"Okay, we've *got* to be near something important," Berg shouted. It was another rush of dog-demons and thorn-throwers. But worse, in an open area up ahead he was pretty sure he'd gotten a glimpse of a rhino-tank.

The rhino-tanks were one of the two most dreaded weapons the Dreen had used in their brief war with humans. About the size and general build of a rhinoceros, they were as heavily armored as a main battle tank and fired a plasma blast from between their horns that could take one out.

Of course, a blast like that inside of a ship was probably the last thing the commander wished. But it just might be that they were close enough to the conn that the "sentient" would make that decision.

"Did I just see what I think I saw?" Seeley asked. The two Marines were crouched on opposite corners, pouring fire down the corridor the purple markers directed them to. Lyle, per usual, was back a bit covering their leakers.

"If you think you saw a rhino, I think I saw the same thing."

"Two-Gun, Chief. There's only two ways for an infantryman to take down a rhino."

"Go, Chief."

"They fire, then they roar," the chief said. "When they do, they tilt their head back and open their mouth. The inside of their mouth is *not* armored. The other way, which I disrecommend, is to stick a grenade up their mouth."

"Gotcha, Chief," Berg said, trying not to giggle. "I'm just trying to get down this corridor."

"Well, we ain't going back, I can tell you that," the warrant replied. "Thick as ticks on a coonhound back here."

"Chief," the first sergeant said. "You've been hanging out with Commander Weaver too much. Lyle, you need to move forward and hose that corridor when I order. Berg, I see a compartment hatch on Seeley's side in your cameras. You see it?"

"I see it, Top."

"Seeley, you've got one on Berg's side."

"Got it, Top."

"By fire and maneuver, move down that corridor. On command, Lyle will move to Berg's position and fire past him. Two-Gun, you will move to that hatch, open it and enter, then resume firing. Corporal Seeley, check fire as Two-Gun crosses. Seelman, you will then repeat. Lurch will need to check fire as you cross. When you have established a base of fire, the remainder of the team will move forward and repeat. Lurch, on my command . . . Move!"

»   »   »

"Top, I've got an open area and a rhino-tank," Berg reported, panting. Crossing the corridor was one of the more hairy things he'd ever done in his life. Fire was pouring in both directions from thorn-thrower and the two Marines in support. Seeley had checked fire just a bit *too* long and a dog-demon had made it down the port-side of the corridor and nearly gotten him. Especially since he had to pause to get the hatch open.

Unlike most of the other small compartments of the ship, this one was overrun with fungus. And it wasn't the green kind. It was the full purple Dreen-spread fungus. If he got *that* on his suit he was *grapped*. Fortunately, it was mostly against the back wall.

"The rhino is not firing," Berg reported. "But I can see it clearly and I have to assume the reverse. Count of others is *high*. In excess of thirty thorn-throwers. Purpose of open area is unclear but it's packed up."

"I've got all that," Top replied. "Seeley, cross."

"*Grapp* me, *grapp* me . . ." Seeley muttered, darting out of the cover of the corner.

The Marine made it across the corridor and to the hatch controls. But while he was wiping at the fungus covering it, a dog-demon Berg had been *sure* was dead opened up its beak, clamped down on the Marine's armored leg and scrabbled forward with its forelegs.

The pressure overbalanced the Marine and he fell backwards right in the middle of the corridor. The Dreen let go of the leg and scrabbled up onto him, ripping at his armor.

"Get it off!" Seeley screamed, trying to roll over using the power of the suit. But strong as the arms were, normally capable of rolling a suit and a full load of ammo, the demon had it pinned.

Berg could see the fight on the ground out of one of his side-cameras. Keeping his head tracked on the fight down the corridor he drew his right pistol and fired out of the corner of his eye.

The round cracked through the side of the demon's head, splattering it all over the bulkhead.

"Thanks, man," Seeley said, rolling over and getting to his feet.

But as he turned back to the controls, a thorn-thrower managed to survive just long enough to put five rounds through the side of his armor.

"Top, Seelman is down," Berg related emotionlessly. "Termination signal."

"Got that," the first sergeant responded, just as emotionlessly. Seeley was one of the very few Marine survivors of the first mission of the *Vorpal Blade*. He wasn't going to be making another cruise. "Two-Gun, you've got to get that rhino to fire."

"What?" Berg nearly shouted. "Say again, First Sergeant?"

"When they fire, they roar," the first sergeant replied. "You can see them charge up. Hell, you can tell when they're about to fire. Shoot it. It won't kill it but it will piss it off. When it gets ready to fire, duck into that compartment. The walls will reduce the blast. Then Lurch and I will finish it off."

"First Sergeant, point of order," Berg replied. "This compartment is filled with Dreen-spread fungus. That series of actions is suicide."

"Sergeant Bergstresser," the first sergeant replied, "it was not a request."

"Aye, aye, First Sergeant," Berg said, firing a long burst into the rhino-tank. "Semper *Grapping* Fi."

26

"Main support frame cracked forward of missile compartment," the XO said. "Communications section destroyed. Science section destroyed. Marine berthing destroyed. Torpedo rooms destroyed. Sickbay vented temporarily, then they got a seal in place. Two injured killed by depressurization. Forty-seven casualties, nine WIA, the rest KIA. About the only areas that haven't taken a straight hit are Conn, Tactical and main Engineering. Oh, and your quarters survived the hits that got the torpedo room."

"Boo-yah," Spectre said. "And three destroyers toast."

"That leaves two more with the battlewagon," the XO pointed out. "And let us not forget the battlewagon. It has begun extremely long-range fire at the Hexosehr fleet."

"Let's hope they have some marginal maneuvering," the CO said. "I want to go in and hit its consorts. Come in from their flank and keep them between us and the battlewagon. Take them out one by one. Tactical, you got that?"

"Aye, aye, Conn," the TACO replied over the intercom.

"Set it up and get me a course," Spectre said, leaning back in his chair. "It's like a good luck thing. As long as my quarters make it, we're still in the fight."

"Aaaah," Red screamed as the medic slammed him onto the table.

"Plasma burn," the corpsman said, panting. He was still in

307

his suit because once out of sickbay the whole ship was vented. "Right leg."

"What right leg?" Dr. Chet said, patiently. The machinist's leg was severed just below the knee and the flesh seared well above it. The knee was most effectively cooked by transmission from the sun hot plasma. The corpsman injected another morphine ampule through the machinist's suit as the doctor reached for a set of bone-saws that were still bloody from the last amputation. "At this rate we might as well replace his whole body with prosthetics."

Nonetheless he hummed as he brought down the laser scalpel. Say what you will about the pleasures of high-end neuroscience, there was nothing like a good amputation to make a surgeon's day.

The rhino had been looking directly at Berg, as if assessing the worthiness of him as a foe. So Berg had no choice but to shoot it on its massively armored front.

All of the rounds sparked off, naturally. The only possible target was one of the slit-narrowed eyes and the slits were actually narrower across than the size of the round. But they apparently had the desired effect. The rhino, without any directly noticeable action, seemed to *focus* on the suit of armor and lightning crackled between its horns. A ball of green fire started off as a pinpoint but swelled rapidly and Berg ducked back and to the side, hoping to avoid the fungus, hoping to survive, hoping to live to see Brooke again.

"Lyle, Move!" the first sergeant ordered as Berg ducked back. He was standing right behind the cannoneer and pushed him forward so that the two bounded into the corridor nearly side by side. For a brief moment they were the target of every thorn-thrower in the ranks ahead of them, then the world went white.

The explosion lifted Berg's heavy Wyvern armor and tossed it against the far wall like a child tossing a ball. It threw him right into the bulged out mass of Dreen-spread fungus, the dreaded scourge that still turned up on Earth. The only known Class Six Pathogen, it actively attempted to escape custody, generated enzymes and acids that worked at any containment, cut through Wyvern armor slowly but inexorably and was nearly impossible to eradicate. The primary method of eradication was fire, the red

hot kind usually with gasoline and kerosene mixed with aluminum and lots of it.

So, in a way, Berg was in luck. Because when the plasma
round hit the doorframe he'd been standing by, the temperature
in the compartment raised several thousand degrees and crisped
the fungus long before it could become a threat to his armor.

Of course, his internal temperature soared as well. He was
slammed into a wall at thirty miles per hour, the room was roasting, the inside of his armor was literally the temperature of a
baking oven, the fungus was fully engulfed and he was wreathed
in flames and smoke. The last thing Berg clearly remembered
was the bright white flash.

The first sergeant took the explosion on his armor and rolled.
The blast was hard enough that he found himself on his face,
back in the intersection of the corridor. But there just *weren't*
any enemies between himself and the open area that held a
rhino-tank. He had only a moment. The tanks seemed to assess
the results of their fire and then roar in triumph. He had just
that brief moment to get to his feet, charge forward and get one
shot. Just one.

There was just one problem. The corridor was trashed. The
blast had smashed both bulkheads, the deck and the overhead.
Strands of wire blocked the way and the deck was open to the
next section down: it was a maze he could make his way through
with luck and time. Charging was out of the question. But he
charged. There was a narrow lip on the port side. If he could
make it across . . .

He could hear the chuff-chuff of the rhino. He'd heard it before,
recalled the stench of burning uniforms, burning skin—some of
it his own—surrounded by dead Marines, a young sergeant in a
battle he didn't understand and couldn't seem to win. He was
not going to lose this one . . .

And he slipped. The ledge was just that narrow. There was no
way that the bulbous armor could make it past and he grasped
the edge of the smoking hole with the arms of his suit as he
slammed into that edge. And knew that he'd lost. Again. That
that fucking rhino was going to kill all his Marines *again* . . .

He saw a smoking, stinking, blazing apparition. There was very
little that could burn on a Wyvern suit. Normally. But being in

near proximity to a plasma blast was not "normally." Space rated joints and aluminum exterior fittings smoking, the very ammunition chain firing in the exploding back-magazine, but this the Wyvern, nonetheless, strode out of the fire and smoke of the compartment, two massive pistols unwavering.

There was a roar.

There were, in fact, other ways to kill a rhino. The chief just hadn't had any time to practice one of them. Like any tank, it could only be heavily armored in certain directions. Most of it was up front.

There was, in fact, one small patch on the *back* of the head that was vulnerable to just about *anything*. Oh, it had enough armor to protect from secondary effects, but a high velocity rifle round would cut through it. The problem was getting up and behind a rhino-tank.

But, leaving Gunny Neely in place and fighting his way through the remnants of the dog-demons facing them, the chief trotted down the corridor. It was a ship and it was surprisingly humanlike. Oh, somebody bigger than humans but they seemed to think alike. SEALs trained *a lot* in the layout of ships. One of their main missions was to take them down, after all.

He found the elevator right where he expected, took it up one level, headed back. He'd used the same system as the first sergeant to examine what Two-Gun was looking at as the sergeant received his suicidal orders. And they were good orders. Top knew what had to be done and he ordered it. Miller admired that in a leader. But there was such a thing as a back-up plan. And while Miller wasn't going to steal First Sergeant Powell's thunder, wasn't going to undercut his authority, it wasn't like Top *outranked* him.

So he trotted down a corridor and found what he thought he'd find, a walkway looking down into something that looked one hell of a lot like a quarterdeck. You had to have *some* place to assemble troops. You tended to put it near the bridge, so the CO or the admiral didn't have to walk too far. And you set it up so people could watch. Whoever built this thing thought *a lot* like humans.

There was a dog-demon guarding it. On the other hand, it was watching the fray below. Like their larger cousins, because biologists had determined that the two were closely related, the dog-demon had this little *patch* right behind its armored head . . .

And so there was no longer a dog-demon guarding the walkway. Miller ducked back as the rhino fired. No reason to stand around when plasma was going off.

He stepped back out as it chuffed, took aim, stopped and waited as Two-Gun—what a *kid!*—stumbled out of the smoke and flames of what should have killed him by all rights and blazed away with his two cut-down Barretts. Of course, the kid couldn't see. Most of his optics had to have been blasted out and the vision plate on the front of his armor was covered in soot. But it was a game show, really game. Damn that kid was good. Miller couldn't like him more unless he was a SEAL.

The chief shook his head inside his armor and fired one round from the 14.5, blowing out the brains of the preparing-to-charge-and-fire-again-I'm-going-to-smear-that-suit-of-armor rhino. Which dropped like a pithed frog just as Two-Gun's pistols clicked back empty. Really, unless you looked real close the damage from a 14.5 through the back of the head wasn't going to look all that different than a .50 through the soft palate of the mouth.

Berg collapsed and the SEAL chief warrant officer ghosted back down the corridor, unnoticed.

"And *that* sounded expensive," Spectre admitted as the ship dropped out of warp. "What do you think, Command Weaver? Over or under a billion?"

In space, nobody can hear you scream. But you could hear a ship scream, it transmitted through the feet of your boots, through hands gripping stanchions and controls. And the *Vorpal Blade* was screaming a death knell.

"Under a billion," Bill replied.

"XO? Damage report."

"We just lost the tail," the XO said over the command freq.

"You mean the towed array sonar?" Spectre replied. "No big deal. Sonar is not a necessary component at the moment."

"No, Captain, I mean the *tail*. The ship just broke apart aft of the main engine room."

"Good, Commander Weaver owes me a dollar," the CO said. They'd just lost the very expensive towed array sonar, yes. But also the propellers, the turbines that drove them, the reducing gear and just about everything that made a submarine capable of *being* a submarine. "However, we don't use any of that stuff in space. It was just more target area. Any casualties?"

"Not on that run," the XO replied. "But if we take a round through the sickbay it's going to get ugly."

"Agreed. How's the neutrino generator holding up?"

"The tribble is still successfully duct taped to the phaser, Conn!"

"Good," Spectre said uncertainly. "Prepare for another run."

"Now *that* was something that I hadn't expected," Weaver said, chuckling.

"And *that* was?"

"That Commander Belts-And-Suspenders was a Voltaire fan. Somehow I'm having a hard time wrapping my head around that image."

"The philosopher?"

"Musician. It's a long story, sir."

"For later then," the CO said. "Pilot, engage."

"Oh, *grapp* me," Berg muttered. "Hello?"

He was roasting. The inside of the suit was like an oven; it had to be over a hundred degrees, maybe two hundred.

"Hello?" he yelled.

"You there, Two-Gun?" a voice sounded through the armor. A claw scrabbled at the vision port and then another came into view. He found himself looking at the first sergeant through the two thick panes of aliglass.

"Top?" Berg yelled. "I think *everything* is out on this thing." He pushed at his actuators and managed to get an arm moving but it was like lifting weights.

"I've been checking it out," the first sergeant yelled. "All your motivators are out but it's functional in manual mode. Drink some water, though. You're going to dehydrate fast until it cools down."

Berg sucked at the water nipple, then shrugged.

"I think the bladder burst from the heat," Berg said, coughing. "That would explain the steam."

Even without motivators it was still possible to roll a Wyvern upright. Not easy, mind you, but possible. But when he got to his feet, he started to sway and shimmy.

"What the hell?" Berg shouted.

"Look at Two-Gun disco," a voice boomed from behind him. "Welcome to the manual version of the Wyvern. They *suck* and I say that as someone with *way* too much time in them."

"What happened?" Berg shouted back, turning stiffly to see the chief standing behind him. Unlike his own and the first sergeant's, the chief's armor was pristine, with the exception of a splotch of blood on one claw.

"You got it, son," First Sergeant Powell shouted. "You got it. Good job."

"Great," Berg said. "How? My machine gun's off-line."

"Here," the first sergeant replied, holding out Berg's pistols. Both were locked back. He didn't even recall firing them.

"Oh," Berg said. "Great."

"Hang on," another voice boomed. "Just hold still."

"Do I got fungus on me?" Berg yelled, suddenly. "Get it off if I do!"

"Crisped," the first sergeant replied.

"Fried to cracklin'," the chief added. "Seriously burned up totally. Not an issue."

"Okay," Berg shouted, suddenly realizing he'd heard the last clearly. "Lurch?"

"I've got the commo module replaced," the former armorer replied. "How's that?"

"Great," Berg said normally. "Motivators?"

"Harder," Lurch replied. "Those I don't have spares for."

Berg's armor rocked forward and his machine gun came into view.

"You can fire one of these things offhand," Lurch said, handing him the 14.5. "But they're kind of heavy without motivators. And your ammo's—"

"Blown up," Chief Miller finished. "Seriously, son, you should see the back of your armor. It's almost funny. The good news is the blow-out panels work."

"Great," Berg said. "What now, First Sergeant?"

"You are going to secure this corner," Top said, chuckling. "Patrol this area and try to avoid contact. Got it?"

"I'm all for that one, First Sergeant," Berg admitted. "You guys can feel free to drive the *grapp* on. I'll happily assume my guard of this position until your return. How long do I give you?"

"One hour, then retreat to the holding area," the first sergeant replied. "Do you understand your orders?"

"Aye, aye, First Sergeant," Berg said.

"Come on," Top said, looking around at the remaining four. "Let's go."

Berg watched their retreating forms and reached up to scratch his face. He felt like he was peeling from a sunburn. Which probably meant burns which he shouldn't scratch so he stopped. Except for his eyebrow which was really . . . there wasn't any hair, there. The claw of his suit, nonetheless, continued to scratch across the face of his trashed sensor pod as he considered his predicament.

All his usual sensors were down. He had external audio, two way, and commo, two way. Weapon traverse out, manual movement only, no cameras. Basically, he could lurch around, look through the soot-covered porthole to see where he was going and maybe lift and fire the machine gun. No water, and the heat from the suit was dehydrating him fast. Internal gravity, which he'd hardly noticed before, seemed over Earth normal. So not only was the suit hard as hell to move, he was trying to do it in a heavy gravitational field.

Maulk.

The machine gun was heavy as hell and there weren't but twenty rounds for it so he leaned it against the bulkhead. He scratched his eyebrow again and considered the bottom of his suit. There was water pooled down there. He was pretty sure it was mixed with urine but drinking your own urine was actually recommended by some doctors, so at the very least it wasn't going to kill him. And he was really thirsty. The problem was, there was no *way* to get to it inside the suit. What he needed was a straw. A really *long* straw.

There was a power feed that led from the reactor to the sensor pod up the starboard side of the armor. It was accessible through a box he could just reach . . .

"Heh," he muttered. Wasn't going to be using *that* insulator as a straw. The entire compartment was one mass of fused wiring, and opening it increased the already serious ozone level in the suit by an order of magnitude. "*Grapp.*"

He picked up the machine gun again, with difficulty, and paused at a skittering sound. Like . . . claws. On metal. Like . . .

He stood stock still as, across the open area, a group of dog-demons headed aft in the direction of the Marines that had just left. When they were past, he backed up, as quietly as he could in an unpowered suit, and fell through the hole in the deck.

"*Grapp,*" he muttered again, looking up at the hole. He must have made a noise that could be heard back on Earth, two hundred light-years away.

He'd been in some seriously *grapped* situations, but this one was starting to take the cake. He hated the idea, but he needed to hide. Find a compartment the Dreen didn't seem to be using, or escape and evade back to the recycling compartment and link up with Norman and Priester. His suit, at this point, was more *grapped* up than theirs. Actually, that sort of cut out E&Eing back to the recycling compartment. He could barely lurch along the corridors like a zombie; escape and evade was going to have to emphasize minimum distances.

He stumbled down the corridor to a T intersection, listened for movement, then looked both ways as carefully as he could. But it necessitated getting in the corridor and moving around in a circle, like an old time helmet diver. Careful was a relative term.

It also was a terrible place to hide because both corridors terminated in hatches that looked as if they went to lifts. And both the control pads glowed light violet. They'd run across those before and they always meant the door was locked.

He turned around again, trying to figure out which way to go, and heard the skitter of claws on metal from the way he'd come. He backed down the corridor, figuring he'd put his back to the elevator at the end of the port corridor and make a last stand. As the claws approached he hefted the machine gun, trying to get a sight picture through the soot-covered porthole.

Just as he figured the approaching Dreen were on the last stretch of corridor before his, he heard a whooshing sound behind him. Turning with difficulty, he found the previously locked elevator was now open, lit by a blue glow.

He stumbled into it and the door closed automatically . . .

"This *grapping* sucks," Miller snarled. They'd found two routes that indicated headed to the purple area, both of them locked. Which just meant they were probably on the right track. "There's got to be a way to blow this door down."

"We might need to figure that out fast," Gunny Neely said from the end of the short corridor. "We've got Dreen closing our position."

"Chief Warrant, if you'd try to convince this door to open, I'd appreciate it," the first sergeant said. "I'm going to join Corporal Lyle and the Gunny in securing this corridor."

"On it," Miller replied. "*This* time I brought demo."

27

"Negative engagement," the pilot said.

Spectre looked around the conn and wasn't surprised that the warp/normal space lash-up they had been using so effectively for so long no longer worked. He could see the sun playing across the rubble where the sonar room used to be. Among other things, there was only half a bulkhead there. For that matter, there was a patch of sun working its way across Commander Weaver's position. Fortunately, the mass driver round had penetrated *behind* the astrogation position, missing the commander. Unfortunately, it had punched through two *more* decks into the crew mess. The mess was overflowing with wounded from the battle; crew were struggling to seal it again before the wounded died of asphyxia.

"Tactical, Conn," Spectre said, struggling to keep the fatigue out of his voice. The battle just seemed to go on and on.

"Tactical."

The voice wasn't the TACO.

"Who's this? Chief Brooks? Where's the TACO?"

"Sickbay, Conn," the tactical chief replied. "Took a fragment to the chest. We got his suit patched but . . . It doesn't look good."

"Understood," the CO said. "Engagement system is down."

"We're on it, Conn. Appears to be overheating of some of the interface chips. We're attempting to repair."

"Enemy status?"

"Sierra One, Sierra Seven, Sierra Fifteen and nine Bandits

remaining in BatRon One. Six more Bandits, Sierra Six remaining from CruRon One. Estimate Bandits attached to CruRon One unable to return for replenishment. Sierra three, CruRon One, will be unable to engage for a minimum of three hours. Sierra Twelve dead in space. Primary threat, BatRon One, continues on course to intercept Hexosehr fleet. Sierra One has been engaging at long range but negative impact on Hexosehr fleet. Estimate, based on Hexosehr maneuvering delta, impact guaranteed at seven light-seconds. Estimate forty minutes to that range for Sierra One."

"Got that," Spectre said. "Conn out. Eng, Conn."

"Go, Conn."

"Status?"

"Primary drive system offline. Working on secondary. Drive is up. Spare neutrino generators ready for replacement."

"Roger," the CO said. "Conn, out."

"Be interesting flying home like this," Weaver said.

Spectre looked at his suit indicator and realized it was on a private frequency. The rest of the conn crew couldn't hear it.

"If we can take out Sierra One, the Hexosehr can patch us up easily enough," the CO said.

"Yes, sir," Bill said dubiously.

"And you have an issue with that, Commander?"

"I just don't think it's possible," Weaver admitted. "If we still had the *Caurorgorngoth*, maybe. As it is . . ."

"Conn, Comm."

"Go."

"Incoming message from Fleet Master Lurca."

"Put it on."

"Boss Man Spectre," the fleet master said. "Your ship is truly *grapped* up."

"Thank you for that vote of confidence, Lurca," Spectre replied. "We need to do some minor repairs on our battle system, but we will be back in the battle soon."

"I am dispatching a fleet collier," Lurca said. "I am transmitting its path. If your engines continue to work, move to intercept it. The collier has engineers onboard that may be of assistance."

"We appreciate that, Fleet Master."

"The engineers have been working on a shield generator capable of interfacing with your systems," Lurca continued. "If it works, you will have some shielding against plasma."

"I cannot begin to express my gratitude," Spectre said. "Be aware, though, that our tacticians estimate only forty minutes until the battlewagon is in range of your fleet. If we have not taken it out by that time, this battle will be for nothing."

"Our tacticians have the same estimate," Lurca replied. "Which is why you must use your engine to intercept the collier."

"On our way," Spectre said. "Weaver?"

"Course transmitted to pilot," the astrogator said.

"Pilot, engage."

Matching course and speed with the collier was not difficult, even using the secondary engine controls. As soon as they were matched, a veritable army of Hexosehr swarmed across the intervening space, disdaining hatches and entering through the numerous holes in the ship.

"Senior Engineer Elirgoth," the lead Hexosehr said as he swarmed into the conn. The ship had shut down engines to permit easier movement by the Hexosehr, the conversion to gravity being an issue on the outside of the ship.

"Commanding Officer Steven Blankemeier," the CO said. "Spectre. This is my executive officer, who is in charge of repairs."

"We see the most critical need being to install the shield generator," Elirgoth replied through his translator. "The specifications for your ship have changed but we should be able to adjust. We will install it on the hull near your power generation system. That will be the shortest run. My peripheral teams have orders to meet with your damage control crews and assist. We will remain on-board the ship, if that is acceptable, during the battle. We have patching material coming across to seal critical areas. In addition we have hull plates we can install in patches to shield critical zones. Show us where to work and we can work *very* fast."

"Follow me," the XO said. "I'll show you where to install the shield generator and talk to you about other critical needs."

"See, what did I tell you?" the CO said as soon as they'd left.

"I still don't see us taking out the battlewagon," Weaver said.

"Oh, I'm going to take it out," Spectre replied.

"Yes, sir. How if I might ask?"

"If it comes down to it we're going to fly right in that damned mass-driver and blow the engines."

》　　　》　　　》

"What *is* this stuff?"

Miller hadn't been joking about bringing demo. If *his* suit had been in Berg's condition, he would have taken out a couple *more* compartments with all the octocellulose he was carrying in his butt-pack.

But despite using the strongest conventional explosive in the military inventory, over four times the power of C-4, even with tamping the blast with the dead bodies of Dreen, he still hadn't managed to scratch the secured door.

He had, however, managed to coat the entire hallway in a very nice shade of light violet from the blood of the Dreen ersatz sandbags.

"I don't know, Chief," Lyle replied. "But you're about out of demo."

"Jeff, I'm getting nothing, here," Miller admitted. The door just mocked him. "I hope you're running out of Dreen, because I don't need any more bodies."

"Alas, no," the first sergeant replied. "And I do believe I just heard a roar from down the corridor."

"In that case, I'll keep some of my demo," Miller said, shaking his head. "There's actually a couple of other ways that rhino-tanks have been taken out. They're just much lower probability. Like, damned near zero."

"Engage."

It had taken a bare thirty minutes for the shield generator to be installed, hard points placed over Conn, Engineering, Sickbay and Tactical, and the overheated nodes rebuilt or replaced by the Hexosehr engineers.

Some had swarmed back to the collier, but others remained, continuing to work even as the ship went back into battle.

The destroyer designated Sierra Fifteen swelled in the viewscreen, its face a mass of plasma bolts, lasers and blazing mass drivers. The improved *Blade* ignored the fire, pausing for a moment to adjust and then flashing out a chaos ball that ripped through the destroyer like tissue paper.

"Conn, Tactical. Sierra Fifteen no longer accelerating."

On the main viewscreen the dots could be seen separating, and the battlescreen updated as the remaining two ships of the Dreen taskforce thundered past their damaged brethren.

"Conn, Tactical. Fighters moving out from BatRon One. Appear to be headed for the Hexosehr corvettes."

"I hope they can deal with them," Spectre said. "Tactical, get us lined up on Sierra One. It's time to go for the heavy."

"Where'd they go?" Miller asked, looking around the corner. The corridor beyond was piled with the bodies of Dreen dog-demons and thorn-throwers. But there were none moving. Well, a couple of dog-demons were trying to drag themselves forward, their bodies ripped by machine-gun and cannon fire. He popped the targets in the head but those were the only enemies in the corridor.

"I don't know," First Sergeant Powell replied. "One minute they were rushing us in a mass wave, the next they pulled back."

From down the corridors there was a roar that shook the ship and a crunch as of a heavily armored tank running into a wall.

"Uh, oh," Miller said.

"I guess they got out of the way for the heavy."

A pair of horns appeared at the end of the passage and Miller fired at them, striking sparks from the refractory material.

"What are you doing?" Powell snapped.

"Behind us is a dead *grapping* end," Miller replied, continuing to fire into the flank of the massive rhino-tank as it inched around the corner. It was having to slam its bulk into the bulkheads, bending the corners, to get around the turn. "If we let it get down to here, we're *grapped*."

The rhino finally got enough of its bulk into the corridor to turn its head towards the two fighters in the intersection and focused on them for a moment. Sparks began to fly between its horns and the SEAL and the Marine backed up.

"Incoming plasma!" First Sergeant Powell snapped as a ball of green fire flew down the corridor. The explosion blasted fire and smoke back down the passageway, but didn't harm the Wyverns.

"You know," Miller said in a thoughtful tone. "If we could figure out a way to get it shoot that *hatch*, and survive mind you . . ."

"It's an elevator," Powell said.

"Okay, point. Guess we'll just have to kill it."

Berg stepped out of the elevator and looked around. As far as he could tell, it was just another of the seemingly endless corridors of the ship. There was a short corridor to a T intersection with the usual color-coded markers. This time, though, one of the purple ones was flashing.

He looked at that and blinked his eyes, then limped down the passage it indicated. There was a hatch about thirty meters down but before he could open it, it slid aside, revealing two thorn-throwers and a dog-demon.

He dropped the machine gun and drew his pistols automatically. One of the thorn-throwers had its back turned but the other fired immediately. Too soon, because the burst of thorns went by Berg with an evil whistling sound.

His .50 caliber round went right into its thorn projector, which, since it was mounted in the thing's snout, meant right through its brain case.

A second round caught the spinning thorn-thrower in the side; a third went through its head. The fourth through seventh of the magazine were expended on the charging dog-demon, which slid to a stop a few feet from his boots.

"I gotta get a better job," Berg said, reloading with one of his few remaining magazines. He was so hot and dehydrated, his vision was wobbly and his coordination was off. For that matter, he swore he'd heard voices a minute ago. Or at least a voice whispering in an alien tongue. He managed to seat the mag after dropping it only once and holstered his pistol. He started to pick up the machine gun, then just left it where it had dropped and continued to lurch down the corridor.

Beyond was a room filled with what looked like control positions and computers. At least, that was what his struggling brain was telling him. He thought he saw a mermaid for a second, but then resolved it as a bunch of the alien script on one wall. Sure looked like a mermaid if you sort of turned your head, though. He tilted his head back and forth and snorted. If you were hallucinating, maybe.

The control positions were arranged sort of like an auditorium with the door entering at the base and the positions stretching up to his left. He wondered for a second why that would be and then looked to his right. He had to lean back, carefully, to see what the operators would have seen. It was a big screen that was actually active, showing a series of colored lights scattered across its face. Some of them had alien script next to them and a few had what looked a lot like arrows. Some were purple, others blue. There were two blue ones right in the middle of the screen and one way off to the side. There was another cluster of blue on the left side of the screen. Near the edge on the left there were some orange ones. And one about halfway up the left-hand side. As he watched, it vanished for a moment, appeared again near the two blue dots, then vanished again, reappearing in its original location.

At almost the same time he felt the ship begin rumbling from fire along the port side. Then there was a thump, felt more than heard, and a klaxon began to ring.

One of the orange dots on the far left had a sort of diamond around it. The diamond began to flash and the whine of the main gun started up again.

"Okay, I know where this is going," Berg said. He really hoped he met the creators of this ship some day because they were so much like humans it was scary. "I am in the ship's tactical room. Purple is the Dreen. Orange is us and the Hexosehr. And the *Blade*'s fighting this thing, now. And I think we hit it. I wonder if I can turn it off?"

"You cannot," a voice whispered over his communicator. "Continue. Follow the flashes."

Okay, either he was hallucinating again or . . . No, that one had been clear. And in English.

"Okay," Berg said, lurching forward. There was another hatch on the far side of the room and the control panel was flashing. "Okay, I can do this. Either it's a fever dream or . . . something stranger. But I can do this."

"We can do this," Miller argued.

"It's *grapping* insane," Powell replied. "But we're all gonna die, anyway, so why not?"

"Lurch, you get the left leg," Miller continued. "Neely, the right. I've got the demo."

"And the duct tape," Lyle said. "Don't forget the duct tape."

"What do I do?" the first sergeant asked.

"Pray like hell this works," Miller said. "And pick up the demo if I drop it. And keep that *grapping* beak away from my armor if you can."

The rhino had managed to make it around the far bend and now was humping into view, grunting under its breath and rolling its beady eyes at the humans in the corridor.

"Wait for it," Miller said, crouching on his knees a bare couple of meters from the stuck rhino. "Wait for it to get stuck in the turn."

The rhino lurched to its left, crumpling the steel of the bulkhead and gathering room for the turn. Then it lurched forward, smashing the other side and tried to spin in place, getting jammed between the forward bulkhead and the port.

"Now!" Miller snapped.

Lyle slid forward on his belly wheels, then came up, holding onto the left leg of the beast. Neely slid forward, also, grabbing the right.

Miller flipped onto his back and pushed off from the bulkhead, sliding under the rhino as the two Wyverns struggled to lift the thing into the air. Its claws raked bare inches from his Wyvern, struggling to gain purchase on its smaller tormentors.

Powell slid forward and straddled the SEAL, grabbing the underside of the thing's beak and straining to lift it. The rhino's eyes rolled bare inches from his cameras and it was *much* closer than he ever wanted to be to a rhino-tank again in his life.

"Emplaced," Miller said, grabbing the thing's legs and sliding out from under the monster. "Get back!"

All three of the Marines released almost simultaneously and Lyle and Neely grabbed the SEAL, dragging him back just as the rhino pawed at where he had been.

"Seven, six, five . . ." Miller counted.

"It's charging," the first sergeant pointed out. "Down!"

The rhino, though, could duck its head now, and pointed the charging ball of plasma right at the four Wyvern suits cowering on the floor.

"Two . . . one . . ."

The plasma fired at *almost* the same moment as the improvised explosive strapped to the beast's underside. Almost. In fact, it fired precisely four milliseconds afterwards. But that was long enough to lift the multiton rhino nearly a foot, so the plasma blasted past the Marines and the SEAL and, in fact, impacted directly on the door of the lift.

Rhino-tanks were, in fact, very well armored. But four kilos of octocellulose duct-taped to its belly exceeded its rated design limits. The center of the massive organic tank exploded all over the corridor, raining intestines, stomachs and other less identifiable bits in every direction.

Furthermore, the SEAL had slid *way* back on the tank, figuring that the armor would fall off the farther it went to the rear. Thus the powerful explosive lifted the massive creature up and forward.

Right on the four cowering suits.

"Well, Todd," First Sergeant Powell said. "This is another fine mess you've gotten us into. My first gunny warned me never to work with SEALs. I knew I should have listened to him."

"Excuse me, First Sergeant," Lyle said. "But do I hear claws approaching?"

"Cool," Berg muttered, leaning back and looking up at another massive viewscreen. This one was speckled with stars, somehow giving an impression of three dimensions. The conditions were too complicated for him to figure out but he was pretty sure it was great intel on the Dreen. Some of the markings *had* to be details of the Dreen empire. Probably other races, as well.

But the control pad on the far side of the compartment was flashing insistently. He didn't know what was at the end of this quest, but it was getting cooler and cooler.

Either that or he was having a very interesting dream as he was being eaten. He was still trying to decide.

"Holy *Grapp!*" Spectre shouted, grateful that his commo was off. The last blast from the Dreen dreadnought had shaken the ship from stem to stern. The defenses of the ship were ten times more powerful than those of either the destroyers or the carrier. If it hadn't been for the Hexosehr patches, the *Blade* would have been cut in half long before.

Looking over his shoulder, though, he would tell that had been a serious hit. Tactical was . . .

"Conn, Damage Control," the XO said wearily. "We're down. We barely made it back into warp. Tactical is gone, half the interfaces are blown. All external cameras and sensors are destroyed. We can't see, can't hear and can barely maneuver."

"Get me a forward view," Spectre said. "I don't care how you do it. And get me in touch with Lurca. It's time to end this fight."

The final compartment was surprisingly small compared to the "auditoriums" of the tactical and navigation rooms, but it was cool. The main viewscreen had been tuned to give a view of a world with cool, crisp mountains beside a crashing sea. It wasn't anywhere on Earth that Berg recognized and the color of the sky wasn't quite right unless he was much mistaken. Other than that, it looked sort of like someplace in Scotland or Ireland.

It took him a moment to spot the massive pile of Dreen fungus built up around a central dais. There was a big chair, apparently for the commander, on top of the dais. From his position, all he could see was the pile of fungus and a bunch of tubes running out of it, wrapping around the chair towards . . .

An occupant. Lurching forward he could see that something was in the seat and as he approached the forward viewscreen and turned he could see that the occupant was small, the size of a human child. An emaciated cat.

A Mreee.

Humans had thought the Mreee wiped out. It was the world of the felinoids that Weaver and Miller had shoved the ardune bomb on top of, shutting the Dreen gates to Earth. The six-hundred-megaton bomb should have wiped the low-tech culture from the face of their planet. Even the few surviving captured Mreee, who despite heroic attempts to keep them alive had all eventually died, thought their race had been wiped out. But here was one commanding a Dreen task force.

"Welcome, human," the Mreee gasped, the voice labored. "Welcome to hell."

"How can you talk?" Berg asked.

"I must command this battle, but parts of me remain, to a degree, free," the Mreee gasped. "What good a voice that none can hear? What good eyes that can only look forward? The Dreen care nought for such. But you must hurry. Your friends are about to die and your ship is sore pressed. When it attacks again, I will destroy it and my security is about to destroy the remaining Marines. Unless you act."

"What do I have to do?" Berg asked.

"Kill me," the Mreee replied. "But first I must give you orders. On the right side of this room as I sit is a panel with purple symbols like one of your L's. When I am dead, press each of these three times. That will open up all of the airlocks and doors on the ship. It is a firefighting measure. The ship will be unscathed; it can handle vacuum quite well; its Karchava builders were thorough. But the Dreen and their fungus cannot survive vacuum. You must empty all the air and that will destroy the Dreen. The two destroyers will remain but your ship should be able to survive then and triumph. But you *must* empty the air. Now, kill me and be about your orders."

"Can't I just pull . . ."

"That would kill me, more painfully," the Mreee hissed. "Your pistol, Two-Gun. Use it. Free me from this hell. Please. Be aware, security is coming. You must act quickly. There are other survivors. If you meet any of my people . . ."

"I will tell them of your sacrifice," Berg said, lifting the pistol. "Go with God."

"And you, Two-Gun."

"Okay, this is going to be all manual control," Spectre said. "The objective is to get close enough to the battlewagon that when the engine goes we'll take it out."

The casualties had been moved to the collier as had all nonessential personnel. That included Miss Moon who had, to everyone's surprise, survived.

"We'll warp in as close as possible, then go in the rest of the way on manual control of the normal space drive," Spectre continued. "Most of our armor is oriented upwards, so we'll try to maintain that relativity. We only have about three minutes until the battlewagon reaches engagement range. Everyone take your positions. And I have to say I'm proud of all of you. No crew in history has fought so hard and so long with such success. I love you all. Now, let's go kill ourselves."

"As a battlecry that leaves something to be desired," Bill said as the crew resumed their positions.

"There's no need for you to be here, Commander Weaver," the CO said. "You know as well as I do when the drive detonates it's just going to be sitting there in space. The Hexosehr have promised to make a new ship from scratch if necessary so the survivors can get back to Earth."

"Might be sumpin I kin do t' git us all kilt," the astrogator said, for once letting his full Southern accent slip free. "Gonna be funner than skinnin' a lahv coon."

"Ayup," Spectre replied. "Pilot?"

"Conn, Commo."

"Go, Commo," the CO replied. "We've *got* commo?"

"Retrans through the Hexosehr collier. Lurca. Voice only."

"Go."

"Ship Master Blankemeier, Fleet Master Lurca. Hold your run."

"You're about to get taken out, Lurca," Spectre replied. "We don't have *time* to . . ."

"The Dreen dreadnought has ceased acceleration," the fleet master replied. "It has opened all its hatches and is blasting air and water into the ether. I do not know the significance of this, but . . ."

"What the hell?" Spectre said. "What about the destroyers?"

"They continue forward," Lurca admitted. "If anything, they are accelerating. But they will require an hour to get in range with plasma weapons and the dreadnought is open to space and has ceased fire. We have time—"

"XO!" Spectre snapped. "I want the combat engagement system back up in twenty minutes! Get to it!"

"*Grapp, grapp, grapp* . . ." Miller muttered, trying to move the beast on his back.

"If we all lift at once . . ." Powell suggested.

"Got it," Miller said. "Ready, one, two . . ."

There was a blast of sound in the background, like a tornado, and the Wyverns could feel a rumble transmitted through the deck. Thumps resounded along the corridor as hatches flew open.

"What the *grapp*?" Lyle asked. "My external air pressure sensor is dropping like a rock."

A dog-demon scrabbled around the corner, coming into Miller's view. But it was clearly struggling. Its beak opened and closed, gasping for air as it collapsed a foot from him. He watched it continue to gasp its last then slowly boil as the external air turned to vacuum. It wasn't a fast process, there was a lot of air in the massive ship, so he got to watch it in slow motion.

"Okay," Miller said as the thing in front of him started to freeze-dry. "We don't have to worry about Dreen, but we've *still* got this mother on our back. So. A one and a two . . ."

EPILOGUE

"I don't see repairing this ship," Lurca said, looking at the *Blade*. "It is so damaged as to be useful for nothing but scrap metal."

"Hey, the engine still works," Spectre argued. "If we could figure out how to survive in suits for thirty days, we could fly it home."

"Where it would be scrapped," the XO pointed out.

"Well . . ." Spectre said. "But it's a *good* ship!"

"It is a most excellent ship," Lurca said. "But it would be better to make you a new one."

"You've got supply problems," Spectre said. "I know you've got good fabricators, but . . ."

"The food you supplied to the visitors," Lurca said, "could you get more to us within a year?"

"A year?" the CO said. "We could probably get more to you in a couple of weeks. How much?"

"As many tons as possible," Lurca said. "But we would need it in no more than a year. But if I have the food supplies, all the rest is easily enough gathered. If you can promise us resupply, I will take you at your word and rouse our full engineering force. Using our repair fabricators, we can build a ship of this size, much more robust and with more of the small chaos generators, in no more than one of your months. But I take you at your promise that you will return with food. Otherwise my crews will starve."

329

"Done," Spectre promised. "Food for a ship? Oh, yeah. I'll take that trade any day."

"We will get started on a new ship immediately," Lurca said. "We'll need to get your technical people involved in design. I understand they are getting on well with my engineers . . ."

"That is *grapping* cool," Gants said, pulling the machined piece out of the Hexosehr device.

He'd taken a metal blank and put it through the wringer. The Hexosehr device cut metal in ways that should have been impossible, actually cutting *inside* of the outer face if so ordered. He'd started with a square blank of metal and ended up with something that looked like a seriously intercut medallion, with bits of metal lingering in the cut-out sections.

"Nice," Red said, slapping his right thigh. "Nearly as nice as this leg. And they built it in a few minutes from design up."

"I wonder if there's some way to buy in on this before anybody knows," Gants said, sucking his teeth. "This is going to change . . . everything."

"Yeah, except for one little item," Red said. "The Dreen are coming."

"Hell, we took out one of their battleships," Gants said, shrugging.

"And as far as we can tell, lost all the Marines that did it."

"Found you," the first sergeant said, walking onto the bridge.

"Figured you would sooner or later," Berg said. He was leaning back against the viewscreen, looking at the shriveled body of the Mreee. He'd been there for several hours, wondering when his air would run out. "I mean, how hard was it going to be?"

"Until we found those blinking lights, pretty damned hard," Miller opined. "Every hatch on this ship is open."

"I figured I should give plenty of time for any of the fungus that got in odd places to die," Berg said, lurching to his feet and returning to the damage control console. When he hit the buttons again, he could feel hatches throughout the ship closing. As the hatch on the bridge closed, air began to flood the compartment.

"Hmmm . . ." Miller said. "O_2 levels are good, pressure's good. I wonder what it smells like?"

"I figure we'll find out in about fifteen minutes," Berg replied. "Unless you brought any spare O_2. I'm getting pretty low."

» » »

"It certainly appears dead," the tactical specialist said.

"We shall be cautious," the corvette master ordered. "If it becomes live, we will quickly die."

"Corvette Master," the commo tech said. "We are receiving broadcast in human method and speech from the ship."

"Put it on."

". . . this net, this is Bravo Company Marines. We have captured the Dreen dreadnought. All Dreen onboard are dead, as is the sentient. We're nearly out of air. Request assistance. Any station this net, this is Bravo Company Marines. We have captured the Dreen dreadnought. All Dreen . . ."

"Contact the humans," the corvette master said. "Tell them we have found their lost fighters."

"Sir, you might want to take a look at this."

The duty officer for the Space Command Central Watch Post walked over to the long-range sensor controls and looked over the staff sergeant's shoulder.

"Is that the *Blade?*" the colonel asked. "About damned time. They're nearly thirty days beyond where anyone thought they could survive."

"I'm not sure, sir," the sergeant said. "Some of its emissions are the same as the *Blade*. Others aren't. More neutrino output, more meson. More output, period."

"Sir," the visuals tech said. "That is negative on the *Blade*, sir."

"What?" the colonel asked, striding over. "Sound alarm. Send a Flash message that we have an unknown—"

"Incoming message, sir," Communications interjected. "It has the *Blade*'s coding on it." The printer started to clatter and the tech ripped it off, handing it to a signal runner.

"Belay that alarm," the colonel said. "But wake up Admiral Granger."

He took the message form and frowned.

"Yeah, definitely wake up Admiral Granger."

"No, seriously, sir, it's us," Spectre said patiently.

"That is *not* the ship you left in, Captain," the admiral said doggedly. "And if you get any closer to the planet you're going to get engaged."

"Yes, sir, I understand that protocol," Spectre replied as soon as he got the lagging reply. Per doctrine, the *Blade II* was standing off at lunar orbit to await clearance. "I'm sending my full mission report. Read it over and make your decision. But, be aware, you're going to have a hard time shooting the *Blade Two* out of the sky. Among other things, the antimissile systems on this baby are *awesome*. The bad news is we're going to need a lot more ships. A *lot* more ships."

"Welcome to the Oval Office, gentlemen and ma'am," the President said, shaking hands. "Sit, please. Glenda, coffee, please. Commander Weaver, my predecessor spoke highly of you. How do you like your new job?"

"I like it very well, Mr. President," Bill said, taking the proffered cup of coffee.

"I feel I ought to offer you all something stronger, but since you're officially on duty . . . But Miss Moon? You, as a civilian . . ."

"I'm allergic, Mr. President," the linguist said.

"Then that settles that," the President said. "Coffee all around. Captain Blankemeier, I was given an executive summary of your report. Then I asked for a more detailed summary. Then I made the mistake of taking your full report and logs with me for bedtime reading, for which I paid the next day."

"Sorry about that, Mr. President," Spectre replied.

"You have a gift for turn of phrase, Captain. You would make a good speech writer. But you've certainly dropped an enormous . . . something probably obscene in my lap."

"Sorry about that, also, Mr. President," the CO said. "But we were sent out to find out what happened to the colony and then it got a little complicated."

"Agreed," the President said, looking over at the secretary of defense and secretary of state. "Are we sure about the Dreen spread?"

"Yes, sir," the secretary of defense said. "I had analysts go over both the raw data that the Hexosehr had and the astronomical data recovered from the . . . Karchava, was it Staff Sergeant Bergstresser?"

"Yes, Mr. Secretary," Berg snapped. He was sitting rigidly at attention, coffee cup and saucer squared on his lap.

"The Karchava battleship," the secretary continued. "The analysis section agrees that the Dreen are spreading in this direction, as well as others. They put the maximum period before they reach Earth as twenty years. However, if they become aware of our location beforehand, and there are more outposts between us and them, that could be accelerated. I'd like to, again, commend Miss Moon on her linguistic ability. Starting from the point that the Marines reached she has cracked most of the Karchava script. With that, the analysis became solid. The Dreen are on their way. Worse, they overran the species that produced the most powerful ship we have encountered to date. No species has so much as slowed them. And they're headed for our region of space."

The President bowed his head for a moment then looked back up.

"Then we have to prepare for war," he said, looking over at the secretary of state again. "I'm now going to do something rather rare in this office. I'm going to ask you," he continued, looking at the assembled group from the *Blade*, "what your suggestions are in this regard. Among other things, you've had a month longer to assimilate the information."

Spectre looked at the President in surprise for a moment and then cleared his throat.

"You're serious, Mr. President?"

"Don't tell me you haven't discussed it," the President said. "I've thought about it, discussed it with my senior advisers. But I'd like your input."

"Uh . . ." Spectre said.

"A coalition of the willing, Mr. President," Berg said, still sitting rigidly upright and looking past the President. "Led by the United States and including, at a minimum, Great Britain, China, India and Japan. It is preferred that Germany, some of the other Old Europe countries, the Eastern European block and the Seven Tigers are included as well as certain countries in South America. It should specifically *exclude* France."

"Exclude the French?" the secretary of state asked.

"Yes, sir," First Sergeant Powell replied. "Though diplomatically difficult, that's actually rather important."

"Explain," the President said, leaning back and putting his hand over his mouth.

"In the two hundred plus years of our country, we have been involved in wars with the French several times," Weaver said reluctantly. "All of them as allies and all but one to our net detriment. Basically, Mr. President, every time the French get involved in anything, they tend to do more damage to their allies than to their enemies. Examples redound but Vietnam, the War on Terror and World Wars One and Two all come to mind."

"In fact, Mr. President, there was significant discussion of what to do on the way back," Spectre finally admitted. "And the last time we can recall the U.S. benefiting from having the French involved with us was in the Revolution."

"Which, I'd like to add, was when they were under the Bourbons," First Sergeant Powell pointed out. "So, basically, if they're willing to bring back the aristos, we'll think about it. Otherwise, our recommendation is that they be excluded."

"Except for the Legion," Miller interjected.

"Yeah, we'll take the Legion," Spectre agreed.

"And we'll take some volunteers if there are any," Berg said, lightening up. "As soldiers, they're fine. It's their politicians and generals that suck. Oh, boy, do they suck." He suddenly whitened as he realized what he'd just said to the President of the United States.

But the President, far from offended, burst out into laughter and looked over at the secretary of state, who was nearly purple.

"Thank you, gentlemen," the President said, grinning, "for making my point for me. And, I'll add, with some additions I hadn't considered."

"What about the Louisiana Purchase?" the SecState asked, plaintively.

"That was bowing to reality, Mr. Secretary," Miriam said. "As well as sucking our treasury dry."

"Either we were going to take over that territory or the British were," First Sergeant Powell answered. "By selling it to us, Napoleon got money to support his wars *and* kept the British from taking it."

"*And* it was a causative factor of the War of 1812," Miller said.

"I disagree, Todd, I think that war was guaranteed no matter what happened," Powell argued. "England was already angry over us using neutrality to covertly supply Napoleon and we were, of course, wroth over the pressing of—"

"I've got the point," the President said. "Mr. Secretary, that has to be understood in the negotiations. The U.S. will retire from any planetary mutual defense treaty if the French are part

of the pact. We'll go it alone before we'll take any cheese-eaters.
And we're not starting from the point of departure of the UN.
Coalition of the willing; we're the top-dog. Why? Because we're
the only superpower on the planet and we're going to take the
brunt no matter how many allies we have. Dress that up in pretty
diplomatic language when you have the meetings."

"Yes, Mr. President," the secretary of state said with a sigh.

"And don't let your department try to weasel around it," the
President said. "I'm serious."

"I won't, Mr. President."

"The Hexosehr, Captain," the President said.

"They're headed for Runner's World, Mr. President," the captain replied.

"And it will take them a minimum of two years to reach it
with their warp technology," the President said. "Two years we
don't have. How do we speed that up?"

"They'll reach Michelin's World in about six months, Mr.
President," Weaver replied. "There's a gate there that opens up
in Alabama. We can easily move it, though, to anywhere we want
to establish a major base. Open a gate that leads to Runner's
World. Perhaps another to the Cheerick. We can drop both off
quickly enough. Bring what we can fit through a gate from their
ships, their people in deep sleep especially, and move them to
Runner's World. Most of them. Many will end up on Earth or
Adar working on defense systems and bringing in their technology.
They were able to build the *Blade Two*, while on the run and
in deep space, in less than thirty days. Everything from soup to
nuts. We're going to need them leading the drive on developing
the new space navy we're going to require to defend Earth."

"If I may, Mr. President," Miriam interjected. "One of the problems is going to be the economic destabilization caused by their
technology. Their technology is leaps ahead of the Adar which is,
in turn, well ahead of our own. Their fabricators, alone, are going
to impact manufacturing across the globe. The way they work with
metals is going to stand the entire machine-shop industry on its
head. Every precision manufacturer in the world could be put out
of business overnight. Which means that their employees, who are
some of the highest paid and most highly skilled workers in any
industry, are going to be out of jobs. Preparing for that onslaught
is going to be nearly as difficult as preparing for the war."

"On the other hand, Mr. President," First Sergeant Powell said, "when you have two problems . . ."

"Sometimes they cancel out," the President said, nodding. "Such workers would be highly useful, with some retraining, in a space navy. The Draft is on the way, big time."

"We're going to need schools," Weaver said. "We're going to need somebody besides me who can astrogate. We're going to need to send grad students to *their* schools to understand the theory behind their systems. *They're* going to need schools, and supplies and lots of food from the Adar for the time being . . ."

"And now we're getting into details," the President said. "For which I have a very able staff. But I wanted to hear what your thoughts were on the broader picture and I'm delighted that they match my own so well. There will be changes and I'm sure that we will weather them as America always has. But a few are more immediate. Captain Blankemeier."

"Mr. President?"

"I know that you love this new ship that the Hexosehr built much as you loved the one scrapped on the arms of Orion. However, you are leaving command."

"Yes, Mr. President," Spectre said, his face falling.

"You're no longer eligible to command it. I just sent your name to the Senate for confirmation of promotion to rear admiral. It was pointed out to me by some senior officers that there were boards and such for such things and that you are very junior to be a flag officer and I pointed out that not only did we need some admirals who had actually been in space combat, I was commander in chief so I trumped them."

"Thank you, Mr. President," Spectre said, nodding.

"I've been told that as a bipartisan show of support, you're assured confirmation. I was assured that shortly after I showed the Select Armed Forces Committee your mission report. Commander Weaver."

"Mr. President?"

"You've been what the Navy calls 'frocked' for some reason to captain," the President said. "Which means you've got the rank but not the pay. I'm told the pay will come along in time. The same people that mentioned boards were somewhat more vehement that you did not yet have sufficient experience as a naval officer to assume command of the *Blade Two*."

"Understood, Mr. President," Bill said. "And agreed."

"I wouldn't say that the Chief of Naval Operations pitched a fit in this very room, but that's because I'm polite," the President continued. "Persons who shall remain nameless, however, were more than willing to accept you taking the position of Executive Officer, despite the bump in rank which would technically disqualify you, after I again had to use the phrase 'commander in chief.' The *Blade*, until we have other deep space ships, will probably be undergoing a series of skippers. We need officers with experience in space, simple as that. To an extent, in your new position as XO, it will be your job to train them. They will, of course, be your superior officers. They will have time in grade on you, not to mention a superior position in the chain of command. But persons who shall remain nameless were in agreement that one captain can say something to another captain, even if that person is their commander, which a commander could not. If that sentence parses out. Are we on the same page?"

"Yes, sir," Bill replied.

"Very good. And we are left with the inimitable Staff Sergeant Bergstresser," the President said. "The *Blade* is about to undertake some tedious but necessary infrastructure missions for what I believe to be the next several months. In other words the necessity for derring-do is significantly reduced. Are you, once again, going to volunteer to go where no Marine has gone before, Staff Sergeant? Or has the long drawn strife quitted you of the desire for adventure?"

"I will admit, Mr. President, that being baked by a plasma ball and having to take off my suit before I ran out of air, on a Dreen ship, has cooled my ardor," Berg said. "But, no, sir. I'm not quitting if that is your question. I already told the first sergeant that I'm on-board for the next cruise. I was hoping for some personal time before we left, though. I've . . . got some things I need to take care of."

"I think that can be arranged," the President said. "Among other things, given the *Blade*'s next few missions, I believe that the first sergeant can spare you, can you not, First Sergeant?"

"Yes, Mr. President," First Sergeant Powell replied stoically. It wasn't like the Prez had just cut off his right arm or anything. Left, yes.

"Very good," the President said. "I'd hate to have to use the dread phrase upon you, First Sergeant. In that case, Staff Sergeant, you're going to school."

"Excuse me, Mr. President?" Berg asked.

"I'm told that if one is intelligent, perceptive, in good physical condition and doesn't break a leg or something, that a young Marine can complete officer's candidate school in a bare four months. Don't break your leg and the next time you run into First Sergeant Powell he'll be required to salute you."

"Yes, Mr. President," Berg said, stunned.

"When I discussed this choice with persons who shall remain nameless, after a long tirade about something called 'mustangs' which I had previously associated with horses, the salient point of sending you to OCS instead of my initial choice, direct commission by order of the dread phrase, was that you'd receive training in your new duties which have something to do with venereal disease and inventories. Since I'm sure you have no experience of the former and minimal experience of the latter, I acquiesced. Have fun in OCS. Oh, I was also told that Force Recon Platoon leaders had to have at least a year 'with troops' in regular units. The dread phrase was repeated at that point. Upon graduation you will become Third Platoon leader of Bravo Company, First Space Marines. If you don't graduate, you will become something called 'a goat' and be sent to durance vile probably somewhere nearby as an instructor in Marine Space Combat, which was the initial suggestion of persons who shall remain nameless. I assure you that would be a tedious assignment. Graduate. Preferably with honors and on time. Barring another emergency, the ship will not leave for its next serious mission until you show up. I didn't have to use the dread phrase that time but I was definite."

"Yes, Mr. President," Berg said, starting to grin.

"And I'm throwing in another medal for capturing a Dreen battleship. Something tasteful, Silver Star or suchlike. First Sergeant Powell? Promoting you to sergeant major would remove you from your present position. Want the pay or the position?"

"The position, Mr. President," the first sergeant answered.

"Eventually we'll be able to put a battalion on a spaceship at which time, if I'm in office, dread phrase or no dread phrase you'll get a battalion. In the meantime, you remain. Want a medal?"

"Got plenty, Mr. President."

"You sure? Legion of Merit? Silver Star? That's always bright and cheery on a uniform. Or a flag for that matter. Something to clutter the wall in your old age and dust? I'd be hard pressed to swing a Medal of Honor but I could try."

"Got plenty of dust catchers, Mr. President."

"Very well. Chief Warrant Officer Second Miller?"

"Mr. President?"

"You just got a jump in pay, Chief Warrant Officer Third Miller. Again, it was suggested that you become an instructor along with a suggestion that maybe a SEAL team would be better off on the *Blade*. At that point, a pointed discussion ensued between two persons who shall remain nameless, both of equal rank but one the other's technical superior because of something called a 'junior service,' which phrase caused the larger and stronger to nearly strike his technical superior. After tempers had cooled, it was agreed that the *Blade* would continue to host Marines. And one SEAL if he's still interested. If not, Coronado or Little Creek, take your pick."

"*Blade*, Mr. President. I hate instructor positions."

"What is it with all you suicidal people?" the President asked. "Never mind. And we are left with Miss Moon. People who shall, et cetera, also discussed the fact that there was a civilian running around on 'their' ship. After pointing out that it was *my* ship, thank you very much, you work for *me* not the other way around, I also pointed to certain details of the captain's most thorough and well-written report. Well-written enough that I suspect he had some help. But the hidden details caused what could best be termed a 'harumph' and a suggestion that certain persons could best be used in any number of training or technical capacities right here on Earth. About which I agree, most wholeheartedly. Or not on Earth. I'm in need of ambassadors to both the Cheerick and the Hexosehr. I could even switch out the one to the Adar although Peter is doing very well. Or, via use of the dread phrase and magic signature powers accorded me by fifty point zero two percent of the American people, you can remain as linguistic officer of the *Blade Two*. Frankly, I think that's a step down, but I leave it up to you."

Miriam looked frozen for a moment, then shrugged.

"The *Blade*, Mr. President."

"Is that your final answer?" the President said. "I have been informed of your almost habitual lack of self-confidence. While

I'll admit that could be a problem in an ambassador, I nonetheless feel that there is no person more suitable to the position of ambassador to the Hexosehr. Your technical competence is what I'm looking at there, far more than your linguistic ability. And the short communiqué you returned with from the Hexosehr mentions you by name as a suitable interlocutor."

"I appreciate that, Mr. President," Miriam said. "Really I do. But I think I'm of more use on the *Blade*. We're going to encounter more species, we're going to encounter more linguistic problems and we're going to encounter more . . . technical problems. I think I can be of more use there than negotiating details with the Hexosehr. Nice as they are, I think it would drive me insane. More insane."

"Very well," the President said, waving his magic finger. "You are permanently, at least as long as I'm in office, the linguist for the *Vorpal Blade*, whatever number it ends up as. If you change your mind, you can of course unvolunteer at any time and options remain open. Ambassador, linguist right here in the White House—heck I could use a technical advisor as easy on the eyes as you are. Whatever you ask."

"Thank you, Mr. President," Miriam said, dimpling.

"There's just one problem with Miss Moon continuing on the *Blade Two*," the CO suddenly said, frowning seriously.

"What's that?" the President asked, blinking.

"It's a brand new ship," Spectre replied. "If it has to take another long cruise, there aren't any pipes to paint! God *help* whoever takes over as CO!"

"Brooke, this is Amanda Bergstresser."

"Yes, ma'am," Brooke said. It had been nearly four months since that one single exchange of messages. Eric's mom was in contact with other families from his unit and all of them were worried. The ship Eric was on wasn't supposed to be able to be gone this long. The Marines weren't saying anything, just that the unit was "overdue."

Nobody was giving up hope, least of all Brooke. Prom was coming, but she'd turned away every offer of a date. She had her dress, she was ready to go. But only if she was on Eric's arm. But a call out-of-the-blue like this from Mrs. Bergstresser could mean only one of two things . . .

"I've received two messages, one for us and one for you. Yours is two words. Can I just read it to you?"

"Yes, ma'am," Brooke said, taking a deep breath.

"From Staff Sergeant Eric Bergstresser to Brooke Pierson. Marry Me. End message."

"Oh *yes*," Brooke said, crying. "Oh, tell him yes!"

"Tell him yourself; he's in Washington, DC. They're back, he's fine and he wants to see you as soon as he can get home. You've got his cell phone number. Use it. And tell him to call his momma."

"The problem with this . . . anomaly is that with the subject's normal irregular data it's hard to pin down. Definite increases in activity in the parietal lobe. But there have been so many described shifts in the record it could just be a new . . . change?"

The two neurologists looked at the results of Earth's most advanced medical scanning and then, almost in turn, shrugged.

"I can't say that there's a notable change," the older said, frowning. "And that is the keystone phrase."

"If we make *any* suggestion of a change, the subject is in for some very invasive procedures," the younger said.

"Be interesting to pull that brain apart."

"I'll put that down as a 'no notable changes,' then," the younger said.

"Spoilsport."